I0599986

ALSO BY ARIA DEVI

The Other Woman

Wanter Dynamics & The Love We Are

THE VELVET CLOVER

THE VELVET CLOVER

A NOVEL

ARIA DEVI

Copyright © 2025 Aria Devi

All rights reserved.

First published in 2025 by Aria Devi Books

An imprint of Prism Business Intelligence LLC

www.ariadevibooks.com

Library of Congress Control Number: 2025919052

This is a work of fiction. Names, characters, places, and incidents are either the product of the author's imagination or used fictitiously. Any resemblance to actual persons, living or dead, events, or locations is purely coincidental.

No part of this book may be reproduced in any form or by any electronic or mechanical means, including information storage and retrieval systems, without written permission from the publisher, except for brief quotations used in a book review.

Cover design by 100Covers

Book design by Aria Devi Books

Printed in the United States of America

First Edition

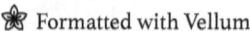 Formatted with Vellum

To New York City,
You are unpredictable, unforgiving, and forever magical.
I never leave you without story.

1

It was eight days before Christmas . . . and I was being dumped.

Elliot sat across from me at our favorite Italian restaurant, twirling his fork through pasta like he wasn't about to shatter my holiday plans. The man had a remarkable knack for terrible timing.

"I just feel like we're in different places," he said, slurping his noodles. His voice soaked in that calm, reasonable tone that made me want to chuck a breadstick at his head.

"Different places," I echoed, my wine glass halfway to my lips. "You mean, I'm here, and you are what . . . in Timbuktu?"

I was already having a bad day—I had spilled coffee on my favorite suit—and now this?

He had the nerve to sigh, as if breaking up with me was somehow exhausting for him. "Ava, you're just so . . . independent. You don't really need me. Sometimes, it feels like you're more committed to your work than to us. It's not you. It's me. I just have things *I* need to figure out."

I stared at him, momentarily stunned into silence. What was the problem? That I had a career, strong opinions, and could assemble IKEA furniture without male supervision?

"I refuse," I said, setting down my glass with a little too much force.

Elliot blinked. "You refuse . . . to break up?"

"No, I refuse to spend Christmas mourning a man whose name and wardrobe could have him mistaken for a fashion designer on *Project Runway*."

He frowned, missing the insult entirely, which only reinforced my point.

I stood, tossing a fifty-dollar bill on the table. "Enjoy your pasta." And I walked away.

It's not you. It's me. That cliché bullshit was the one he had to pick, of all the sentences one could use to break up with someone? He couldn't muster the energy to come up with something original after nearly a year together? And not only had he broken up with me, but he had broken up with me eight days before *Christmas*.

Was my ego slightly bruised? Of course. But while I'd love to say I was heartbroken or even sad, my shock quickly faded into relief. Elliot had been a convenience. Nothing more than a companion. We'd met at an event hosted by the PR company I work for. He was the hot up-and-coming chef. We'd hit it off, went on a few casual dates, and before I knew it, we were spending weekends together at the local farmers' market and going out to dinners in the city every Friday. But it never really felt like more than a close friendship with occasional sex. He was nowhere near a core shaker. He had never been someone I saw myself with long term. But somehow, I'd stumbled into a relationship I never intended to keep.

Maybe this is a blessing, I decided as my feet took me farther from that chapter of my life.

A month ago, Quinn Carter, a recruiter from one of the top

headhunting firms in New York, had been blowing up my inbox about an atelier who'd had their eye on me. I'd put it on ice for the time being, out of courtesy to Elliot, who never would have gone for anything long distance. But the truth was, I'd been craving a change for a long time. A new city. A new life. A new version of myself.

And now, obviously, I regretted saying no.

Ironically, I had it marked in my calendar to break up with him by February 15th—after all the major holidays. I didn't want to be a total bitch and make him have to explain to his family— who, of course, adored me—why his hot, successful girlfriend wasn't coming home for Christmas. Him beating me to the punch was both the best and worst part of this breakup. The best, because now my calendar was clear to take the meeting with the atelier. The worst, because I hadn't gotten to end it on my terms. And I always liked to end things on my terms.

But also, now I would be single on Christmas.

That's right; the holiday that sucked the absolute *most* for singles.

My thoughts spun as I tried to figure out a change of plans. I hadn't been home for Christmas in nearly a decade. Work always came first. There was always a holiday campaign to wrap up and a January launch to prepare for. Plus, not going home meant I could skip the awkward family dinners and dodge the inevitable "single again?" looks and comments from my mother, over pie. Don't get me wrong; my family wasn't terrible. I just had no desire to sit across the table and explain why I was, yet again, a tragic thirty-three-year-old woman without a ring.

Yet, I reminded myself, Elliot's family would have done the same. I guessed I should be thankful to be saved from that same awkward conversation over Christmas. Honestly, I almost felt bad for *him*. Now Elliot Harris was the one flying home . . . alone. Visiting his family . . . alone. Most likely being relegated to the kids' table . . . alone. He'd be the one forced to explain why his girlfriend wouldn't be there this year. Spinning his own nearly-forty, no-ring tragedy to his family. Explaining to his mom why he was now single. How he'd lost his most viable and likely option to procreate with.

I couldn't help but smirk. His family would be heartbroken. I could hear them now—his sisters slapping him upside the head, telling him how stupid he was to mess things up with a "ten" at his age. His dad wouldn't be listening, probably changing the subject to sports, or asking if he was finally going to get a real job. His mom? She'd be crying over what she'd believed was her last hope of continuing the family name through her only son. God, Susan loved me. I'd miss her.

The tension drained from my shoulders knowing I'd be nowhere near that cringey mess. His life would suck. And mine? Mine would be great. Why? Because I refused to give even an ounce of my power away to a man. I, Ava Hawthorne, did not allow men to ruin my life. Never had. Never would.

I straightened my spine as I looked ahead with confidence, weaving through strangers on the sidewalk. I wasn't the type to take to the bed, wallowing in self-pity, crying, eating a dozen donuts, and drinking myself into weight gain and sugar-induced acne oblivion after a breakup. I made lemonade out of lemons. I was the kind of woman who turned a crisis into what looked like a totally strategic and intentional rebrand. When it came to PR, no one did it better than me, so why not apply that same zeal to this breakup?

I didn't think I truly believed you could have both—a thriving career and passionate love. You had to choose. One or the other. Since Elliot wasn't anywhere near a passionate love, my choice had been made clear. A thriving career *was* my passionate love. And men would be no more than sprinkles on my sundae. Nice to have, but I'd still enjoy my ice cream without them.

I would, however, have to figure out the Christmas dilemma and how to avoid my mom begging me to come home once she found out that I was newly single. Now that Elliot had blown my excuse for not going home, it was time to make some calls, avert that crisis, and come up with a new plan.

I didn't break my stride as I fished my phone out of my pocket.

"Hello?" Lila answered like she didn't have caller ID.

"Hey . . . it's Ava." A long pause. "Your sister? What—has life with Simon digressed you back to a landline?"

"Oh, hey, Ava! No, not at all. I just didn't expect to hear from you. I thought it might be a butt dial. I figured you would be pretty busy at work or flying to Oregon with Elliot."

I supposed Lila's reaction was warranted. I only called her about once a year. What could I say? My life was busy. I did, however, do my best to be a great auntie to her kids. I even had my assistant send them each a birthday card every year.

"I'm not going to Oregon anymore," I said in as bored a tone as I could muster, digging at a speck of errant dirt that somehow got lodged under a perfectly manicured nail. "Elliot just ended things with me—"

An end-of-the-world gasp came from her. "Oh my gosh. Ava, I am so sorry to hear that. Can we do anything to help?"

Of course, *we*. Ever since Lila had gotten married, she spoke exclusively in plural, as if the concept of a singular pronoun, or her own identity, had vanished from her vocabulary.

"No, I'm fine. Thanks," I dismissed. "Actually, I was calling to see what *you* had planned for Christmas this year. Are you going home to see Mom?"

"No, Mom came here last year. We're going to Simon's family's this year. We alternate each year," she said, her voice filled with poorly disguised disgust.

From what I had heard, Simon's mother was the spitting image of Jane Fonda's character in the movie *Monster-in-Law*.

The epitome of making her favorite son's wife as miserable as humanly possible whenever she got the chance. And Christmas was her grand stage, her Super Bowl of passive-aggressive behavior and snide remarks.

"Do you even *want* to go?" I asked.

"Does it sound like I want to go? Moms rarely get to do what they want to do," she said.

In the background, I heard a bit of all-too-familiar sisterly bickering. "Hey, Rose! Stop taking Violet's markers—those are hers!" Lila scolded then dropped right back into our conversation without missing a beat. "But you are more than welcome to join us. All of the kids will be there. Simon's side of the family, too. Except for his mom, they are all really great."

A weird feeling came over me at the mention of family, and kids.

I stopped for a traffic light, clearing my suddenly scratchy throat. A little pinch or lump—it felt like the early onset of a cold or something. *I should have that checked out.* I swallowed it and shook it off.

"Judging from that tone, it sounds like the absolute last place I would like to be on Christmas. Honestly, I'd rather face Elliot's family tribunal after the breakup. No offense."

"Oh, none taken," she said. I could almost hear her multitasking—half-here, half in Mom Land, like she was wrapping presents and decorating a tree, all while folding laundry on the other end of the line.

It had been years since I'd seen my sister. When we did get together, we had a great time, but with her raising a family in Colorado and me married to my career, finding time for each other had become more of a wish than a reality.

From what I'd seen online, though, Lila had fully embraced the Christmas mom aesthetic—matching pajamas, handmade wreaths, a holiday playlist on repeat from November first until mid-January. It was cute. Meanwhile, I still had a plastic jack-o'-

lantern on my kitchen counter, left by Elliot when he tried to hand out candy to trick-or-treaters who never showed up because, well, I live in a luxury apartment building that was basically a "no kids allowed" zone.

"Let's play hooky," I said, inspiration hitting as suddenly as my scratchy throat. This could be the perfect and only plausible solution for both of us. To run away from our problems, all the way to a dream vacation. And the location I had in mind would have an added benefit for me.

It was the perfect solution.

"Very funny, sis. You can't be serious. I can't just ditch family Christmas. Simon's mother would shame me well beyond the time she reaches her grave."

"Sounds like a reason to go somewhere far, far away."

"I don't know, Ava. As fun as that sounds, I just missed Rose's dance recital last week. My mom guilt is at an all-time high already. What kind of a mother would I be if I ditched Christmas?"

No, she couldn't refuse.

"But it could be perfect. Just blame me. Make something up. Tell everyone that I am super sad after I broke up with Elliot or something, and that I need some sister time."

"But, Av . . . *he* broke up with *you*," Lila said in her sweet yet annoying way.

"That's not the point," I snapped, rolling my eyes even though she couldn't see it. I walked past some guy who gave me a dirty look. I glared back and flipped him off as I walked on by.

I needed a vacation, time away from this city, from my life, and it seemed my sister needed one, too. I hadn't taken a vacation since, gosh . . . ever. I doubted Lila had either. I imagined her in sweatpants she'd likely worn for a week straight.

"Well, I guess they would probably buy that you were struggling after being dumped," she answered uncertainly.

Ouch. Was that a diss coming from my stay-at-home-mom,

sweatpants-wearing sister. Despite my offer to blame me? Whatever. I'd take one for the team if it meant she'd say yes and I didn't have to spend Christmas with my family or completely alone. Of course, I *could* be alone. I had no problem being alone. Especially on Christmas. It was just another day. But I couldn't have anyone thinking I'd been tragically dumped right before the holidays; I had to have *some* sort of backup plan.

"What about your work?" she interrupted my inner musings. "Would you even be able to take time off?"

Lila understood the difficulties of taking time off work. She'd had a respectable career as a journalist before she had Violet, her oldest. Once Rose was born—yes, both of their daughters were named after flowers . . . I know—she stayed home with them full-time and never went back to work. Despite the shift, the journalist in her never truly went away. She was always observing, questioning, and searching for a story to tell. I wondered if she missed it.

Nonetheless, while I appreciated her consideration, I knew this was just her sneaky way of trying to get out of it. Hoping by doing so, she'd somehow earn a fake "Mom of the Year" trophy by staying there and spending time with Simon's terrible mother. I didn't have the heart to tell her that would never happen, no matter how amazing she was to the girls. Or to Simon's mom.

"Won't be a problem. I already have the time off since I'd planned to visit Elliot's."

Another long pause from her end of the phone. Then, "I guess I could go for a few days. The girls probably wouldn't even notice if I'm there or not. They are at that age where their mom is so uncool. They will be busy playing with their cousins the whole time, anyway. And I already finished Christmas shopping and wrapping, so I wouldn't leave Simon on the hook for that. Maybe I could plan to come back right before Christmas . . ."

Yes, I had her.

While she was talking through her plans, I pulled up my Delta app and started booking our flights. Even if she couldn't stay through Christmas, it was fine—it gave me just enough of a reason not to have to go home for the holidays *and* an excuse to explore that job opportunity. And, of course, get to spend some time with my sister. It was a win-win.

". . . and I would need to talk to Simon to confirm it was okay with him, but I'm sure if he knows you are having a mental breakdown because of the breakup, he would totally understand."

"I am not having a mental anything," I barked, coming to a halt and pausing my flight search. I stepped closer to the curb and braced myself on a bench as I took a breath and regained my cool.

"You know what I mean. I'll have to beef it up for him to say yes," she said. "Ugh, Ava, I don't know."

Clearly, she needed to see more of the picture. "Come on, Lil. You are almost what—thirty-*one*? With two kids and a mother-in-law who hates your guts. I turned thirty-three last month. I just got dumped before Christmas by my boyfriend. Neither of us are getting any younger. Besides, what sounds better than being free on vacation with your sister that you haven't seen in years? We would have such a fun time together. Imagine being free on vacation for a few days to sleep in, go out to eat, no responsibilities, no laundry."

There was silence on the other end.

I added, "It will only get harder to do stuff like this. For Christ's sake, we haven't taken a trip together since Mom dragged us to Mount Rushmore after Jeff left—what was that, when you were two and I was four? Right after Christmas. It would be good for us to spend some time together."

"You do make some good points," she reasoned. "But, *if* Simon were to be fine with it and the girls didn't care, where would we even go so last minute? Won't it be hard to get a motel in most places this close to Christmas?"

I scoffed. "*Motel*? Lila, please. You think I'm going to spend Christmas in some sketchy roadside motel? I have *never* and will *never* sleep in a motel," I declared. "Ew."

Lila laughed. "Okay, okay, I get it. No motels. But still, any place we go will most likely not have availability."

I smiled. "I guess that means we will have to go to a place where you can fly in and out on a whim and there is no shortage of hotels or restaurants—ever."

Lila paused, waiting for me to announce my idea.

"I just emailed you your flight confirmation and added it to your calendar. You leave tomorrow at eleven," I announced. "We are going to New York City!"

"Ava! Why would you do that? I haven't even talked to Simon yet."

I ignored her. "Also, when I see you, remind me to get you a new email address, one that doesn't end with AOL.com, for God's sake." I shook my head. When did my sister go archaic?

"Oh, hush it. I've been out of the career game for a while, so don't judge me. I've been a bit busy raising human beings."

"I respect that," I said. "But you better get going, sis. You don't have much time to talk to Simon and pack those bags of yours. Do you prefer an aisle or window? You can pick 1A or 3C."

"Ava Hawthorne. You did not book me a first-class seat," she exclaimed. "That is so unnecessary."

"Either thank me or shut up," I bossed—what I was best at. "Aisle or window?"

"Ah—um . . . aisle, I guess. My bladder was never the same after having Violet," she confessed.

"See, this is why I don't want kids. They fuck up everything. Even your bladder," I said. "All right, giddy up, Colorado mountain girl. And pack your dancing heels, because those hiking boots won't be up to the dress code at the places we're going to be dining in the city."

"Av, I have to talk to Simon and the girls first to make sure it's okay. I'm sure it will be fine. Oh, I may need to borrow a few of your clothes. I haven't been out on the town in a while."

God, what would this woman do without me? Stay under the rock she had been living under since giving birth years ago? I smiled to myself and resumed my walk home.

"I got you covered, sis. You can borrow whatever you need."

I used to hate when Lila wore my clothes. She would sneak into my room and steal my new things before I even had a chance to wear them. She'd act all innocent. I would stand there and make her take them off and usher her out of my room, locking the door behind her. The classic dance between younger and older sisters. Interesting how those little melodramatics disappeared once you were an adult.

"I'll see you in the city tomorrow night," I said brightly.

"Av, thank you so much for this." Ah, yes, now she was committed. "I will let you know what Simon says."

"He's going to say yes. You will make sure of it. Because that first-class ticket is nonrefundable," I said, hoping she would lean on my confidence in her conversation with her husband.

"Right. Well, if he does say yes, I am excited to see you. I can't wait to spend time with you. It's been way too long."

"You can do it. And we can always fly you back home right before Christmas if it's a dealbreaker. We've got options. See you tomorrow, Lil." I hung up, effortlessly switching to my email as I walked through the door of my apartment building.

I quickly drafted a response to the recruiter:

Quinn,
    There has been a change of plans. I will be able to make it to

New York for an interview after all. Let me know the time and place to meet with the atelier.

- Ava Hawthorne

A twinge of excitement cut through the shock of the Elliot breakup and the change of Christmas plans as I rode the elevator. New York. Lila. A potential job opportunity that would get me out of this city and already made my heart race faster than Elliot ever had.

I didn't need Elliott's family Christmas. Mine would be just as great—better, in fact. Lila and I hadn't spent the holidays together in years. I couldn't wait to see her. And now, with this interview, it felt like the universe was giving me a second chance. A fresh start. New opportunities. Maybe even a whole new life.

The view from my window caught my eye as I shut the door behind me. My apartment was perched forty floors above San Francisco in one of the city's most luxurious high-rises. Yet it didn't do much for me. Despite the festive time, not a trace of Christmas existed in my apartment. It was luxurious but empty.

Sometimes, I felt like a bird trapped in a cage here. God, I couldn't wait to get the hell out of this city.

I had the sudden urge to burn my apartment to the ground, along with every last thing I owned, and start fresh in New York City, if I decided the job was a good fit, of course. Maybe that was just the Scorpio in me. We loved a dramatic death-and-rebirth moment.

And with that thought, I turned on my heel and headed to my closet to pack enough for my sister and me.

2

_____

Apparently, Lila's conversation with Simon and the girls went well, because less than an hour after we spoke, she messaged to say she'd see me in New York. I wasn't sure how long she'd be staying, but we could sort out all of the details once we got there.

Against my better judgment, I let Lila choose the hotel. I figured since I didn't clue her in to the vacation destination until after I booked her flight, I should at least let her book the hotel of her choosing.

Big mistake.

I figured with my American Express card and unlimited options in one of the best cities in the world, she would have at least found her way to the Four Seasons or The Ritz Carlton. Rather, while I was midflight, I received an email confirmation for a hotel called The Fitzgerald Hotel on 57th and Lex.

From the pictures, it looked far from the luxurious robe, spa, and room service experience I had imagined. After a quick

Google search, I found that it was an Irish Hotel, which meant a few things. Musky sheets, thin walls, small showers with cold water, and a hotel bar that served a lot of two things I didn't prefer: Irish Whiskey and Irish Bacon. It didn't look terrible by any means, but it felt more like a motel tucked away on the outskirts of a small town than anything resembling a five-star destination in Manhattan.

I would have texted Lila to cancel the reservation, but, one, she was midflight, and I knew for a fact she wasn't the type to pay for in-flight Wi-Fi, so she wouldn't get my message for hours anyway; and two, I figured she should have at least one thing her way on this trip, even if I was highly confident she'd be much happier at The Ritz Carlton, where the concierge would have known her name the moment she walked in and the room would have overlooked Central Park, offering the perfect backdrop for her kid-free, morning coffee.

After a six-hour cross-country flight on one of the busiest travel days of the year, in a snowstorm, and an hour-long ride from JFK to the hotel with a cab driver from Bangladesh who nearly got me killed six times, I was vibrating with exhaustion and adrenaline. But I respected Ahmed's efficiency. I really did. Nearly dying aside, I love a man who's about his money. And since he got me to the hotel in one piece, and in record time, I left him a tip so generous he insisted on hugging me when he dropped me off.

Despite my terrifying death ride into the city, I already felt freer here in one hour than I had in years in San Francisco. Plus, my style? It fit more seamlessly in New York. No-nonsense. Fast-moving. Brusk. I was practically a New Yorker already, based on street metrics.

By the time I stepped into the hotel, all I could think about was checking into my room, getting some focused work in, and pairing it with a strong drink.

Work was my preferred form of relaxation. It always had

been. Even when I traveled, I liked to work. My relationship with my career was the most consistent thing I had going for me. And yet, even that relationship had been far from perfect recently.

I'd been at Atlas & Grey PR for almost seven years—built a name, built a solid industry reputation—but lately, I hadn't felt the same passion I had when I'd first started. I wanted to do more than just make money. I wanted to be part of something bigger than helping pharmaceutical companies and massive corporate conglomerates sell to the masses. For a while now, I'd been feeling the pull to explore new options. Ending things with Elliot felt like the permission slip I needed to finally go for it. Hence, one of the many reasons I was here—New York had options.

I wrestled my luggage through the entrance of The Fitzgerald Hotel because, of course, in true old Irish fashion, there wasn't a single automatic door in sight. Just a musky smell, dim lighting, *lots* of mahogany, and a staircase that looked like it had seen some things. I rolled up to the check-in desk, slightly winded and fully over it. Jeremy, the bellhop, concierge, doorman—not a good one, I might add—and judging by the keys dangling from his belt, probably the valet, too, gave me the kind of polite smile reserved for high-maintenance guests and B-list celebrities.

"Tell me I have options for dinner," I said. Lila's flight wouldn't arrive until eleven, so I needed to stay busy and awake for as long as possible.

"Ma'am," he said with a smile. "Depends. How adventurous are ya feelin'?"

I looked outside, where the wind was hurling fat snowflakes sideways, burying cars and street signs. "Not freeze-to-death-in-a-blizzard adventurous."

"Well den, ma'am, ye've got one option," he said in a thick

Irish accent, nodding toward the dimly lit restaurant just off the lobby.

"*One*? One restaurant. In this *entire* hotel?"

Jeremy shrugged. "Sorry ma'am. Unless vending machine food is to your likin'?"

I exhaled sharply. "Fan-fucking-tastic."

He grinned. "'ey, at least da drinks are strong."

"Are you the bartender, too?" I asked, raising an eyebrow.

His expression quickly turned into a look of utter confusion. Jeremy, the man of many talents, master of none, didn't seem to appreciate my humor. Maybe it was my delivery? Hm.

I hauled my *own* luggage to the elevator, rolling it down the pre-war carpeted hallway so narrow it barely fit. *Great pick, Lila. Jesus, I gave you one job.* Not only was I carrying my own bags, but I was also navigating a hallway that seemed to be designed for literally nothing wider than a morbidly obese Irish man. Maybe this was why no one in Europe was overweight—they wouldn't be able to stay in their own hotels.

There were only six rooms on my floor, and as I made my way down the hall, I could hear at least three conversations going on behind closed doors. I was shocked that many guests were staying in this hotel, let alone on my floor.

I used my key to open the door to my room—no, not a scan key, but an actual old-fashioned put-it-in-the-lock-and-twist key that looked eerily like the one from the first *Harry Potter* movie, when Harry got on the broom to find the Sorcerer's Stone and all the keys started flapping their wings and attacking him.

And not just the keys—everything about this place felt like a scene from a movie. But not the lavish Hollywood film type. It was more like a strange mix of a historical documentary and a horror film. Like the kind of hotel room where the police would find a dead celebrity who had seemingly overdosed on pills but had actually been whacked by the mob.

I suppose you could say the place had *vintage* charm. I'd give it that much. Dark wood framing the creaky bed, an old armoire-styled dresser, off-white sheets with gold trim, velvet accent pillows in deep purple, and walls that had probably been white in the 1900s. They looked like they'd been smoked in daily by hotel guests ever since, tinged with a faded yellow-brown hue.

I unpacked my things, barely able to open my luggage in the small space. Turned out, I was right about the musky sheets. However, I was wrong about a few things. There was a robe, so that was a win. Though, when I leaned in to smell it, I was met with more musk. I made my way to the bathroom, finding the shower had two settings: freezing or scalding—on brand for a European-styled hotel, so I couldn't be too mad.

I pulled the shades open, hoping for at least a decent view. Instead, I was greeted with the sight of another cement building so close I could practically tap on their window from mine. In fact, I could see directly into one of the rooms. I didn't know whether to wave or look away. I opted for keeping the shades closed for the remainder of the trip.

"Welcome to New York," I muttered, scanning the room, dreading the thought of spending any more time in here until Lila arrived tonight. There was no way I was going to stay in this gross room and get any work done.

Before heading down to the restaurant, I grabbed my laptop and scrolled through emails for anything urgent. Down, down, past the hundreds that flooded my inbox every day. It came with the territory in PR, and I was built for it.

Down. Down. Down. There it was.

Re: Meeting Confirmation with The Aislinn Atelier

· · ·

Hi Ava,

I'm so thrilled to hear you can make the meeting happen! I just spoke with Ronan's team (the founder) and they're eager to meet with you.

We're cutting it close to Christmas, but as I am sure you know, the fashion industry never takes a break. I've secured the meeting for tomorrow, December 19th, at 3 P.M. Once you confirm, I'll send over a calendar invitation with the address and details.

Looking forward to hearing from you!

Best,

Quinn Carter
Senior Recruiter | Beacon Search Partners

I would never admit to anyone that I was excited for this interview, but I was. Atlas & Grey PR had been a great place to learn in my twenties, but at this point, I could have run the place. It was great for building my skill set, but something about the corporate culture felt stale, like milk that had passed its expiration date.

I had googled The Aislinn Atelier once I'd decided to come to New York to meet with them. It had been tough to find anything online. No wonder they were in desperate need of PR. I would completely agree. They were stuck in the early 2000s, which was common for a smaller, family-run brick-and-mortar business. But despite the lack of online presence, I sensed a lot of potential. The only thing I could dig up online was the owner's name—Ronan Broderick—and that they specialized in custom bespoke suits which, lucky for me, I was an expert in.

Fashion had always been my first love. It was a path I wanted to pursue when I was young, but it never felt like the right time or place. Once I found my way to PR and worked my way up, starting over in a completely new industry didn't make sense. Still, my closet was packed with nothing but three-piece custom-tailored suits from the best bespoke tailor in all of San Francisco.

I loved bespoke suits. The craftsmanship and attention to detail . . . it was like wearing art. It wasn't just about looking good; it was about feeling like the suit was made for me. Every stitch, every seam, hand made for me. A bespoke suit wasn't just clothing—it was a complete, custom, artistic luxury experience.

If this worked out and they passed my thorough process of vetting, this could be a fabulous fit, from both a career and getting-the-fuck-out-of-dodge-and-restarting-my-life-from-zero standpoint.

My stomach growled like a small animal was trapped inside, making it impossible to concentrate. I sent a quick email back to Quinn, confirming the meeting, before changing into a fresh suit, touching up my makeup, grabbing my computer, and heading down to the bar to get something to eat and, hopefully, a very strong drink.

It was a charming place, fantastically Irish pub vibe— quaint, with Christmas lights and decorations everywhere. The few servers had cute little Irish accents, adding a nice touch of authenticity. It reminded me of the Russian nail salon I went to in San Francisco, where all the women were legitimately from Russia, giving it the feel like they knew what the hell they were doing and you shouldn't ask questions or tell them how to do their job. Of course, that never stopped me from trying.

"What'll I be gettin' for ya?" the bartender asked. He was short and stubby, wearing a Santa hat. I guessed he was in his sixties, and based on my reliably sharp ability to read people, I assumed he'd been working here since college.

"Old fashioned and"—I looked around for a menu as I took a seat at the bar—"what do you have for food?"

"Well now, dat all depends on what yer after, ma'am."

I had been thinking more like a menu . . . but sassy quips and small talk worked, too, I guessed.

I narrowed my eyes and forced a straight smile, mustering, "I'll have french fries."

"That *all*?" he said, eyebrows lifting in disbelief. His tone was overly jolly despite his confusion. Like my simple order of just fries had genuinely rattled a man who was otherwise having a great night.

"Unless you can manage sparing me a menu, I suppose that is all I am confident this place will have for dinner," I said, gesturing around the near empty bar.

He raised his brows before walking away with a shit-eating grin across his face. I wasn't sure if he was being an ass, or if he was just cheeky as hell.

I had just opened my laptop to dive into some more emails when Mr. Sassy Quips returned with my drink.

"Sorry, darlin', but in about thirty minutes, ye'll have to put dat thing away. We stop lettin' patrons use laptops at nine twenty-five p.m. each night," he said, blissfully unaware of how much he was ruining my evening.

"Are you *kidding me*?" I turned to the group of people who didn't exist around me. "No one is even here! And why nine twenty-five?"

He wiped some sort of wetness off his hands with a towel, shrugging. "I don't make da rules, darlin'," he said, completely ignoring my second question.

"Jesus fucking Christ," I muttered, pinching the bridge of my nose, elbow propped on the bar, wondering how else this Irish hotel might ruin my trip in record time. I'd figured New York City was full of hustlers, people who worked at bars on their laptops well into the night. At least in San Francisco, everyone had an appreciation for technology.

"I still have thirty minutes," I said, checking the time.

He nodded and took a few steps back, probably scared of me at this point. I seemed to have that effect on people.

I spent the next thirty minutes with my head buried in my laptop, knowing I was on a countdown. I was even considerate enough to turn the screen brightness down on my computer, you know, to be mindful of the other "patrons" around me.

As the clock on my laptop struck nine twenty-five p.m., Mr. Santa Hat was on my ass to close it down, tapping his wrist that did not, in fact, contain a watch on it.

"Can I at least get another old fashioned?" I asked, stifling a yawn as the thought of retreating to my musky room with no view sounded even more terrible than sitting at this laptop-free bar. If I stopped drinking now, I'd be asleep in minutes.

I wondered if I should just go to sleep, let Lila find her own way in—she's a big girl, right?—but I knew better. My sister was flying into New York City, in a snow storm, alone, and I needed to stay up long enough to get her checked in. She couldn't handle New York by herself. I had to stay busy— drinks, work, anything to keep me from passing out before she arrived.

"We stop servin' alcohol at nine twenty-five, as well, ma'am," he said, grimacing, bracing for the wrath he could probably sense simmering beneath my seemingly sweet, blue-eyed, blonde-haired exterior.

Enough.

I stood, pissed. "What the *hell* kind of hotel is this? I can't use my laptop? You stop serving alcohol when most people are just starting to *think* about going out in New York? Don't Irishmen drink more beer and whiskey than any other demographic in the world? Where am I right now—the fucking Bible Belt? The Salt Lake City Airport with all their weird, limited alcohol rules? Honestly, this is just bad business."

Mr. Rule Enforcement Man didn't react; he just stood there, smiling, assessing me, like I hadn't just gone completely ballistic on him. Now his stupid Santa hat was really starting to piss me off.

I leaned in, raising my brows, waiting for him to speak.

Nothing.

"Okay," I said, taking a deep breath, my hands together in a prayer position, hoping it would give me some sense of peace and help me channel my inner Mother Teresa. "If I can't use my laptop, and I can't get a drink here, where do you suppose I go for at least one of those activities tonight, what with the snowstorm outside? Hm?"

Mr. Santa Hat leaned against the bar behind him, eyes narrowed on me, chewing his cheek, thinking of what to say next—or at least, I hoped he was. If not, whatever he was doing just came off as creepy. He folded his arms like he was weighing his next move.

Suddenly, a wave of anxiety hit me. I was the only patron in this place. Was this the part where he killed me in the kitchen? My serial killer radar hadn't gone off with him, though. He seemed harmless enough. I was usually spot-on at reading these things. It was how I'd managed to survive this long as a woman in a big city.

A heavy silence hung between us before he wagged his finger at me, clicking his tongue like he had some secret grand solution to my dilemma. Tilting his head, he then gestured toward the right side of the bar—my left—as if something mysterious was hidden behind the velvet curtain. "Come dis way, ma'am."

I narrowed my eyes on him. "Oh, no. I don't think so. Last time someone said that to me, I ended up with a flat tire and no cell service. You think I'm falling for the 'come this way behind the dark curtain' routine?"

He didn't answer. He remained infuriatingly calm. Smiling.

He gestured again, palm up, toward the curtain. Then, as if to tempt me, he pulled it back just enough to reveal a dim glow spilling from behind a mysterious doorway. "Ye know," he said, leaning his elbow on the bar, still holding the curtain back a sliver, "people tend to fight da hardest against the thing they need the most."

I glared at him. Why was this guy speaking in riddles?

I inched closer, arms crossed. Maybe I could just sneak a peek.

"Is this the part where I disappear into an alternate dimension? Or is that just where you keep the really good whiskey?"

"Ye'll have to see for yerself to know for sure," he said, a hint of amusement tugging at the corners of his lips.

I hesitated. Every instinct screamed this was a bad idea. But me and bad ideas, we had a bit of a flirtation going. I never liked to admit it, but I secretly loved living on the edge. Just a little. Historically, I hadn't gone there often, and when I did, it usually worked out for me. Other times? It left me with a flat tire and no cell service. But since there were no cars in sight, I figured, *What the hell? Might as well take the risk.*

"This is a terrible idea," I muttered mostly to myself. "But what else do I have to do for the next few hours, I suppose?"

He stepped aside, holding the curtain open with an exaggerated gesture. The fluffy ball on his ridiculous Santa hat flopped to the other side of his head as he basically bowed at the waist.

"Enjoy, Ms. Hawthorne," he said, a chuckle following me as I passed through the door behind the curtain. As I stepped through, a shiver ran down my spine—wait, how the hell did Mr. Santa-Hat-Wearing Bartender know my name?

The air changed immediately, intensifying as it swallowed me, pulling me deeper into a room that felt like a completely different world than the one I'd just left.

3

THE ROOM BEHIND THE CURTAIN WAS SO DIMLY LIT I COULD barely make out the faces of the people just a few feet away. The bar looked like something out of a whiskey ad—hand-carved mahogany, dark wooden chairs placed around the low tables, and worn leather booths. Rows of whiskey bottles lined the back wall, with what looked like only one or two sad rum options. A stench of tobacco and smoke filled the space—it was definitely not legal to smoke inside anymore, but somehow fit perfectly in here. Vintage art hung on the walls, and heavy, black velvet curtains covered the windows.

The room was packed. The men looked like they'd just stepped out of a time machine—three-piece suits, shiny shoes, hair slicked back. The women? Full flapper mode. Beaded drop-waist dresses, feather headbands, pearls down to their waists.

I blinked, taking in the sight. Did I just stumble into a *Gatsby* cosplay night? A themed birthday party? A niche cult gathering? It was almost like I had walked into a different era entirely.

I stepped further into the room, trying to make sense of

what I was seeing. A pianist played in the corner, and the soft hum of murmured conversations filled the bar.

"Welcome to Da Velvet Clover, ma'am," a voice pulled me from my thoughts.

The hostess greeted me with a tone that felt strangely formal, but kind. Judging by her accent, she was Irish, with dark hair cut into a short bob. She had a mysterious, cinematic look. She couldn't have been more than fifteen or sixteen. She looked like a gothic Daisy Buchanan.

"Will anyone be joining ye this evening, ma'am?"

"Table for one."

Why would that bartender hide this speakeasy from me this whole time? So rude. This place was incredible. I couldn't help but wish I'd been here, enjoying some music and a themed party instead of wasting the last hour dealing with his annoying self and all of his rules.

"I'm terribly sorry, ma'am," the hostess replied, her voice polite but apologetic, "but we're extremely full at the moment. The only option I have for a single patron currently is at our communal table. Would that suit ye, all right? If anything else opens up in the meantime, I'll be more than happy to move ye to the first available seat."

For real? I glanced around, my frustration bubbling. Suddenly, I was starting to question if I even liked this city. Single people couldn't get tables and no one let you use your laptop?

"Fine. If there's really no other option . . ." I sighed in resignation. "Sure, that's fine."

She gave me an apologetic look as she gestured for me to follow her to this "communal table."

She took me to the back corner booth, tucked away, hidden, wooden, but with a perfect view of the entire place. Great for people watching. The booth was empty.

"I thought you said this was a communal table?" I asked.

"It is indeed, ma'am. I believe there was a gentleman sittin' here moments ago. I am sure he is around here somewhere," she said, turning to scan the space. "Da bartender will be right with ya," she added, placing her hand on the table. Her arms were covered in white gloves to her elbows. "Also, I love yer hair, ma'am. It is so long and beautiful. I've never seen anythin' like it."

I narrowed my eyes. "Do you live under a rock?" My hair looked just like every other basic bitch out there on the streets of New York, or anywhere else in the world, for that matter.

She pursed her lips politely. "Enjoy yer evening at Da Velvet Clover, ma'am," With that, she walked back toward her station.

"Don't you have a drink menu?" I called after her.

She turned, tilting her head, looking confused, then offered a polite smile. "We offer a bit of rum, and gin, but mostly whiskey here, ma'am."

No menus, either? Odd. Maybe it was an Irish thing. At least they were still serving. It was more than that bartender on the other side of the velvet curtain could say.

I shook my head, settling into the corner booth. If I was going to have to share it with someone, at least it was a decently sized table.

I scanned the room and couldn't help but notice the guests smoking cigarettes. Was smoking still allowed indoors in New York? Then again, maybe this place was one of those relics where the rules didn't apply and no one tattled.

A Christmas tree stood in the corner, covered in lights and ornaments that looked older than me. Candles flickered on each table, the only real light aside from a few antique sconces on the walls. Garland was draped across the fireplace and wound around the bar, giving the space that old-world charm everyone seemed to eat up these days. Despite my general disdain for the holiday itself, I had to admit the place was charming. I could see why it was packed.

I couldn't believe Santa Hat Bartender let me sit at that lame-ass bar all night without telling me about this place. No wonder no one was there—the party was here. He was an evil man for making me suffer that long. I would be having a word with him tomorrow.

I glanced up at the bartender as he arrived at my table. He was huge. A middle-aged man with a gut and a pencil behind his ear. He looked like a dorky dad who had just finished mowing the lawn or changing a tire. He had some dirt or grease on his face—I couldn't tell which. I leaned in to peek behind him, scanning my drink options. From what I could tell, it was mostly Irish liquors. My stomach turned. Not my first choice, but whatever.

I sighed. "All right, one Irish whiskey, I guess."

The bartender gave me a smile. "Comin' right up, ma'am." He nodded, and I settled back into my booth.

I looked around as I waited for my drink. This place felt incredibly authentic, with the themed dress code and Irish staff. It was like stepping into an actual Irish speakeasy from the 1920s—at least, I imagined this was how it would be. Who handled their PR? I needed to ask the hostess on my way out. This place definitely needed more exposure.

The costumes were impressive, and I couldn't tell if the twenties dress code was permanent or just for a special Christmas party. And no one was on their phones, which was a nice touch. Most speakeasies required you to check your phone at the door, but the hostess hadn't asked for mine.

I'd searched online earlier and found nothing else to do in the hotel—no hidden speakeasies, no tucked-away lounges. This place seriously needed a PR overhaul. Our in-house generalist, Jeremy, hadn't mentioned it, either. With the way it was set up, it was practically begging for some attention. I'd love to meet the owner and see how I could help get the word out about this place.

"Yer Irish whiskey, neat," a man with a thick Irish accent said, placing my drink on the table in front of me. But it wasn't the voice of the bartender from whom I'd just ordered.

"You aren't my bartender." I looked up, glaring at him. The last thing I needed was some random guy hitting on me and spiking my drink. *It's not my first rodeo, buddy*.

"No, alas, I am not. But I am the next best t'ing," he said, sitting down catty-corner from me at the table. "I'm yer table-mate at this fine communal table, for the evenin'."

"Great." I rolled my eyes, scooting a few inches away from him. I inspected my drink, checking for any signs of something off—drugs maybe—before I took a sip.

I peered out of the corner of my eye. He was sipping what looked like a matching whiskey. He had the most piercing blue eyes I'd ever seen in my life. His dark brown, nearly black hair was styled with an undercut, the sides and back shaved short, creating a stark contrast with the longer hair on top. He wore a wool vest and trousers, with a buttoned-up, high-neck collared shirt, and a pinky ring. Very Ralph Lauren catalog.

His face was sculpted, sharp features that could carve the air around him. He took another sip of his whiskey, his jaw flexing slightly, his gaze drifting to me with an air of boredom. I acted like I didn't notice, keeping my focus locked across the room.

"Well, aren't ye gonna say thank you?" he asked, his eyes boring into the side of my face.

"Thank you? For what?" I finally turned to look at him, my brows raised in annoyance.

"For bringing ye yer drink," he replied, his voice monotone. Cold.

"I didn't ask you to do that. That's why I tip the bartender. Would you like me to tip you instead?" I asked.

What was this guy's deal? He sounded and looked too bored to be trying to hit on me.

The smallest hint of a smirk tugged at the corner of his mouth. "Nah. I'll just chalk it up to good karma. Besides, a percentage of all da tips make their way back to me, eventually."

I ignored his comment, muttering under my breath, "Who the hell creates a communal table at a speakeasy?" while dropping my head back slightly to study the ceiling.

"Well," he said, pulling a cigarette case from his inside jacket pocket then placing one between his lips and lighting it with a flick of an old-school Dunhill lighter. This guy was really into his character. "This communal table was created fer people like yerself. Da lonely ones. da ones who come to Da Velvet Clover, wishin' they could be here, enjoyin' it all with someone they love. But they don't have anyone to bring. The lonely ones still deserve a drink, even if no one's bothered to join 'em."

"I am not lonely," I protested, my blood boiling, though I refused to let him see. This type of guy thrived on making women squirm, and I wasn't about to give him that satisfaction. "My sister is coming in from Colorado as we speak."

He looked at me, his already large eyes widening even more, as if I were crazy. "Colorado? Well, lovely, sounds like ye'll be waiting quite a while then, won't ye?"

"She will be here tonight. And for your information, buddy, you're sitting here, too . . . alone," I snapped, taking a sip of my drink to calm myself.

"Well, dat don't count," he said plainly, the cigarette flapping between his lips.

"And why not?" I snapped.

"Because"—he took a big inhale before grabbing his lung cancer stick with his fingers—"dis fine place you're sitting in, Da Velvet Clover"—he paused—"tis me bar."

If this actually was the owner, consider my PR interest officially revoked.

I let out an extremely sarcastic cackle. "This is *your* bar? Yeah, I highly doubt that."

He said nothing, continuing to smoke and stare boredly in front of him, out at the people having a great time with their loved ones, giving a one-shoulder shrug before tapping his ashes into the glass tray in front of him.

"If this is your bar, then why do you sit at the reject table?" I asked.

"Communal table," he corrected calmly.

"If this is your bar, why do you sit at the *communal table*, the lonely table—whatever the hell you call it?"

He huffed, his face staying stoic . "Because . . ." he paused. "Sorry, I didn't catch yer name?"

"Ava," I said, still staring straight ahead.

He nodded, looking down at his lap then back up to the bar. "Because, Ava, I, too, am a lonely soul who wants to have a drink, but has no one to join me."

"Hm." I bit my cheek.

We sat in silence for what felt like years, but my best guess was it was about thirty seconds. I could feel his eyes flicking to me, and I tried to resist the urge to look back at him. I couldn't help but glare at him. Just once. Just to show him he couldn't affect me. That he couldn't get under my skin. But there was something about this guy, something that made my skin prickle with irritation and curiosity all at the same time.

I took another sip of whiskey and watched the people in front of me dancing, kissing, and laughing. I glanced back at my irritating table mate, only for a moment, but he hadn't looked away. His piercing eyes were still locked on me with an intensity that made the air between us feel charged with electricity.

I shot him my best stop-staring-at-me glare, sharper than before, holding it for a beat longer than I probably should have.

But he didn't look away. Like he was trying to figure me out in the same way I was trying to figure him out.

It was a standoff—neither of us willing to blink first. But then, his demeanor shifted. He looked almost amused, the corners of his lips turning up just slightly, but not a full smile. No, I didn't think this guy was capable of smiling.

He continued to stare at me. What the hell was wrong with him?

The discomfort mounted until I couldn't handle it. Finally, I broke the silence, my tone shifting just slightly, as I offered a small, almost begrudging gesture of peace.

"Well then, how about two shots of whiskey for the lonely ones?" My voice edged with a mixture of sarcasm.

He nodded, blinking slowly. His gaze felt like it had just cast a spell on me. When he finally looked away, he called over the bartender who had taken my order but sent the drink running to this guy.

"Oi, Eddie, sir. Me and Ava here, we will take two shots of whiskey, 'eh?"

Moments later, the bartender appeared, bringing two shots over with a quick nod.

I raised my glass, meeting the eyes of the man next to me. "Well then, cheers to the lonely ones."

"Cheers to ya, Ava, for making me evenin' a little less lonely," he said, and then we both knocked back our drinks.

I was pretty sure that was something Irish people loved—good toasts—right?

"I'll say this much, this place is fucking amazing. But what's with the 1920's thing?" I reached out for the cigarette dangling between his lips. When in Rome, I guessed. I had never been shy about taking what I wanted before, and apparently, tonight that included his cigarette. "Is this just a holiday party, or is it like this all the time?"

He looked confused as he handed it to me, eyes narrowing

at the cigarette now resting between my fingers before I took a drag.

"No, t'is pretty much like this . . . all da time." It sounded like a question.

"People come here every night dressed like this?" I asked.

He nodded, scanning the bar. "Yes ma'am, I suppose they do. But ye are one to make mentions of everyone's outfit here." He took out another cigarette from his case and wagged his fingers my way. "Is it appropriate for a woman to be wearing pants like that?"

"Appropriate?" I scoffed. "There isn't a room I enter these days where I'm not the most well-dressed woman there. Women are so lazy these days when it comes to fashion."

"Hm," was all he said, his voice deep, gruff, slowly scanning me up and down.

"Can I help you?" I snapped, giving him the best irritated eye roll I could muster.

"Nope." He looked forward once more. "No, ye can't . . . Ava. I do suppose all da clothes are much more baggy and formless these days."

I harumphed, trying not to let him get to me. Why was he *getting* to me? No one got to me. Ever. Especially some pathetic 1920's-themed speakeasy owner who had to sit at his own damn communal table to hook himself a drinking buddy.

"Wait—what time is it?" I peeked at my phone in my pocket, but it was dead, the screen black. I would have pulled it out, but I didn't want him to yell at the hostess for not collecting my phone at the door. I turned to him expectantly. This guy moved at a fucking glacial pace. "*Hello?* The time?"

His face remained straight on, but his eyes darted sideways to me, the near-bored look driving me insane. Then, slowly, he pulled out his pocket watch.

"A pocket watch? Seriously?"

"How else is one supposed to tell da time? Ye sure couldn't."

"Very funny, Mr. . . ."

He held the stopwatch up for me to see.

"Oh shit, it's almost twelve thirty?" There was no way I had been sitting here that long.

Why had Lila not called me yet? Right, my phone was dead. Or maybe this dumb place didn't have service. See, more proof that bad ideas lead to no cell service. She had to have landed by now.

"I have to go. I think my sister is here." Thank God I'd brought cash. I didn't have all night to wait on the world's slowest bartender, or for this so-called *owner* to run my card. I tossed a fifty on the table.

"She has arrived from Colorado already? That was quite quick, I must say." His tone was cheeky, his demeanor calm. Too calm. He held up the fifty. "Are you implyin' somethin' with this?"

"I assume that will cover the drinks, yeah? If it's more, just tell me," I said, reaching back into my pocket for my wallet. I hated carrying a purse. That was why the suits worked for me —lots of pockets to carry money, my phone, and lipstick. All a woman's necessities.

"No, no. That is perfectly fine. I will give the leftovers to Eddie. I can imagine he will be quite happy to use the extra at Christmas."

All I could do was frown at this strange man. "Uh, yeah, I guess. Well, see you around," I said, grabbing my glass of whiskey, throwing the rest of it back, and then clinking it against the glass in his hand before setting it down on the table. "Hope some other lonely loser wanders into your speakeasy to keep you company tonight." I clicked my tongue and turned around.

"I am certain none shall rival da great Ava," he called after me as I walked across the bar and back toward the velvet curtain.

Despite my better judgment, I glanced back, just once—part curiosity, mostly ego. I caught sight of him still watching me. A smile tugged at my lips as I quickly turned away, praying he hadn't seen it. I wasn't about to let him think I might actually be intrigued.

———

Lila was sitting on the couch in the hotel lobby, looking like she'd been waiting for me. Honestly, she really was helpless outside her usual routine.

"Ava!" She looked tired, like she'd had a long travel day and was ready to get some rest without her kids waking her up at five a.m..

"Lila, why didn't you call me when you got here?"

"I called you like ten times."

I grabbed my phone again, which seemed pointless because I knew it was dead—

So strange. It had been completely dead in the speakeasy. Now all her missed calls and texts started flooding in. How was it suddenly back on?

"It's okay; you're here now. Isn't this hotel *amazing*?" She pulled me in for a hug. "I tried to check in and go up to my room, but they said they only had one reservation for us." She sucked a breath between her gritted teeth, looking guilty.

"What? How is that possible? Let me figure it out. One second." I stormed toward the concierge to see what was going on.

"I am sorry, Ms. Hawthorne, as I shared with yer lovely sister, we only have da one room booked for the two of ye," Jeremy, the beyond unhelpful bellhop, valet, doorman, and concierge, said. "And, with the holidays, I am sure ye'll understand that we are fully booked, or we would be happy to accommodate yer sister in a room of her own. We are so sorry for the inconvenience."

I stared at him. "Are you seriously telling me there's no way to get another room? Not even one?"

He shook his head.

"How is that possible?" This place sucked; who would *choose* to stay here?

"I'm sorry, Ms. Hawthorne. Really I am."

I sighed, the energy to fight drained out of me. "Fine. I'm too tired to argue about this right now. I'll check again tomorrow and speak to someone else who can actually help me." I turned and walked back to Lila, who looked up at me with hopeful eyes. I forced a smile, despite wanting to throw her luggage at Jeremy.

"Looks like we are roomies for now. I'll come down tomorrow and iron it out."

"I'm so sorry. This is my fault, Ava. I could have sworn I booked two rooms. With the price being what it was, I just assumed it *was* for two rooms."

"Welcome to New York, sis. Land of outrageously expensive hotel rooms." I wrapped an arm around her shoulders, easily towering over my five-foot-five sister in my heels.

Grabbing her suitcase, I rolled it toward the elevator. "All good. Happens to the best of us. Let's get some beauty rest and recharge for our vacation." I forced a smile, doing my best to mask my annoyance. My already packed room was about to feel a whole lot smaller with her crammed into it.

Note to self: Having kids and quitting your job may result in a complete loss of common sense, basic life skills, standards, and any semblance of reliability. Attention to detail? Gone.

As we headed up the elevator and toward our room, I tried to shake off the strange night like it was nothing. The weird

Santa-hat-wearing bartender, the bizarre speakeasy, the stoic speakeasy owner with his stupid pocket watch. None of it mattered now. It had been an odd night. Nothing more. I had bigger things to focus on, like this interview with the atelier and enjoying a few days of sisterly bonding.

But I couldn't help my thoughts from returning back to that lonely bar owner. There was something about him. Something infuriating. Something intriguing. The kind of man who got under your skin and infiltrated your thoughts, despite your best efforts. And somehow, I had a feeling tonight wouldn't be the last time I saw him.

4

Lila and I spent the morning shopping on 5th Avenue. Christmas in the city was magical—sickeningly so. The air was different, crisp with the scent of roasted nuts and desperation. Joy buzzed through the streets like a seasonal drug people lined up to dose.

We made our way to the Rockefeller Center tree and ice rink, holiday cheer was practically being sold by the square foot.

I didn't believe in Christmas anymore. I didn't think I ever really had. I never thought Santa was real, and I never saw the season as some warm Hallmark fantasy. Even as a kid, it looked more like the commercialization of Christianity than anything sacred—a shiny, manipulative excuse to capitalize on sentiment and sell people things they didn't need. Still, the city did it well. New York didn't pretend Christmas was about anything other than spectacle and spending. At least here, the lie was honest.

It was a far cry from Christmas with Elliott's family—all

matching pajamas and conversations so polite they bordered on robotic. And definitely not like Christmas at home, which was quieter, lonelier, and somehow still exhausting. This version was loud, tacky, and completely over the top. Plus, in the city, I didn't have to spend three days trapped with people I'd rather never see again.

Lila sipped her hot chocolate like she was an elf at Santa's workshop, while I held my double espresso, bracing myself against the manufactured magic. We watched the skaters—children clinging to their parents, couples attempting spins only to crash on the ice. It was chaotic, messy, and ridiculous.

And yet, despite my deeply rooted cynicism, I couldn't help but notice how, for a moment, everyone seemed happy. Even the ones cracking their tailbones on the ice. And, just for a second, I figured it wouldn't hurt to let myself enjoy it, too.

"Are you any good anymore?" I asked Lila, nudging me.

"Oh God, no. I haven't put on a pair of skates since we were really little and Mom's boyfriends would shovel off the lake by our house and we would skate out there. Remember that?"

"Of course I remember. We'd skate till it was too dark to see. I haven't skated since," Lila said.

"God, I would never subject myself to that humiliation now," I laughed, even though a part of me missed the feeling of spinning in circles so freely, without a care in the world.

"You were way better than me at most things, but especially at skating. Sometimes I thought you were going to become a professional figure skater or something," Lila laughed.

"I would have loved that. Mom told me she didn't have money to invest into lessons back then. I was so pissed at her."

"I forgot about that. I think I was a little too young to remember. That was before her writing took off, right?" She frowned.

"Mhmm," I murmured. After Jeff left—our dad, though it was hard to even call him that—our mom started seriously writing. A few years later, she went from stay-at-home wife and mother to *New York Times* bestselling author. I guessed that was just another testament to what leaving a toxic relationship could do for a woman's career. I always assumed that was where Lila got her knack for journalism.

We walked past vendors serving roasted chestnuts, candy canes, holiday souvenirs—anything you could want or need when it came to Christmas cheer and holiday spirit. It was nice to be with Lila. It was like we were kids again. Like I didn't have to be *on* all of the time. When I was with her, I could just be myself. Why hadn't I thought of going on a trip with her until now?

"So, I guess Simon was okay with you coming? He didn't get upset, right?" I asked. Being around Lila always brought something out in me—this reflex to protect her. When we were apart, it was easy to forget. To forget what we'd been through and that there was a time I'd felt responsible for her in a way that never fully disappeared. When we were together, it came rushing back. Like muscle memory. It wasn't just because she was my sister; it was because, for a while after Jeff had left, I had been the one who had made sure she was okay. And maybe some part of me still believed it was my job.

"Oh my gosh! You know Simon. He was so excited for me, for you and I to have time together. I think he might be a little sad I won't be there these days leading up to Christmas, but your 'mental breakdown,'"—she used air quotes with her fingers—"helped him understand. But, if he reaches out to you, just make sure you sound a little neurotic."

"Shouldn't be too hard for me to 'fake it,'" I joked, air quoting back at her before giving her a light shove. "And the girls?"

"They couldn't have cared less. I think Violet's exact words were, 'Mom, you deserve some time away,' and Rose's were more like, 'Violet, I bet we'll get to stay up later, and Dad will let us have ice cream for dinner.'"

"Classic. I'm so glad it all worked out and you could make it." I glanced at her. "Do you know how long you want to stay? Are you thinking of heading back before Christmas?"

She shrugged. "I was thinking maybe the twenty-third. Or Christmas Eve morning. I haven't totally decided yet. Now that I know they are okay with me being here, I don't feel as guilty. You know, like I have to rush back too early. I feel like I can just relax a bit and really enjoy my time here."

I knew Christmas meant more to Lila than it did to me, and I tried to understand why she'd want to make it home for all the festivities. Though, truthfully, I couldn't quite wrap my head around it.

As we stopped, leaning against the wall of the skating rink, she asked, "So, what do we have on the docket while we're here? Anything exciting?" She knew me too well, probably figuring I had a full agenda mapped out for us, from morning until night.

"I have a few items in mind, but is there anything specifically you would love to do while you're here?" I wanted her to *feel* like she at least had a say in the matter.

"I've never been to New York City before, so I guess I don't really know."

"Wait!" I shrieked. "You've *never* been to New York?" My jaw might as well have been on the ice it dropped so low.

Lila shrugged with a grimace on her face as if to say, *I don't know what to tell you. I am a mom with two kids.*

"Holy shit. Well, in that case, while we're here, I have to take you to The Met, to Central Park, West Village to Carrie Bradshaw's and the *Friends* apartment. We have to go to Meatpacking and L'Artusi. Maybe even get drinks in Soho. God, we have so much ground to cover," I said, clenching my coffee, shaking it with excitement.

"Do we have time for all that?" she asked, looking concerned.

"Of course we have time. New York time is different. It's magical. You can get more done in a few hours than most do in a week." My voice was laced with conviction.

"Okay, whatever you say. You're the boss!"

I had discovered over time that there were two types of people in this world: leaders and followers. I was a natural born leader. Lila was designed to follow. She wouldn't initiate anything this weekend, so I had to be the one to show her a good time. It never felt like a burden—it was my natural gift—and there was no better place to flex it than in my favorite city in the world.

"I do have one meeting this afternoon on the Upper East Side. And I need to stop by the hotel's restaurant to grab my laptop. I left it there last night after . . . losing track of time and my phone not working," I said. Not to mention the semi hostile but incredibly attractive and smug bar owner and one too many shots of whiskey. In fact, I was pleasantly surprised I'd woken up with almost no sign of a whiskey and cigarette hangover this morning.

"Ooo, what meeting? Can I come?" Lila asked.

"Do you even remember what it's like to work? Of course you can't come to the meeting. It is a *meeting*. You can't just sit in and listen like it's a college class." I laughed. "But you can shop while I'm there. The Upper East Side has the best high-end shopping and great coffee shops that don't have homeless people in the bathrooms."

"That sounds great. Was the restaurant good last night? Maybe we can go there later."

I hadn't brought up the speakeasy to Lila yet. Part of me knew she would love the space—it was one of the coolest places I'd been to in the city. If it weren't for the weird, Santa-hat-wearing bartender who acted like some kind of gatekeeper and the bar owner who had something about him I couldn't quite shake—something that scared me a little—I'd probably be dragging her there already for drinks.

"Ugh. No," I said, rolling my eyes and chugging the rest of my espresso before tossing it in a trash can. "You can barely even call it a restaurant. It's a long story. I'll tell you on our walk back to the hotel. Let's go; I want to show you the Museum of Modern Art on our way back."

———

I had planned to get us two separate rooms at the hotel once we arrived back from our walk, but Jeremy was manning the front desk again. After last night, I didn't even bother engaging with him. I let it go and accepted that one room would have to do for the rest of the trip. It would be just like when Lila and I were kids and had bunkbeds.

We walked through the lobby back to the hotel bar, Lila chatting about all the things she saw at the Museum of Modern Art while I mentally braced myself for whatever interaction might lay ahead to get my laptop back.

As we reached the bar, I called to the bartender, who was wiping down the counter, the bright purple streaks in her hair noticeable from the entryway. "Excuse me, where is the bartender from last night? Old, Santa hat? I left my laptop here and he was working."

"Don't know who you're talking about," she said in one of the most monotone voices I had ever heard. Now *this* was a New York City bartender. Cold, edgy, and not helpful at all. "I only work during the day. I'll check in the back to see if your laptop is there. One sec." She stepped back into the kitchen.

Only a few patrons were using the space; mostly old couples having lunch—or what they considered dinner—and what looked like a couple college students studying.

"If it weren't for that stupid bar owner, I would love to do the PR for the speakeasy," I whispered to Lila.

"*This* is the speakeasy you were raving about on our walk back?" she asked, looking around the restaurant with mild disgust. Which was saying something considering her idea of a nice vacation included a motel.

"No. Yuck. Hell no. I mean The Velvet Clover behind that curtain over there." I pointed to the left of the bar.

She squealed, "I need to see it. Please show me."

"Come on." I grabbed Lila's elbow and guided her to sneak behind the curtain before the bartender came back. I pulled the curtain open just enough for her to peek through the door.

She turned the handle then stuck her head in while I stood watch. She came out only seconds later.

"That was fast. Did you even look?" I asked.

"Ava, that is literally a broom closet. Very funny. Ha-ha." She rolled her eyes.

"What? No. This is where that bartender had me go." I stepped back to look at the wall for another curtain. This was the only one. I pulled back the curtain and opened the door that she had just looked inside of. But she was right. I peeked in, and there it was—a small broom closet, not much bigger than my entryway closet at home. It was filled with storage items, cleaning supplies, and stacks of rolled silverware.

"Maybe the door is behind the shelves and they block it during the day so people can't get through? Did you maybe walk through there to get to it and you just forgot? Simon and I went to a couple speakeasies when we were first dating, where you have to walk through a restaurant kitchen or a fake book-shelf. Maybe it's like that?" she offered, always the non-judg-mental one.

"I only had one drink before I went in there," I snapped. Not at her. "I think I would remember going through that shitty broom closet."

She started chewing her cheek, like she didn't know what to say.

"We'll come back when Santa Hat is working. I'll have him show you," I mustered, trying to brush off the embarrassment. "It's an incredible space. I'm telling you. Everyone's dressed in 1920's costumes, super vintage. Some of the patrons even pretend it's the 1920s, like method acting. Kind of corny, but so chic. You'll love it." I knew what I had seen. I knew who I had talked to. It had been real. Eddie the bartender, the hostess who'd complimented my hair, and the nameless, brooding owner. I wasn't *that* drunk.

"That sounds good. I can't wait to see it," Lila said, trying to hide the confusion that was so clearly on her face.

"Found it." The bartender came out holding my laptop like it was a dead fish. "Sorry it took so long. It was under a huge stack of papers back there."

"No need to be sorry," Lila said. She had a horrible habit of appeasing everyone around her. How did she grow up to be so nice and me so . . . not?

"It had a sticky note with what I assume is your name on it." She peeled it off and read it, "*Ava . . . Hawthorne*, yeah?"

"That's me," I said, grabbing it. "Appreciate it."

I considered asking her about the speakeasy but couldn't bring myself to do so. The bartender likely already thought I couldn't even remember my own laptop, and bringing up a speakeasy that clearly didn't exist in the light of day would only add to my humiliation.

I turned to head back to our room. Lila followed.

"Thank you so, so, so much for all your help!" Lila called back to the bartender on my behalf.

I glanced back at her trailing behind me. "Come on. Giddy-up. We've got things to do," I said, waving for her to catch up.

She skipped over, and we went back to the room so I could prepare for my meeting, doing whatever I could to forget about the speakeasy that I must have dreamed about. Then, the smallest part of me, felt a twinge of sadness that I never got the lonely bar owner's name.

But I couldn't think about that right now. I had a meeting to focus on. A chance to start my life over. To reinvent myself. A life outside of Elliot, outside of San Francisco, and maybe, a life outside of Atlas & Grey PR.

5

"ALL RIGHT, I AM GOING IN," I TOLD LILA AS I STOOD ON THE corner of 83rd and Madison, which was a prime location for an atelier shop like this.

"Good luck, sis. You are going to crush it!" she cheered, giving me a tight squeeze and pulling on my hair. She had no idea what meeting she was sending me off to but, as always, she showed full support, like the good sister she was.

"Hey!" I pulled back. "Don't squish the hair." I ran my fingers through it, fluffing it back up. "Thanks, but I don't need luck." I grinned, whipping my hair behind me. "Now, here is my card—go do some exhausted-Midwest-mom-retail-therapy on me."

She looked at my black card, her jaw dropping. "Ava, I-I couldn't . . . I—"

"You can, and you will. You need to have some fun, and that allowance that Simon gives you, I am sure is not enough. Consider it payback for me missing your bridal shower and both baby showers." I squeezed her shoulders.

"Yeah, that's fair. You really have been a terrible sister when it comes to things like that," she admitted, flinching at her own words.

"Hey, you don't have to agree with me," I laughed. I didn't see why I had to show up to every overly themed event just because someone else chose to have a baby. If that was your life decision, great. But I should be allowed to RSVP *no* without getting side-eyed. That was what online registries were for—to send a gift, skip the awkward small-talk, and get your Saturday back. Just saying.

"I love you. Now have *fun*," I told her.

Lila nodded, smiling.

I turned, took a deep breath in, and headed into The Aislinn Atelier to see if this place might be my future.

———

As I stepped into The Aislinn Atelier, the brass chandelier caught my eye, casting a warm light over the dark wood paneling, detailed wood carved in the ceiling, and worn wooden floors. The space was stunning, elegant. Mannequins were draped in tailored suits, and the shelves were lined with vintage—near rusty—tools and gorgeous fabric bolts. There was a collection of old-school sewing machines in the corner that looked like they were hundreds of years old. The arched windows let in just enough natural light to make the room feel alive.

It was hard not to be impressed by the space. Still, as much as I'd love to get out of Atlas & Grey, I wasn't about to make it obvious. I couldn't act desperate. Or, at least, I wouldn't let them know I was—if I was. This team had their work cut out for them if they thought I'd just walk away from my cushy job for a small family-run shop like this.

On paper, I had all the leverage. They didn't know I had broken up with Elliot and wanted a reason to escape San Francisco. They didn't know I had been hoping to find a new, more aligned work environment. They didn't know anything about me.

I told myself it was just another meeting, and I'd been to plenty of those before. Some disappointing, others forgettable. I never wanted to get my hopes up only to get let down, so I did my best to keep expectations low.

But something about this place already felt different. I had no way of explaining it, but for the first time in a while, it was like I was starting to head down the right path, even if I couldn't see where it led yet.

As I stepped farther into the space, appraising every detail, I was curious to learn if the man behind this stunning space—Ronan—was a savvy businessman or if he had simply inherited this place and had no formal training. If that were the case, a place like this was sure to go downhill from here, like most family businesses that declined once handed down from generation to generation.

Within seconds, a voice echoed from across the space. "Ms. Hawthorne, welcome to The Aislinn Atelier." The words were soon followed by a woman approaching from a back room. She was fit, wearing a skintight burgundy dress that revealed every curve of her body, and heels that were so high it boosted her to be able to match the eyelines of the men she faced daily. Her hair was brown, cut shoulder-length, pin straight, and she wore narrow, black-rimmed rectangular glasses. I assumed she was in her mid-thirties.

She walked up to me with her hand out in confidence, wearing a warm smile. "We are so pleased to have you here this afternoon, Ms. Hawthorne. Thank you for coming so close to Christmas. I'm Sofia Lundgren, Ronan's personal assistant."

I gave her hand a firm shake without as much as a smile. I had been in the game long enough to not exude too much warmth up front. As a woman in this world, showing the slightest bit of warmth revealed slivers of weakness.

"No worries. I don't do much in the way of celebrating Christmas. It's just another day. It's a pleasure to meet you, Sofia. Where will I be meeting with Mr. Broderick?"

"Mr. Broderick and yourself will be meeting out here, Ms. Hawthorne."

As if on cue, a man entered from the same room Sofia had emerged. The man I assumed to be Ronan commanded attention with his tall frame and quiet confidence. His features were sharp—dark well-groomed hair, bright eyes. He was dressed in a tailored buttoned-up shirt and a tie, his sleeves rolled up his forearms like he had just been cutting a pattern for a suit. He carried a silent authority that filled the room, a confidence that only a master in his craft could have. He looked familiar, but I couldn't place him—either he had one of those faces, or I'd just seen one too many pictures of him while researching the atelier.

Sofia smiled and moved aside. "May I get you two something to drink?"

I raised my brows at the suggestion.

He turned to me. "Do you drink?"

"Absolutely," I replied.

"Then fetch us two glasses of whiskey, Sofia—the Redbreast twenty-one-year-old in the cabinet."

The fact that his assistant was fetching a three-hundred-dollar-bottle made it clear he wasn't a man who settled for less than the best. And so, my evaluation of this place and this man began.

I felt a rush. It was quite fun to be interviewed by a company when they *needed* you, when you had all the power. Well, the perceived power, at least. It's like dating a guy who's more into you than you are into him. It has a way of boosting your confidence.

He turned back to me with a smile across his objectively handsome face. "Welcome to my home, Ava—The Aislinn Atelier. We were overjoyed when we heard from Quinn that you were going to make it to New York for a meeting after all."

"I'm glad it could work out for both of us," I said coolly.

He led me to the tailor's bench that took up a large part of the shop, where a vintage sewing machine sat, along with a large variety of bolts of fabric, tucked just beneath the table's edge.

Sofia returned with our drinks. Placing them on the bench in front of each of us.

"Please lock the front doors, Sofia. We don't need anyone disrupting our meeting," Ronan said, grabbing his glass and holding it up to me. I wasn't a stranger to businessmen preferring to seal deals over a few drinks. Refusing his offer might have been seen as a slight, so I mirrored him, raising my glass.

"Cheers to the future of The Aislinn Atelier," he said as we clinked our glasses, the sound of crystal ringing through the space.

As we each took a sip, he paused to appreciate the taste. "So, straight to business," he said, tapping his bare fingers on the table.

Thank God. I loathed small talk. I would rather grab those sewing machine needles and poke my eyes out.

Mini test numero uno: passed. No bullshit small talk.

"Ava, what we are in need of is a bit of a facelift here at the atelier. We are over a hundred-year-old company."

"Congratulations," I said with a straight smile. Meaning, he had definitely inherited this place.

Test numero dos: failed. Nepo baby.

"Thank you," he said. "And if you did your research, you have probably noted that our presence in the media is limited. Dismal at best. This is due to a few things." He took another sip of his whiskey. "First off, I am an artist. Due to the nature of being a tailor, we use our hands all day, focusing on creating our pieces, our art, which leaves little bandwidth to create content and keep up with social media trends, or to create PR opportunities for the atelier to expand. I spend sixteen to eighteen hours a day working on my art." He gestured around. "We need someone who can help assemble the team that could bring the vision we have to life.

"Second, because we are a family-run company, and always have been, we prefer to keep our approach highly tailored and exclusive—much like the bespoke suits we create. Our clients are loyal, lifetime clients. Many of them are extremely wealthy and powerful individuals. The fear I have is that we will lose that essence if we expand beyond our four walls, beyond the locals of New York, and those who travel from other cities and countries to work with us. We are looking for the perfect person who can blend the two, but keep the essence of what we have true. The perfect person to help us brand Aislinn and share our story with the world in a way that doesn't dilute the integrity of our brand."

I kept my eyes locked on him, listening intently. I did my best to extend the times between blinks if I could help it.

He paused to see if I had any questions, but they could wait —I wanted him to keep talking.

"Now, we are a successful *and* profitable company," he said. "We always have been. But it is time to finally bring this company into the twenty-first century and reach the potential of what we are here to do."

"Which is?" I asked. A brief and potent question.

A smile tugged at the corner of his mouth. "I am glad you asked, Ava. Our vision is to merge the timeless craftsmanship of traditional tailoring with the innovation of the modern world, creating bespoke garments—pieces that are custom-made, crafted by hand, and tailored to the individual. Not just in fit, but in essence. To empower each individual to express their unique identity through the garments."

I gave only a slight nod, prodding him to continue.

There was something about his words that aligned deeply with me—a sense of purpose and soul that had been missing from the projects I had been involved with recently. The idea of creating and sharing something truly personal—custom, not just another mass-market copy and paste product—felt like a breath of fresh air. Here, it wasn't about the generic, the mass-produced. It was about individuality, about real craftsmanship. About bespoke, which I had such a passion for. I liked what I was hearing.

"Just as the world pushes the boundaries of technology, we at The Aislinn Atelier challenge the norms of modern fashion, reviving the artistry of tailoring in an era dominated by mass production. In a world where fast fashion has stripped clothing of its soul and burdened the environment, we bring back the craftsmanship, elegance, and tradition that make fashion an art form, not just a commodity."

Then it hit me. The Aislinn Atelier, if I chose to be here, wouldn't be just another job. It wouldn't be a stepping stone to something else. It would be different. It would likely demand more from me, push me in ways my current job never would. But that was the point—it would challenge me to do work that mattered, to create something lasting, not just another product or marketing scheme to churn out. This was a rare space where art wasn't rushed, where tradition wasn't sacrificed for convenience. A place where I could make an impact.

And, as if my internal filter had lifted, words left my mouth before I could second-guess them. "I can work with that."

As the words settled between us, I realized they weren't *just* words—I meant them.

"Yes?" he asked.

"Yes. I believe that the bespoke tailoring industry is truly a dying industry. Without passing it down from generation to generation from tailor to apprentice, which is happening less and less, there is the very real potential that it could eventually fizzle out completely. Without a vision like yours, it's inevitable that in the next one hundred years, the industry, sadly, may not exist at all.

"With advancements in technology and A.I., it is rare that anything is made *entirely* by hand anymore. But the irony is that today's customers, especially the high-end clients that you serve, are the smartest generations of purchasers the world has ever seen. Because of the dissolution in quality and the rise of fast fashion, I believe the pendulum will eventually swing back in the opposite direction, causing individuals to seek quality rather than quantity once again. Your vision is on the forefront of that swing back to quality." I completed my thought by taking a sip of whiskey.

He left space for me to continue.

"The Aislinn Atelier. If I'm not mistaken, *Aislinn* in Irish means 'dream' or 'vision,' and *Atelier* means 'workshop.' At least, I'm assuming you're Irish, what with the name of the shop, Ronan being a very Irish name, and this Irish whiskey." I held up my glass. "Am I correct in that assumption?"

It was almost too perfect—Lila booking us at an Irish hotel, completely clueless that I'd be interviewing at an Irish-owned atelier. It had given me a chance to do some general research, preparing me perfectly for today. It felt like another sign that I was on the right track.

"You would be correct." He nodded slowly with a smile stretched on his face, revealing the straightest, whitest teeth I had ever seen.

"So, the name of this space is literally The Vision Workshop. *That* is what we are doing here. Bringing people's visions to life. The vehicle in which we do so is through custom bespoke suits. You aren't just a place where people buy suits;

you are a reprieve for people who come and create *with* you. To build something from nothing. From scraps of fabric, a thread and needle, and your bare hands. It is incredible. This gets to be shared with the world as a magical, mystical, historic space —a workshop that transforms someone into the most confident version of themselves, with every single stitch in mind.

"Clothes alter and transform how we feel about ourselves. And with every stitch and cut, you are infusing Aislinn—aka Vision—into the fabric of your clients' lives." I leaned forward, my elbows on the workbench, as I finished my thought.

"Ava," he said as he leaned back in his chair, "I could not have said it better myself."

"Well, that's why I am the best at what I do." I shrugged. "I already have several ideas we could implement immediately that would impact you as early as February 2026. For instance, we could develop a campaign centered around the concept of 'The Vision Workshop,' showcasing how this space transforms not just clothing but people's entire sense of identity. We could highlight the rich history of The Aislinn Atelier and its dedication to craftsmanship, weaving that narrative into feature stories across top fashion and lifestyle publications. A series of behind-the-scenes content could also be created to bring attention to the artistry and tradition behind every bespoke suit made here, with a special focus on the legacy of the family-run business. Because your PR and branding efforts have been near zero until now, there is huge potential over the next decade to scale your efforts when it comes to being seen."

Ronan took a slow breath, his eyes fixed on me as he processed. He nodded slightly, a thoughtful expression on his face. He set his glass down and tapped his fingers lightly on the table. There was a flicker of recognition in his gaze, as if he was seeing the vision come to life in front of him. Then, with a quiet, approving nod, he said, "I completely agree."

I smirked. Of course he agreed.

"I am curious, however," I started, "why haven't you already pursued this path? Sought out someone to help with this? It is such an obvious growth vertical. Especially if you are profitable enough to hire the correct support needed to bring it to life."

"It has been our intention for quite a while, as I mentioned. We have just been looking for the right person." He huffed out a laugh. "Actually, we have been looking for years. We were close to pulling the trigger with a few, but it didn't feel quite right. Either their values were not aligned or I felt they didn't truly appreciate the craft, or Aislinn, for what it truly is. They were trying to get us to become something we weren't."

"I understand," I said. "That is the reality of what most PR firms do. They try to fit companies into *their* mold. It keeps costs down and limits ideas that haven't been proven and tested." As a matter of fact, that was what Atlas & Grey did. It was another reason why I was considering leaving. But I couldn't just jump ship if this place didn't pass all my tests.

"So, Ronan, that leads me to the question: why do you think *I* would be any different?"

"Well, Ms. Hawthorne, I may be a businessman, and while I do make many decisions on data and numbers, I am also an artist, like I mentioned. When hiring, my artist instinct will rise up. I am not right about a lot of things in life, but I am almost *always* right when it comes to people. Every person I have brought on board here at The Aislinn Atelier has stayed on for years. Shoot, Sofia has been with me since she graduated college."

"That says great things about your leadership and management style," I said, seeing in his eyes how proud he looked of his company.

Test trois: passed. High employee retention.

"We are like a family here, so if we interview someone, a great qualitative metric I like to use is: would we want to spend time with this person during Christmas? If not, they are not the right fit."

"And do you think I'd be a good fit for the team? Like someone you'd want around for Christmas?"

Something felt good about this place. Really good. Like a place I could grow and be challenged. Not like Atlas & Grey, where the companies I represented were corporate and lifeless. This place felt warm, like a family. Ronan had heart. Only now, walking in here, did I realize how cold Atlas & Grey had been—how cold I had become.

"From the moment Quinn told me about you, I knew you could be the ideal fit for this job. I normally believe in hiring slow and firing fast, but there was something about 'Ava Hawthorne'"—he air quoted my name—"that stuck out. And after reading about your work history and client testimonials, it only made sense. You really have some raving fans.

"But I needed to meet you in person so that you could see the heart of our company—my family's legacy. This place is everything to me. I needed to ensure you weren't going to try to completely change us, that you were only going to enhance what we want to create and who we are. I needed to make sure you were one of us." He paused. "From this brief conversation, it is an obvious yes for me."

His tone was so grounded that it made me feel oddly trusting of his judgment. Like this certainty made me feel ready to dive in with them immediately. But I needed to show him I wasn't going to pick up and run across the country and change my entire life because he wanted me to. I would not give my power away to any man. Not in romantic relationships, and especially not one in business.

I leaned in, my forearms now resting on the workshop bench as I stared straight into his eyes—those familiar eyes. "Ronan, this all sounds great, but I'd love for you to tell me: why should I leave my comfortable, cushy life at Atlas & Grey

PR? A stable job with a massive salary, benefits, commission—everything I need to coast through life? To leave all that for a role in New York City where I know no one, for a small mom-and-pop shop—The Aislinn Atelier? The Vision Workshop."

My question sounded mocking, but it wasn't. It was honest. Most people shied away from asking the tough questions when considering jobs, afraid of seeming too forward. But I'd learned the hard way that avoiding uncomfortable truths only led to regret. I'd seen it too many times—people stuck in jobs they hated because they never asked the real questions upfront. I didn't live like that. If something didn't feel right, I walked away. No hesitation. Life was too short to settle for less than what aligned with who I truly was. Well, when it came to work, at least. I'd be the first to say I could have been a little faster to jump the gun and dump old Elliot.

Ronan didn't flinch. Didn't blink. He leaned in even closer, completely unbothered by my directness or the discomfort of my question. Green flag. I needed people who didn't get flighty, who could handle tough conversations without breaking a sweat.

"Because, Ms. Ava"—his eyes locked on me—"you're bored. You haven't been challenged in years. I can see it in your eyes. Your enthusiasm hasn't been stoked for your work *until* today. That is what this place will do for you—it will light that fire in your belly that has been stamped out for much too long."

His words hit home, and I couldn't hide my surprise. My eyes went wide at his spot-on assessment. Maybe he really did know people.

"I could see it earlier when you were talking about the vision we have here. A person like you—someone with ambition and drive—starts to wither when they're not challenged, not passionate about what they do. That's why, deep down, I know you haven't felt truly alive in a long time.

"When you come to The Aislinn Atelier, I promise you it

will revive that fire in your belly. The vision you have for your life. You will be seen for your gifts, and you will actually make a difference in this world. You will have complete autonomy to run the show. You will be the boss. Which I assume is where you thrive." He flashed a grin as if he was reading me like a damn book. "I am confident that it will be the best decision of your entire career. Plus, with New York as the backdrop of that choice, I am certain that it may even be the best decision of your entire life."

I stared at him, determined not to let any sign of weakness slip through. I refused to blink. This was my next test—to see if he truly stood behind what he said, if he questioned his own prediction, or if he would backpedal under my unblinking gaze.

A full minute of silence passed. The only thing I gave him was one slow, deliberate blink, drawn out to its fullest. I wanted to see if he would close the deal. If he would ask for the sale.

"So, Ava, what do you say? Let's make it a merry Christmas for all of us. Join The Aislinn Atelier family."

There it was. Straightforward, no hesitation.

Test four: passed.

I had to give him credit—he'd passed one of my final tests. He hadn't offered me time to "think about it," "sleep on it," or question the moment. He went straight for the close. But I already knew I wouldn't make the decision on the spot even if I knew my answer.

A smile spread across my face as I stood from the workbench.

His gaze didn't waver. He knew this game, too, which made me like the guy even more. He knew business. We would work well together.

"I'll think about it, Ronan," I said confidently. "You have an excellent pitch; I will admit that. But I never make a big life decision on the first meeting. Especially when it comes to my career and a move this big." I added, "I'm sure you can understand."

Shock flashed across his face. Did he really believe I would be that easy to sway? Like a little sweet talking from a handsome face could have me packing up my whole life after one meeting? I could practically hear his mind racing. He'd assumed I'd be quick to jump at the offer, swept up by the excitement of the moment like some young woman getting her big break.

I placed my hand on his across the workshop bench. "Don't worry, Ronan; this is a good thing," I said. "It means we can set up another meeting. I'm sure you're not used to hearing no, but this isn't a no. I just need to think on it for a couple days." I gave him a neutral, unreadable smile.

He looked to his side, like he was trying to figure out where he went wrong. "Ava, what can I do to have you seriously consider joining us?"

"I *am* serious. If I wasn't, I wouldn't have offered to set another meeting. I'm here until January first and would like to make my decision before I leave."

"All right. We will make that happen," he said, waving two fingers, a quick motion that summoned Sofia.

She floated over to the bench, her hips swaying with each step.

"Sofia, please schedule a time for Ms. Hawthorne to meet us here again before Christmas to discuss whatever she will need to see or hear to join us at Aislinn."

Did he handle rejection with class and poise? Yep. The final test. What was that? Quatro? Cinco? Passed.

Sofia nodded with perfect posture, holding her iPad. "Yes, sir. How is December 22nd at this same time, Ms. Hawthorne?"

"Fabulous. For your preparation, when we meet, I would like to dive into your current PR and marketing plan, if any, and get a brief overview of the company's history to help shape the storytelling for our potential future campaign strategy. Once I see those two things, I will know if I am able to help you get what you want, Mr. Broderick."

"That sounds wonderful. I so appreciate your thoroughness, Ava. I see why they say you are the best of the best." He guided me to the front door of the atelier. Sofia slipped in front of us to unlock the door.

"We look forward to seeing you on December 22nd." Sofia smiled.

"Indeed," I said as I walked out the door, Ronan holding it open behind me.

"Ava," he called after me. "Nice suit. I know a bespoke when I see one."

"My tailor in San Fran and I worked on it for years. It's no Aislinn Atelier, though."

As I turned, our eyes locked, and something shifted. A jolt shot through me—sharp, sudden. My pulse spiked. There was a pull, a strange familiarity that gripped me. Like the universe was trying to get my attention, to tell me something. I didn't know what it meant, or why it happened. Only that it mattered somehow.

6

LILA FLOPPED DOWN ON OUR SHARED HOTEL BED, WHERE, IF I hadn't already mentioned, I had been sleeping like shit. "Wow, there is so much walking in this city. My feet are killing me." She took her tennis shoes off, throwing them across the room. "How the heck are you walking everywhere in those tall heels?"

I shrugged. "My feet are just shaped like this after so many years of training them. I'm like a reverse Barbie. You know that scene where her feet go from arched to flat when she becomes human? Well, I'm the opposite. Now they are just permanently arched."

"You are insane," she said, shaking out her legs.

"You should lie on your back with your butt against the headboard, put your legs up in the air, it'll flush the lactic acid out so they aren't sore tomorrow. We have another big day of walking ahead of us. You better rest up."

She did as I suggested, scooting her butt to the wall, lying back, her legs up in the air. "So, what was this mysterious meeting you went to?"

"Well, I don't want to say much unless it actually becomes something, but I went there for an interview."

She took her legs down and flipped onto her stomach in shock, jaw dropped. "Wait—what? You are leaving Atlas & Grey? Would you be leaving San Francisco? Would you move to New York?"

"Here come the questions. See? This is why I didn't want to tell you." I took off my heels then headed to the bathroom to brush my hair. "Nothing is decided yet. I am just looking at my options."

"Did you already have this interview planned, or did it just come up in the last few days?" Lila asked.

"This atelier has been trying to get me into a meeting for months, but until Elliot and I ended things, I wasn't considering it," I huffed. "When I called you to see if you wanted to go on a vacation, I figured it would be a good way to knock out a trip with you and see what was up with this place."

Lila jumped to her knees, clapping her hands together. For a moment, I forgot she was a mother of two. She was all energy, like we were back in high school, gossiping about boys and our dream jobs.

"Oh, Ava, I am so, so excited for you! I've always thought it'd be good for you to get out of San Francisco. But to move to New York? That's straight out of a movie!" she gushed, setting her chin on her laced fingers, now propped on the bed. She was fully engaged, and her legs seemed to have forgotten their pain. "What's the company?"

"You are so ridiculous."

"Living vicariously through you, is all," she admitted. "Go on."

"It was an interview with an atelier. They need major help with their PR, and from what it sounded like, building out and hiring an entire marketing team, as well. The founder seemed really sharp. The company has been handed down for generations. It is a really cool place."

"Oh, an atelier. You mean . . . like . . ." She scrunched her face. "What does atelier mean, again?"

"It is a custom bespoke suit atelier. Basically, they make suits. Atelier just means workshop. Bespoke means that everything is done totally custom for each client and made completely by hand. Everything is hand stitched. It is really amazing what they do. This suit"—I gestured to the suit I was now taking off—"is bespoke. Each one takes about a hundred hours to make and costs anywhere from ten to twenty thousand dollars. Or more, of course, depending."

"Twenty thousand dollars!" Lila shrieked, as if I had just told her I'd committed murder.

I laughed. "Yes. I know it's ridiculous. But I would love to work with a luxury product and high-end clientele like this, with a cool history. All the companies I work with are software, tech, or pharmaceuticals, which is great, but I am so tired of mass market, low-ticket items. It is like I am building these companies and managing their public image, and it's not even something I believe in. I am just helping them sell to the masses and making the sick sicker and the rich richer. I think I'm ready to be a part of something more meaningful." I hung up my suit on the rickety hotel hanger, standing there in nothing but my bra and trousers. "Being in that meeting today, I could tell that Ronan actually *cared* about what he did. There was real passion in his voice. He has a heart for his clients. He's not just about profit. You know?"

"Wow. First of all, this is amazing. But where did this change of heart come from? Last time I saw you, you were, and had *always* been, about the profit. Not really caring what businesses you work with if it meant you made money."

"I know. I didn't really think I cared until recently. But today, I got a glimpse of what it could look like to have a job that pays well *and* that I could actually be passionate about." I brushed it off, trying not to make a big deal out of it. "I never thought that was possible. That you could have both. Anyway, what's the second thing?"

"Is this Mr. Ronan cute? He sounds really cute." She emphasized the word *cute* in a way that was so annoying. So Lila. *Ca-ute.*

I threw a towel at her face. "Shut up. I am not going to, nor would I ever consider, dating my potential future boss. I'd never give my power away like that at work," I scoffed in disbelief at the hopeless romantic in front of me.

"I am just saying, how cute would that be?" Her hands were clasped at her chest. "You move to New York after a devastating breakup, explore a new job opportunity, and it leads to finding the love of your life that you build on hundreds of years of legacy with," she said dreamily, staring off into the distance.

"The breakup was not devastating," I corrected. "Lila, you were really in the wrong profession. You should have become a screenwriter for romcoms or something." I laughed. "Or a matchmaker. Definitely not a journalist."

"I wish. Being a journalist was tough. But honestly, being a mom is the hardest job ever. I hate to admit it, but sometimes I wish I could just go back to working full time. Even if that meant being a journalist. It was way easier. I had so much freedom before kids." I could see the mom guilt painted on her face for even thinking it.

"It's worth it, though, right? Don't you love it?" I asked.

Part of me wanted to offer reassurance, but the thought of giving up my freedom to raise kids felt suffocating. I'd never dreamed of having a family. I liked my life just the way it was—free and on my terms. Lila, though, had clearly found meaning in it. I couldn't imagine living that life. Still, I respected her path, even if it wasn't a path I'd ever take myself.

"Of course," Lila said. "It's so fulfilling, but sometimes I look at you. You can do whatever you want, with whoever you want, however you want, whenever you want. Sometimes, I would love to just drop everything—all my responsibilities—and write romcoms in New York City cafés. I don't know. It's probably just my hormones talking."

Sympathy, mixed with something else, stirred within me. "Well, sis, this week, you can be whoever you want to be. We're in New York. Maybe you can take my laptop and write in a *ca-ute* coffeeshop for fun? Live the dream while you have the free time away from everything?"

For a second, I considered how different our lives were. She had a family—real responsibilities—and I had freedom, but I couldn't help but feel a strange, deep, buried longing for a piece of what she had, even if it wasn't something I could ever see for myself.

Lila considered my offer then perked up. "You know what? You're right; I will. How often do I take a vacation without my kids? Never! This is the first time I have been away from the girls since they were born."

"Yes, that's the spirit. Embrace your freedom, Lila. We will do it together. I am newly single, as well." I wiggled my brows. "In a way, we both have a freedom here that we haven't had in a long time."

"Speaking of, maybe we can check out that speakeasy tonight if the bartender you mentioned from last night is there?" Lila was being disturbingly supportive, considering I'd shown her a broom closet earlier. Maybe that closet *did* lead to the speakeasy.

"Yeah, I mean, we can try. Or we can chalk it up to me being drugged by that strange bartender and none of it actually happened," I scoffed. "It was all just some mushroom-alcohol-induced hallucination."

"Well, now I really want to go to get some inspiration for this romcom I'm going to write this week." She grinned.

"Immediate implementation—I love it. I knew you were still you somewhere deep in there," I leaned on the bed to give her a high-five then went back to the bathroom to brush my teeth. "But for God's sake, just do *not* use my life as your muse for this little writing project of yours."

"What time did you say the bartender stopped serving drinks?" Lila shouted over the running water.

"Nine twenty-five," I mumbled with a mouthful of fluoride-free toothpaste. "How fucking weird is that?"

"Well, maybe that's when the speakeasy opens? Why don't we get a drink and try to get some information from him, then see if at nine twenty-five, anything is different? It's a speakeasy, after all. They are kinda supposed to be hidden in plain sight. Hard to find. Right?" she offered.

I spat out my toothpaste, wiped my mouth, and then stared at myself in the mirror. "I guess that could work," I said. I came out of the bathroom and leaned against the doorframe. "The only catch . . ." I trailed off.

"What?" Her voice was frantic.

"Did you happen to pack a flapper dress or pearls, by chance?"

I walked into the nearly empty restaurant with Lila, both of us dressed in a way that *could* technically pass for 1925—me in a simple black suit and silk scarf, Lila in a high-waisted skirt and blouse, her hair in finger waves.

The moment I spotted the bartender across the room, I couldn't help myself. "Thank God you're here!" I yelled, beelining for him. I nudged Lila and pointed discreetly. "This is our guy," I whispered, excited to get some answers.

"Good evenin' to ye ladies, what can I get started for ye tonight?" he asked, his cheery smile insinuating he hadn't drugged me and thrown me into a broom closet, leaving me to hallucinate alone for several hours the night prior.

"Hello sir. I am Lila Carrington," my sister interjected before I had a chance to unleash on this man. "What was your name, kind sir?" she said as I shot her a death glare.

Why was this girl so damned nice? I swear we were raised in the same household, but you would never be able to tell.

"Me name's Christopher, kind ma'am," he said, reaching across the bar to shake my sister's hand.

I rolled my eyes. *Christopher*? Mr. Santa-Hat-Wearing Chris Fucking Kringle? It had to be a joke. His real name was probably Harold. Or Eugene. Maybe Reginald. "Christopher" sounded like the kind of alias you used around Christmas to lure young women into a speakeasy that's actually a broom closet, right after slipping something into their drink.

Everyone trusted a man named after Good Ol' Saint Nick.

"Well, Sir Christopher, I think you met my sister, Ava, last night." She gestured to me.

"Oh, I most certainly did," he said, maintaining his smile but widening his eyes and raising his brows suggestively to Lila.

She let out a knowing laugh.

"Jesus Christ," I muttered, walking a few steps away to emotionally compose myself.

"Well, Chris—do you mind if I call you Chris?" Lila asked.

"Of course, m'lady," he said, sounding like a fourteenth-century knight.

I couldn't stop my eyeballs from rolling to the back of my skull this time in complete resignation.

"Thank you," she said, sitting down on one of the bar stools in front of us. "Chris, to start, could my sister and I please have two espresso martinis, please?" Did she just say please twice in one sentence? That had to be some kind of politeness record.

"Comin' right up, darlin'," Chris said, turning to whip up our drinks.

I sat at the bar, my head dropping down to rest on my forearm. "Lila, you just said please two times in one sentence. What are you doing? If we want information from this man, we need to put him under pressure. Not *please* him to death. I don't need him spiking my drink again," I protested.

"*This* man? This man doesn't have a dangerous bone in his body." Lila laughed. "You spend too much time in business meetings with sleazy salesmen and liars. You're just paranoid. If we can get him casually talking until nine twenty-five, maybe he'll offer for us to go to the speakeasy again."

I checked my watch, which I had purposely worn in case we needed it when we went back to the cell phone service-less time warp tonight. "Fine. I'll give you ten minutes, and if you haven't made progress, I get to take over."

She smiled like she did as a kid whenever she got her way—proud, accomplished.

It took him five minutes to make our drinks, giving my sister only five minutes to get information before the clock struck nine twenty-five.

I tapped my watch at Lila, mouthing, "*Tick-tock, Cinderella. Your time is running out.*"

She stuck out her tongue just as her phone started to ring. "Oh, it's the girls. I promised I would talk to them at bedtime each night. I have to get this. I'm sorry."

"Your loss," I said, returning the victory smirk she'd given me moments ago. "Tell them hey from their favorite Auntie Ava.

"I will," she said as she stood to step away.

"Oh, and Lila!" I called after her.

"Yeah?"

"Stop saying *I'm sorry* so much. It makes you sound kind of pathetic."

"Okay, you're right. Totally. I'm sorry," she replied automatically then caught herself, holding up a finger as she stepped into the lobby. "Hi, girls . . ." Her voice trailed off.

I rolled my eyes. Exactly my point.

I turned back toward the bar. Back toward my prey. Mr. Santa-Hat-Wearing Christopher. Chris Kringle, making his way over with our drinks.

"Where did dat kind sister of yers go?" he asked.

"She's got to check in with the little gremlins before bed.

Kids, such a time suck, right?" I said, attempting Lila's befriending approach to get him talking.

He belly-laughed, setting my drink down and staring at me like I was some sort of circus act. "Yes, indeed, those children can occupy much of one's time."

"What the hell was that place you sent me last night?" My tone was as blunt as ever, all semblance of pleasantries and small talk gone.

"Ah, yer talking about Da Velvet Clover?" He grinned from ear-to-ear, his cheeks rosy, flushed.

"Yeah, I came back to show Lila today, and it was a broom closet. Is there a secret entrance I forgot about walking through, or did you drug me last night? Because I doubt your *boss*, the one who sets all these *rules* for this bar, would like to hear about that little incident." My stare was as threatening as my words.

He only laughed a deep belly laugh, which caught me completely off guard. It felt like I was punching air. Nothing threw him off his jolly demeanor. He was so obnoxious.

"Oh, don't ye worry, Ms. Hawthorne. Da Velvet Clover is very real, and ye certainly went dere last night. But how you got dere is part of the speakeasy's magic. 'Tis supposed to be hard to find, impossible without knowing how to use the secret door. After all, dat is the whole allure of a speakeasy—it's hidden in plain sight," he said, glancing at his bare wrist, as if his scattered freckles and sunspots somehow kept time.

I followed his lead and checked mine. Nine twenty-five on the dot.

"In fact, not everyone gets the luxury of being invited into Da Velvet Clover. It really is for those who are ready for it. Or for those who need it," he said, his stupid smile still across his face. He walked over to the left side of the bar where the curtain hiding the broom closet was and pulled it back.

"I am *not* falling for this. I checked earlier—it's a broom closet. And I don't *need* some stupid speakeasy. Or anything, for that matter."

He raised his brows, hand open, palm up, as if ushering me through the curtain, just like the night before. "I never said you did, Ms. Hawthorne."

I looked back toward the lobby. Lila was still on the phone with the girls. It looked like she was going to be a while.

I cocked an eyebrow. "Do I have to go through this door at exactly nine twenty-five, or . . . what—the secret speakeasy self-destructs? The portal shuts down at nine twenty-six, then no trespassing?"

He just grinned, silent for a beat, then shrugged and said, "Well, timing *is* everythin', Ms. Ava."

A few seconds of a staring standoff passed before I rolled my eyes and muttered, "You're impossible." I stood from my chair, grabbing my drink from the bar, rolling my eyes as I walked past him to open the door, fully prepared for a stupid smelly broom closet. Before I walked through, I paused and leaned back to say, "If you drugged me or spit in my drink again, I swear to God, I'm coming back tomorrow and suing your ass."

"Sounds like a wonderful plan, Ms. Hawthorne," he said, still wearing that stupid grin.

"Stop calling me that. Make sure to tell Lila I'm in here. She will come looking for me." I figured if Lila got in after she talked to the girls, that meant we'd be able to get in after nine twenty-five and Chris Kringle was full of shit.

I walked through the doorway into the broom closet behind the velvet curtain. Only, this time, it wasn't a broom closet. And there were no cleaning supplies, or wrapped silverware, or mops in sight.

As I stepped through the doorway, a rush of cold air swept past me and what waited on the other side was the same dimly lit, 1920's-inspired speakeasy, still dressed in holiday decor, just like last night. Only, tonight, there was a live jazz band in the corner; four men, with variations of hats, bow ties, and suspenders. One man on the piano, the others on the bass, trumpet, and saxophone. They played across from the Christmas tree, which stood beside the bar. The reject table I had shared with the elusive man sat in the opposite corner. The devastatingly attractive, elusive, brooding bar owner man.

"How the fuuuc—" I muttered under my breath as I stepped up once again to the hostess stand, where the same woman with the short bob stood there, smiling.

"Good evenin', Ms. Hawthorne. Will you be joining us again this eve?" Impressive. She remembered my name. "I am happy to seat you at da communal table once again, if ye prefer. Or we have a few great spaces available at da bar this evening, if ye're here alone," she offered.

"The bar. Anything to keep me away from that communal table," I said, sipping the espresso martini I'd brought with me. What the hell had Chris Kringle put in these drinks?

I followed her, looking around in disbelief. I wasn't crazy. I hadn't dreamed it. In fact, it was better than I remembered.

"How is this seat for ya, ma'am?" She gestured to a barstool with a perfect view of the band, at the corner of the bar, as far away from the communal table as possible.

"This is fabulous, thanks." This time, I did not ask for a menu. "Do you guys check phones upon entry, or is it just everyone being polite? There has to be a no-phone policy here, right?" I asked, reaching for my phone to hand in.

A look of confusion flashed across her face before she plastered on a smile. "Ma'am, if ye are in need of our resident pay phone, it's in the back room, next to the wash closet. It is five cents per call. Let me know if ye need any help workin' it." She smiled and walked back to her station.

Man, these people really were committed to the whole 1920's theme. Maybe it was some kind of murder mystery party, where everyone stayed in character until they figured out who offed the bar owner. It was always the butler or the maid, right? Or, maybe this time, it would be the giant bartender, or the woman in the suit named Ava.

"Okay . . ." I said, clicking my tongue. I threw back the rest of my drink within a few minutes. I had to admit, Kringle made one damn good espresso martini. Why were espresso martinis so good?

As I set the glass down, my gaze drifted toward the reject table. No one was sitting there. No mystery man. Then I noticed something I hadn't the night before—a door I hadn't seen, tucked near the table. Maybe it led to another restaurant. A second hotel entrance? An exit to the street?

I hoped Lila could find me all right in here. She was going to love this place.

I snuck a peek at my phone to see if I had any messages from her. Maybe being seated closer to the entrance, I could connect to Wi-Fi, but nothing. Once again, a black screen. Odd.

The same bartender from last night—Ed or Eddie, I think was his name—made his way over.

"Ms. Hawthorne!" he called, waving enthusiastically as he hurried over. His eagerness startled me so much I nearly fell out of my seat.

"Ma'am, Ms. Hawthorne," he said, his hand placed over his chest, breathless. "I wanted to thank ya so much for the kind tip ye left last night. Cill told me ye left it for me. I just wanted ye to know that it made all the difference for me family this Christmas. I'm able to buy gifts for all me kids now, and me wife, too. They'll be so excited. Me wife insisted I make the next drink ye have here on da house. What can I get for ye on this wonderful eve?" His smile was filled with gratitude, like any dad just trying to make Christmas special for his kids. But he acted like I'd left him a winning lotto ticket. I swore I had only left a fifty. Not sure how he did all that with fifty bucks minus a round of whiskey, but that wasn't any of my business.

"Oh ... that's great, Ed—" I said, testing the name.

He nodded eagerly, so I continued.

"Eddie, I'll have an Old Fashioned." Then I added for some reason I couldn't quite explain why, "And make it with Irish whiskey." I always thought I hated Irish whiskey, but last night had proven me wrong. I guessed I was still surprisable.

"Yes, ma'am, right away." He said, like he himself was a kid on Christmas Eve, waiting for Santa to fill his stocking after being a good boy all year. Then he turned and headed off to make the drink with a smile so big I half-expected him to break into song and dance.

"Ava Hawthorne."

How the fuck does everyone know my name in this godforsaken place?

The voice came from behind me. The deep, strong accent. The voice that sounded like music. The hair on the back of my neck stood up. I *knew* that voice.

I turned to my left and saw none other than the stoic, brooding bar owner leaning against the counter, a microscopic look of amusement on his face, one he clearly didn't show often.

"Interesting to see you outside of the reject table." I said. "You know they say that seeing someone outside of their usual environment is like running into a teacher on a date—odd and confusing to the mind. No other lonelies to harass tonight?"

"Only one, but she has recently convinced me hostess to seat her on a barstool, even though she is alone in my pub and should technically have been sat at my *communal* table," he said, completely devoid of warmth. "And, as of last night, has managed to bribe and befriend me best bartender." Sarcasm seemed to be his tone of choice. Like mine. I guessed we had at least one thing in common.

"Yes, in fact, my buddy Eddie here tells me your name is . . . *Kill*? What kind of name is that?" I meant it as a snide offense, but it came out more like a genuine question.

"Cill for short. Cillian is Irish. I was born in Ireland. If ya couldn't tell."

"Oh, I could tell," I said, trying to keep my tone equally as cold as his. I didn't trust guys like him—too smooth, too charming, too mysterious, too unreadable. "So, what brought you to the States? A fake marriage to get your green card? Or you just didn't have enough anxiety living in Ireland? Figured New York was better for that?"

He darted his eyes to me, but his frame was still facing forward, his forearms resting on the edge of the bar. "Nah, none of that. I came here after da war."

A long pause lingered between us as I waited for the punchline to the joke that didn't come.

"What war?" I asked incredulously, letting out a laugh. Was he seriously under the impression that he lived in the 1920s? Was this place some kind of joke? Maybe this really *was* one of those themed restaurants where everyone had to stay in character.

He looked at me like I was—how would his people say it?— daft.

When the blank look must have stayed plastered on my face a few seconds too long, he cleared his throat and straightened. "Uh . . . Da Great War . . . the largest war in history?"

"Wait—I'm sorry. Just to clarify, you're saying you *fought* in The Great War?" If my memory of freshman-year history serves me right, that's what they called World War I before World War II happened, right? If this *wasn't* a murder mystery, stay-in-character, 1920's-themed bar, then what the hell kind of drugs were these people on? And if it *was* a 1920's murder mystery party, then he was a phenomenal actor and should move to LA.

I paused, watching his unchanged expression. He only raised his brow.

Well, if he wanted me to play along, I'd humor him. But before I left tonight, I'd need to leave the hostess the number for the nearest psych ward for this guy. Just in case. I felt as if it was my civic duty. Call me Mother Teresa.

"Wow, I can imagine how crazy of a time that must have been," I offered. It came out like I actually meant it. Man, maybe *I* would be a great actress, maybe I will win the murder mystery game I'm not totally sure we're playing.

"Indeed. But dat time is over now. Now I'm here in New York, the greatest city in the world. And tonight, I'm in me pub, next to one of da most fascinating creatures I have ever encountered." He took a slow sip of whiskey, turning forty-five degrees toward me but still looked bored.

His words jolted through me, straightening my spine with a sudden rush of energy. I didn't expect that low ball—what was it—compliment?

"Here ye go, Ms. Ava." Eddie dropped off my drink, and I couldn't say I didn't second-guess it before I took my first sip.

I guessed I was in the land of make-believe tonight. On the plus side, this would be great content for Lila to write about while she was here. Speaking of, where the hell was she? She couldn't still be talking to the girls. I checked behind me to see if I'd missed her coming in.

"Lookin' for someone?" Cillian asked, now seated on the bar stool next to me, bringing my attention back to a conversation I had tried to forget.

"I'm waiting for someone, hence why I am not at the lonely loser table tonight."

He raised an eyebrow. "Ah. Is it a date, then? Who's da lucky gentleman?"

I rolled my eyes. "So, is all you do just sit and drink at your bar all day and harass innocent patrons?"

He huffed. "Oh, I wish I could. No, me life is much more complex than that."

"How so? This decade is so simple. No complexity. No technology. What could be so hard about it?" I played along.

He glanced at me. "Tings that seem easy to ye may not be so easy to others."

Now *this* guy was talking in riddles? "What makes *your* life so complex?" I was curious what story he would spin. I had to admit, this role play thing *was* kind of fun. Maybe it was his preferred foreplay, or his fetish. Yuck.

"I am a businessman, Ms. Hawthorne. That means da game is never finished. Dere is always someone to hire, to fire. Someone to pay off, someone to pay out. Me mind never stops, never sleeps."

"So you own the speakeasy as a what—stress relief, a free place to come drink and flirt with women." Not a question.

He smirked. "Dere are many reasons I opened this speakeasy—stress relief bein' just a small one of them. But, in all my years of ownin' this place, dere hasn't been a woman worth flirtin' with . . . till you."

He stared at me. I froze. Then I forced another eye roll. What a line. The way he'd said it, though—calm, detached—made it impossible to tell if he actually meant it, or if he was just delivering the same old spiel that had worked a million nights with a million women before this one. I guessed it was the latter.

"I find that hard to believe. You are in New York, 'the greatest city in the world.' Plus, I bet women love the stoic, brooding bad boy act."

"Act?" He shook his head. "Isn't an act, Ava. Haven't ya met men after da war? This is it. We were left as shells of ourselves. Like all the rounds of bullets we shot, only the shells left, lyin' in the dirt."

I pursed my lips in somewhat fake sympathy. "That is really

. . . sad. I guess you are the first one I've encountered." I patted his shoulder.

He glanced back, looking at my hand, then me. I couldn't tell if his look was one of appreciation, or if it triggered some sort of fake PTSD and he was about to fake kill me.

I removed my hand. Just in case.

"So . . ." I did my best to smoothly reroute us to a much happier 1920's-esque topic. "What other businesses do you have, Mr. Big Time Business Man?"

What looked like an almost smirk almost crossed his face, but he caught it before it fully formed. "I have many. Many I can't tell ya about."

"What about the ones you *can* tell me about?" I asked.

Cillian looked at me. "Ye are a persistent one, aren't ya, Ms. Hawthorne?"

The way he said my last name shot a sensation down low that surprised me—unexpected and unwelcome. I brushed it off. Biology was a traitorous son of a bitch.

He took a deep breath then let his chest fall. "Well, we 'ave dis lovely speakeasy, Da Velvet Clover, here." He gestured around. "I 'ave an importing business with the Irish military. I 'ave a book printing shop, a tailor shop, and a . . . construction business." He glanced at me before he finished the sentence, like it was a joke. All of it fabricated. I couldn't tell what was true to save my life. Man, he was *good*. If it wasn't true, then this man was quite the storyteller. Truly, he could win an Oscar for this performance.

I stared at him, narrowing my eyes as much as I could with the amount of Botox I had to eliminate my 11's—those deep lines in-between the brows from all the frowning I'd done over the years. My team joked that I had the worst case of Resting Bitch Face they'd ever seen.

"Fascinating . . ." I paused to decide which direction to take this conversation. "A tailoring shop, tell me more about that." I could talk tailoring shop. Maybe I could pick up some tips from him, with the atelier as a strong candidate for my future.

His head stayed down while quickly glancing at me. I held his stare. Then he leaned in, his scent wrapped around me—smoke and whiskey, leather and something darker. It was intoxicating. Dangerous.

"I tell ya what, Ava. I will tell ya about my tailoring shop, if ya tell me about yerself," he said.

This time my name on his lips did something to me—something unexpected. It was like a jolt of electricity, sparking a rush of warmth to my cheeks and a flutter deep in my stomach. I couldn't tell if I was into it. Or terrified.

I shifted back on my stool. "What exactly would you like to know, *Cillian*?"

A corner of his mouth turned up slightly at the sound of his name, the closest thing to a smile I had seen from him.

"What do *ya* do for work? Office clerk? Nurse? Teacher? I can tell ya are not a wife and mother who stays home."

"Well, you're right about the latter," I said with pride, not offended at his limited career choice suggestions—if we were playing the 1920's game. "I am in public relations. I work at a large firm in San Francisco. But I am considering taking a position here in New York, at an atelier of all places."

"Ya came all the way to New York for *one* interview?"

"I guess you can say I am seriously considering it," I huffed. They probably didn't have a ton of commercial flights in the 1920s.

I stared at him. There was something about this guy—despite the brooding mysterious act, an odd, unearned trust seemed to settle between us. Like we had been cut from a similar cloth in some unexplainable way. Maybe it was the reject table that had bonded us, positioned us both as outcasts. Misunderstood. Too cold to be truly loved and accepted as we were. Against my better judgment—or maybe nudged by the Irish whiskey—I let my guard slip, just a little.

"Truthfully? My boyfriend and I broke up last week, and I figured I shouldn't put my life on hold any longer. This company has been trying to recruit me for a while, and once he ended it, I told them I would be out here as soon as possible for an interview." *Why was I telling him all of this?*

"Ah, so ya are heartbroken, are ya? Eh?"

"I am not. Half the time, my ex would annoy the hell out of me, and the other half, I wasn't even into him," I said. "Relief is how I would more properly put it."

He let out a laugh—an actual laugh—one that revealed his teeth. Well, almost. It was breathtaking. *He* was breathtaking. Jesus. It felt like I had just unlocked something in him. Something few ever got to witness. That smile was enough to make me want to chase it, to do whatever it took to see it again . . . and again.

"Was that *a laugh* I just heard from the depressed, brooding businessman?" I gasped, my hand on my chest in feigned disbelief. "That seems very off brand for you."

He ignored me, and his smile faded. "So, ya are considering it, then? This job at da atelier?"

I mourned the loss of that smile but continued on. "I am. The founder I interviewed with today is great. And he passed almost all of my tests."

"Your tests?" he asked. "Wasn't he interviewing *you* for the job?"

"I've been in PR long enough to know what to look for on the job hunt. The green flags, the red flags. So I shit test these places pretty harshly before I even consider working there." I shrugged. A wave of realization hit: *I am sharing way too much. It must be the drinks.* "Anyway, enough about me. On to your tailoring shop; come on." I tapped his arm with the back of my hand.

Cillian's gaze was steady on me, unreadable. Bored. Then he exhaled a short breath, almost amused. "It's quite impressive to meet a woman who knows business." He tilted his glass slightly in my direction. "Extremely refreshing."

Man, he was really deep into this role play thing.

"You don't deal with many women in all your different lines of work?"

"Nah, hardly any. Unless dey are clerks or assistants."

"Hmm," was all I said. "'Kay, go ahead. Tailoring shop . . ." I gestured for him to get on with it.

"What exactly would ya like to know, Ava?" He mimicked my earlier question.

"Well," I said, "why do you have one? How did you start it? You don't seem like a tailor."

"Ava!" A high-pitched shriek rang out behind me.

I turned in my chair to see Lila at the hostess stand, her jaw practically on the floor.

"Are you freaking kidding me? This place is *insane!*" she shouted over the music and the hum of the crowded room.

I blinked, somewhat shocked she had gotten in. I *had* ordered Chris Kringle to let her in, but I had no idea if he actually would, or could, what with all his no-laptop–no-drinks-after-nine twenty-five rules. He'd made it seem like nine twenty-five was the one and only time I could enter this place. He was so full of shit with his "timing *is* everything," making it seem like I couldn't wait for Lila.

"Hey, Lil," I shouted back, waving her over. Then I leaned in to whisper to Cillian, "My sister."

"The one from Colorado," he recalled.

I glared at him for remembering, despite being many shots of whiskey deep when I'd told him that menial factoid. He had actually remembered?

"Right," I said, eyeing him with suspicion

"Christopher told me he wasn't technically supposed to let

me in after nine thirty, but he said he'd make an exception—for me," she squealed, clearly pleased with herself.

Guilt pricked at my chest. I had basically ditched Lila for no reason. But she'd made it in somehow, and she didn't seem mad, so I guessed it worked out.

"I'm so sorry that took so long! The girls would not stop talking about everything they did at school today—it's their last day before Christmas break."

After all that talk about not saying sorry, here she was, apologizing.

I shot her a sharp look.

"Oh," she seethed. "I am *not* sorry. Sorry, Av—I mean . . . I *apologize* for taking so long," she corrected, pausing to analyze her words, like she was checking to see if she'd accidentally managed to apologize again.

"Lil, saying 'I apologize' is just another way of saying I am sorry."

"Ya have children?" Cillian cut in, clearly attempting to steer the conversation toward something more interesting than my sister's ongoing struggle with apologizing for existing.

"Lila, this is Cillian," I said, pronouncing his name slowly, raising a brow. "This is his speakeasy. Cillian, this is Lila, my sister."

"It is a true pleasure to meet ya, Lila." He stood to offer her his barstool. "Please, sit."

"Oh no, no, you don't need to do that," she said, waving him off.

"I insist," he said, standing back as I noticed, once again, he wore a gorgeous three piece navy suit. It made me want to know more about this tailoring shop of his. Damn my sister and her timing.

"Thank you so much, Cillian," she said, blushing—swooning—as she shook his hand and slid onto the now-vacant stool. "My feet are killing me in these heels," she added then turned to me with a look that screamed, *oh my gosh, this is the most gorgeous man I've ever laid eyes on.*

I clenched my jaw to stop the smile that threatened to peek through.

"Ava here told me about your amazing speakeasy last night, and wow, does it live up to the hype."

"Why, thank ya, Lila," he said. His demeanor was one hundred percent more pleasant than it had been with me. "May I ask: how old are ya children?"

"I have two, Rose and Violet. Five and six." She smiled, sitting up straighter in her seat with pride.

"Phenomenal," he said, his tone warm.

"Do *you* have children?" she asked.

I shot her a wide-eyed look, and she immediately realized she probably shouldn't have asked.

"Lila," I hissed, shaking my head. If looks could kill . . .

She clenched her jaw. "Oh, sorry—you don't have to answer that. It's none of my business," she backtracked. "*Sorry,*" she mouthed to me.

"Lila," I muttered, exasperated. Now every other word out of her mouth was *sorry*.

"It's fine," Cillian said, waving me down before I could say anything else. "I had two as well. One passed away, complications at birth. His name was Eoin. But my eldest, we call her Saoirse."

"Freedom?" I blurted out. This Irish whiskey was strong.

"Very good, Ava," he said, his eyes filled with surprise. "You have been studying your Irish names, eh?"

"I did a lot of research for the atelier I am interviewing at. It's owned by an Irish family," I said.

"I am so sorry, Cillian," Lila offered, her sympathy far more natural than mine. That time, I had no urge to correct her. I figured it was one of the only times when saying "I'm sorry" was actually appropriate. Lila continued, "That has to be one of the hardest things for a parent to go through. I can't imagine how challenging that must have been for you."

"Thank ya," he said, taking a sip of his whiskey. "Happened long ago. I am just grateful I still have my Saoirse."

I snuck a look at his hand. No wedding ring. That must mean the mother—his wife—had died during birth, maybe? Nasty divorce?

Lila and I exchanged glances like we were both thinking the same thing. Neither of us dared to ask. I couldn't believe he was sharing all of this. Unless it was all part of the façade, all of it bullshit. If that were the case, he was just a dick.

Lila had this way about her, where people just offered information and were willing to help her with things so freely. Things they would never offer to help me with. Prime example: Chris Kringle letting her into the speakeasy *forty-five minutes* late. He hadn't had any trouble following the rules when it came to refusing to serve me drinks right after nine twenty-five last night.

"How about another round?" I had to change the conversation to something else. Anything else. "I'll have Eddie start while I run to the restroom. Whiskey for everyone? Lila, you will love their Irish whiskey."

"That sounds . . . great," my sister appeased. She hated whiskey but probably felt so guilty for bringing up Cillian's dead child that she wasn't about to offend his country's national drink.

"Restroom?" I asked Cillian.

He stepped closer, his hand lightly brushing my lower back as he pointed me in the right direction. The heat of him, the scent of oak and smoke clinging to his jacket, sent a shiver up my spine. Time slowed.

He leaned in, his lips just beside my ear, his breath warm as he murmured, "Just dere, love." He gestured toward the back, where an old wooden door had the brass letters "*WC.*" The way he'd said it, the way his hand stayed on my waist for a second too long, made something stir low in my stomach again—that same biological urge that had betrayed me earlier. It was just a simple direction, a simple touch, but the intimacy of it—of him —caught me completely off guard.

I exhaled. "Right. Thanks," I mumbled, stepping away.

I told Eddie the drink order then slipped into the "wash closet," my pulse going a million beats a minute.

I gripped the sink, staring into the mirror, trying to catch my breath. The restroom was as immaculate as the speakeasy itself. Dimly lit sconces, black walls, and hand towels for washing.

I couldn't believe Cillian had a child . . . and a . . . dead child. And potentially a wife? I had no idea why I cared. But after hearing him say it, I did. And that touch. Holy shit, his touch on my low back still burned as if I could feel him even through the multiple layers of my suit. It was like his hand had been lit on fire, incinerating any clothing between his hand and my skin.

I closed my eyes, took a deep breath, held it, then slowly exhaled. He could spend every night here, escaping into a 1920's fantasy to avoid his real life. Not my problem. Not the type of man I'd ever get involved with.

I was here to decide if the atelier was the right next move for my career and to have fun with my sister. Not to entertain some guy who couldn't even face his reality, who had to hide in his own speakeasy and spin stories, hitting on random women at his reject table just to get through his miserable life.

I wouldn't be surprised if everything he had just told me— about his dead child, his businesses, maybe even his name— was all a lie. Nothing more than an added layer to his carefully crafted persona. How could I believe a single word that came out of his mouth? I knew nothing about him, really. Just the fragments he chose to reveal, wrapped in a cute Irish accent (which also could be fake). All of this was a lie. A façade. Some cosplay game speakeasy.

I finally looked up and met my own gaze in the mirror. Then I saw it. There, just behind me in the reflection, was a massive wall of pictures. Black-and-white photographs, each in antique frames. My eyes locked onto one in particular. A flicker of recognition sparked a sense of unease in my stomach. Unease and nausea.

I turned, drawn to it, rushing over to the wall. Only inches away, I blinked—three, four, five times—testing reality. Was I imagining this? Was it a trick of the dim lighting and too much whiskey? Or maybe just a series of well-crafted photoshop edits to make the place feel more authentic?

On the wall of the women's restroom, hung a collection of photographs, undeniably from the 1920s. Impossible to have been photoshopped. The grain, the fading, the creases in the paper—these weren't fabricated photos. Women in flapper dresses, covered in pearls, feathers, and sequins. Couples kissing in the leather booths of this exact speakeasy. Dancers caught mid-twirl, jazz musicians playing behind them. These weren't replicas. These were *real*.

But so what? Maybe he was a collector of old relics. There was a chance he had collected these and the bar had actually been around since 1920, and they were trying to keep tradition alive. Weird but okay.

Then I noticed each photo had a date scrawled in pen at the bottom right corner. *April 1920. August 1918. January 1923.* I skimmed over them—all of them—until I landed on the one that had stopped me cold.

Cillian.

The man I'd just been talking to at the bar. The one whose touch had burned like fire against my waist. The one who was very much alive.

And yet, here he was. In this photograph. Standing amongst

soldiers, ready for battle. His gorgeous face streaked with mud and blood. His light blue eyes, somehow dark and cold beneath the weight of a tin helmet. Surrounded by weaponry and military vehicles.

Undeniably him.

Undeniably real.

Undeniably a soldier of *war*.

My breath caught as I stared at the bottom corner of the image.

The date was inked in pen.

The Great War – October 1914.

8

_____

"Holy shit." The words left my mouth louder than I had intended.

A woman washing her hands shot me a nasty, disapproving look. I ignored it. She looked like she'd stepped out of a Gatsby fever dream—beaded drop waist dress, feathered headband, gloves that ran up to her elbows.

"Excuse me," I said, figuring I would rather look like a psycho to this random stranger than to Cillian. "Do you know the date?"

"December nineteenth, ma'am," she offered with a polite smile—she was being surprisingly helpful for a New Yorker.

"No. What _year_?" I pressed, my irritation unhidden.

Her eyes flickered with amusement then annoyance. "1925," she said, frowning, her tone now laced with sass. She shot me one last look before rushing toward the door.

"This isn't some elaborate party where everyone's just _pretending_ it's the 1920s, right?" I muttered, more to myself than to her.

Her expression shifted—just a flicker, but enough. Pity. Fear. "Are you feeling quite all right, or should I have the bartender fetch a doctor?" she asked, like *I* was the one who had lost my grip on reality. But there was something in her eyes —something that told me she wasn't putting on a show for the bar. She truly believed that this was 1925.

"No, I'm good," I said, staring back at the photo of Cillian on the wall.

She gave me one last concerned look before walking out of the bathroom.

"There is no way," I muttered under my breath. I couldn't think straight, couldn't figure out what was going on. I needed to find Lila and get us out of here.

As I stepped out of the restroom, I noticed Eddie had delivered the three shots of whiskey across the bar. They sat in front of Cillian and Lila, who seemed to be having a swell time without me. For a second, I seriously wondered if the drinks were laced with some kind of maniac-inducing, time-traveling hallucination drug.

No, that wasn't a thing. Right?

I shook my head at my own mental chatter. Maybe I *was* going crazy.

As I approached, Cillian glanced over his shoulder. "Ya have yerself an amazing sister here, Ava." He pointed to her with his lit cigarette.

"Yeah, so I've heard," I said, not making eye contact with him. "But she's married, so you're out of luck."

Why the hell had I said that? He wasn't . . . interested in her. Right? Even if he was, I wouldn't care. He was—allegedly— from 1925, for God's sake. Those pictures in the bathroom were real, and that only made everything more confusing. I needed to get out of here—away from all the noise—so I could try to make sense of those photos, this place, the weird feelings Cillian made me feel, before I lost my mind.

He didn't defend himself. He just shook his head and clicked his tongue. "Oh, Ava . . . ya have no idea."

Why was it so damn hard to rile this guy up? Was he immune to everything? I suppose if you'd spent a century on this Earth and fought in a war, you'd become a little unshakable.

"Don't talk about me when I'm not here," I snapped, trying to find something to get upset about. This guy could be dangerous. This place could be dangerous. I needed to protect myself and my sister. "Thanks." My voice must have sounded cold enough that they both noticed.

"*Are you okay*?" Lila mouthed.

"Yep. Lil, we need to go. I forgot I have some stuff to prepare for that interview."

"But the interview isn't for a few days—" Lila stopped, noticing the death glare I gave her.

"Eh, come on, the night's just begun. Ya can't get much done this time of night, anyway, especially not after all dis whiskey," Cillian said, glancing at his pocket watch, showing me that it was now nearing midnight. This place was a fucking time warp. "Just stay for one more drink," he said, sounding as close to begging as I bet he ever got. "If ya're really going to get work done tonight, what's another half an hour?"

"Can't." I shrugged as if my hands were tied.

"Cillian, I need ya!" Eddie shouted across the bar, gesturing for him to come help him with something.

This was our chance to get the fuck out of here.

"I will be right back, ladies. Give me two minutes. I will come send ya two off properly for the evening so Ava can get her work completed for her interview," he said, leaving me and Lila alone at the bar.

"What the hell does that even mean?" I called after him. Send us off "properly?" Who was this guy?

Lila's eyes went wide, wondering if I'd turned insane while peeing. "Ava, what in the world is happening? Are you okay?"

I let out a deep sigh. "This is going to sound insane, but I'm pretty sure this place is some kind of portal to the 1920s. I asked a girl in the bathroom about the date—she said it was 1925. I could tell she was telling the truth." I paused, watching Lila for any sign of a reaction.

This could go one of two ways: she could either believe me, or she could send me to the looney bin. And then I'd spend Christmas in white, which was definitely not my color, sitting in a wheelchair, looking like Angelina Jolie's character in *Girl, Interrupted*.

"Wait, Ava," she said, grabbing my hands. "I have been thinking the *same thing*."

Well, that was a relief. She actually believed me. Maybe I wasn't going insane.

I let out an incredulous laugh, feeling a small weight lift off my chest.

Then I stopped, furrowing my brow. "Wait, are *you* serious?" Now I was starting to think *she* might be the crazy one. Then again, her skin tone was just as pale as mine, so white wouldn't suit her either. "Why do *you* think that?" My tone shifted, skeptical, like suddenly I needed her to prove it to me.

"Well, for one, this place turned from a broom closet earlier into a speakeasy. We both saw it. Cillian mentioned what he does for work, and it doesn't seem like he is lying—no one is that good of an actor. And no one has businesses like that these days. Plus, I've noticed a few people paying for their drinks with actual *quarters*. There is no way this place would be able to survive in 2025 serving a drink for a quarter."

Her list of reasons was longer than mine. Yet, despite her laundry list proving our potential time travel, she still wanted to stay and drink with Cillian? Was she nuts?

She continued, "Also, the likelihood of his child dying in childbirth would be way more likely back then. *Plus*"—now she was on a roll—"Cillian literally talks like he's from the 1920s. I just don't think everyone in this place could keep up the act day in and day out for years if it weren't real." She paused. "Wait, besides the girl in the bathroom, why do you think so? She could have just been playing along with the whole 1920's theme, too."

I raised my brows. "Wow, okay, that's actually a way more solid list than I had. When I was in the bathroom, there was a picture of Cillian fighting in World War I, dated 1914—definitely not photoshopped. I know Photoshop when I see it. Before you got here he mentioned something about the war and how it affected him and other men in 'his generation.' I figured he was just some method actor, committed to keeping the 1920's vibe alive here or something.

"Oh, and another thing—they don't confiscate phones, but I've never seen anyone have one out. Plus, I have zero Wi-Fi signal. No service. Every time I've been here, my phone just goes black. When I asked the hostess if I needed to check my phone at the door, she just stared at me like I was speaking another language and told me about some phone in a room somewhere I could use for a nickel." I exhaled sharply, trying my best to stay calm. "I also couldn't find this place anywhere online when researching places to eat at the hotel." The evidence was mounting.

Lila gasped. "My phone isn't working, either! Oh my gosh," she said, her voice dropping to a whisper. "Ava . . . have we time-traveled to 1925?" Her eyes were as wide as saucers.

"No. No way. There is no possible way," I said firmly, more to convince myself than her. "Come on; let's go." I gestured for her to get up with both hands, like I was herding a cat.

"What? Why?" Lila protested, her eyes lighting up with excitement rather than the expected panic. "Who knows if we'll ever get back in? Christopher barely let us in the first time. Plus this is literally a once-in-a-lifetime experience," she said, the free spirit in her fully taking over. "This would make such a fun story for me to write about. Great inspiration for a rom-com.

Plus, Cillian seems good for you—he actually gives you a run for your money." She waggled her brows.

Why was she not more concerned than this? She had kids, for God's sake. A family. A life to go back to.

"No." I threw my hands up. "Lila, this is not some little adventure where you meddle in my love life and you can be 'inspired' to write a rom-com. This is insane. We should be freaking out right now, not treating this like a story for your next major motion picture!"

"It's just one night, Ava. We never have to come back again, but what's the harm in gathering as much information as we can while we're here?" She nudged me. "Besides, you could at least enjoy yourself while you're stuck in the past, with a man who is very clearly smitten with you. At the very least, let him distract you from being rejected by Elliot."

"I was not rejected," I snapped. Then I let out a dry laugh. "Yeah, great. The bar owner I like might actually be a ghost from the past. *Super* hot."

"Ha! I *knew* it. So you admit you like him," she said, pointing at me like she'd caught me red-handed.

I crossed my arms. "Please. He barely reacts to anything I say. And if he does, it's with sarcasm. If anything, he seems more interested in you and your army of children than anything I've had to say. He was a total scrooge last night, and tonight, until you showed up. Pretty sure he has a crush on your married ass."

She rolled her eyes. "Oh, that is just because I am nice and opened him up for you with the whole kid similarity thing. But, when you went to the bathroom, all he did was want to know about the 'Ms. Ava Hawthorne,'" she mimicked his accent, sitting up straighter in her seat. "He couldn't stop asking about you. Come on; just flirt with him a little bit, please. What's the worst that could happen?"

I dropped my head into my hand, elbow propped on the

bar. "Christ. Great idea, Lila. Post-breakup, why don't I just dive headfirst into a romance with an Irish war-hero with PTSD from 1925 that we time travel to each night?" I mustered a look that I hoped silently communicated *what the actual fuck are you thinking* without having to say it out loud and hurt her feelings. I lifted my head just enough to add, "Not to mention, he has a child . . . and potentially a wife."

She rolled her eyes. "First of all, he's not wearing a ring. Second of all, *details*." She threw her hands up, exasperated. "Come on; this is the first time I've gotten out of pajamas and left my house all year, and something like this happens? It's too good. It's meant to be. We have to carpe diem—seize the day!"

When was the last time my sister had *carpe diem-ed* anything? I guessed she used to be all about it, but since the kids had come along, that side of her had vanished. She'd traded in her free-spirited ways for routine, structure, and the constant pull of responsibility and motherhood. Maybe she needed this more than me. Maybe, deep down, she was longing for a bit of carefree joy. Maybe this was her chance to feel that rush again, to remember who she'd been before life had gotten so complicated. Or maybe the whiskey had just been fully absorbed into her blood stream. I had told her we were going to have an adventurous trip. This definitely counted as fulfilling on that promise.

But I couldn't wrap my head around what was happening here. Had we really stepped into some kind of time warp? Was this all just a clever set designed to make us feel like we'd slipped into the past? Or maybe, just maybe, there was some strange magic at play. Dare I say, Chris Kringle Christmas magic?

My blood boiled at the thought of him alone. How ridiculous. This stuff only existed in movies, in stupid fantasy books. There was no way this was actually happening. We would have to figure it out tomorrow.

"What about the girls?" I asked. "What if they try to call and can't reach you while we're here?"

"Oh, please." She waved me off. "They just spent forty-five minutes telling me how much fun they're having with their dad and how excited they are that I'm getting a vacation. Violet even said, 'Mama, you should stay for Christmas—we're having so much fun. Every night is like a sleepover. And Auntie Ava deserves some time with you, too, after Elliot.'"

"Geez, when did the girls get so grown up?"

"I know, right? They're like actual little people now. It's crazy." I could hear the relief in her voice, like her mom guilt was starting to lift, just a little, now that she knew the girls were okay without her for the holidays. I secretly hoped she would be willing to stay through Christmas.

I looked at her, her puppy-dog eyes unwavering and, for a second, I could have sworn I saw a tear welling in the corner of one.

I sighed. We were already here. I guessed staying a little longer wouldn't kill us. And like she said, we'd probably never come back.

"Do you really want to stay?" I asked. At the very least, I could figure out more about this strange place while we were here.

"Yes! Please, just one drink. I never get to do anything fun like this anymore," she begged as if she didn't have two girls who did the same thing to get what they wanted. Like mother, like daughter.

I stared at her to make sure she was serious. More puppy dog eyes.

I sighed. "Fine. We can stay, but we are *not* coming back after tonight. I don't know how this place works, and I am not about to get stuck in 1925 with that guy for the rest of my life."

"Deal!" she squealed.

As if on cue, Cillian walked back into sight, running his hand down the breast of his jacket, straightening it.

"Sounds like ya ladies are havin' a lovely time over here. I apologize for bein' rude and leavin' you both. Ol' Ed needed me attention with somethin' in da back." He pulled another cigarette from his pocket. "Ava, I wish ya could stay. But if work calls, I can have a car ready for ya." He nodded toward a door across the bar—not the one we'd come through. I wondered: was that the entrance to 1925?

"Yer career is important, and I'd hate to hold ya back from doing yer best at yer meeting."

Why did this guy have to speak my love language: career support? Elliot would have begged me, shamed me, into staying and "hanging out," *especially* when it was at the expense of my career goals. He was always much more about "living for the moment" than "planning for the future."

"Oh, Ava, you are so screwed," Lila whispered from the side opposite Cillian.

I glared at her.

"Can I try one of those?" Lila asked, gesturing to the cigarette, and I spat out my drink at the question.

"Lila!"

"What? It is just *one*—it won't kill me."

"I mean, technically, it could," I said dryly.

"Plus, I am on vacation." She shrugged.

Who was my sister? I didn't even know her right now. Apparently, that happened when you didn't see each other for years—shit changed.

Cillian gave my sister a long look before slowly reaching in and grabbing another cigarette. She placed it between her lips, clearly having never done this before. He leaned in to light it.

"What do I do?" she murmured, holding the cigarette between her lips.

"Breathe it into your lungs," I said, rolling my eyes and

looking toward Cillian. But he was already staring at me. Like he had been the entire time.

It startled me. I think my heart actually skipped a beat. That or I had a mini heart attack.

Before I could think of something witty to say to get him to stop, Lila took a slow inhale then exhaled a stream of smoke from her first-ever cigarette. She coughed a few times. Then she grabbed it between her fingers, tilted her head back, trying to look cool. Coughing again.

I couldn't hold back my laugh. She was ridiculous.

"By the way, Cillian," she said casually, "we changed our minds. We're going to hang out a little longer. So tell Eddie to keep the drinks coming."

"How wonderful," Cillian said, as he pulled away from lighting her cigarette, his arm brushed mine, but he didn't pull away.

Those eyes. Those deep ocean eyes. Heat flooded my body, warming my cheeks, coursing through every inch of me. It was like he knew how much it affected me. The smallest, most imperceptible smirk tugged at his lips.

I did my best to swallow my reaction. His eyes dropped to my throat, watching the lump in it bob, making me feel completely exposed and vulnerable. Like I was stripped naked.

I forced myself to look straight ahead at Lila, who just took her first puff of a cigarette in a 1920's speakeasy—a place we'd somehow time-traveled to while on vacation. *What was happening?*

I watched her, searching for any sign of sadness. It was just a few days until Christmas, and my sister had left her family behind to be here with me. I knew she was probably enjoying the kid-free time—no screeching, no packed lunches, no monster-in-law trying to ruin her life. But I also knew her well enough to guess there was a soft ache somewhere beneath the excitement of being here—an ache from missing her family, missing those little moments, missing creating memories with them. Maybe staying in this bar, at least for the night, helped her forget that ache.

I hated Christmas. I always had. And this year, I had no one to miss. No memories I was missing out on creating back home. I was glad. Glad I didn't have to be around my family, or Elliot's for that matter.

As I scanned the bar—the jazz band playing old-timey Christmas tunes, the tree glowing through the smoky haze, fresh garland that smelled like Christmas, if that was even possible, people laughing and dancing—I felt something close to warmth. Like maybe, just maybe, this wasn't the worst way to spend the holidays.

We were pretty sure we had just time-traveled to 1925. There was a chance we might never come back, or that we wouldn't make it back to 2025 at all—I had no idea how any of this magic-portal-speakeasy business worked. Still, maybe a small part of me, like Lila, felt that staying in this bar—at least for the night—softened the ache of loneliness I didn't want to admit was buried inside me.

While I wasn't the sentimental type, I figured, if I had to spend Christmas trapped in a hundred-year time warp with anyone, a man with a jaw like that, eyes like that, a voice like that, wasn't the worst company.

Then I looked at him—Cillian, otherwise known as the brooding bar owner with the kind of face, and eyes, and voice, and charm, and smell, who made me forget my own name, who made my knees weak and heat flood my cheeks—and a strange sensation stirred deep in my chest, something so foreign I didn't know how to name it.

Lila was right.

I was so fucked.

9

After the clock struck midnight and we decided to stay, the night hummed along. I did my best to keep my distance from Cillian, yet he was always in my periphery. We shared a few drinks before Lila fully surrendered to the 1920's fantasy—twirling to a piano number with her eyes closed, a whiskey in one hand, and a cigarette in the other.

Meanwhile, I stayed put, doing my best to blend in to the 1920's scene. Cillian seemed to enjoy every second of my discomfort. Whether he was helping Eddie behind the bar or mingling with other patrons, his eyes always found their way back to me, a grin forming on his mouth whenever I shot him a glare—like he was fully aware of just how much he was getting under my skin with a single look.

Then the trouble started.

Some man—drunk, half my size, and much too confident—sidled up beside me at the bar, grinning with the kind of self-confidence only whiskey could provide. "Haven't seen ya here before, little lady," he slurred, leaning in way too close. His breath wreaked of liquor.

"*Little* Lady? Jesus." I stiffened, firing him a look of steel, one he was far too drunk to register as *get the fuck away from me*. "That's because I haven't been here, genius."

"Well," he said, setting his drink down with a too-loud clink, "a little lady like you shouldn't be sitting alone."

I wasn't alone, and I certainly wasn't little, but I wasn't about to waste my energy correcting him.

"I'm fine, thanks." I bet as soon as I stood up and towered over him, he would stop those "little lady" comments pretty quick.

He laughed like I'd just told a joke. "Come on now; don't be like that. Ya are more than fine." He brushed my arm with his fingers, then a lock of my hair.

No one touched my damn hair.

Before I could shake him off, or slap him, a shadow loomed behind him.

"Think ye've had enough for da night, mate."

Cillian.

His tone was calm, but hard underneath. He didn't raise his voice, didn't have to—just *was*, standing there like an immovable force.

The drunk rolled his eyes at me before scoffing. "She doesn't look spoken for," he called behind him without looking back.

Cillian's mouth twitched with the slightest hint of amusement—or maybe annoyance. "She's not." His tone: final. He took a slow drag from his cigarette, exhaling smoke without breaking his gaze from the back of the douchebag's head. "She's also not interested, Phil."

Cillian might have annoyed the hell out of me, but he did speak the truth. I certainly was not interested in this man who looked like he was one of Snow White's seven dwarfs.

Then little-lady Phil's expression changed, as if recognition of Cillian's voice sobered him up, finally clicking in his alcohol-soaked brain who stood behind him. His eyes went wide as he slowly turned to face Cillian. "Didn't mean no harm, Mr. Cillian, sir."

"Of course not," Cillian said, his tone heavy with boredom. Still leaned back, smoking his cigarette with one hand in his pocket.

Every ounce of the drunk's bravado deflated at Cillian's frame towering over him, and with a quick glance at me, he muttered something unintelligible and backed off, fading into the crowd.

Cillian stood there for a moment longer, making sure "little-lady Phil" was gone before his gaze shifted back to me.

I exhaled as sharp as I could manage. "I didn't need you to do that. I had it handled."

Cillian barely spared me a bored glance. "Didn't do it for ya."

"Then why?"

He took another slow drag of his cigarette, smoke curling around him. "Couldn't stand the idea of some fool ruining yer night before I got the chance to."

I blinked, caught off guard. "Excuse me? What's *that* supposed to mean?"

"Well, that ol' Phil there creeps a lot of the ladies out. It's me job to keep the integrity of the bar, to make sure the women feel safe enough to come back." He totally ignored my question. "Stay out of trouble, would ya?" he said, before turning and disappearing into the crowd as quickly, as smoothly, as he'd arrived, flicking his cigarette ashes in a nearby table's ashtray.

For the next hour, I kept stealing glances at him, no matter how hard I tried not to. Something had shifted—something different in the way he carried himself after stepping in, and—I hated to admit it—protecting me. The way he watched me now felt less like he was trying to get under my skin and more like he was keeping an eye on me. Like he cared. The more I looked, the harder it became to ignore the invisible pull between us.

What was he thinking? More importantly, what was *I* thinking? This guy wasn't even alive in 2025.

I did my best to shake it all off, to enjoy the evening. I committed to ignoring him as best as I could until Lila was ready to get out of here.

Unfortunately, my commitment didn't last long.

Less than an hour later, I found myself slinking into a nearby booth after Lila dragged me out for a dance. She was still out there, lost in the music, trying to do the Charleston or whatever dance they did back then—or these days.

Cillian sat in the seat next to me like he belonged there, which I guessed, since it was his bar, he technically did. His presence immediately too large, too all-consuming. He set two glasses on the table, one for each of us. He didn't say anything, just tapped his fingers against the table in a slow, steady rhythm, emptying his cigarette ashes into the tray in front of him every few minutes.

I ignored him. Or, at least, I *tried* to.

He exhaled a slow, deliberate breath of smoke and, without even looking in my direction, said, "Have dinner with me tomorrow night, Ava."

I choked on my drink. "Excuse me?"

He turned his head toward me, unfazed. "Ya heard me."

I turned back to him, narrowing my eyes. "That wasn't a question. And it's not possible." Neither of them were total lies. More like half-truths.

"Didn't feel the need to make it a question. Of course it is possible."

I scoffed, swirling the last of my whiskey. "And what exactly makes you think I'd say yes?"

He smirked, tilting his head slightly. "A hunch. And the way ya haven't rolled yer eyes in this conversation yet."

Ugh. Infuriating.

I rolled my eyes. I was determined not to let him get under my skin. "For your information, I haven't left because I promised my sister, who is a mother of two, a fun trip. Also, I don't even know you."

"Ya know enough," he said smoothly, leaning in slightly.

I hated how much I wanted to say yes. Why the *hell* did I want to say yes? He was literally a corpse, six feet under, in 2025. Reduced to bones and dust. This was ridiculous. I couldn't even explain how I was here, or if I could get back after tonight.

But how easily I could imagine what a night alone with him would be like. It made my stomach turn. And the way he was looking at me, like he already knew my answer, was infuriating. And incredibly attractive. I was too drunk for this.

"No. Not interested," I said as coldly as I could muster.

"Hm. So ya're not interested," he mused "And yet, ya keep sitting here, arguing with me instead of leaving me pub."

I opened my mouth to tell him exactly where he could shove his arrogance, but he beat me to it.

"One dinner," he said, his voice lowering an octave, making it feel like a secret.

I needed to say no. I should say no. I had to say no. But something about the way he looked at me—like he knew I was going to change my mind—made my pulse do something annoying. Beat erratically.

Just as I was about to respond, Lila appeared beside the booth, all smiles and flushed cheeks from dancing. "All right, I think it's time to go. My feet hurt *so bad*. And I am *really* drunk. You ready, sis?" She was practically glowing from the sweat running down her face, still dancing a bit, clearly enjoying every moment of the night.

Before I could answer, Cillian stood. "Let me walk ya to the door." He leaned in and whispered, "It will give ya a few moments to consider me invitation, Ava."

I opened my mouth to protest, but Lila was already slipping her arm through mine, pulling me out of the booth.

"Oh, don't be rude. Let him walk us. I will leave you two to talk," she teased, winking at me.

I shot her a look, but she was already skipping toward the door.

I could feel Cillian's gaze as he followed me, guiding me toward the exit. There was a tension between us that I couldn't escape—like we were two magnets, needing to fill the space between us. He had to feel it, too.

His hand hovered just above the small of my back, the heat from his fingers radiating through the fabric of my suit, once again. Like an electric current. I was acutely aware of his every step, every breath.

As we reached the exit, Cillian turned to me, gently brushing his fingers along my arm. "So, now that ya've had much time to think about it—what do ya say? Dinner tomorrow night?"

"You really don't take a hint, do you?"

He grinned. "I take every hint, Ava. I just don't always listen to them."

Lila, who had clearly been eavesdropping, let out a dramatic gasp. She grabbed my arm and shook me. "Oh my God, yes! She says yes. She absolutely says yes."

"Excuse you?" I ripped my arm away.

"Oh, come on." She rolled her eyes. "Live a little, Ava. When was the last time you went on a date with someone who looks like *him*?" It was official. She was too drunk to have any sort of legitimate say in this.

Cillian chuckled, shoving his hand into his pocket. "I like this one. She's got excellent taste."

Lila clutched my arm tighter. "Ava, please. You *promised* me a fun trip. What's more fun than watching your sister go on a hot date?" She winked at Cillian.

"My God." I groaned, rubbing my temples. "That is *not* the fun that I promised."

"Close enough." She clasped her hands together. "Just *one* date. One *tiny* little dinner. If it's awful, I'll fake an emergency and bail you out." She paused to wink at Cillian again, his new number one fan. Some guy from 1925. This was unreal. Laughable. I needed to get out of here and get her to bed.

Cillian smirked.

I exhaled sharply, glaring at both of them. "Fine. But I'm doing this for my sister, who clearly won't remember any of this tomorrow."

I figured agreeing to it so I could get Lila to sleep would be less painful than standing here, fighting about it with two drunk people (three including me) until the sun came up. Besides, we didn't even know if we could get back here tomorrow. Hell, I didn't even know if we could get back to 2025 for sure when we walked through that door right now. For all I knew, it might be just another broom closet.

Since I'd made it through the night before without any problem, I silently prayed it would be just as seamless tonight, that we wouldn't be trapped in 1925 forever.

Cillian stood there, staring into my eyes.

"Don't get any ideas," I said.

His smirk deepened. "Too late for dat, Ava."

Lila squealed, and Cillian's grin widened.

Damn him.

Damn her.

Damn this stupid speakeasy.

Why did I ever think coming here for Christmas was a good idea?

10

"I CANNOT BELIEVE HE ASKED YOU OUT FOR DINNER," LILA SAID, clapping her hands together as we walked through Central Park the next morning.

"First, I'm shocked you even remember that conversation happened with how drunk you were. Second, how are you focused on *that* when we may have just—casually—time-traveled to 1925 like it's nothing?" I said, kicking a rock.

Lila shrugged. "That's fair, but we're back now. Central Park looks normal. I don't feel any side effects. No wormholes. No weird déjà vu. I don't even feel hungover. And I always feel hungover after drinking."

"I know. Me neither," I said, slowing my pace. "But what if we imagined it? What if that was some shared psychotic break or hallucination? Should we be, like . . . concerned about that?"

There was a pause.

"No," Lila said. "If we both went crazy, or were drugged, I don't think we would be this self-aware about it. Or feel normal today."

I gave her a look. "That's exactly what a crazy person would say."

"Well, if we *weren't* insane before, we definitely are now." She laughed.

I sighed. "Anyway, if Cillian really *is* from 1925, I'm not surprised he asked me to dinner on the spot. That was a hundred years ago. No phones. No dating apps. No Google. You had to shoot your shot while you had the chance."

"He is so gorgeous, Av," Lila said dreamily.

"Gorgeous, drunk, and lonely," I replied, brushing my hair out of my face.

"Sounds a lot like someone I know on a Saturday night," Lila snorted, elbowing me in the rib.

"Wow. Rude."

"Accurate," she corrected. "Anyway . . ."

"Also—bar owner. Red flag."

"He isn't *just* a bar owner, Ava. He is a multi-talented businessman. I mean, yes, the time travel thing is freaky," she admitted, "but maybe it's a sign. Maybe the universe is throwing you a bone after the whole Elliot breakup. Cillian is kind, and handsome, and mysterious, and he looks at you like a king looks at a queen. And hey, maybe you'll even pick up some inspiration from him for the atelier."

I shook my head, laughing. Lila could spin anything into a sign from the universe. She was the type to crash into a pole on the way to work and take it as confirmation that she should quit her job and start a family. Which, if I remembered right, was exactly how that had happened.

I ignored her comment. "I just don't understand how this is all possible," I said, racking my brain. "And what if it doesn't work again? What if we go back to the speakeasy, and it's just a broom closet? Or what if we go back and get in but can't get back to the current time at the end of the night?"

Lila smirked. "Then I guess we're stuck in 1925 forever, and I'll have to get used to smoking cigarettes and wearing fancy gloves and pearls every night."

"That isn't funny."

She sighed. "I know, I know. I've thought about that, too. I mean, I have a family. I have kids. If something glitched—if we got stuck there—" She paused, pursing her lips. "It's not like I can just disappear into some Gatsby fantasy world forever. As fun as it is to play pretend, that would be terrible."

I nodded, aware of the stakes—not just for me, but for her, too. "Are we *sure* we time-traveled? Is there any other possible explanation?"

"I don't really know what else it could be. We'll just have to be careful and try to get some answers from Christopher," she said. "So far, it's been pretty consistent—we know we can get in around nine twenty-five when he's working the bar. And you haven't had any trouble coming back out yet. Besides, I doubt Christopher would let us go in if it were actually dangerous. Maybe when you go tonight—for your date with Cillian—you can get some real answers."

"Are you sure we should even try to go back in? It feels too much like a high risk, low reward situation," I said.

"Ava, you promised Cillian you would be there for your date."

"Well, technically, *you* promised. But I never miss an appointment. But . . . did it actually even happen? Does Cillian exist, or is he just dead and it won't affect anything if I miss the date? Is it actually history? Or do you think it is more like a simulation? If that speakeasy is like a portal, would what we do there affect anything in the present? Or is it just a nightly looping speakeasy that never advances past 1925? Like that movie *Groundhog Day!*"

We walked in silence for a beat before she said, "I guess I have no idea. Still, if the universe *did* drop a magical man from 1925 into your lap, the least you could do is get dressed up and enjoy yourself with him while you can."

I snorted. "I like how you're willing to send me in as bait.

And if I disappear into the space-time continuum, or get lost in the void, you'll be safe and sound, free to return to your life. You're incorrigible."

"I may be. But you are curious. Which is why I know you're going back. How could you not?" she asked.

We reached the Bethesda Fountain and sat to do some people watching.

"This place is beautiful. The city is so magical. I absolutely love it here," she said, tilting her head back to catch the sun. "How could you not want to pick up your whole life and move here?"

The park looked peaceful in that quiet, wintery way—bare trees, frost on the ground. The bite of winter air was refreshing. "It is an incredible city, and there really isn't any reason for me to stay in San Francisco anymore. We'll see how the second meeting with Ronan goes, but I'm becoming much more certain that this is where I want to be. But it's a big change."

Lila gasped. "Maybe you will end up moving here and falling in love with Cillian, and starting a family, and he could help you with the atelier!"

"Lil, if what we think about the speakeasy is true, I highly doubt I could convince him to move from 1925 to 2025, or if that would even be physically possible. He may walk through that door and evaporate into mist or something. I am not even sure if that place—if he—is *real*. Plus, he has a kid. Besides, I thought you were just team Ronan?"

"Is team Ronan an option now?" she asked.

I shook my head. "Anyway, I don't even like the guy. I am telling you, the first night I met him, he was so cold. I'm confused as to why he even asked me out." I could hear myself lie, but I couldn't admit I had a pathetic, girlish crush on a man who might not even exist. That would just sound delusional. Or pathetic. Or both.

"Well, based on first impressions, you come off pretty cold, too—no offense. But look at you." She leaned back and gestured to me. "He was probably intimidated. You gave him a run for his money. I am sure women are scared of him, never call him out or talk back. I don't think women were even allowed to wear pants in 1925, let alone talk back to men. I bet he liked that you weren't like that." She paused. "Wait—do you think he knows that we aren't from his time?"

"The only thing less believable than finding a time-traveling speakeasy in 2025 is being from 1925 and realizing someone is from the future. There were barely even phones back then. I doubt he deduced I was from one hundred years in the future—he probably figured I was from some other big city."

"Totally." Lila shook her head and giggled. "I'm just so happy that you said yes to the date."

"*I* didn't. *You* did. I only agreed so I could get you out of there and off to bed. I also wanted to keep the option open for us to go back and snoop around, try to figure out what's really going on with that place. I bet you're right; Chris Kringle has to have some answers," I said, staring off at the bridge where a man played a mandolin, filling the space with music.

"Who is Chris Kringle? Chris Kringle like . . . Santa Claus?"

"No. Like the bartender," I said. "It's what I call him in my head."

"Oh, Christopher! You always did love giving people terribly rude nicknames." She wrapped her arm around me.

"That isn't rude," I protested. "He literally looks like Santa. And acts like him. I'm just calling it as it is."

"Well, since you got in the last two nights, I can't imagine it would be any different tonight. Maybe the portal there just turns at nine twenty-five and there is a small window of time we can go in."

"Maybe. I would just hate to go in and get stuck there with him in that speakeasy."

She shook her head confidently. "That won't happen. If it was going to trap you, it would've done so by now."

I raised an eyebrow. "Oh. Okay, Mrs. Time-Traveling Professional." I couldn't help but laugh at her sudden resolute confidence when it came to something she knew absolutely nothing about.

"Remember, you've made it back the last two nights no problem. Why would tonight be any different?"

I couldn't tell if she was saying it because she actually believed it or because she wanted more content for her writing project and was too attached to me falling in love with Cillian, or Ronan, or anyone with a pulse.

"Are you at all excited for the date?" Lila asked.

"It's not a date. It's dinner. At a bar," I snapped. "Basically, what we've done the last two nights, but with food. Not exactly what I would consider a proper courtship."

She gave me a look, as if asking: *Do you want him to court you?*

I considered her unspoken question, shrugging a shoulder. "I don't know. He's handsome, so at least I'll have something nice to look at. There was also a little bit of a . . . a spark when he touched me last night. But nothing will come of it, for obvious reasons." I brushed it off, hoping to change the subject to something else. Anything else.

Lila clapped her hands. "I cannot wait to get the full report tonight. Stay out as late as you'd like," she said. "Don't even worry about coming back to the room if it goes well." She wiggled her eyebrows.

"Stop." A laugh escaped me as I slapped her hand away in annoyance, a smile sneaking on my face. "I'm not even sure either of us could leave the speakeasy together without the time-space continuum blowing him to smithereens—or me, for that matter," I joked. "And I highly doubt we'd have a one-night stand in the middle of a crowded bar. I'm confident I'll be home earlier than the last few nights. I also have my meeting with the atelier to prepare for. I need all the sleep I can get. I'm not going to stay out late, letting some odd time traveler risk me being anything less than one hundred ten percent for that meeting."

We both stared ahead, taking in the sights.

"So, what are your thoughts on Central Park at Christmastime?" I asked.

She shook her head slowly. "It is everything I imagined, times a million."

"Right? It's the best. Even more beautiful in the summer," I said.

"Well, maybe if you move here, I will get to come visit you in the summer?" she offered, always the hopeful one. Maybe moving here would be good for our relationship. She might finally *want* to come visit me.

"Are you sure you're good with me going tonight? I don't want you to be bored all alone. I didn't drag you away from your family during the holidays to leave you to fend for yourself in the city. What are you going to do? Are you sure you don't want to join us?" I offered as my last saving grace for this date to not be an actual date.

"Puh-lease." She threw her hand up at me. "A night all alone in this city? With no kids? It is like a dream come true. There are a million and one options. I think I'm going to go out to dinner and do some of that writing we talked about."

"That sounds great. I'm so happy you're deciding to do that while you're here. Have you decided what you're going to write about yet?"

"I don't know, but this city is inspiring me so much. I'm going to find some sort of story within it."

"Great idea. Maybe we can head to the Upper East Side and do some shopping. Pick you out an inspiring dinner outfit to get your creative juices flowing . . ." I offered.

"For real? That would be amazing," Lila said, her eyes wide with excitement.

". . . and for my date night with Cillian." I added casually.

"Ha! So, it *is* a date."

"Shut up," I said, standing and holding out my hand to help her up. "Let's go shopping." I rolled my eyes. "If it *were* a date, I should at least try to look nice. And appropriate . . . by 1925's standards."

———

"You're going to look so good in that dress, Ava," Lila said from the bed, watching me as I got ready in the bathroom again. The less time I spent lying in those musky sheets, the better. Getting ready for the night was the best alternative.

I was holding up the dress she'd forced me to get at Jacumeaus. My French stylist, Samuel, had loaded us up with items to try on. After too many glasses of champagne and many runway walks later, we had narrowed it down to a tea-length silk slip dress, with Art Deco details. It was a gorgeous deep burgundy color that went perfectly with my blonde hair and pale skin. I could wear my fur coat with it in case it got cold in 1925.

I wanted to get a suit, but Lila had informed me—courtesy of her Google search—that a woman wearing pants in 1925 was a big no-no. Despite my long list of reasons why I didn't give a shit, both she and Samuel had insisted the dress was the way to go. And Samuel had never steered me wrong. Ever. Lila, on the other hand, occasionally. But his vote gave hers more weight.

I couldn't even remember the last time I'd worn a dress. Probably when I was three. When Mom and Jeff had made us go to church at Christmastime. I vaguely recall a velvet emerald dress, paired with white tights and little black Mary Jane flats.

As if he could sense me thinking about him for even a

second of my life, my phone rang. I grabbed it from the bathroom counter, cluttered with makeup and barely any space to spare. *Jeff (Deadbeat) Hawthorne.* Decline.

I shook my head in annoyance—a gesture Lila recognized instantly, even after years apart.

"Was that Dad?" she asked. How the hell could she tell?

"Yeah," I muttered, holding the silk dress up to my front, debating how to wear my hair. Big, old Hollywood curls seemed fitting. "I'm sure he's calling for his yearly Christmas 'check-in,' just enough to convince himself he's *Dad of the Year.*"

"I can't believe him sometimes," Lila said, as if this was somehow out of character for him. She had always held onto hope that, one day, he'd show up for us—really show up—that he'd suddenly stop being a total piece of shit.

I, however, had given up on that fantasy a long time ago. Because it was nothing more than that—a fantasy.

"I find it ironic that he always calls at Christmas, right around the same time he left us. Like he thinks a holiday phone call erases the fact he walked out on us *during* the holidays."

Lila frowned. "Yeah. It's totally messed up."

He would never change. No amount of wishing, waiting, or holding our breaths would make him care any more than he already did—which was not at all. Maybe that was why I hated Christmas. Because it always reminded me of when Jeff had abandoned us, ruining all of our lives.

Lila's phone started ringing. She let out a frustrated sigh and held it up for me to see. *Dad.*

"Now he's calling *me*," she said, her grip tightening around the phone.

"Go ahead. Answer it," I said, rolling my eyes. Knowing she secretly—and desperately—wanted to talk to him.

"Are you sure?" she asked, a cocktail of hesitation and excitement flashing across her face.

I raised my brows at her as I brushed them in the mirror.

"You better hurry before he hangs up and you don't hear from him till Christmas of 2026."

I closed the bathroom door behind me, but with these thin Irish walls, I might as well have left it open.

"Hey, Dad!" Lila answered. Hearing the hope in her voice nearly killed me.

I'd watched her suffer through his absence when we were little. Mom had told us he wasn't coming back. That he had a new family. Lila was so young—barely two years old. His leaving had always affected her more. I had defaulted to the protector, the caretaker. The strong one. If she had seen me upset or crying, she would have followed suit. I had swallowed any feelings that I had about it down and held it together—for her, for us. For our mother. Our heartbroken, beautiful mother.

"Oh, I'm actually in New York with Ava," Lila said from the other room. "Yeah, I know. We haven't hung out in years, but it's been really good for us."

Why was she telling him anything about our lives? What right did he have? He had lost that privilege a long time ago.

"No, I think her phone is usually on silent. I'll tell her you called."

Classic. Lila covering for me, apologizing for my actions. Hoping that if we played nice, maybe he would keep calling. That maybe, just maybe, it would make him want to come back and right all his wrongs.

"All right, sounds good, Dad. Thanks for calling. Merry Christmas to you and Patty, as well. Of course, I will."

Once I was confident she had hung up, I opened the door again then went right back to applying mascara.

"How's the ol' deadbeat?" I asked, as if I hadn't heard the pathetic once-a-year, surface-level conversation through the door made of paper.

"He's good. He says hello and wants you to call him."

I snorted. "Yeah, well, I wanted him to be a present dad, but we don't always get what we want just because we want it, now do we?"

"Av," she pleaded. "Come on; he has changed. He really has. He is trying to be better. To make amends."

"Yeah?" I said, cocking my head to the side. "And how many times has he called you this year?"

No response.

"Exactly. He may say all that stuff, but he doesn't do anything about it. One call a year at Christmas does not a father make." Now *I* was talking in riddles. It really did add good emphasis, though. "Maybe I will send him a trophy in the mail for calling this year."

"All right. Well, you don't have to forgive him, but at least give him a call before Christmas. I think he would really appreciate it," she said. "Besides, what do you have to lose by hearing him out?"

"Fine, all right, I will," I lied, only so she would stop bugging me. I had absolutely zero intention of speaking with him this year, or any year after, for that matter. "You are a good daughter, Lil. And a good sister."

"So are you, Av. I love you."

And then, as if both our parents' ears were burning, Lila's phone buzzed again.

"He's calling you *again*?" I asked, annoyed.

"It's Mom," she said, flashing the screen at me. "Want to say hi?"

I hesitated then gave a small nod. She picked up and put the call on speaker.

"Hi, my lovely Lila!" Mom's voice rang out. "Are you two still playing dress-up in that magical city?"

"Yes! You're on speaker," Lila said. "Ava's here, too."

My chest tightened a little, but I managed a casual, "Hey, Mom." I hadn't called her in weeks. Not since long before the trip. Or before the Elliot breakup. And now, with Christmas so close, I felt a small pang of guilt for totally avoiding going home —for not even offering. For not even calling.

"Oh, my girls," she sighed. "I'll miss you both at Christmas. But I'm so glad you're getting this time together. Maybe next time, all three of us can go."

"Me, too," I said.

"Yes, next time, we will make it a Three Musketeers trip," Lila added. "It's been so nice to get away. I didn't realize how much I needed it."

"That makes me happy to hear, my two sweethearts," Mom said. "You each deserve some fun. You both work so hard."

Lila smiled. "Thanks, Mom. That means a lot. Oh, and you'll laugh," Lila went on, "tonight, Ava's going to a 1920's speakea—"

I shot her a sharp look and shook my head.

Lila cleared her throat catching on. "—uh, themed bar. It's a . . . really cool place—very retro—like a Gatsby-themed thing. She showed me last night."

"Oh! That sounds fabulous, Ava, darling. Just be careful with that bathtub gin."

Lila laughed nervously.

"Mom, guess what!" I chimed in, steering the conversation away from dangerous territory. The last thing I needed was these two hopeless romantics dissecting my love life. "Lila is writing while she's here."

"Oh, honey, that is wonderful. That's the magic of New York. Did I ever tell you about the time I went there by myself in my twenties, right before I had you girls? I stayed in this cheap little studio in the Village and started writing a novel."

"You never told me that," Lila said. "Was that your first novel?"

"Oh yes. It was the first time I had written anything in my life. But I didn't finish it, not then. After that trip, I didn't write for years. Not until your father left. When he did, something in me just cracked open. I picked it back up, rewrote the whole thing. I didn't publish it until recently. That trip really changed me, though. It was the spark for it all. I always hoped one of you would have your own New York writing moment one day."

"Which book was it?" I asked.

"*The Choice of a Lifetime.*"

"No way," Lila said. "I had no idea that you wrote that one in New York. That's so inspiring, Mom. Maybe this is my writing moment."

"It just might be, honey," Mom said with her usual warmth.

"Mom, I just feel so bad leaving Simon and the girls during the holidays." Lila glanced at me then back at the phone. "Actually, I've been meaning to ask you something. Did you ever feel guilty for doing things just for yourself when we were little? Like . . . trips, or writing, or just anything that's *not* being a mom or a wife?"

"Oh, yes. Of course, I've felt that—every mom does at some point," she said. "But you have to remember who you are outside the role of mother and wife. Because, one day, your girls will be grown and might not even come home for Christmas. Then what? You have to hold on to your own identity, so when they become adults, you're not left realizing that you spent the last twenty years living for them and feeling like a shell of who you once were."

Lila's voice caught. "Thanks, Mom. That helps."

"You're allowed to enjoy New York fully, Lila," Mom said. "You don't have to rush home to convince yourself, or anyone, that you are a great mom or a great wife. You're allowed to have a life that inspires you, that fills *you* up. And I think your girls will be better for seeing that example. Who wants to have a mom who doesn't have a life? The best thing you can do for those girls is be a woman who chases her dreams."

Lila and I exchanged a look. I squeezed her hand. Our mom really was amazing. Man, Jeff really screwed that one up.

"I love you girls," she said. "Call or text me later this week if you have time, all right?"

"We will," Lila promised.

"We love you, too, Mom," I called out.

After Lila ended the call, I stood up and began smoothing the edge of the bed, keeping my tone as casual as I could. "Lil, I didn't mean to cut you off about the speakeasy. But that's why I didn't want to go home this year. I haven't told mom about Elliot, and I just don't want her asking a million questions about my love life, especially when I don't have any answers. You know how she is. If we even mentioned Cillian's name, she would start to assume things, telling people I am in a relationship, or planning an imaginary wedding."

Lila nodded. "Yeah, she can tend to get carried away."

I looked at her, brows raised. "Like someone else I know. I just don't need any more pressure, or questions, with all the uncertainty I have in my life right now."

"Fair," she said. "But for what it's worth, I think she'd understand more than you think."

I didn't respond, steering us back to a more time-sensitive topic. "Are you going to get ready for your solo date with the city? I want to see your dress on you," I said, grabbing the light blue, structured dress Samuel had picked out for her. The perfect dress for Lila. Clean lines. Classic. Feminine. He truly was a miracle worker, that man.

"You really didn't need to spend all that money on this dress," she said, slipping it on.

"Yes, I did. I want you to feel inspired to write—and to feel sexy on your solo date," I said, zipping her in.

She took a spin.

"To die for," I said, bringing my fingertips together and kissing them. "Chef's kiss."

She laughed then hesitated. "Will you help me do my hair

and makeup? I honestly don't even know if I remember how to after having kids."

I caught the flicker of embarrassment in her light blue eyes —eyes that, not-so-coincidentally, matched the dress perfectly.

"Of course." I smiled. "Come on." I gestured for her to come sit on the toilet seat lid, like we had as kids. "Let's start with hair." I grabbed her equally long blonde hair behind her, brushing through it. "I'm thinking a sexy blowout?" I didn't realize it until we were next to each other in the mirror—except for the five inches of height difference—that we could pass as twins.

"You mean, like those Victoria's Secret models we used to watch on the runway?" she asked, her voice rising an octave in excitement.

"Exactly. Plus some light blue eye shadow to match the dress," I said, like I was leading a glam squad, making it feel like her idea, even though I already had a clear vision of how this was going to turn out.

"I've never done blue makeup. Are you sure that will look okay?" she asked, digging through my makeup bag like she was searching for buried treasure.

"I'll make it look classy. Trust me."

"You've never once led me astray, sis."

For the next hour, we played with our hair and makeup, just like we had done as little girls, rummaging through our mom's stuff. It was the most fun I'd had in a long time. I threw myself into it—because it was easier than thinking about the fact that I had a date with a man who'd been alive one hundred years ago. A man who, by all logic, shouldn't even exist in my reality.

But for now, I shoved that thought aside and focused on perfecting Lila's winged eyeliner.

11

"WELCOME TO DA VELVET CLOVER, MS. HAWTHORNE," CILLIAN welcomed me as I stepped through the door at nine twenty-five p.m. sharp. A rush of cool air hit my skin, along with the smell of tobacco, old wood, and something faintly floral. The speakeasy was exactly as I'd left it.

Part of me exhaled in relief—relief that the speakeasy, somehow, still opened like clockwork. I hoped it meant I had a better chance of getting back to 2025 after the date.

The other part of me? Still highly convinced I might be losing my mind.

Unfortunately, Chris Kringle hadn't been working the bar tonight, so I couldn't get any questions answered. I had hesitated at the door, wondering if I should even go in—just in case. But I figured, what the hell? Like Lila had said, I hadn't had any trouble getting back and forth so far. Besides, I was never one to skip out on my commitments, and I had told Cillian I'd meet him at nine twenty-five, so I didn't really have another option.

He was wearing his usual three-piece suit. Tonight, it was in gray wool, paired with a blue and white striped collared shirt, with his usual chain and pocket watch. He stood tall, his hands clasped together in front of him, a look of amusement on his face. It was the most expressiveness I had seen from him. There was even a glint of genuine pleasure in his eyes, like he was glad I'd arrived. It threw me off a bit.

I looked around. He was alone. "Did you fire your hostess? Or did she quit?"

"I told her I wanted tonight to be special, so I let her 'ave the evening off. This is a stunning dress," he added, his gaze traveling over me. But it wasn't the usual look of a man admiring me—there was something in it that made me feel not objectified but admired.

The speakeasy was empty. Not a flapper dress in sight. Not one lit cigarette being smoked. Only Eddie, sitting on the edge of the bar, arms crossed, staring off in the distance. Lost in his own world.

"I hope you didn't send the cooks home—I'm starving," I said.

He turned and offered his cocked elbow for me to take, guiding me to the table.

"I can walk by myself, you know."

"Well, of course ya *can*—your legs aren't broken, are they?" he asked, checking my lower extremities. "Doesn't mean I can't be a gentleman and walk ya meself."

I studied him. If I grabbed his arm, did I automatically lose all my power?

I stared into those piercing eyes, and my knees went weak. Maybe it wouldn't hurt to let him stabilize me—guide me across this slippery floor in my heels—just a little.

"Fine," I conceded.

He raised an eyebrow.

I slipped my arm through the space he'd made available, and it fit perfectly. The itchy wool of his jacket and the firm press of his bicep beneath it reminded me of the night before—

when he had touched me. But this felt different, more intimate. Touching Cillian's arm, through three layers of fabric, felt more intimate than anything I'd ever experienced with another man.

He glanced at me with a side-eyed smirk as we walked toward a private room behind two sliding doors. And there it was—another Christmas tree, like the first one had cloned itself out of sheer holiday optimism. It was decked out in home-made ornaments. The fireplace crackled, garland was draped over the mantel, and an old wooden clock ticked, unaware it had missed a century.

I normally would have rolled my eyes at the holiday over-load, but I didn't. Weirdly, this place made it harder to hate Christmas. It wasn't the usual noise and pressure—it felt quieter, softer. Real. Like maybe Christmas had meant some-thing once, before it had all gotten commercialized over the last hundred years.

As I looked around, I couldn't believe how easily I had accepted the idea of time travel. But something about being here muted my logical mind. The risk felt distant, like the danger had simply dissolved.

There was only one table in the room—one table with two place settings across from each other. Set with antique china—some of the finest I'd ever seen—with multiple sets of forks, knives, spoons, and glasses.

"What are we having—a four-course meal at a speakeasy?" I laughed.

"Six," he said plainly, taking my fur coat from my shoulders. He draped it over his arm before moving to hang it on a nearby coat rack. He was so smooth.

He returned and stood by my chair, waiting for me to sit, holding on to the back of it. "After ya, Ms. Hawthorne," he said, with a slight tilt of his head, his voice commanding.

I hesitated for a moment, reluctant to give in to the old-fashioned formality. Finally, I lowered myself slowly into the chair, and without missing a beat, he gently scooted me in. I suppressed the urge to roll my eyes so hard they might get stuck. But maybe this was what chivalry looked like in the 1920s. Women hadn't really worked back then, couldn't vote or own property, and Jesus, they couldn't even get a credit card until the 70s without their husband signing. So, I figured I'd play along. In honor of all the women who never had the opportunities I have now—letting a man push in my chair felt like the absolute *least* he could do.

His action felt almost too intimate for a simple dinner—his hand just barely brushing my back as he adjusted the chair beneath me. I couldn't decide if it was charming or irritating, but there was no denying that there was something powerful in the way he made these small gestures feel so deliberate. So significant.

"Thanks."

He paused and looked at me. "Was dat manners I heard from Ms. Hawthorne's lips?"

A smile escaped me, which I quickly covered with a shrug and an exaggerated eye roll. I couldn't help myself.

"Why would you send everyone home if we are just eating in this private room?" I asked.

"The reason," he said as he sat, unfolding his napkin and placing it across his lap, "dat I sent everyone home and shut down tonight . . . was because I *can*. Because I'm the boss. And I wanted to make dis evening special for two lonely people to have dinner and not be so lonely." He leaned back in his seat with a grin. "Together."

I kept my spine as straight as I could. "Or did you bring me here to kill me and didn't want any witnesses? Isn't that what people do in the 1920s—just kill people? Shoot them in cold blood?"

"Ava?" he said slowly, pulling out a cigarette and handing it to me. I took it. FYI: Cigarettes were way better in the 1920s.

"Yeah?" I asked as he reached across the table to light mine, then his.

"Why do ya speak of today as if it were da past?" His words were mumbled, his cigarette bouncing between his lips.

"I don't." I scrambled for something to say, but my mind went blank. *Change the subject now. You will sound insane if you tell him you are from the future. Then he might actually try to kill you.* I grabbed for something—anything. "I think the better question is: why did you ask me on a date?"

Of every first date topic, I pick that one. Great job, Ava. Jesus.

"Is dis a date?" he asked.

"I ... uh ..." I stammered. "I-I don't know."

He smiled like his life's mission was to fluster me.

"Stop avoiding the question!" I said, a laugh escaping me.

Cillian stifled a laugh himself, his shoulders subtly shaking with the effort. He slowly leaned in, his forearms now on the edge of the table. "I wouldn't close me pub for a *non-date*, Ava."

"But why would you ask me on a date when you act like you hate me? You were nicer to my sister than me." I tried to pass it off like I wasn't fishing, even though I most certainly was. But why *was* I? Why did I care what he thought or who he liked? I didn't. But God, if I was honest with myself, I did. I really did. I cared more about what he thought and who he liked than I should. And I had no idea why.

"Well, I was nice to yer sister, because she was kind to me," he said.

"I *was* nice to you," I argued.

He raised a brow. "*That* is your version of nice?"

"Well, I didn't want to be sitting with some strange man at a reject table, at a random speakeasy."

"Communal table," he corrected me, leaning back in his chair, crossing one leg over the other (somehow making it look cool). "But, for yer information, speakeasies are supposed to be hidden. If they weren't, they'd just be called bars. And they'd be legal." He cleared his throat.

I hadn't even realized that 1925 was mid-Prohibition. Alcohol was illegal. Did that mean his whole bar was illegal?

I stared at him, and for a second, it was like looking in a mirror. He was using my own tricks against me—the ones I pulled at work with colleagues and clients. The lean-back posture, the subtle provocation, the smug little fact-checking routine. The worst part? It was working. I could feel myself getting riled up. Damn, he was good. He was giving me a real run for my money.

I took a deep breath. "Okay, smartass."

He raised a brow.

"If I'm so rude, why did you ask me here tonight?"

He brought his hand to his face and ran it across the corners of his mouth. "Because, Ava—"

"Why do you keep saying my name ... like that?" I snapped. He needed to stop it. It was affecting me in ways I couldn't admit.

He sat in silence for a moment and a half. "Ava—*Ayva* in Irish—it means 'life,' 'living.' And it suits ya perfectly." He didn't rush, his words deliberate. I wasn't mad at what he said; I was mad at how it made me feel. "You, Ms. Ava, are full of life—"

"Now you are just saying my name to annoy me," I cut him off.

"Ava. I say your name, because your name is beautiful," he said, staring at me.

My body tensed and released each time my name crossed his lips.

I gave him my best fabricated bored look.

"Like you," he added casually, as though it was the most natural thing in the world. "You are beautiful."

Oh no.

"Now, can I answer your original question, or would ya like to continue to interrupt me?"

His words made me sit up straight in my seat. I hadn't even noticed I was interrupting him. "Yeah, of course. Go ahead." *Shut up, Ava. Let him talk.*

"I asked ya here on a date, darlin'," he said, and my lips parted as I gasped for air at that one word, his accent adding at least two points to his already outrageous attractiveness, "because ya're the first woman I've met in a long time, if ever, who isn't scared of me. Not intimidated. Ya're also the only woman I've ever heard utter a word about business and wear pants—of all things—into me pub. How could I not want to know everything about a woman like that?"

I was sure I seemed like an alien in his world. I guessed that was what one hundred years of evolution and women's rights did. Maybe this time travel thing brought me up a few points on his subjective dating scale.

"That just sounds like you need to get out more," I said.

He chuckled at first, the laughter building until it erupted into full-on amusement. I couldn't help pursing my lips to try to hold in my own laughter, but a smile escaped me.

His laugh was low and unexpectedly warm, his eyes lighting up in a way I hadn't seen before—something genuine, a part of him that had clearly been buried for a long time. I had never heard him laugh, and now that I had, it felt like I'd unlocked a new side of him, one that didn't belong to the man I thought I knew. The man whom I thought he was.

It was like the laughter dissolved an invisible but real barrier that had been between us. It was then that I came to the conclusion that this could be the perfect situationship for me while here in New York. There was no real possibility of a future with this man, given the incredibly strange time-travel phenomenon that I couldn't even begin to understand.

Not that I could explain it, but the one hundred years

between us would ensure there was no future together. Which took the pressure off. It meant, while I was here for the next week or so, I could spend some time with a sexy, charming, amazing-smelling war-hero-man with an accent that made my knees weak. One who pushed in my chair and walked me arm-in-arm to our dinner table. He would probably even open a door for me if the opportunity presented itself. As much as I hated to admit it, I liked it.

Of course, there was the whole time-travel element to figure out—the risks, the rules. Could I just come and go each night without causing a mess? Did what Lila and I did here affect the future? I figured since nothing was going to get serious in such a short time, how much of a difference could one week really make?

This could be the perfect distraction from the Elliot breakup, and I'd keep all my power intact. After the new year, I'd check out of this hotel and never look back. Never have to see him again.

"How're the two most gorgeous people I know doin'?" Eddie asked, sliding the doors open just enough to peek his head in, as though Cillian had told him not to come in unless otherwise prompted. "Cill, she has got ye laughing in here? I haven't heard that laugh from ye since before da war."

Cillian looked at me, but I pretended not to notice.

"You know, Eddie, I think I may have just met me match," he said, his gaze still burning into me while I kept up my act of indifference. I couldn't tell if he meant it as a challenge or something else entirely. "We'll have two glasses of Cabernet."

"I'll have dat right up, sir." He saluted Cillian then headed back to the bar.

"No whiskey tonight?" I asked.

"It is a special occasion. And that wine will go much better with our third and fourth course."

"Whatever you say," I said, playing along.

———

What I assumed to be hours, a bottle and a half of cab, and six of the most delicious courses of my life later, Cillian and I finished the evening with some dessert and coffee. The entire night had flown by. Time felt different here. Time felt different with him.

Throughout the evening, I had played along with his old-fashioned mannerisms and language. Dropping a few 1920's references I'd picked up from *The Great Gatsby*, mostly to see how he'd react. Lucky for me, he had no way of knowing those nods came from a book that hadn't been written in his time— yet. I couldn't help but wonder if he knew more about this whole time-traveling situation than he let on.

Once our Cold War shtick had faded with a few drinks and conversation, I found that he was actually quite pleasant. He was easy to talk to. Not like most snooze fests from the modern day. He was sharp, witty, intelligent. And, of course, easy on the eyes.

I figured it was like the universe's way of, however Lila said it, "throwing me a bone." *Here you go, Ava. A perfectly unavailable man—in more ways than one—for you to play with over the holidays. Your reward for putting up with Elliot for so long. Enjoy!*

I took a sip of my coffee, setting my cigarette in the ashtray beside it, as I grabbed the last bite of cake sitting between us. "I have a question."

He leaned forward, clasping his hands together, fingers interlaced. "Wouldn't be yer first, or yer last, I am sure," he said. "Well then, get on with it."

"Did your wife . . . die during childbirth? With Eoin? Or . . . was his mom your wife?"

He took a deep breath out through his nose, biting a small piece of his cheek. "Yes." He clicked his tongue, like that would ease whatever pain resided. "She was. And she did." That cold look returned to his eyes that had lived there all the nights before. Like this woman, whom he had loved and lost, was the cause of all of his pain and suffering. His coldness.

I shook my head. "We don't have to talk about it. I shouldn't have asked."

"Ya have every right to know, Ava," he said.

Did I, though? I was basically a stranger to him. Did people not casually date back in 1920? Or was he trying to ruse me into becoming Saoirse's new mommy after only one date?

My eyebrows twitched, but I left space for him to share.

He took a slow breath before speaking, his voice distant. "We got married and had the children before da war." He looked at his near-empty wine glass, gliding his finger around the edge, mesmerized by his own movement. "We were very in love. When she was in labor with Eoin, we were home; my mother and sister were dere helping with the birth. She had abnormally terrible pain when the contractions came on. Our doctor was in another town and wasn't able to make it in time. Eoin came out as a stillborn. My wife was fine for a few hours, devastated, of course, by what had happened. As was I. We aren't fully sure what happened. She passed away that night in her sleep. A part of me wonders if she was so heartbroken that she couldn't stand to live knowing Eoin wouldn't be a part of her future."

His eyes stayed on his glass while I gaped in shock. I had no idea what to say. Instinctively, all I knew to do was reach across the table, grab his hand from the glass, and hold it in mine.

"I'm so sorry," was all I managed to get out.

He looked up at me. "That is da first time I have heard those words from yer lips."

"What words?" I asked.

"I'm sorry."

I shrugged. "I don't like saying sorry unless it is warranted, and it usually isn't. Women say it way too much. Like my sister.

Every other thing she says is *I am sorry. I'm sorry this. I'm sorry that.* It's like she feels obligated to apologize for taking up space in the world, for existing. But this—this *I'm sorry* is definitely warranted."

"Thank you. Very kind of ya to say. But ya have nothin' to be sorry for. 'Tis what it is." He cleared his throat. "It was many years ago now. It happened for a reason, and there's always a bigger plan in place."

I gave him an empathetic look, and he returned a knowing one.

He pulled his hand out of mine, only to take both of mine into his, cupping them gently, his warmth seeping—burning into my skin. He gave them a small squeeze, like a silent thank you he couldn't quite put into words.

My hands being in his felt natural. Like the most natural thing in the world.

This man, who had lived through war, buried a child, kissed his wife goodbye, and still managed to sit across from me like the whole world hadn't shattered beneath him. I had to ask . . . "Are you scared to die?"

I shouldn't have asked. I wasn't sure why I had. Maybe I asked because I didn't understand how someone survived that much death and grief and still showed up every day. Maybe I asked because I wasn't sure I would be able to do the same, if I were in his shoes. Maybe I asked because I was terrified to die. It felt like the scariest possibility out there.

He paused before saying, "When ya agree to a life, ya agree to a death."

"Okay, Shakespeare," I said. "Seriously. After the war, after your son, after your wife, are you less scared of dying or is it still just as terrifying?"

"War certainly changed me views, as did my wife's and Eoin's deaths. Out there, I saw men meet death with a cigarette and a joke, others with tears and fear. In the end, it takes us all da same. We all owe God a death."

Nodding, I lowered my eyes to the floor.

"When I first arrived in America, I met a Native American man here in da city," he said. "We struck up a conversation at a pub, and he told me his people don't fear death. In fact, they honor it. He said that when they had teepee living, each and every day, they would open the flap of their teepee, stand tall with their back arched, heart open, head back, and call to da Great Spirit, 'Today is a great day to die. And therefore, I shall live,'" he said, letting out a deep laugh, as if he were reliving that moment. "I thought it was a beautiful way to look at death —welcoming it with open arms. Not afraid of it or avoidin' it, but truly embracin' it as a real and inevitable part of life. Because any moment could be the last one."

"That is beautiful," I said.

"What about you, Ava? Is da fearless woman in front of me tonight afraid of death itself?"

All sense of inability to be vulnerable vanquished after how much he'd shared with me. He had a way of softening me like butter sitting in the sun.

What the hell was happening to me?

I took a deep breath in. "Terrified, actually."

His forehead wrinkled in surprise. My hands still in his, he gave them a squeeze. "Go on," he coaxed. "Why?"

"We work our whole lives to accumulate all this stuff— success, money, material things, wisdom, knowledge, love. Then we die and lose it all, and what—have to start all over in the next life? Sit up in heaven for eternity? Devolve into a house plant? Reincarnate into a mosquito? Or who knows, maybe even end up in limbo? Hell? If it's anything like the rules from that church I grew up in, then hell is probably my next stop. I lied all the time as a kid. I curse a lot and definitely didn't save myself for marriage. If you know what I mean. So, what? I am just stuck down there for all eternity? It all sounds fucking terrifying, no matter which way you cut it."

"If it was between the two of us as to who got the next seat in hell, I am sure I would go long before ya, Ava." He squeezed my hands in his.

Little did he know, his statement was factual, purely due to chronological timing and the fact that I technically didn't exist in this reality for another hundred years. He'd probably been dead and buried for decades before I was even born. So, yes, based on that alone, that was a pretty safe bet to make. Plus, he had probably killed a lot of people in war. That definitely had to gain you an admission ticket into hell.

"Well, after you, I won't be far behind." I laughed. "Maybe we can go together." *Great, Ava. Now you sound like some clingy weirdo. Why would I say that?*

I paused, not sure why I was about to share what I was. "I don't think I'm as afraid of dying as I am of falling in love. Finally finding the love of my life after all the years of searching, and then . . . just dying. How tragic would that be? To finally find that love, after decades of searching, and searching . . . and then I die. Or they die. It sounds just as bad as going to hell."

I stopped, realizing what I had just said—and to whom. *His wife, the love of his life died, you stupid bitch.*

My mouth dropped open. "Fuck, I'm so sorry. Shit, Cillian. I didn't mean . . . I just—"

"It's okay." He smiled. "It *is* tragic. Probably one of the most tragic tings dat can happen, which is why it's a common fear. And why many of us avoid love altogether. But at some point— whether we're young or old, whether it's after finding love today or decades down da road—we all end up losing it all. It's inevitable. We all leave this life the same way we came into it . . . . alone."

"So depressing," I said.

"I have found that, with enough time, the more ya think of it—the more you embrace it—the less tragic it all becomes. In a strange way, death has made me a better man. It was such a terrible shock dat it snapped me out of me daze enough to get me life together and start anew. To become better. To try every day to be better."

He continued, "We come into this life alone, and we leave it alone. But while we're here, we might as well love as much as we can, while we can. What's the alternative? Going through life alone? Miserable? It's such a brief moment in time dat we are here, and if we're lucky enough to find someone whom we love dearly, why not make the most of it?"

I hadn't expected him to be so wise. Or such a romantic. It was like he'd actually lived one hundred years. He had come off like such a lonely cynic when I'd met him.

"Do you believe you will find love again?" I asked.

His blue eyes looked straight into mine. Staring into the depths of my soul, he said, "I do." His words knocked the wind out of me. "And ya?"

I looked down at my hands in his before speaking. "I'm not sure I'll ever find someone I'm compatible with. I've always felt like something's wrong with me, like I'm broken in some way. Some—most . . . well, all of my exes would probably say I am impossible. I'm in my thirties and single. At this point, I've come to terms with the fact that maybe it isn't in the cards for me."

"Nah," he said. "Ya just have to find someone who has felt as broken as you. As lonely as you. Someone who sees you for who you truly are and still accepts you, despite it. *Because* of it." He stared at me, but I acted like I didn't see it.

"You are right, I guess I will keep up hope." I looked at him, we exchanged smiles.

"If *I* can find love, Ava, so can ya." He pulled my hands to his lips and gave them a warm kiss.

I wanted to be disgusted by it. I wanted to say some sassy, rude comment telling him to stop. Like I would any other guy who had invited me to his own bar for a first date. But I couldn't. I didn't want to. I liked it. No . . . I loved it. Every second of it. I loved every second of him touching me. Every second of him holding my hands in his. I wanted more of it. I wanted all of it. It felt good to let him in.

No. Stop, Ava. This is just for fun, just for the week. Nothing more.

But even I knew that was a lie. I felt something for Cillian. Something real. And it scared the absolute shit out of me.

In that moment, whatever it was that he was doing to me, the way he was making me feel, scared me more than death itself.

Maybe even more than love.

———

Cillian walked me to the door that led back to the hotel bar, once again with my arm laced in his, his free hand resting over mine. After all that wine, I actually needed the stability.

My heart pounded in my throat, the anticipation of how we would say goodnight knotting in my stomach. Cillian had asked Eddie to give us some privacy, so we could "have a proper goodnight"—whatever that meant.

Why was I so nervous? I was *never* nervous.

"Well," I said, turning toward him as we arrived at my exit . . . portal . . . door? What would happen if he walked through it with me? Would he stay in 1925 or end up in 2025, right beside me? Would he evaporate, unable to cross into the future, or would he step through it just like I had, into the past? I really needed to figure out how the hell this all worked.

"Thank ya for having dinner with me tonight, Ava. I had an

amazing time. One of the best nights I've had in . . . a long, long while."

I braced myself for the usual male games—the pullback, the manipulation, the "I'll call you," followed by radio silence.

"So did I, Cillian. Really, I'm shocked. But it was amazing. I'm glad I gave you a chance," I said, my voice sounding higher than normal.

He stifled a laugh, looking at his feet, then me. "Ava, earlier ya asked me why I asked you on this date, and I told ya. Now, ya have to tell me: why did you say yes?" He grabbed the hand dangling by my side, bringing it up and holding it with his hands at his chest. My breath caught.

"Weren't you there? I said yes because Lila volunteered me," I answered.

He stood there, waiting for the real reason.

"Well, if I'm being honest, I decided to come to see if you had any good tips for the atelier that I'm considering working at. But that was a dry well." I winked, pressing my knuckles into his chest to push him off balance. He didn't budge. We'd been so deep in conversation that we hadn't talked about any of that. I hadn't even thought to bring it up.

He looked down at my hand, still firmly clasped in his. "Oh, I have plenty of advice when it comes to dat. Wait for date number two." He smiled.

Just the mention of a second date made me soften, relaxing into the strange sense of safety I felt with him. There were none of the usual games. No mixed signals. No emotional gymnastics. I could get used to dating in 1925. Which, of course, was exactly the problem. My mind said *one-week-fling*, but my body? My body was yelling, *When will you see him again?* My biological clock screaming, *Mate for life*.

I rolled my eyes. "Fine, really, I said yes because, much like you, it has been a long time since I have come head-to-head with someone who could feed me as many dry and sarcastic comments as I feed them. You told Eddie you have met your match . . . I think I might have met mine, as well."

The wrinkles on the corners of his eyes became more defined from his full smile, revealing a joy that I wanted to see a million more times—that rare sparkle in his eyes.

He took my hand and kissed it. "When can I see you again?"

I tilted my head slightly. "I can see how you have so much success in business. Booking the second date before I even leave the first? Very impressive."

"How else would ya expect I get a hold of ya, unless ya were to magically have a phone in your hotel room."

"Right. Of course," I said, remembering the generational tech gap—no cell phones.

I acted like I was considering his question, giving him a playful look. "I guess I could see you again. When?"

"Tomorrow," he said without hesitation. "Here again. I promise I won't close down da place. I will have the band come. You like jazz music, eh?"

"Love," I said. He was going to get a band to come for me? "I suppose I can make tomorrow work. I may bring Lila. I have that meeting with the atelier and don't want her to feel like I am ditching her *all* day."

I noticed his brow twitch when I said "ditching," like he didn't know what that meant. Reminder to self: stop using modern slang in 1925.

"We wouldn't want dat. Of course Lila can join us," he said. "How does nine o'clock sound?"

"Nine twenty-five?" I negotiated.

"Quite an odd time, but nine twenty-five it is. I will see ya tomorrow." He grabbed my hips—high enough that it was respectful, but low enough that he had full control over my body.

A bolt of lightning shot through me.

He leaned in and kissed my cheek. I inhaled sharply. Then

bit my lip, trying to stop the lightning bolt of energy. Anything to stop the moan that threatened to escape my mouth.

What on earth was this man doing to me?

As he pulled away, he looked at me like he could read every thought in my mind. I did my best to maintain my composure.

"Thank you, Cillian. I'll see you tomorrow," I said, barely able to think after such a simple yet intense touch.

I turned toward the door, feeling his eyes on me until I walked through the velvet curtain and back into the hotel—the door that led me back to 2025.

12

MY PHONE DINGED SIX TIMES AS I LEFT THE SPEAKEASY AND headed out of the hotel to get some air. The sudden brightness of the streetlights felt like the brightness of the sun. I couldn't tell if the dizziness was from time-traveling a hundred years in a split-second or from that last glass of cabernet—and no Cillian to hold me steady. Everything felt different—sharper, louder, clearer, like the volume of the world had been turned up too fast.

I grabbed my phone out of my pocket. Lila.

> Hey, how is it? Amazing I bet. Text me when u r done.

> Oh my gosh, I just got hit on at this bar by the creepiest guy. Ew.

> I can't wait to hear how ur date was, living vicariously through u!

> I'm at The Mark Hotel Bar, meet me after. It's really fancy!!

Hellooo? I know you have no cell service there. Did Cillian have his chefs chop u up into a million pieces and send you off into the abyss of another dimension?

Txt me so I know u r ok. Mom instincts kicking in. I would hate to lose you to 1925—or the aliens.

I rolled my eyes and sent back a message:

Just finished.

Grabbing a cab, see you in 10.

———

"Finally! It's about time. I thought I lost you to that speakeasy," Lila said, standing from her barstool to hug me as I rushed over to meet her.

"Thanks for waiting. How have things been going here? Did that creepy man leave you alone, or do I need to kick someone's ass?" I asked. "You can't be too nice here, Lil. People will take advantage of you. You wreak of 'kidnap me energy.'"

Her jaw dropped in offense. "I do *not*. It's fine. I told him to eat rocks, and then he left."

"You *said* that? Out loud? Where did you get that line—the fucking playground?" I scrunched my face in disgust.

"Okay, that is so not important right now," she said. "I need to hear *everything*. What happened with your enchanting 1920's speakeasy man? It must have gone well; you were there forever." She patted my shoulder like she was a dog begging for a treat. "Tell me, tell me!"

"Can I get a glass of cabernet?" I asked the bartender as they came by. Then I took a deep breath, centering myself. I hadn't even taken a second to process what had just happened. I had spent the entire cab ride over, reviewing some emails that Sofia had sent me with their 2025 campaigns and PR opportunity records.

"Okay . . . wow," was all I could breathe out, settling into my seat.

"Wow good or wow bad?" Lila grimaced.

"I think wow good. Like, wow, *really* good," I said with a smile that I couldn't contain, now spreading across my face. *Dammit.*

Lila gasped, clapping her hands, bouncing up and down on her chair, shrieking with excitement.

The people next to us shot us a look of annoyance. I shot a look right back that made them mind their own damn business.

"God, I feel like I am in second grade again when I found out Derek Armstrong had a crush on me," I said, without specifying if that was a good or bad thing because, quite frankly, I had no idea.

"Tell me everything," Lila begged. "Tell me about the conversations. What did you talk about? Did he kiss you? I need to know everything!"

"Okay, okay, calm down, and I will." And I did. I told her everything in detail. Cillian greeting me at the empty restaurant. That one got a big reaction from Lila. More cheers. I told her about the deep conversations. The hand holding. The cheek kiss. The full body tingles. The follow-up date for tomorrow.

"*Death?* The two of you *would* talk about death on a first date. And this close to Christmas? You are sadistic," she said with disgust.

"I wouldn't be a true Scorpio if I didn't dive into a conversation about death on night one with a stranger," I said, sipping my wine.

She elbowed me. "He isn't a stranger *now*."

"Oh, stop." I swatted her away. "It was . . . great. But nothing can come of it, Lil. Was it surprisingly amazing? Yes. But it cannot go anywhere. I can't get too emotionally involved without it getting messy."

Lila slouched, pouting at my comment. "But he is so perfect for you. Can't you just let yourself like a guy for once?"

"See where that got me last time?" I said. "Not to mention he's from *1925*. I can't exactly date a man who's not even supposed to exist in this time. It's a dead end—literally."

"But Cillian is different, and you know that. And clearly, he likes you," she whined.

"Of course he likes me. There were probably five total viable options back then when it came to dating. They had to jump on a good one if they walked by. Besides . . . what? I just have a relationship that is solely confined to a 20's speakeasy in an Irish hotel in Manhattan that only opens at nine twenty-five p.m.?"

Lila gave me a hopeful look. "I mean, would you consider that?"

"No. I mean, maybe . . . I mean, no."

"But you clearly like him. What's the harm of just enjoying the week together?"

"I do not like him!" I tried to fight through the damn smile that kept creeping onto my face every time she brought him up. I covered my face with my hand. "Fuck . . ." I said, dropping my head back, looking up at the ceiling. "Maybe I do like him, just a little. But I can't. It doesn't even make sense. Lila, how could you let this happen?" I slapped her arm.

"It isn't *totally* my fault. You said yes to the date."

"No, *you* said yes to the date, for me. When you were hammered."

"Touché. I'm sorry. So, what are you going to do?"

"I'm sticking to my plan," I said firmly. "I'll enjoy him while I'm here, let myself be wined and dined, have some fun—why not? After Elliot, I deserve a fun rebound. Or, at least to have an enjoyable holiday since he fucked mine up last minute." I paused, shaking my head at the sheer absurdity of it all.

Time traveling. My sister and I were actually time traveling, and neither of us found each other clinically insane. And not only that, but I was now entertaining a Christmas fling with a man from the past.

"Do you think we'll be able to keep getting in every night?" Lila asked.

I shrugged. "I didn't have any trouble tonight, and Chris Kringle wasn't even there. It seems pretty reliable so far."

"I wonder if it's a Christmas magic thing. Like it only opens during the holiday," Lila said.

"I mean, that'd be absolutely ridiculous. Christmas magic is not an actual thing. But . . . maybe." Honestly, of all the explanations, that sounded like the most reasonable one. "Either way—whether I were to go back to San Francisco, stay here in New York for the new job, or the speakeasy portal closes on its own one day—that'll be it. I could never have a long-term thing with someone if I always had to check into that hotel and step through some portal to see him. Not to mention having to deal with Chris Kringle every time. No thank you. Once we check out, that'll be the end of it. A week of fun doesn't have to lead to anything serious. I just want to have a good time while it lasts."

"But what if Cillian catches real feelings for you?" she asked.

I frowned. "Well, when I am here in 2025, it doesn't matter much since he technically isn't alive. But I doubt that man is truly capable of catching real feelings after everything he's gone through. I'm sure he is just having some short-term fun, as well."

"Do you think you would tell him about us being from the future?"

"No way," I said. "I just don't think it needs to come up. This thing isn't going to last more than a few days; why put a wet blanket on it with that information?"

"Even if it got serious? Or either of you caught real feelings?"

"We won't."

Lila curled her bottom lip down. "Fine, fine. I support you whatever you decide. But I think you should let yourself have fun, lean into the feelings if you feel them. It would be good for you to experience a gentleman and allow yourself to receive—"

"I am *not* giving my power away to this guy!"

"I'm not saying you are. I'm just saying it would be good for you to be cared for. Not have to be on edge or protective of your heart all the time. Just allow this strong, sweet, handsome, masculine guy to do things for you. It's good practice for you to be in your feminine."

"Now you're making my plan sound terrible," I said.

"Okay, okay, I'll stop," she said. "Sis, just have fun with him in whatever way feels comfortable to you, and I will fully support you." She forced a smile. "So, his wife is for sure dead?"

"Yeah, terrible isn't it?" I said.

"I mean, yes, terribly awful. But at least you won't have to deal with the crazy ex." She grimaced. "Or the baby mama. Not sure how they referred to them back then."

I gaped. "Lila Carrington, when did you become so morally bankrupt?" I scoffed. Though she had put words to what I'd been thinking all night.

"Just saying, those exes can be crazy," she said like she had personal experience in this arena.

"Did you get any writing done?" I asked, changing the subject.

"Indeed, I did! Thanks for asking," she said, her voice filled with pride. "I wrote like ten pages."

I was happy for her, that she got some time to do what she enjoyed, kid-free.

I took a sip of my wine as she organized her papers on the bar top.

"Will you share what you're writing with me?"

"No, not yet. I'm still too shy about it. But I'll tell you soon. I just want to get further into the story before I share it with anyone. Is that okay?" she asked.

"Of course, sis. I would love to hear about it whenever you're ready." I gave her an air kiss. "P.S. Tomorrow night, Cillian said that you are more than welcome to join us, when I asked if you could come."

She started to say something, but before she got a chance to answer or protest, I leaned in to order us a night cap. Whatever it was, she kept it to herself, and we enjoyed our final drink before walking off our buzz, twenty blocks back to the hotel.

13

The next morning, I took Lila to the Union Square Market to grab some green juice—our attempt at offsetting the prior night's drinks. Strangely, the wine buzz I'd left the speakeasy with had completely lifted by the time I'd met up with Lila, like it had never happened. It wasn't until Lila and I had our night cap at The Mark when the familiar buzz had crept back in.

I wasn't a farmers' market fan—and I loathed useless trinkets—but I was patient as Lila picked up a few things for the girls and wandered. Once she'd made her rounds, we stopped at ChaCha Matcha for lattes and croissants before wandering toward Barnes & Noble—five stories of books in every direction.

"This is my favorite location," I told her, dragging her across 17th Street to the entrance. "This might be good inspiration for your book too, Lil."

"Oh, great idea," she said, glancing both ways before hurrying to catch up.

"What kinds of books are you into these days?" I asked as we stepped inside. Was it sad that after more than thirty years, I didn't even know such a simple fact about my sister?

"Oh my gosh, it's so cute here for Christmas!" Lila squealed, taking in the holiday decorations scattered throughout the store. She rushed over to the Christmas book table. I followed behind her.

"I haven't had much time to read since the girls were born," she admitted, trailing her fingers along the display table. "But I've started getting into fiction again. *Romantasy*, they call it."

I stopped in my tracks. "What the fuck is *romantasy*?"

"Romance and fantasy!" she exclaimed, leading me toward another table.

"So, like . . . werewolves and humans having sex? Think they call that bestiality, sis. Or *Twilight*."

"Ew. No, Ava!" she shrieked, slapping my arm before shoving a bright red book into my hands. The cover featured a wolf with an arrow shot through it.

I held it up. "Exactly my point," I said, pointing to the wolf.

"This series will *literally* change your brain chemistry," she crooned.

I gave her a sidelong look. "There is no way that's *your* saying. Where did you even find this series? Some internet trend?"

"It's called *BookTok*, Ava. Try to keep up," she said, continuing on her soap box. "Oh, especially this one. *Chapter 55*." She showed me another—this one bright green, with an eagle clutching a wedding ring on the cover—another massive book, another animal.

"Hence my original comment about bestiality." I flipped through it. "Lil, this thing is like eight hundred pages! I thought you said you didn't have a lot of time to read. And there are what?" I counted them on the table in front of me. "Five of them?"

"Sixth one should be coming soon, thank God," Lila squealed again. "Come on; just read it. I promise you'll love it."

I sighed, flipping it over before setting it back on the table and grabbing the pink one next to it. At least this one didn't have an animal on it.

"All right, I'll give it a go . . . sometime in the *very* far distant future—maybe. Like when I am retired and have time to read five thousand words about wolves and birds having sex."

"Honestly, you and your one-hundred-year-old boyfriend would fit right in with the Stone Age—completely out of touch." She tipped her nose into the air.

"Alright, I can see this is a sensitive topic for you," I said.

She grabbed the book out of my hands and pulled it tight to her chest. "Do *not* question my reading preferences. Time invested into this series isn't like normal reading; trust me. For the romance alone, you would read ten million pages," she said, her voice ethereal, like she was reliving the fantasy.

"The romance? You mean the scenes where the wolf and human have sex?" I laughed.

"Av! They aren't always animals. There are faeries, too." She gestured dramatically at the front cover with a huff and an eye roll.

"Yeah, that sounds much better . . ." I mocked. Offense washed over her face. "I love watching you get flustered. It's hilarious."

"Okay, we are done with my books. You don't appreciate them." She grabbed a few more, hugging them into her chest before moving on. "We can talk about them when you are more open-minded," she said, sticking her tongue out and walking away.

"Great, then we will never need to revisit it," I said, knowing the day would never come that I would read bestiality for women, and we continued to browse.

"If you're so smug about my books, then what types of books do *you* read, Miss Romantasy is Beneath Me?"

"I mostly read non-fiction these days—business books, psychology, quantum physics stuff," I said, running my fingers along the spines of the books as I walked past them.

She trailed behind me. "Ugh, you're so annoying. Does anyone actually like reading that stuff? Or do you just tell yourself you do so you can feel superior when you walk into a Barnes & Noble?"

"No, it actually helps me in my work. A lot. I see reading less as a fun pastime and more as part of my job—career advancement," I said, picking up *Psycho-Cybernetics*, a book I had been meaning to read.

Lila stood there, tapping her foot, looking around, bored out of her mind. "What's upstairs?" She gestured toward the escalator.

"There are five floors. The third and fourth are where we want to focus—fiction, business, and what I'm assuming is more of your . . . *romantasy* . . . smut? Isn't that what they call it?" I gave her a challenging look as we headed for the escalator.

"Ha, so you *have* heard about it!" she squealed.

I smiled and changed the topic. "Have you ever read the classics? *Wuthering Heights*? *Anna Karenina*? *Crime and Punishment*?" I asked.

"No, never have. I know I should, but they're just so boring." She shrugged.

"Same," I admitted. "I did watch *Pride and Prejudice* once—the movie—but that's the extent of my literary adventures."

"You should probably start studying, though. You're basically dating a character from one of those books."

"Lil, he's not from the 1800s." I laughed.

My sister, who was far superior at mental math, gave me a serious look. "I mean, Av—Cillian was literally born in the late 1800s."

I stopped in my tracks and gasped, staring ahead, as if her words had just unlocked a groundbreaking piece of information. "Jesus, that's freaky to think about." It was like I had forgotten for a second that he was a dead guy in today's world. That he had an old gravestone somewhere.

"I mean, unless he is"—she paused for a quick calculation —"one hundred thirty-eight years old, which would make him the oldest man to ever live, then yeah, he was born during the Victorian Era."

"This whole situation is messing with my mind," I said, shaking my head. "How is this even possible?"

She shrugged, still clutching her smut as if she didn't already have three copies of each of those books at home. "I don't know, sis. But maybe this speakeasy isn't meant to be understood by your mind. You just said you are always reading those quantum physics books. I bet they talk about infinite timelines, parallel dimensions, alternate realities. Maybe this place is meant to be felt. Not everything has to fit into a theory that we can understand to be real. Some things just can't be explained by science."

"I would prefer to stick to the things I can comprehend," I admitted. As soon as I said it, I realized I was a walking contradiction. I had been so quick to accept time travel as reality. In fact, I had gone back last night, even though I knew I'd never be able to fully understand how it was possible.

When I was in the speakeasy, it was like I was open to the unexplainable magic. But back in 2025, grounded in my reality, I questioned everything. My mind came in, and the reality hit differently.

"By that logic, only the things we can comprehend are possible," my sister said.

I paused. "Are you sure you haven't been reading the same books I've been? Those smut books seem beneath your IQ, sis."

"Not possible," she said, turning to pull the books away from my reach. "I'm just saying . . ." She trailed off.

"No, you're right. Maybe I need to stop figuring it out with my mind. It's just so hard not to when there is no logical explanation."

"Well, the alternative is you going insane in the process. Or you can just relax and enjoy the mysteriously perfect man who's been presented to you at Christmastime, post Elliot breakup. Maybe consider it an early Christmas present from Santa," she said as we continued to peruse.

"Yeah, that's what I'll do," I said. Just what I needed, Christmas *magic* to complicate the chaos of my current life.

Lila gasped. "Ooo, look! The history section. Let's look for an Irish World War I book and see if we can find Cillian."

I scrunched my face. "I highly doubt we will. Are you sure those sex books aren't making you believe that unrealistic plotlines exist in real life? Sorry to burst your bubble, but werewolves that rip your clothes off in the forest don't exist. Well, they do . . . but they wouldn't exactly pillow talk with you afterward. You'd be dead."

"God, wouldn't it be great if they did, though," she said dreamily.

"Ew."

She turned to me with doe eyes that even I couldn't resist.

"You've taken way too many notes from your kids with this begging stuff, Lil." I nodded toward the history section. "Fine, let's go then."

I was shocked that Lila found twelve books about World War I, with exactly two of them covering Ireland's involvement —one of which had pictures. Lila sat on the floor, books scattered all around her. She was still flipping through the picture book, looking for Cillian, while I started reading *Psycho-Cybernetics*, standing close by, totally bored by her journalist's version of *Where's Waldo*.

Yet another gasp, even more dramatic than the first, came from Lila. She grabbed my knee with a death grip. "Ava."

"What? Did you find our ghost of Christmas past?"

She flipped the book toward me.

And there he was.

The image was labeled, "*The Distinguished Service Order (DSO) was awarded to the below officers for having distinguished themselves by meritorious or courageous action during active operations in World War I.*"

I shook my head. I couldn't believe it. I mean, I could, but it was still shocking. It was the exact same photo from the bathroom in the speakeasy. Handsome Cillian, still recognizable, even in the throes of war. Stone-cold. Death living behind those eyes.

Until this moment, a small, minuscule part of me held out hope that maybe, just maybe, the speakeasy had manufactured those photos for an authentic vibe. That it was all some giant prank. But this? This photo was in a book at Barnes & Noble. The exact same damn photo. This wasn't some elaborate ruse.

It was history.

And unless the Irish government and World War I were in on Cillian's speakeasy ruse, then he was, in fact, from 1925. Meaning, I had, in fact, been time traveling each night. Which meant that, I, in fact . . . had feelings for a dead man and had been spending my evenings one hundred years in the past. Unless, of course, he somehow survived all those cigarettes and whiskey and set a world record for becoming the oldest man in history.

She looked at me with wide eyes. "It's real, Ava."

"What the actual fuck?" was all I could muster, still staring at the photo.

While I stood frozen in shock, Lila—forever the journalist —wasted no time. She grabbed her phone and began to google something.

"Okay, there isn't much online, but I found one old article about this speakeasy called The Velvet Clover, attached to The Fitzgerald Hotel in Manhattan," she said, slapping my arm like we were making progress. "The article's titled, '*Legendary Prohibition Speakeasy Shuts Its Doors After Thirty Years.*' It says, '*A popular underground speakeasy shut down in the 1950s, but was one of the few that stayed open nearly the entire Prohibition.*'"

"Does it say why they shut down?"

Her eyes stayed glued to her phone as she scanned. Then she shrugged. "It just says the family decided to focus on their other business ventures in the 1950s."

A part of me was relieved it didn't mention anything about Cillian's death, even though I knew he was gone. For some reason, it still made me feel better.

I leaned in closer. "Does it mention Cillian?" I couldn't help but smirk when I said his name, the thought of last night lingering in my mind. I bit my lips together. "Or Saoirse? Maybe his daughter took it over?"

"No. It talks about the 'legendary speakeasy' that opened in the early 1920s and was kept hidden from the government for almost all of the Prohibition. Apparently, that's one of the things that made it so renowned. But it says the family who owned it wanted to remain as anonymous as possible." She paused, looking up at me. "I guess that makes sense, considering it was illegal to serve alcohol back then. They probably could've gotten into a ton of trouble if they were too high profile."

"This confirms that we aren't getting drugged or hallucinating, but it doesn't explain how we can still access it," I said.

"Av, we just talked about this. It isn't explainable with the mind. But it *is* happening. Maybe there's no logic to it. Maybe it's one of those things that doesn't need to make sense. It is just a gift that has been given to you. You just . . . enjoy it."

"And why would I need the gift of a speakeasy from one

hundred years ago, during the holidays, post breakup? I don't need that. Besides, *you* are the one googling it." I laughed, pushing her over with my knee as she still sat cross-legged on the floor.

"I know, but I'm not attached to it like you are," she said.

"I'm not attached," I shot back defensively.

"Puh-lease, you're swooning over this man like I've never seen before. You can't even say his name without smiling."

She finished reading and clicked off her phone. "Unfortunately, there isn't much more than that. Basically, it's just an article saying the speakeasy eventually shut down and the family didn't want to be named. They had the article written to thank everyone for all the years of business."

"Stupid. God, he really needed a PR team. I totally could've helped him," I said, rolling my eyes.

"You *would* turn this into a business thing," she chortled.

"What? I'm just saying," I said innocently.

She shot me a look, clearly not buying it. There was a long pause. "Do you think what we do while we are in the speakeasy will affect the future?" she asked.

"What do you mean?"

"I don't know, like . . . if we say the wrong thing, or change someone's mind about something they were going to do, could that ripple out and mess everything up? Change the future?"

I blinked. "Like a butterfly effect kind of thing?"

"Yeah. Or maybe we're already part of how it was always supposed to happen, and we just don't know it."

I opened my mouth to say something then closed it again. I couldn't help but think about all the books I'd read on parallel worlds and branching timelines—how a single moment could fracture everything, sending time spiraling in a new direction. I'd once read that *everything affects everything affects everything*. It sounded cool at the time. But living it? Not so much.

I didn't want to believe it. Not really. It was too real. Too much. Too overwhelming to comprehend. The idea that just being there each night might completely change the future, or even stranger, that we were always meant to be there, that this was how the future got created in the first place, it was too much to wrap my head around. While I believed there could be alternate realities, I never believed you could actually physically *visit one.*

I shrugged. "I guess I don't know, and I don't think we can ever know for sure. But we should definitely be careful when we're there. I can't imagine us doing anything that would drastically change things. But let's make sure, when we go back, we lay as low as we can, just in case. Not draw too much attention to ourselves."

She nodded. "Agreed."

"Okay, Nancy Drew," I said, "I think we've hit a dead end for now. No need to keep searching." I stood and reached for her hand, pulling her up off the ground.

But even as I pulled my sister to stand, I couldn't shake the strange mix of disbelief and intrigue settling deep in my chest. The more we uncovered, the more this whole thing felt surreal —like I was teetering between two worlds, both real and imaginary. A part of me—the logical part—wanted to dismiss it all as some strange coincidence. But another part—something deeper—kept nagging that there was more to this than I could understand. Like it was fate? Destiny?

Maybe it was the way my heart raced when I thought of him. Or the feeling that something inside me had already crossed a line I couldn't uncross. He was real, and yet he wasn't. He was alive, and yet he wasn't. My mind went wild trying to make sense of it all.

"Come on; let's go look at these Tinker Bell fairy books."

"They are *faeries,*" she defended with all of her petite self, paling in comparison to my height.

Despite our literary differences, and height differences, we locked arms and headed to read about bestiality together, as sisters.

14

"CHRIS!" LILA ROSE TO HER TIPTOES, UNNECESSARILY SHOUTING and waving across the—as usual—empty bar as we approached later that night.

"Ava, don't interrogate him right away. We need him to warm up to us first so he'll give us the information we're looking for," Lila whispered, scowling at me as if the look alone would scare me out of asking him questions.

"All right, all right." I said brushing her off. "Go on."

"Mrs. Carrington!" Chris replied, matching her enthusiasm with a broad smile and a wave before turning back to the drink he was mixing—probably for himself. As we got closer, he said with a plain, almost indifferent, "Ava," not even glancing up at me.

"Chris Kringle." I offered him an equally hostile look.

He just chuckled, unbothered by my name calling. "Are ye ladies all prepped for Christmas? Get all yer shopping done?" He topped off his drink with a sprinkle of cinnamon before setting it on the bar for a server to deliver—to whom? That was the question. I didn't see a soul in here.

I let Lila answer, knowing she'd be eager to share.

"Oh, yes! I shop all year for my husband and the girls. I've been done for months. December is just a matter of wrapping everything and decorating the house to be festive."

"Very nice, Mrs. Carrington. I could tell yer one to fit right in with the holiday spirit," he said, leaning back with his arms folded over his belly. Then, with a shift in tone, he turned to me. "And ye?"

I waved a dismissive hand. "Oh, no. I don't believe in Christmas presents. It's all just a big capitalist corporate scam to boost Q4 sales and hit year-end quotas."

Chris let out a deep belly laugh, shaking his head. "Why does that not surprise me?"

"I think she'll change her ways once she finds that special someone, you know? Become a little less Scrooge-ish?" Lila interjected, nudging me.

"Love seems to find a way of changing us, even if we resist it, at first," Kringle mused.

"Looks like the two of ya are dressed for the occasion," he said, scanning our outfits. Lila had gone full flapper mode—fringe and pearls—while I'd opted for a deep burgundy suit, tailored at the waist. "In fact," he said, checking his watch, "it's about time. Are ya both ready?"

I looked at Lila expectantly. "Are you going to ask him or what?"

Her doe eyes went as wide as ever, in terror. My sister feared confrontation more than death itself.

I refocused my frustration onto Santa Hat. "Look, Christopher, you need to tell us what the hell is going on. Is it actually 1925 in there? Or are we part of some elaborate setup with the Irish government? Are we actually time traveling?"

He just stood there, smiling like a deaf idiot, as if he hadn't heard me at all.

I glanced back at my sister to make sure I hadn't just imagined saying it out loud. She only shrugged. Not helpful.

"Why did you even show this speakeasy to us in the first place? Can we keep going back, or is there some kind of risk to our health or our mind?"

Another pause. Nothing. Just a wide smile on his annoying face.

"And what about bringing someone back with us from the speakeasy to the future? I mean today. I mean the present. Can that happen? Is that possible?" I asked, now flustered.

Lila cut in, holding her hand up as if she were about to hold me back in case I physically started attacking him. Not that she ever could. In all our years growing up, she hadn't won a single physical fight against me.

"Christopher," she said with a smile, "sorry. I think, what my sister means is . . . we'd really appreciate some clarity. Any clarity. Just a little explanation so we know we're not losing our minds."

Dammit. I was finally getting somewhere with him. And did she just say sorry *again*?

Santa Hat smirked. "I can't give away all me secrets, Ms. Hawthorne and Mrs. Carrington. Some things aren't meant to be understood. Besides, if ya knew everythin', it would ruin the Christmas magic." With a wink, he pulled back the velvet curtain, his eyes gleaming with mischief.

"Useless. Absolutely useless." I sighed in resignation. "Can you at least tell us that we will physically be okay? That we will make it back to 2025?"

He smiled. "Ms. Hawthorne, I can promise ya yer health will be just fine. Just fine, indeed. And ye shouldn't have any issue with getting back here at the end of yer evenin'." His response wasn't totally convincing, but it did make me feel a little better.

"Oh, thank you, thank you, thank you, Christopher," Lila gushed, gripping his hand and bouncing on her toes in excitement.

Maybe Lila was right. Maybe this whole thing was just some strange, freaky, magical Christmas portal. It still didn't explain the time travel in general, but at least it meant everything might end after the holidays. And I responded well to deadlines, so that was good enough for me . . . for tonight, at least.

I rolled my eyes as I stepped past him. "I'd stay and pester the full truth out of you, but I don't have time. I have an appointment that I can't be late for."

"An appointment, Ms. Ava? Or a date?" he asked like he had me figured out, winking at Lila as she nodded like a bobblehead.

How the hell did he know I had an appointment-date-thing? Who *was* this guy? Some kind of time-traveling match-maker who lured unsuspecting women into magical speakeasies during Christmas? Was the dating pool in this dimension really that sparse? Now matchmakers were having to jump timelines to find us our one perfect match? I don't remember signing up for whatever this weird dating service was.

I stopped, my hand on the entrance to the speakeasy, turning just enough to meet his gaze. A slow, slightly malicious smile spread across my face. "Oh . . . I can't give away all my secrets, Mr. Kringle. That would ruin the Christmas magic."

Just as I was about to push the door open, Chris called after us, "Oh, and ladies?"

"What now?" I asked.

"Don't go out da other door."

I paused, glancing at Lila. "Which door?"

"That door opposite this one, toward the far side of the speakeasy."

I remembered it. It was where the regular 1925 patrons came and went. The one I'd noticed last night, near the communal table.

"Why? Where does it go?" I asked.

"Just trust me."

I raised an eyebrow. "Why would I do that? And why are you just now telling us this?"

He didn't answer, just smiled in that infuriatingly calm, cryptic way of his, and turned back to polishing a glass.

I checked my watch. Nine twenty-five. I didn't have time for his shenanigans.

I sighed. "Kringle, as long as we will be physically safe and can come back here tonight, I really don't care about some other door. Come on, Lila." I said, pushing through the door.

Chris's deep laugh lingered in the air, gradually fading as we stepped through, leaving the present behind and stepping into a moment that felt both like the past and my future unfolding all at once.

The scent of aged whiskey hit me immediately, married with the jazz music filling the air. The past welcomed us like it had been waiting for us all night.

As we stepped through, I couldn't stop thinking about Chris's words. What would happen if we went through that other door? Would we disappear? Evaporate? Be sucked into oblivion? Get stuck in 1925 forever? Wearing dresses and pretending to enjoy not having any real rights?

Maybe the speakeasy wasn't just a place. Maybe it was an in-between. A limbo of sorts, suspended between two real worlds. And maybe, we weren't as free to move through it as we'd thought.

"Ms. Hawthorne, welcome back to Da Velvet Clover," the hostess greeted us with her usual polite smile. "Mr. Cillian has yer table ready. I can seat ya and yer guest dere now if you would like?"

"Thank you, yes," I responded as we followed her to the table—a cozy corner booth.

Lila shot me a playful look, as if to say, *He's so chivalrous, Ava. Maybe you should marry him.*

I glanced at the hostess, a small smile crossed her face. As we sat, she handed us what appeared to be menus, encased in an embossed leather sleeve. "Here are our drink lists, ladies. Please take a look, and Eddie will be by shortly to take yer orders."

"I thought you didn't have menus?" I asked, lifting an eyebrow.

"We didn't," she replied, her thick, dark eyeliner perfectly matching her sleek black bob. "After yer brilliant suggestion the first night ya visited, I mentioned the suggestion to Mr. Cillian, and he had 'em made immediately." A shy smile tugged at her lips. "Ladies, have a wonderful evening. If ya need anythin' at all, don't hesitate to find me."

Lila's jaw dropped as her stare went from the hostess to me. "He had leather bound menus *made for you,* Ava," she said, reeling. "I can barely get Simon to take out the trash half the time."

"That's not true. Simon is great," I refuted.

"You're right; he is amazing, but this is . . . wow." She tapped the menu. "So romantic."

"Incomin'!" Eddie said with a grin, dropping off two festive holiday drinks—one a vibrant green with whipped cream and a garnish, the other a deep red with cranberries and a cinnamon stick, each loaded with way too much seasonal spirit. Seasonal spirit and about a pound of sugar.

"What is it?" I held it up to inspect.

"Eddie's Christmas Special." He winked.

"Wow, Eddie, these look amazing, but we didn't order them," Lila said, confused.

"A special surprise from yers truly," he said, putting a hand on his chest. "I just love havin' ye girls here. Ye bring so much joy to the place. And Ava, I can't thank ye enough for what ye did for me family this Christmas," he added, reaching out to grab both of our hands.

"So much for laying low," Lila whispered to me before

turning to Eddie. "Thank you so much, Eddie. We love you, too!"

"Yes, we do," I added.

He leaned in to whisper to us. His crooked teeth couldn't be hidden behind his smile. "And between ye girls and me, I haven't seen me Cillian dis happy in years . . . maybe ever. Keep up whatever it is ye're doing, Ava." He squeezed my shoulder before heading back behind the bar.

"What the heck did you do for his family?" Lil asked.

"The first night I came in, I left a fifty on the table because I was rushing to grab you from the lobby slash running away from Cillian. And, apparently, the conversion on a fifty dollar bill one hundred years ago is like nine hundred dollars." I laughed.

"So he thought you left him a thousand dollar tip?"

"Inflation's a bitch, but the conversion for him was great. I just went with it." I shrugged.

"Again, so much for laying low and not drawing attention to ourselves." Lila laughed nervously.

"I didn't know I was leaving that much cash," I said, taking a sip of my sugar-filled Eddie special. This was definitely going to get me very drunk and leave me with a sugar high.

Before Lila and I had time to sit and gossip like little school-girls, I felt the soft squeeze of a hand on my shoulder. I knew it was him before I turned to look—the energy from his touch surged through me like a lightning bolt.

Lila glanced up at him, her eyes widening slightly, before flashing an excited look at me. Yep, it was definitely him.

"Ladies." Cillian's voice was smooth and steady as I turned. There was a softness in his blue eyes now, a warmth that hadn't been there the first time I'd met him. It was like he'd shifted from a cold statue to something more human, lighter somehow. "Welcome back, and thank ya for coming," he said, leaning into the booth.

He kissed Lila on both cheeks, offering her a quick, friendly hug. "Lila, ya look lovely, as always. I hope yer trip to New York has been wonderful." He took her hands and squeezed them gently before letting go.

"It has been great. I *love* this city. I am praying Ava moves here so I can visit," she said, shooting me a hopeful look.

"Quite the journey from Colorado," he said. Then his focus shifted to me.

I tried to hide the flush I knew was already showing through my cheeks from his presence alone.

"I hope I'm not interrupting your date. Ava told me you insisted I come. I can always go sit at the bar and chat with Eddie if there's an open seat," Lila offered.

"No," he replied, his eyes still fixed on me, a smile tugging at his lips. "I truly insist ya stay and spend time with us, Lila. It is Christmastime, after all."

"All right, if you say so," she said. I could feel her gaze flickering between us.

"You look absolutely stunning, Ava," he said, taking my hand and giving it a gentle squeeze before raising it, as if showcasing me. "This color suits ya beautifully."

"Thanks," I giggled.

Lila looked at me in surprise.

I cleared my throat, suddenly aware of how girly I was being. "Do you want to sit?" I asked, scooting toward the center of the leather booth.

"I'll be back in a moment, me dear. I just need to grab a drink for meself," he said. "Ye'd think, when ya own the place, ye'd get better service. Certainly not the case. Can I get ya ladies anything?"

"We're good, thanks," I replied, trying my best to suppress my smile, though I failed miserably.

He patted the table with his hand, bare except for the small ring on his pinky finger, which for whatever reason I found wildly attractive. It gave him a bit of a gangster vibe.

As soon as he was out of earshot, Lila leaned over the dark wooden table, slapping it with her hand. "The. Way. He. Said. Your. Name. I. *Cannot.*" Her jaw hung so low I could have tossed an apple at her and she would have swallowed it whole.

I leaned on the table, resting my head in my hand, trying to hide the smile. "I know, right? I'm in trouble, aren't I? I mean, he's ... amazing."

"Not to mention, thoughtful, handsome, sexy, witty, chivalrous. He's got great style. And swagger, he's totally a 'cool guy.' You need to date a cool guy," Lila said, glancing over at him standing at the bar. "And he's got a great butt."

"Lila!" I shrieked, my face flushing. "Stop it." I slapped at her as she giggled.

"I really shouldn't be crashing this party. You two need all the time you can get together ... alone." She wiggled her eyebrows.

I sighed, staring at him. "He really does have a nice butt," I admitted, not quite sure how I was just now noticing it. As if he could feel my gaze, he turned to meet my stare then bit his cheek, trying to suppress a laugh. It couldn't have been more obvious that we were checking him out.

"God, that's so embarrassing." I looked back at Lila. "You can't leave me now—he just saw me checking him out."

"Oh, please, are we in second grade? It's obvious you two are attracted to each other. You already went on a date. You can check him out all you want. You can tell he's already so in love with you. And honestly, it's great to see you more in your feminine energy around him," she teased.

"I am not!" I protested.

"Av, it's a good thing. A relationship won't work if you're always carrying all the weight. From what I can see, you've finally met someone who matches your energy. Someone who's strong enough that you don't have to be on all the time. And he lets you be fully yourself, without feeling like you have to hold everything together alone," Lila said.

Was she right? It did feel good to be around him. Like I could lean back a bit. Relax. Breathe. Like he had everything under control, and I could just . . . be.

"I guess you're right," I said, leaning back in the booth and scanning the room. Then my eyes drifted to the far side of the speakeasy. "Lil, what do you think Santa Hat meant when he said not to go through that door?" I asked, gesturing in that direction.

"I was hoping you knew," she said, taking a long, slow sip of her drink.

"I was thinking maybe it's the door to 1925. But I wonder if it actually *goes* to 1925, or if it's more like a frozen moment in time. Like limbo. What if we disappear if we go through it?"

"All I know for sure is that we should avoid it at all costs. Neither of us needs to get stuck there. Wherever there is."

I frowned. "Do you think if Cillian—or someone from this time—were to go back through our door, it would be the same? Like they might not exist—"

"Oh, Av, he's coming back." Lil tapped my arm.

"Quick. Let's act like we're talking about something else—your writing?" I suggested.

Lila picked up on the cue immediately, thank God. "Yes, it's been amazing. I'm finding so much inspiration around the city for my book," she began.

"Am I interruptin' anythin', ladies?" Cillian's voice broke through as he returned with a whiskey in hand.

"Nope," I said quickly. "Lila and I were just talking about how she's taking some time to focus on her writing while she's here in the city."

"Beautiful," Cillian remarked. "Yer a writer?"

"I used to be a journalist before I had kids," Lila said,

slightly overcompensating. "Now I stay home with the girls. I've always dreamed of being a writer since I was a little girl. Ava encouraged me to start on this trip."

"Wow, two career women. So rare. Yer parents must've raised ya both well. I am sure they are very proud," he said.

Lila and I exchanged a glance, both of us recalling that women hardly worked in the 20s, especially in fields like PR or journalism. At my age, I was probably considered an old crone for not being married yet.

"Uh," Lila began, trying to recover. "Yes, I worked as a . . . stenographer—mostly assisting at a newspaper office. Nothing too exciting. I had to support myself before I settled down after meeting my husband," she lied so smoothly I was impressed. *Stenographer?* Nice touch.

"Ah, yes. Well, women are truly the greatest gift we men have. Without ya to care for us men and love our children, we'd have long ago driven the human race to extinction," he said with a smile.

It was wild, the power of context. If this were 2025, I would have stood up and walked out after a comment like that—condescending, even if wrapped in a compliment. But in 1925, I found myself pleasantly surprised by his progressiveness for the time.

"And, of course, we'd have no beauty and much less fierceness in this world, without ya ladies." He held up his glass in a cheer. "To women with fire in their hearts and wisdom in their words. May they always be as powerful as they are beautiful." He looked at me with those newly softened eyes. Once again progressive. Hmm.

Lila and I glanced at each other and smiled, then at him, and we drank to that.

15

HOURS AND MANY DRINKS LATER, THE SPEAKEASY WAS PACKED. IT was like everyone in Manhattan wanted to be here tonight, or in 1925. There really was a magic about this place and, apparently, serving alcoholic drinks when they were illegal was a big draw.

At some point, the tables and chairs in the center were cleared out, pushed against the walls, and the floor opened up for dancing. The Foxtrot. The Charleston. No bumping and grinding like in today's Manhattan clubs. It was cute. Innocent. Pure.

"This is so fun," Lila said, snapping her fingers and bopping to the music, watching everyone out on the dance floor.

"It is. People love to come here and dance and drink. Makes 'em forget about da last decade and everything we've gone through," Cillian said, watching the couples dancing.

The band started playing "White Christmas."

"Oh, I love this song . . ." I mumbled under my breath, only to realize I'd said it loud enough for Cillian to hear. *Dammit.* I stared at the band, hoping maybe he wouldn't say anything.

This was the only thing I liked about Christmas: this song. I had no idea why.

Cillian looked at me in surprise then stood. He held out his hand for me to take, the other arm wrapped around his back. "Ava Hawthorne, may I have this dance?" It was like that scene from *Pride and Prejudice*, where that rude guy asked the brown-haired girl to dance at that ball even though it seemed like the last thing on her priority list.

"You can't be serious," I said, glancing at Lila, trying to hide my embarrassment.

"Oh," he said, leaning in, bent at the waist, kissing my hand, his gorgeous face right in front of mine, "I am dead serious, love." He enunciated each word with his beautiful accent, his eyes charged with a fleck of sweetness and challenge. "Join me, eh?"

Lila's jaw dropped in my periphery.

I narrowed my eyes on him, a long pause. He didn't as much as blink.

"Fine."

A pleased look crossed his face. Without taking his eyes off me, he called back to Lila, "Oi, Lila! Ask Eddie to take ya for a spin—he's a phenomenal dancer. Or so I've been told . . . And don't worry; he's happily married, too, so there'll be no funny business from him."

Cillian led me to the center of the dance floor, his movements as deliberate as ever as he guided me into his arms. One hand extended to his right, mine resting atop it, while the other wrapped around the small of my back, pulling me in close. Our chests pressed together. The warmth of him made my breath hitch. The scent of him was intoxicating—whatever pheromones this man had, had been designed just for me.

"Are ya having an enjoyable night, love?" he asked. I knew the choice of the word "love" was just some sort of Irish pet name, but it didn't stop me from being completely affected when he said it.

"I'm having an amazing time." I chose not to make eye contact with him because if I did, I was afraid of what might happen to me. I was genuinely concerned, for the first time in my life, that I might actually melt into a puddle on the floor.

He held me close as we swayed to the music.

"I wouldn't have expected you to be a dancer," I said, breaking the silence.

"And I wouldn't have expected ya to like an actual Christmas song." He pulled back and looked at me. "Ya doubt me dancing abilities, eh?"

"No, it's not that. You just seem like . . . I don't know. You seem so serious all the time. Not one to let loose on the dance floor."

"My darlin', it's 1925—everyone dances. 'Tis the only thing that gets us through at times." He pulled me closer again. His hardness softened me, no matter how much I resisted it.

Relax, Ava. Just let yourself relax. Release control. Stop thinking so much. Let yourself enjoy this. Just for the next few days.

As if he could read my damned mind, he pulled back more to look into my eyes as we slowly swayed back and forth in one spot. "Ya know, I am not going to hurt ya, Ava." It was too intimate, even in all its innocence. I could tell he was telling the truth. "It's safe to let go and relax with me." As he said that, he held me tighter, in a way that made me feel like if I fell, he would catch me. In more ways than one. In every possible way.

I took a sharp, deep breath. Slowly, hesitantly, I brought my hand from his shoulder to the nape of his neck. My fingers grazed the skin there, unsure at first, but it felt so natural that I couldn't stop. I ran my fingers back and forth, my touch tentative. I wasn't sure if I should be this close, but something inside me whispered to let go.

Let go. Let go. Let go.

I stared into his eyes like they held some sort of answer I was looking for within them. I took another deep breath in, then out, emptying all the air out of my lungs. Hoping the next breath I breathed would be the one that helped me surrender.

As the band continued to play "White Christmas," a memory flashed. Christmas, years ago. Mom spinning around in her favorite dress, Jeff holding her close, both of them smiling like nothing could go wrong. Dancing and in love. It was the last time our family had felt whole before everything had fallen apart. Before Jeff had torn it apart. Dancing with Cillian now, the memory hit me—sad, but somehow comforting. Maybe that was why I liked this song. It was my last happy memory of what it was like to have an unbroken family during the holidays. The last memory I had of not hating Christmas. Of not hating Jeff.

Cillian took my hand, which was still clasped in his, and placed it on his chest. His other hand resting at the nape of my neck, his fingers lacing in my hair, warm against my skin. He held my gaze, his eyes locked with mine, waiting. Waiting for me to give some sign—a touch, a tug, a lean.

I wanted to. God, did I want to. The part that craved something reckless and fleeting, something that would remind me I was alive. Something that made me feel. Something. Anything. But just as quickly, the responsible voice within me stirred, the one that kept the emotional stiff-arm up. The voice that protected me from allowing a man—or anyone—to have any power over me. The one that reminded me that we were in 1925 and none of this was real. I mean, it was real, but not, all at the same time.

We stopped moving, frozen in the center of the dance floor. The world around us continued, everyone dancing to "White Christmas," but all I could see was him. His hand on my neck radiating warmth. I could feel my heart pounding in my chest. I closed my eyes, trying to steady myself. I felt safe. He made me feel so safe.

He was so beautiful.

Fuck it. With that, I quieted the voice that gave me all the reasons I shouldn't.

I turned my palm from his chest to the lapel of his jacket, running my fingers along the fabric before I tugged ever so slightly, giving permission.

His sign.

Not rushed, not urgent, but in utter and total control, he slowly pulled my face to his, and our lips touched. He was warm, smelling of whiskey, and cigarettes, and *him*. He moved slowly. Deliberately. I opened my mouth for him as he slipped his tongue in just slightly. As he did, I let out a soft moan. He pulled me in deeper, his hand firm on my neck, lacing his fingers deeper in my hair. Our mouths worked in tandem, like we were made for each other, cut from the same bold of fabric. The passion between us was so deep, but both of us knew we couldn't go there, or there would be no going back. Plus, there were people around us, for God's sake.

As the song came to a close—way too soon, I might add—I wanted more. I wanted all of him. But with the kind of restraint that only someone who had fought in a world war could possess, he pulled back. He took his hand now resting on my hip and gently brought it to join his other hand on my neck. He held my face in front of him like he wanted to stay with me there forever, frozen in this moment. His eyes pierced so deeply into mine that I felt undone with just a single look. Exposed. Naked. Vulnerable. He could see all of me—the parts I never let anyone see. Every crack, every hidden piece. Every jagged edge. He could see me because we were the same.

A look crossed his face I hadn't seen yet. A sweetness about him. He smiled, his tongue caught slightly between his teeth, adding a playful edge to his expression. It was life. Life brought back to his soul. Like a seed that had been trying to bust through the surface of soil, finally sprouting through.

His smile made me giggle. Who was I right now? What had this guy done to me? I was not a person who giggled.

Cillian pulled me in for another soft kiss before moving his hands from my face, down to the small of my back. I wrapped both my arms around his neck, wishing I could stay here forever.

"Wow," I breathed.

The band started playing the next song.

He said nothing, just squeezed me tight.

I rested my head on his shoulder. It felt unnaturally natural. I hugged him back, feeling the warmth of his body seep into mine. A slight bulge in his lower extremities reminded me of the tension between us.

Something inside me released. The kiss had done something to me, something I hadn't expected. I didn't think I could surrender like this, yet, with him, it felt easy. Inevitable. Like a tide pulling me under. My body relaxed fully into his, as if it could no longer stand without him.

I gave myself over to him, even though a small part of me still wondered if this was too much too soon. But in that moment, I didn't care. Couldn't care. Yes, the drinks lowered my defenses, but more than that, the kiss had done what I'd been trying to do all night—to let go.

And Cillian held me. All of me. I felt him smile as he leaned his cheek against the side of my head. And it felt good. Safe.

I scanned the room as we danced. Lila was dancing with Eddie. Both of them were already staring at us, smiling and giving us a thumbs-up. I rolled my eyes, trying to hide the sense of embarrassment creeping up my neck. I noticed the hostess smiling in our direction, as well. Suddenly, I felt self-conscious. She was looking at us like she was happy to see him happy. It struck me how effortlessly he seemed to be the center of attention, admired by everyone around him.

"Looks like we have an audience," I said.

He turned us to look, not taking his head from mine. He let out a laugh. "Yeah, we got the nosey crew here, focused on me instead of their jobs. Remind me to fire dem later, would ya?"

"It would be my honor." I laughed as the music began to shift into something more upbeat, the intimacy of the moment pulled right along with it. "We should sit. I don't want Lila to feel all alone."

I had noticed her dancing with Eddie, but it was the only excuse I could come up with to regain some sort of control. That feeling—the feeling of fully letting go—now felt terrifying. Like I was freefalling.

"Yes, ma'am," he said, gesturing for me to lead as we headed back to our booth.

Lila made her way back, as well. "You were right, Cillian. Eddie was the perfect dance partner. He knew all the guests' personal drama, so I got the lowdown on this place."

Cillian let out a light huff. "Of course he did."

As we settled back in, Cillian placed his hand over mine on the table. Lila stole a glance and quickly looked away, failing miserably at pretending she hadn't noticed.

It felt so good. Normal. Right.

Shit. *I cannot get attached. I can't get emotionally involved with a man who literally doesn't exist in 2025.*

When I was here, it felt like my rational and logical senses dimmed—forgetting the stakes, the risk of being here, how none of it was forever. Christmas magic, according to Kringle.

I pulled my hand off the table and into my lap. He did nothing except let a small smile cross his face, totally unfazed by my sudden coldness. Like he knew me better than I knew myself.

I furrowed my brow at his smugness. He kept looking straight forward, biting his cheek before grabbing for his drink.

"So . . . Ava," Lila cut the tension. "How are you feeling about the interview tomorrow?"

"It isn't as much as *my* interview as me interviewing them," I said, trying to bury my emotions. The sharp edge returned to my voice.

"Well, I for one cannot wait to hear how it goes," Lila said, lifting her shoulders. "What was the name of the atelier again? It had such a pretty name."

"The Aislinn Atelier," I said.

There was a quick flicker in Cillian's eyes, and his jaw clenched for a beat, but it was gone as soon as it had appeared, his face shifting back to neutral.

"Do you know it, Cillian?" Lila asked hopefully, like we might be able to piece more together about this time-traveling speakeasy.

He shook his head, his brows knitting together, and he cleared his throat before speaking. "Nah, I don't think I have heard of it. Do ya feel prepared, Ava?" There was something odd in his tone, but I brushed it off.

"Of course I am. I just want to shit test the owner a bit more; see if he is the real deal." I clicked my tongue.

"Well, I can't wait to hear how it goes," he said, sitting close enough that his knee brushed mine under the table. His touch alone shot sparks through my entire being.

"Thanks," I said, trying to stay cold, stoic. But, as soon as our eyes met, I couldn't help but soften once again. He was like an oven, enveloping me in warmth that melted even the toughest parts of me, despite my best effort.

"Ladies, I almost forgot," Cillian said. "My staff convinced me to hold a Christmas party on the twenty-third of this month —Tuesday. I'd love for the two of ya to come. It truly wouldn't be the same without ya." He placed his hand on my leg, giving it a gentle squeeze, a touch so sweet, so tender I couldn't bear to pull away.

I didn't want Lila to feel like she had to spend her entire trip in this speakeasy.

"Duh!" Lila chimed in. "Eddie already invited me, and I asked him if he could reserve a table for us. He said he was on it." She was now sipping her third Eddie's Christmas Special of the night. Well, I guessed that took care of that.

I turned to her. "Wait, Lil, were you still thinking about heading back on the twenty-third?"

She shrugged, lifting her glass again. "I was thinking I could leave the next morning. Maybe we can talk about it later, Av."

I made a mental note of her vagueness—it wasn't like her. Maybe she wanted to stay. Maybe the extra time away was exactly what she'd needed. Simon and the girls had assured her they'd be fine if she stayed through Christmas. The thought that she might actually want to be here—choose to be here—with me, made me happier than I thought it would.

Cillian clapped his hands together once. "Yes! So glad to hear ya will stay and join us."

"Well, I am going to have to check my schedule and get back to you. I don't know if I can make it," I said, trying to seem semi-annoyed that Lila just RSVP'd for me.

Lila looked at me in abhorrence. Cillian's look wasn't much better.

"Really?" Cillian asked.

The corners of my mouth twitched. "I'm kidding," I said dryly, the softness returning in that moment, and it felt good. Really good.

"Oh, she's got a sense of humor now, does she? Eh?" He wrapped his arm around me, pulling me into him, holding my face still, planting a kiss on my cheek. I pulled back in playful resistance, batting at him, fake wiping off his saliva.

I could never be playful like this with Elliot. I'd never once felt like I fully let my guard down around him. But with Cillian, it felt like the most natural thing in the world. Like breathing.

"Well, this is lovely. Now be sure to wear yer best Christmas attire," he said. "Our patrons go all out here on Christmas."

Lila gave me a knowing look—another shopping day! "Is this place open the rest of the week?" she asked.

"We're closed on Mondays, open the rest of the week," he said with a nod.

"Even on Christmas Eve and Christmas Day?" she followed up.

Why was she asking? Maybe she was trying to figure out when she would fly home.

"Yes, ma'am," Cillian said. "I have always liked to stay open for those people without families, without places to go." His arm was still firmly wrapped around my waist. I didn't pull away.

"What about your family? Do you spend the day with them?" she prodded.

I looked at her, confused.

"Nah, it's just me and Saoirse," he said, looking around as if she might be nearby. "She's never too far from hangin' around here. In fact, all those gifts under dat tree are hers. She decorated it herself. We've been doing our celebration here every year. A tradition of ours since she was little."

I smiled. Somehow, it wasn't weird that he had a daughter. Maybe because I knew there was no way to have an actual future with him, or maybe it was the fact that he didn't exist in my current world, like there was no reason to sweat the small stuff.

Still, the idea of a holiday event with my time-traveling situationship who didn't exist in 2025 made something inside me tense.

"That is so cute!" Lila squealed. "Maybe, if I do stay, we can stop by on Christmas Day. We don't really have anywhere else to go. What do you think, Ava?"

I caught the way she avoided my eyes, her voice a little too high. Maybe she was trying not to think about what it would really mean—to choose not to spend Christmas with her family. To stay here rather than fly home and spend Christmas without Simon and the girls.

She'd left them behind to be with me. Because of me. The least I could do was make sure we had some fun if she stayed—enough to make it feel worth it, maybe even a little less heavy on the actual day. Worst-case scenario: she would change her mind, and I could fly her home on Christmas Day.

I forced a small smile. "Let's just get through the Christmas party first. We'll figure out our Christmas Day plans after that."

She slouched into the booth, pouting. When had she become such a child?

"Well," Cillian exhaled, patting my leg with his free hand, "you are both more than welcome anytime ye'd like. Christmas Day included."

It was a sweet offer—absurdly sweet. Based on what we knew, nine twenty-five p.m. was our golden hour for slipping into this speakeasy, not exactly a flexible visiting window. Still, the way he'd said it made me wish it were true. Made me wish that we really could come by and enjoy this magical space anytime we wanted.

Lila perked up, holding up a hand like she was hiding her words from me. "I'll talk her into it," she whispered to Cillian across the table.

"I can hear you." I laughed, shaking my head. "You are unbelievable. Come on, Mrs. Drunky." I checked my watch. "It's time to get you to bed before Eddie's special drinks knock you out for good."

"No," she protested.

I raised one eyebrow.

"Okay, fine. You're right. I need sleep," she said, her words slurred.

I rolled my eyes as Lila got up and put on her jacket. "I'm going to go say bye to Eddie. Have fun, lovebirds," she said before skipping off.

"Looks like those sugary drinks really got to dat one tonight." Cillian laughed.

"And to think she has two kids and a husband back home."

I paused, realizing it was now just us. All the energy shifted, settling back into the space between us. Me and Cillian. Cillian and me. The two of us. The atmosphere felt as charged and intense as it had when we'd been dancing. I became hyper-aware of his arm still around my waist.

I turned slightly toward him, bringing my bent knee up to rest on the booth cushion. He looked at me. Those eyes. Those damn eyes.

Cillian ran the back of his fingers against my cheek. I leaned into them, guiding his hand to open and cup my face, and I took a deep breath. I looked up at him, fully aware that he might be the death of me.

"What are you doing to me?"

"I suppose maybe you, too, have met your match, Ms. Hawthorne."

Without thinking, without considering the repercussions of time travel, the strangeness of it all, or the fact that this man didn't exist in the future . . . I mean, present. In 2025 . . . you know what I mean. Without weighing the consequences of my actions, I followed what I thought was my heart.

I leaned in, grabbed his face, and kissed him with all the passion that had been tingling beneath my skin. He met me there, tugging the back of my head, pulling me even closer. His fingers laced through my hair, and even though our bodies were pressed together, it still wasn't close enough. Nothing would ever be close enough for us. I wanted to be in his skin and have him in mine. Even that wouldn't suffice. Even that wouldn't be close enough. Everything about us fit together so perfectly.

Just as I started to realize what I was doing, I pulled away. *Have some self-restraint, Ava, Jesus. This is just a Christmas fling. Nothing more. It can't be.*

Staring into his eyes, inches away, I felt his breath on my lips.

"Tell Eddie no more of those special Christmas drinks," I said, standing to find Lila and get the hell back to our hotel room. Back to a safe zone, where I had a chance of putting distance between us and stopping myself from taking this any further. From feeling anything more.

As I began to walk away, he reached out and grabbed my hand, still sitting in the booth.

"Ava," he said, and God, the way he said my name unraveled me.

I closed my eyes, breathing deeply, gathering myself before I turned back to him—partly from the dizziness of standing too quickly, partly from bracing myself for him to say my name again.

"Yes?" I replied, trying to sound as composed as possible in my current state.

"Thank ya for coming." He pressed a kiss to the back of my hand.

What happened next was a blur, thanks to Eddie's stupid drinks. I remembered him kissing my hand, and then I remembered thinking, *I am going to kiss this man like I've never kissed anyone before.* It wasn't what I wanted to do. I *had* to do it. And that was exactly what I did.

I was bent at the waist, hovering over him, my knee pressed into the booth seat for balance as he stayed anchored below me. My tongue was in his mouth, his in mine, exploring, tasting. I tangled my hands in his hair, desperate for more. I braced myself, feeling his hands on my hips—not gently resting, but holding me firmly, completely in control of my body.

"You ready, Av?" Lila called from across the bar above the band.

I showed world class restraint as I pulled back, ripping myself off of this gorgeous man.

"Okay, I'll see you tomorrow?" My words alternated between heavy breaths.

He was breathing heavily but somehow didn't seem flustered by that core-shaking kiss. "I'll be waiting, Ava." He clipped my chin with his fingers before poking my side.

Was this man made of fucking stone? If anything, he was calmer and cheekier than ever.

I squealed, swatting at his hand. "Stop it. I'm ticklish." I giggled, blowing him an air kiss as I turned and ran toward Lila. As I glanced back over my shoulder, I caught him catching the kiss and tucking it into his pocket, his lazy smile still in place.

Something about him—about *us*—felt dangerously natural, like we'd skipped a hundred steps and landed in the deep end of the pool. And maybe, if this were a different time, a different life, I'd let myself actually believe we were meant for each other.

But it wasn't. And we weren't.

I convinced myself it was the Christmas drinks, the music, the energy of the speakeasy during the holidays. I could enjoy myself. I could have fun for the week. A beautiful, impossible week. Then I could go back to my life, and business, as usual.

And I decided, for now, that was a good enough plan.

"Have a lovely evening, ye two. We'll see ya for the Christmas party," the hostess called after us as we headed out the door and through the velvet curtain.

"See you then!" Lila called behind us.

I turned to wave, and we stepped through the door and the velvet curtain, straight into 2025.

The change hit like whiplash.

The buzz of the speakeasy vanished, replaced by the modern day Fitzgerald Hotel. Everything was sharper here— the lights too bright, the colors too harsh, the air too cold. The warmth from Cillian's touch evaporated like mist. I blinked, the weight of reality slamming back into my body like a bucket of ice water being poured over me.

The buzz from the Christmas drinks dissipated almost instantly. My head cleared too fast, and it left me dizzy in a different way. My heart still raced, but now for a different reason entirely.

He was gone. That world was gone. And I was back. Back in my own time. Back in my own—real—life. Back to reality.

I pressed my palms to my temples and exhaled, but that ache in my chest didn't ease. A part of me—my *heart*, maybe— missed him already. Missed the way he looked at me like I was someone worth waiting for. Someone worth being with. I missed how the world felt slower, softer, better, when I was with him.

But my *mind* came in hard, snapping everything back into focus.

This couldn't work. He was from another century. I had a life here. A career, responsibilities, *reality*. And even if I wanted to pretend otherwise, I knew better than to believe I could ever have any sort of future with someone from the past.

Still, for just a few hours, I'd let myself feel something real. Even if it was unreal, by every other logical or scientific measurement, except for how I felt. And God help me, all I could feel was that I wanted more.

16

"Wasn't last night so magical?" Lila gushed, still sprawled out in bed in her pajamas the next morning.

I, however, was nearly ready for the day. I wanted to take Lila to The Met before my meeting with Ronan—at the least, to see the Egyptians. I figured it would distract me from spending all day thinking about Cillian. About last night. About what I'd been feeling.

I couldn't figure out why, when I was there—at The Velvet Clover, with Cillian—everything felt right. So real. So good. Like we were meant for each other. Like it might be more than just a week of fun. But once I came back to the present, it felt like waking up and realizing the dream I thought was real had been just a dream, sobering me to the reality of the situation.

When I was with him, I operated from my heart, forgetting about the future—my present life circumstances. And when I was here, I operated from my head, realizing how crazy all of it was. Using logic to talk me down. The time travel. The things I was feeling.

In some ways, both places felt like a dream. And yet, they both felt completely real. I felt like I was starting to lose sight of which was my reality and which was fantasy.

No matter how much I tried to convince myself to stay away from the speakeasy, to not go back . . . I couldn't. It was like an invisible force pulled me there each night, despite my better judgment. Despite the best logical reasons as to why I shouldn't, I looked forward to each meeting. To escaping my life and stepping into one that felt just as real—and maybe even better—than the one I was supposed to be living.

I straightened my favorite black suit with sharp pagoda shoulders. "Kay, come on, lazy bones. Get ready for the museum," I told my sister.

"Did you hear what I said?" she yelled into the abyss that was me in the bathroom.

"Yes," I managed to say as I lined my lips with a deep mauve liner, trying to focus on the precision rather than the flutter in my chest at the mention of last night.

"You didn't think it was magical?"

"I mean, I guess so." I did my best to play it cool. "I am just glad I don't feel hungover after we go there."

"That might be one of the coolest parts. I should be bedridden after all those Eddie's Christmas Specials, but I feel great," Lila said. "Come on, sis; you don't have to hide your feelings. You and Cillian were"—she smacked her fingers and lips in a chef's kiss—"to die for. Eddie and I were in awe just watching it unfold. Like watching two people fall in love right in front of our eyes."

Fall in love? No. It wasn't that. It couldn't be that. It was just the magic of the moment, the fantasy of it all. Like Lila's little books.

But, even as I thought it, a warmth spread through my chest, betraying me. I bit my lips together, doing what I could to stop the smile from sticking on my face for the rest of the day at the mere memory. I let out a breathy laugh, throwing some clothes at her for her to change into. My face now telling all.

"Maybe it was a *little* magical," I admitted.

"Thank goodness. I thought you might actually be broken if you felt nothing today." She flopped back into bed in relief.

"It's so strange, Lila. When I am there, it feels like a dream. No consequences to my actions. Like me and Cillian really could become . . . something. When I'm back here, reality hits me. My better judgment. It feels like two separate lives."

Lila was quiet for a moment then shook her head. "I don't know what to say to that. I mean . . . it *does* sound confusing. Kind of incredible. Kind of terrifying." She forced a soft laugh, like she wasn't sure which direction to lean. "What are you going to do?"

I did what I could to shake it off. "I have no idea. I'll figure it out. I always do. Anyway, did you have an okay time? I felt bad just leaving you with Eddie all night." I tried to clear my conscience. Maybe if she had a horrible time, we wouldn't go back, and I could have an excuse to escape the dangerous game I was playing.

I held my breath, waiting for her answer, hoping—maybe even praying—that she'd say it was dull, that Eddie had bored her to tears, and that she never wanted to step foot in that speakeasy again. Instead, she lit up like a damn Christmas tree.

"Are you kidding?" she gasped. "Eddie is a dream! I had the best night of my life watching you fall in love, with Eddie as my commentator. We talked about our families, our kids, and what it's like being in relationships with people like you and Cillian. I had a ball."

My stomach sank. *Damn.* There went my chance.

"Wait, what do you mean, people like me and Cillian?"

"You two are insane—bossy, temperamental, semi-tyrannical, moody, and bloody brilliant. Also, you are demanding as hell. But we love you for it," she said, clearly reliving the conversation with someone who understood her struggles all too well.

"Bloody brilliant? What are you—Irish now?" I laughed.

"Oh, shush." She rolled her eyes. "So now that you and Cillian have played tonsil hockey, what happens now?"

"Lil, that's so gross."

She giggled, tucking her legs to her chest, wrinkling all the clothes I was loaning her.

"Nothing is going to happen," I said, more to myself than to her. "It's just a fun thing. That's all. Nothing can happen—you already know this, and I've said it a million times. A kiss doesn't change anything." Right?

But even as I said the words, my resolve felt like a lie. Because, deep down, that traitorous part of me ached to see him again. Still, I refused to be the kind of woman who lost herself over a man, especially one from a hundred years ago.

As I brushed my hair, she started to sing, "Cillian and Ava, sitting in a tree . . . K. I. S. S. I. N—Ouch."

"That's what you get," I said, sticking out my tongue.

"Did you just *throw your hairbrush* at me?" she shrieked. "You haven't changed at all since we were kids."

"Yes. And neither have you. Now get up. Let me help you get ready," I demanded.

"See? You are bossy. It's who you are," she said, dragging her tired body from the bed, over to "Ava's Salon" that was apparently open for service twenty-four seven until this trip was over.

"Well, someone has to be, or nothing will get done," I told her as I brushed her hair for our adventurous day ahead—in the *real* world.

. . .

We wandered through the Egyptian wing of The Met, my heels echoing against the marble floors. The place was quiet, with hardly anyone around. Lila stopped to read a placard about a burial ritual, while I made my way toward a glass case holding a golden funerary mask. Its eyes stared back at me—cold, hollow, eternal.

"They really thought they'd live forever," I murmured, more to myself than to Lila.

She joined me, arms crossed. "Well, in a way, they kind of did."

"Yeah, but not the way they meant to. Not as people. Just—displays. Symbols of how temporary everything actually is."

Lila turned to me. "Are you okay?"

I nodded, but my throat tightened. "Cillian said something that first night at the bar, about how it all ends, that we leave the world just like we came into it—alone. Standing here . . . I get it. Proof that we don't have time to waste."

She watched me then tilted her head. "Are you talking about the job? Or Cillian?"

I let out a slow breath. "I think I'm done with San Francisco. Like really, truly done. I thought maybe this trip would just be a break, a reset, to see if I really hated being there or if I just needed a vacation. But now I see clearly: I am done."

"You're going to take the job at the atelier?" she asked.

"I've spent my entire career focused on managing brands and chasing metrics—media impressions, client acquisitions, driving profit. I think I'm ready to finally do something more meaningful with my life. I know I can do that at Aislinn with Ronan. Looking at all this, it's a reminder that life is short. Too short to waste it on anything less than what I love, what fulfills me. Think about it—these people probably believed what they were doing was monumental in the grand scheme of things. But in the end, they're just a blip in history."

Lila looked at a nearby tombstone then back at me. "If we're just a blip, then we owe it to ourselves to live fully. To push for what makes us feel alive, even if it's scary."

"Exactly. If this is my blip, then I'm done settling for anything less than that."

The Aislinn Atelier was where I wanted to be. This was the next chapter for me. I was sure of it. Every part of me said yes. When I imagined going back to my life at Atlas & Grey PR in San Francisco, my body recoiled, like a physical rejection. But when I pictured myself at the atelier, I felt light, expanded, like I could fly—if I just had some wings, of course.

Normally, I'd be making graphs and charts, weighing pros and cons, to decide something so life-changing. But today, I decided there was no better time than the present to follow my gut instinct.

I pulled out my phone, standing in front of a display of hieroglyphs, and without hesitation, typed out the email to Atlas & Grey PR. Resigning. My heart rate steady. No second-guessing, no indecision. With a deep exhale, I hit *send*.

It was done. I was officially leaving my old life behind, burning it to the ground, and stepping into a completely new one.

I walked into the atelier five minutes before our meeting was scheduled. Sofia and Ronan were nowhere in sight. It gave me a chance to look around the shop.

The walls were lined with tailored shirts, a few gorgeous custom jackets. I walked past a table with an assortment of ties. There, on a velvet pad, lay a stunning pocket watch. It was silver with ornate detailing on the cover. An "A" for Aislinn was engraved on the front of it. Gorgeous.

It couldn't help but remind me of Cillian and the pocket watch he always wore.

"Ava Hawthorne, welcome. So sorry to keep you waiting. Have you been here long?" Ronan's voice echoed in the space.

"No worries," I said with a smile.

His brow twitched, eyes narrowing slightly, studying me. "Apologies, you just sound . . . different," he remarked, gesturing toward the workbench where we were supposed to meet.

"How so?"

He shrugged. "Just different. Softer."

"I thought, if anything, New York would toughen me up." Softer was not what I was going for. Damn Cillian. Damn men.

Ronan's eyes shifted. "How have your last few days in the city been?"

"Interesting, to say the least."

"The city always seems to have a way of surprising us." He grinned as he slicked his hair back. "I am glad we were able to make time to meet before Christmas. I figured today we could go over—"

I held out my hand to stop him. "Ronan, do you mind if I say something before we start?"

"Why, of course not."

"I would be honored to accept the position at The Aislinn Atelier," I said, watching his expression brighten. "I've put a lot of thought into it, and I truly believe this is the perfect place for me to put down roots in the next season of my career. After reviewing everything you sent me this week, I'm confident I can help execute a plan that brings the vision you have for The Aislinn Atelier to life." I clenched my jaw—not out of nerves, but to give him space to speak without over-explaining myself.

"Really?" he asked.

"I wouldn't say it if I weren't sure," I replied, offering a small smile. "These types of hires can be big decisions, but like you said about this position and New York being the best decision I may ever make, I'll say the same for you. I can promise you that when you look back at the history of this atelier, hiring Ava Hawthorne will be a pivotal moment. There will be a Before Ava and an After Ava. It may even be the best money you ever spend," I said with a playful wink.

"You're really in, huh?" he asked, like he was trying to convince himself it was real.

I raised my brows. "Indeed. I put my notice in at Atlas & Grey this morning. I let them know I'll be starting my work elsewhere in the New Year. My things are already scheduled to be moved to the city by January first. And I've got a real estate agent on the hunt for the perfect apartment here in the city, as we speak."

"Christ, you move fast, Ms. Hawthorne." He laughed, a mix of disbelief and admiration in his voice.

"Well, we have work to do. No time to waste." I shrugged. Then, shifting gears, I said, "Actually, before the holidays, like I mentioned, I'd love to dig into the history of the company— past campaigns, origin story, any press coverage, even old design archives, if they exist. I want to understand what this place used to stand for and what people *used* to fall in love with. If we're relaunching the atelier in the new year, I want it to be rooted in the original intent of why this shop exists in the first place." I paused. "But first, do we have a deal?" I asked, catching myself—I may have been a bit too bold with the assumptive close.

"Heck yes, we have a deal." He threw his hand out to shake mine. As we did, he pulled me in for a hug. "Welcome to the family, Ava."

I tensed at his hug before realizing that it was . . . nice. The corporate executives at Atlas & Grey never would have hugged me upon hire; that would have been a major HR no-no.

"Sofia, break out the Dom Perignon!" Ronan yelled toward —where I assumed Sofia was—the back room.

Moments later, she emerged with not two but three glasses

and a bottle of champagne to join us in a toast. "Welcome to The Aislinn Atelier, Ava," she said, smiling at me as she poured my glass, her black-rimmed glasses making her look like a mysterious and sultry assistant straight out of a movie.

"I love your style, Sofia," I said, scanning her, running my hand through the air from head to toe.

"Oh, please, look at you," Sofia scoffed. "I wish I could pull off menswear like that."

"Whoa, whoa. Okay, lesson number one. When someone gives you a compliment, never—and I mean never—turn it down or throw it back on the other person. Receive it," I said, wagging a finger.

"Oh, fine. Thank you for the compliment," Sofia replied, blushing.

Ronan had stepped away during our mini Female Compliment Acceptance Course and returned with a large coffee table book. I *loved* a good coffee table book. Across the top read "*The Aislinn Atelier Est. 1919*," with a gorgeous photo of a workbench —the same workbench I was sitting at, with a beautiful bolt of fabric marked and hand-stitched. It was a stunning book. If they could transfer this beauty internally to the public, game over.

"This is where your company history lives?" I asked.

"Yes, brilliant, right?" Ronan said, patting the seat of the workbench next to him. "Come. Sit." He rolled up his sleeves to his elbow, exposing the best part of every man—their forearms.

He showed me photos of what the place looked like back in the day when it had been a simple tailoring shop.

"You have been in this same building for over one hundred years?" I asked.

"Wild, isn't it? There is so much history in this place," he said, looking around. "I used to play over in that corner as a kid." He gestured to a wall with what looked like an old sewing machine station, probably an original from the opening. "After school, I would walk over here with my little backpack. I was such a cutie." He laughed, nudging me. "I would play under that machine while my mother would work on our clients' garments."

"So your mother started all this? Well, no, it would have to be your"—I did some quick mental math—"great-grand-parents?"

"Not exactly. It's quite a complicated family history, as is everyone's. But, since you want to know, I will show you. I think it's important for you to have the full background."

I watched as he flipped through the pages of the book.

"So . . ." I could see him gearing up for his history lesson. He had a teacher quality to him. He was patient. Grounded. Warm. "It was my great-grandparents—really, my great-grandmother. She wanted to create something to help people after the war. Her only real skillset, besides being a mother, was sewing, as it was for most women back then. Once her husband, my great-grandfather, got home after the war, he was a very savvy busi-nessman. He helped her open it while she worked and ran it. It was originally called The Broderick Atelier."

He continued, "I am not sure why but, at some point, my great-grandfather changed the name to The Aislinn Atelier. That is a piece of history that we are still, and probably forever, will be a bit fuzzy on."

Ronan turned the page again, his fingers brushing over the edges of the book with a sense of reverence. "Ah, perfect. Here he is," he said, pointing to an old black-and-white photo. "This is my great-grandfather, Cillian Broderick."

I froze. Did he just say *Cillian*?

I blinked, swearing I could feel my heart stop in my chest as I focused on the photo. The man in the picture was unmistak-able. He wore a black bow tie, his hands casually tucked in the pockets of a tuxedo. A white scarf hung loosely over his shoulders, and a cigarette dangled from his lips. His grin was faint, almost imperceptible—distant.

The man in the photograph was Cillian. *My* Cillian. The same Cillian I had kissed so passionately just the night before, standing by the fireplace in his speakeasy—The Velvet Clover —where we'd shared our first date only days ago.

As I stared at the image of him from nearly a century ago, the world around me seemed to fade. He looked timeless, as though no more than a day had passed since that moment.

My pulse quickened, a rush of heat spreading through my body as I tried to make sense of the collision of past and present—and my new future. The room started spinning, my mind struggling to connect the man in this photo to the one who had set my heart racing only the night before.

The date at the bottom right corner of the photo was marked in pen, just like all the photographs in the wash closet at the speakeasy.

December 1925.

"Wait—Cillian Broderick is your great-grandfather?"

17

My entire body went cold. Then hot. My eyes widened. *Oh. My. Fucking. God.* There was no way. There was *no* way.

I set my champagne down on the table. I couldn't be trusted with a glass in my hand right now—it might shatter from the pressure of my grip.

Stay calm, Ava. Stay fucking calm. You cannot freak out in front of your new employer about your time-traveling speakeasy boyfriend. You're a professional. You've handled worse PR crises. You can handle this.

I took a shaky breath. *Breathe in. Breathe out.* You can process all of this later. Though, God, he did look so handsome in that picture.

Stop it. Focus.

I tried to slow my breathing, to quiet the pounding in my chest. It didn't work.

Chill the hell out, Ava. You already knew he was from the past. How big of a surprise is it that he's the founder of the company you just committed your career to?

Now that Ronan had laid out the pieces, it was shocking I hadn't put it together sooner. It was so obvious. Cillian had said he owned a tailoring shop. The timeline matched Ronan's story —his great-grandfather, the war, everything. How had I missed it? It had all been right in front of me.

Say something before he thinks you've completely lost it.

"Wow, Ronan, you look so much like him," I finally managed, leaning in and squinting at the photo like I needed to study it. Which was true. His eyes. *Both* their eyes. That was what I couldn't put my finger on about Ronan when we'd first met. He had Cillian's eyes.

Also, why had Cillian never told me that his last name was *Broderick*? I guessed I'd never asked—but seriously? That felt like a pretty fucking important piece of information.

He turned to the next page. "My great-grandmother was never photographed. It was rare to get even one photo of someone back in those days. Her story is tragic. She died giving birth to what would have been my great-uncle—his name was Eoin. Just terrible."

"After Eoin and my great-grandmother's deaths," Ronan said, flipping through more pages of the book, "Great-Grandpa Cillian started a hidden speakeasy during the Prohibition. Illegally ran it, of course. He was like an old-school gangster, really. I think it was his way of coping after his wife's and son's deaths, and after the war. Getting people together under a common roof, rebelling against the rules. A true vigilante. Trying to find some kind of freedom after everything they endured. I can't imagine how hard that must have been for him," Ronan said, shaking his head.

"An illegal speakeasy, huh?" was all I could manage through the wave of shock.

You are a PR professional, I reminded myself. *You handle crises for a living. Handle this.*

I needed to flip the switch—emotion off, business mode on. At least for now. I could freak out later. I could process later. I could tell Lila everything later. Right now, I needed to collect as much information as possible.

Grabbing my champagne once I could be trusted with glass again, I slipped into my PR crisis manager mode.

"So, who took over the atelier after your great-grandmother passed?" I asked, taking a big gulp, downing the rest of my champagne.

"Great-Grandpa Cillian, then my mother," he said, refilling my glass then his. "Well, that's where the story gets a bit funky," he admitted.

Oh honey, you have no idea how weird this already is. If he only knew.

"My great-grandparents had another daughter earlier on, before Eoin. Her name was Saoirse. She was born, I believe, around 1910, right before Ireland got involved in the war," he said. "Saoirse is my grandmother. She had my mother out of wedlock, which is why the name Broderick got passed down. It was quite the scandal, from what I've read," he added with wide eyes.

I painted on a smile and offered a huffy laugh, but my mind was racing.

Saoirse. Cillian's daughter. Saoirse was Ronan's grandmother? This was spooky.

"I considered Saoirse my mother. My real mother died in an accident when I was just five years old. Grandma Saoirse took me in." He flipped to a photo of his mother and himself. "This is my biological mother, Maeve *Broderick*," he said, nudging me as if to emphasize the Broderick name and its implications.

"That's so tragic. Her death," I clarified. I tried to offer him as much condolence as I could manage in my current state. Which was hardly any.

"Obviously, Saoirse was already old when I was a boy, but I'd come to the atelier with her every day to learn everything I possibly could. Even as a child, I was the only one in line to take it over when she was gone. So, I learned how to measure shoulder slopes, select the right wool weight for the season, the intricacies of hand-stitched lapels." He smiled. "That woman would have me practicing buttonholes until my fingers were raw and bloody. Thank goodness she lived to almost ninety-eight and kept a sound mind until the end. She was teaching me up until her very last day."

He paused, running a hand over a photo of a client in a suit that looked straight out of the 70s. "I was around twenty when she passed. Took over the atelier the day after the funeral."

"That young?" I asked, somehow managing to ask a coherent question. "When did you all switch from being a tailoring shop to designing custom suits? That's a big jump."

"That was my great-grandfather, Cillian. After his wife's death—from my research—he poured himself into trans-forming the shop into something that would live on as long as possible, to honor her. He knew that wasn't a tailoring shop. So, he married his business savviness with the art of tailoring. He went to Saville Row in London to become a Bespoke tailor after the war. It was a real craft for men back then. Very cutting edge. Very progressive."

Ronan flipped back to the picture with Cillian. It was like seeing a ghost. It took my breath away. I couldn't look away. I wanted to memorize every line of his face, every detail, as if staring long enough might make sense of it all.

"He would spend the days with Saoirse in the shop, teaching her everything he could about bespoke. Then, in the evenings, he would spend it at the speakeasy. They called it The Velvet Clover. Isn't that a wonderful name? Managing his many other businesses in-between somehow. He was an incredible man."

I couldn't believe what I was hearing. Confirmation after confirmation. I had just quit my job to commit to working at the same place that was run by my time-traveling speakeasy boyfriend's great-grandson.

I took a deep breath. "Can I see a photo of Saoirse?" If I was in this deep, I might as well get some damned information on the man I was falling for. I wanted to at least know what his daughter looked like.

"Of course." He flipped through the pages. "Here," he said, "this was her back in the 1920s. Looks like she was at the speakeasy in this one." He pulled the image off the page and handed it to me to take a closer look.

You have got to be fucking kidding me.

I grabbed the photo out of Ronan's hand and held it close to my face in utter disbelief. "This is Saoirse? Your grandmother who raised you? Cillian's daughter?"

"Yes," he said, his eyebrows raising. "Is something wrong?"

"No . . ." I said, forcing myself to keep it together. "She just looks . . . so familiar."

The hostess.

The hostess of The Velvet Clover was Saoirse.

How was it possible that the hostess of The Velvet Clover—the hostess with the cute black bob—was Cillian's *daughter*? The hostess was *Saoirse*? Was it possible for this to get any more *Twilight Zone*? How had I not caught that? Had I been so wrapped up in Cillian that I'd missed the obvious? That his daughter had been there, right under my nose each night, and I had absolutely no idea?

My head spun as everything in my world tilted, the ground beneath me threatening to crumble. A thousand thoughts slammed into me at once, each one more impossible than the last. My stomach churned. Was I sweating? This wasn't real. It couldn't be real. This had to be some terrible multi-day dream or hallucination. I knew it wasn't, but I couldn't help but hope.

You'll have time to process later, I reminded myself one final time, forcing myself to breathe slowly, to stay in the moment, despite the fog closing in around me.

"Wow. This really is some family history." I forced a smile. "Ronan, I am so glad you showed me this. It makes a huge difference in how we are going to tell the story of The Aislinn Atelier." Oh, and did it ever.

It hit me then—something odd (well, more odd) about all this. "Speaking of," I started counting on my fingers. "Maeve, Saoirse, Eoin, Cillian, Ronan. With all this history and Irish family pride, where did Aislinn come from? You would have thought your family would have gone with a family name for the atelier. Broderick makes more sense than Aislinn. Did Cillian choose it because of its meaning? Vision. Dream." I noticed I said his name with a little too much familiarity, like my tongue had just been down his throat the night before.

"Oh, I can't believe I forgot to tell you my favorite part of the story," he said, tapping his forehead. "Aislinn, which is so perfect for its meaning, of course—vision. That was Saoirse's mother's name. My great-grandfather, Cillian's wife. Aislinn."

"He named the atelier . . . after his late wife?" I asked, trying to mask the stir of emotions that I couldn't quite define.

"Indeed," he said, a look of nostalgia crossing his face.

"That is one of the sweetest things I've ever heard," I said, my heart tightening. I couldn't help but wonder what it would feel like to be loved so deeply, to have a legacy like that left in your name. It was beautiful and heartbreaking.

"Well, that, and around that time, everyone knew Broderick to be an Irish surname. My best guess: it was better for business to have it sound a little more generic. It probably opened more doors and made things easier back then. From my research and how Saoirse always spoke about Great-Grandpa Cillian, he was a smart and kind man, but a real brooding soul. Troubled after the war. But a man's man, no doubt." He let out a low laugh. "Saoirse used to call him a pain in her arse."

"I can imagine," I said, knowing all too well. "It seems like he sacrificed so much so that his family could have it all."

"He really did," Ronan said. "I am so grateful for him every day. I always wished I could have met him while he was alive."

"Well, I'm sure he's here in spirit," I said, looking around the shop as the truth started to sink in. Then I realized he wasn't just here in spirit—he was everywhere. I just hadn't noticed. In the furnishings, the old leather chairs that had been here for decades, the dark wood that matched the speakeasy bar. The suits hanging like a perfect reflection of his attention to detail. Every single thing in this shop had a piece of Cillian in it. This place *was* him. It was so obvious now that I couldn't believe I hadn't put it together sooner. That I hadn't seen it. His soul, who he was, his heartbeat—it was woven into everything here, stitched into the fabric of this place. For a second, I could feel Cillian in the room, his presence thick in the air.

And then, just as quickly, I swore I could smell him. That damn scent—cigarettes, whiskey, and sandalwood—wrapping around me like he'd just walked past. It felt real. Like if I turned around, I'd find him standing there, his eyes locked on mine. Those damn blue eyes.

18

Oh, did I have a bone to pick.

Not just out of anger, but anger was the only emotion that didn't completely undo me. Beneath it was confusion, disbelief, maybe even hurt, all tangled together in a way that made it impossible to think straight. So, I chose anger. It gave me something to hold onto. It kept me moving.

I left the atelier, speed-walking back to the hotel as much as one can speed-walk in five-inch heels, a mix of fury and complete confusion trailing in my wake. My heart hammered against my chest. How could he not tell me his wife's name—*her* name—after I had mentioned the name of the atelier I was going to be working at? He'd said *nothing*. Had he just chalked it up to some wild coincidence? Did he know something? Did he know about me being from the future?

There *had* been something when I'd told him. A pause. A flicker in his eyes. I'd seen it. But I'd brushed past it, too caught up in my own excitement to ask about it. I couldn't stop replaying it over and over.

Either way, he had kept it to himself. And now I was left walking through Manhattan, choking on a hundred unasked questions, clinging to anger because it was the only thing that stopped me from crying.

Aislinn. He had named it after *her*. His late wife.

Part of me wanted to be angry about that, too, but I couldn't quite get there. There was something painfully tender about it. Fragile. Tragic. There was a devotion between them that lived on in his choice to name his shop after her. It was so . . . sweet, wasn't it?

I hated how that softened me, too. How I somewhat understood why he'd done it. Maybe that was why he hadn't said anything. Maybe it was too personal. Too complicated. Too vulnerable. Then, there was a sliver of me—a pathetic sliver— that felt jealous. Jealous that he might never feel that way about me.

Cillian had also conveniently left out the detail that his daughter, Saoirse—*Ronan's grandmother*—was the hostess of The Velvet Clover. That she had been there every night. Yes, he had briefly mentioned that she was usually around, but he'd never told me that she was the *hostess*. That couldn't have been an oversight. That had been a choice. He hadn't introduced me to her. A deliberate decision to keep me in the dark. My throat tightened.

Did he owe me that? Did he owe me any truth at all? We weren't together. And I supposed I hadn't quite been fully honest with my whole life and the fact that I was from the future. He didn't owe me his full life history. Just like I didn't owe him mine. Maybe he'd been caught off guard and hadn't known how to introduce Saoirse and I properly, or how to tell me about his wife. Or maybe—my stomach twisted—he'd just decided I wasn't important enough to tell.

I huffed, slowing my pace as I turned a corner. My hands curled into fists at my sides, doing my best to remain angry with him. I had every right to be angry.

But underneath the anger was that sinking feeling that kept

poking through the surface. An understanding as to why he hadn't told me. And that scared me more than anything. That I was reasoning with his lies.

The cocktail of emotion was confusing me more than I cared to admit. I didn't know quite what I felt, but I was feeling a hell of a lot of all of it.

Maybe I shouldn't work at the atelier after all. *Should I call Ronan and tell him I revoke my application? That I quit?* Maybe this was a sign—a tangled mess of history and half-truths I had no energy for.

I could always go back to San Francisco, slip into the clean life I'd built there. I could probably still recover my job at Atlas & Grey. This was what I got for acting preemptively—dammit.

If I did go back, there would be no ghosts from 1925, no questions, no wondering what someone wasn't saying. Life would be simple. But also boring. Vanilla. Elliot. Terrible. *Ick.*

No, I couldn't do that. I wouldn't let Cillian, or his lies, or his past dictate the future I had decided on for myself. I wouldn't.

God, this place—*him*—had already pulled me in way too deep.

I stormed through the front door of The Fitzgerald Hotel, my heels clacking against the wooden floor. I stepped over the velvet rope blocking off the restaurant that wasn't open yet— empty, as usual. I glanced left and right, scanning the dimly lit lounge. Behind the bar, no Chris Kringle, no bartender, no one. Perfect.

I stomped to the velvet curtain, ripped it back, turned the handle, and stormed through the door. It wasn't until I was standing on the other side, in The Velvet Clover—empty—that I realized it wasn't nine twenty-five p.m. In fact, according to my watch, it was only four o'clock. My stomach flipped. This portal time-travel shit made absolutely no sense.

How come, when I'd brought Lila here around this same time, it had been just a broom closet? And why the hell did

Chris Kringle only let us through at that stupidly specific time?

I kicked myself for not trying to figure out how this whole thing worked sooner.

But none of that mattered right now, because I was here.

I looked around the speakeasy. The same soft haze hung in the air, but something was . . . off. Different. It was like a ghost town. No Eddie. No jazz music. No hostess who was Cillian's *daughter*.

The space felt different during the day. Empty. Lifeless. Like some of the magic had drained out with the sunlight.

"Hello?" I called into the abyss. If anyone was here, I didn't want to get shot or shanked for surprising them—people used to shoot first and ask questions later back then, right? At least, that was what I had seen in the old 1920's gangster movies. No DNA, no evidence, just a body outlined in white chalk, with some unqualified and equally unskilled detective shrugging and moving on with the case with nothing more than a "hunch." The last thing I needed was to lose my damned head more than I already had.

I walked further in, trying to keep my heels from clicking too loudly on the wood floor, my rage still simmering beneath the surface.

As I snuck through the space, a noise broke the silence. Faint mumbling. Muffled words. My pulse quickened. I followed the noise, creeping toward the private room where Cillian and I'd had dinner the other night. The heavy sliding wood doors were cracked open just enough for me to see in without being seen.

The once intimate setting had changed—where just a single table had been set for two on that night with Cillian, now there were several, neatly arranged, including one massive table in the center, capable of seating a crowd, covered in hundreds of papers.

There.

Cillian.

He was alone, leaning heavily over the table, his arms braced against its surface, shoulders tense. His head hung low between them, a lit cigarette dangling from his left hand. I couldn't help but watch, just for a minute—sue me. He was too beautiful to look away from, even with those little Benjamin Franklin-like glasses that I was seeing him wear for the first time.

Part of me didn't care how old he was, how young he was, or how decomposed his corpse was in 2025. Part of me wanted to stay pissed, to let that fury stay locked in.

But seeing him like this—vulnerable, messy, in his chaos—dissolved some of it. A reminder of his humanity. Still, I wasn't about to let him off the hook. Not yet.

His jacket was off, the first time I had seen him without one. He had metal sleeve garters at the elbows of his shirt. A well-fitted vest over his button-up. One sleeve was rolled up just like Ronan's had been today. God, Ronan really was a spitting image of him. I couldn't believe I hadn't seen it.

Total side note: If there was a competition for world's best forearms, even from all the way over here, Cillian would take the fucking cake yesterday, today, and tomorrow. And one hundred years ago.

I shook my head. *Focus, Ava. You are mad at him.*

Papers were scattered all over the table that he was bent over. Some were strewn on the floor. A few crumpled. He looked . . . distraught.

He grabbed his glass of whiskey and downed it in one gulp before slamming it back on the table. Okay, he seemed angry—really angry. But damn, that was hot.

He took his glasses off, rubbed his eyes with his free hand, then slid it into his pants pocket, leaning back, staring down at the desk. God, even the way he stood was perfect. It was almost maddening how effortlessly he did everything, like he owned the world. But something about the way his shoulders were so tense, the furrow in his brow, made him seem stressed. What was bothering him? Could I do anything to help?

Something shifted in me, like a protective instinct I hadn't expected kicked in.

I took a step to brace myself, but my heel caught on the wood, making a skidding sound. Shit. Heels and sneaking were no bueno.

"Oi?" he called out, walking over to the doors. I could feel his anger radiating off him.

I slowly pulled the doors open, revealing myself standing there, trying not to look guilty.

"Ava." He said, clearly confused. There was a softness that didn't match the intensity I'd just seen. As though the mere sight of me calmed him. "What are ya doing here? How did ya even get in?" A hint of a smile flickered on his face, like he couldn't help but be relieved to see me.

But I wasn't about to let that soften me. Not this time.

"How could you not tell me your ex-wife's name was Aislinn when I told you about the atelier I'm going to be working at?" I figured I should go right at him, not give him time to come up with a lie.

"How did ya figure dat out?" he shot back, sounding just as offended as I was.

"It's none of your business!" I snapped.

"Well then, Ava. My *dead* wife's name is none of yours," he said, his focus returning to the papers on the desk.

"You didn't think it to be a little weird when I mentioned it? Why didn't you say anything? You lied to me."

His head dropped back, gazing up at the ceiling. "Honestly, I figured it was just a coincidence, me darlin'."

"But you didn't say anything about it. What about your last name being Broderi—"

"Jesus, Ava," he growled. Cillian stood rigid, his eyes hardening. "I don't have time for dis." He clenched his jaw, visibly trying to rein in his impatience. "I have other tings to deal with right now dat are more critical than me last name or the name of some atelier ye are going to work at being the same as me dead wife's." His words were cold, dismissive, cutting off any further discussion.

"Like what?"

"Like running fuckin' five businesses at Christmastime, keepin' them all open with no help from anyone. Like raisin' Saoirse, who's turnin' into a damn emotional rollercoaster with no mother around to help balance her out. Every day's a new challenge with her. I'm not equipped for this. Every single night, I'm tryin' to figure out how to keep this speakeasy from getting' raided by the coppers for serving alcohol." He rubbed his forehead. "The last fuckin' thing I need is dis woman I'm falling for, coming in here, upset about somethin' in the fucking past that I had no control of. Like my dead wife's fuckin' name!"

His words hit me differently, lowering my defenses just enough to stop me from fighting back. Even though I still wanted to pick a fight, part of me knew it wouldn't help anything. I'd always enjoyed a good fight with someone who could handle it—Cillian probably being one of the best potential contenders—but something in his voice took the edge off that urge. It wasn't about being right. I didn't *want* him to hurt. I wanted to . . . help? I wanted to help him.

What is happening to me?

He rested his hands back on the table, leaning into them, letting out a heavy sigh. His shoulders slumped.

I walked over, gently gripping both sides of his face, giving his cheeks a squeeze as I pulled his face closer to mine, wedging myself between him and the table. "Hey," I said, locking eyes with him. Then I gave his cheek a sharp slap. "Snap out of it."

His brows raised, eyes widening.

"You need to snap out of this shit, Cillian. You can fucking do this. I'll help you with the business stuff. And I can help with Saoirse—I was a bitchy teenage girl once—hell sometimes, I still am—and we can figure out the speakeasy stuff. But having a pity party alone? That's beneath you, and you know it."

Something shifted. The anger didn't disappear, but it faded just enough for me to feel something else underneath. I cared. I didn't want to, but I did. I wanted to help him, to take some of the weight off his shoulders. I hadn't let myself admit it before, but the truth was: he mattered to me. More than I thought.

He said nothing. He just stared at me with all the intensity and power of the tsunami that lived in those blue ocean eyes.

"Oh, and no fucking yelling at me," I chided.

Darkness flickered in his eyes before the corner of his mouth twitched.

A comfortable discomfort washed over me. How was it possible for me to have the upper hand in this conversation yet still feel like he held an invisible power over me? How did he keep beating me at my own game?

"What?" I demanded.

"Women don't speak to me the way ya speak to me, Ava," he said as the space between us felt like it had just gotten a lot closer.

My balance faltered, and I reached behind me to brace myself on the table with both hands.

"Well, that isn't really my problem," I said, trying to keep my wits about me as I felt his energy field and mine mingle. Then I had a wild and unexpected thought.

Should I tell him that I'm from the future? But it caught in my throat, and I pushed it away. I couldn't. He had enough of his plate already. Plus, that would make what I was feeling for him too real. Too permanent.

Temporary. That was all this was ever supposed to be. Temporary.

He let out a breathy laugh, wagging a finger in front of my face. "That is what I need in me life." His eyes locked on mine, unblinking. "A woman who not only sees me potential but actually pushes me to achieve it," he said then took a drag from his cigarette and blew the smoke to the side as he lingered just inches from my face before setting it in the ashtray on the table behind us and stepping even closer.

I sucked in air. What the hell could I even say to a comment like that? *Yes, I am a bossy bitch. You are welcome?*

He said nothing as he reached up to brush back a strand of hair off of my face. He looked at my lips.

In situations like this—and hostile negotiations—whoever spoke first lost.

I caught myself biting my lip, my throat bobbing as my eyes drifted down, unable to resist looking at his beautiful mouth, just inches from mine.

"Where did ya come from?" he muttered, searching for the answer somewhere on my face, his voice dropping an octave.

My mind went blank. No sarcastic comments, no snide remarks. It was as if he had stripped away all my walls, and I couldn't joke or jab my way out of it. A pulse rippled through my body with every second he stood there, staring at me.

"What do you want from me?" I managed, though it came out more like a plea than the defensive question I intended. A deep need in my voice.

"You, Ava. I want *you*," he said, wrapping his hand around my neck as he crashed his lips to mine. And just like that, I was pulled back to the night before.

Our tongues tangled, like no matter how much of each other we had, it would never be enough. My hands found their way to the nape of his neck, grounding me, keeping me balanced.

He stepped me backward toward the table behind us. The bulge in his pants sent a jolt of lightning straight between my legs, igniting a desperate need for friction, for release.

I needed him. All of him. Now.

He kissed my neck, and a deep moan escaped me. He lifted me, placing my ass on the edge of the table. I fumbled with the buttons on his vest as he did the same with his shirt—too many buttons. I gave up, pulling at his pants. My own pants—screw the shirt.

Before I could fully comprehend what was happening, he had my coat off.

His scent. I needed it. If I could bottle it up, I would. I would spray it on everything, on every inch of me, forever. I would bathe in it. Every part of me craved that smell. Craved him.

With one hand, he held my head, pulling me into a deep kiss, while he interlaced his other hand with mine. My toes curled as I wrapped my legs around his waist to keep him close. He slid his hand up my half-buttoned shirt, brushing over the peaks of my nipples, sending a tremor of pleasure down my spine.

"Cillian," I let out a breathless cry, the sound barely escaping my lips as his smile curled into something knowing. Something teasing. Like he could feel every part of me, like he knew exactly how much he was torturing me, savoring it.

His erection pressed hard against me, sending an electric shock through my core, making everything inside me ache for him. I barely had time to process it when he started pulling off my pants, one leg at a time, deliberately, painfully slow.

I felt a flush spread across my skin when I realized that he was pleased to notice I wasn't wearing any underwear.

"Ye've got to be fuckin' kidding me," he said, dropping his

head back as if he'd just lost it, or won the lottery, or was praying, or thanking God above.

A part of me wanted to shrink away, to protect myself, but the rest of me couldn't help but revel in the rawness of it all, in how exposed I felt, and how badly I wanted him, despite it.

He kissed down the length of my body until he was kneeling before me, his lips grazing the insides of my thighs. My whole body quivered, the space between my legs trembling with anticipation. I felt completely vulnerable, completely exposed.

"Please, just fuck me," I begged.

Cillian looked up at me with those piercing blue eyes, a dark, sexy smirk tugging at the corner of his lips. "We'll get dere, Ms. Hawthorne," he said, his voice deeper, rougher than I had ever heard it before. His accent made my pulse race. "But first, I need to taste dis beautiful woman before me."

I leaned back on my elbows as he pulled me closer, gripping my ass and holding me firmly in place. My head fell back, my hair spilling, cascading onto the pile of his scattered papers.

With one lick of his tongue, I was undone, soaking wet. He groaned in pleasure. He circled his finger at the apex between my legs. Using his tongue and fingers pumping in and out, the energy from his touch alone pushed me over the edge. The pleasure, unimaginable. Like meeting God Himself. Or herself. . . if God was, in fact, a woman. If I knew one thing, it was that this man knew how to please a woman. And in record fucking time, I was climaxing, seeing stars in a way I had never experienced before.

Panting and breathless, I had a wave of release, but I needed him. *Him.*

He was there, staring at me, kneeling before me like he wanted to stay there and worship me for the rest of eternity. But he slowly stood once he knew he had finished me off. His lips had a plumpness to them. He raised his brows to see if I was ready for more.

I was.

"Please," was all I could manage between breaths. Not able to hold myself up, I stayed flat on my back.

Cillian stood slowly, his shirt still on, half unbuttoned. He pulled down his underwear, revealing the full length of him. I caught a glimpse before I rested my head back on the table. The sight of it alone caused another moan to escape my throat.

"It's fucking perfect," I said, now looking at the chandelier above me.

He laughed. "I only need it to be perfect for you, me love." And with that, as if I was not already undone enough from his words alone, he guided himself into me. Slowly. Generously. Until the entire length of him filled me.

His low growl rumbled through me, eliciting an uncontrollable moan. "Fuck, Ava."

Those two words coming from him were everything I had ever needed to hear. I could officially die happily now. I was no longer afraid of death.

He pumped in and out of me. Every next one better than the last. Completing me, making me feel whole. He laid over me, running his hands over every part of my body, holding my neck, sliding his hand down my back, squeezing my waist.

I locked my fingers in his hair, running them over his shoulders and chest as he pumped in and out harder and harder. Like ravaged animals. Like we had been waiting our whole lives for this.

He pulled my hair. I let out a whimper. He buried his head in my neck.

I had been waiting for this—for this moment—my entire life. For him my entire life. I just didn't know it until now. Didn't know I could actually find this. This feeling. I didn't know it actually existed. Until now.

I could feel him getting close, but as he did, he slowed down torturing us both.

"Please, don't stop," I pleaded.

"I am about to come, Ava." His voice was deep, calm, collected. Like he wasn't having amazing sex. Like he was doing something as normal as picking out tomatoes at the grocery store.

"But I am not comin' without ye," he said, standing and assessing me, as if he was completely willing to walk away if I didn't.

"You're a man of great restraint," I panted. "But I can promise you, there's no way I'm not coming with you—"

A smile crossed his face, and an instant later, before I could get the last word out, he grinded his hips into me harder than before, moving in and out at the most perfect angle I had ever felt.

The pleasure was overwhelming, unlike anything I'd ever experienced. Like seconds and years were colliding, time stretching and breaking apart as we both released together. Our energy swirled, combining into the stars, the moon—pure ecstasy. Breathing together, eyes locked, never breaking the connection.

My body was still trembling, His strength, his control, his tenderness—they all came together in a way that had me feeling completely seen, completely understood. Known. This wasn't just physical; it was a connection deeper than anything I'd ever experienced. This would be the memory I carried with me forever—with the—technically dead—man who defied time and made me feel more alive than I ever thought possible.

An hour later, after two more rounds that were just as amazing —if not more so, Cillian sat against the wall. I lay beside him, my head resting in his lap, surrounded by our tangled clothes. He ran his fingers gently through my hair.

"Have I told ya dat ya have da most beautiful hair I have ever seen?" he said, staring into my eyes, holding me captive.

"No, you haven't. But thank you. I do have great hair," I responded. "Have I told you that you have the most amazing"— I let my eyes drift down to his lap before winking—"eyes," I teased with a playful grin.

He let out a deep belly laugh, taking an inhale of his cigarette. "Ya know? I *have* been told I have great . . . eyes," he said, gesturing with his eyes toward his cock. I felt it twitch beneath my head.

I sat up, propping myself on my elbow. I puckered my lips to kiss him, and he leaned in and kissed me with so much sweetness and desire that I melted all over again. I ran my hand through his hair, tugged his head back an inch, exposing his neck and kissing it. He pulled me into him, our bodies warm, one in the same. It was right. Like everything I ever wanted, or didn't know I wanted, was right here with him.

Holding me still, his head buried in my neck, he whispered into my ear, "Ya make me very happy, Ava."

I kissed him in a way that I hoped made him know that I felt the same way.

"Wait," I said. "I meant to ask, before all of . . . that." I gestured to the room where papers were now scattered all over the floor, even more disorganized than before. "Can you actually make custom suits?" I asked, trying to keep the mood light.

He looked at me dreamily, like he was still thinking about the last hour. "Where do ya get all this insider information on me so suddenly? Eh?"

"Not important," I said, standing to get dressed. Now that I wasn't sweating, I realized how cold it was in here. "Answer the question," I said, throwing his underwear into his lap to cover where my head had just been.

He held a cigarette between his lips. "Indeed, I can. Why?"

"No reason, just curious . . ."

"Ya are a fascinatin' woman, you," he said, wagging his cigarette laced between his fingers at me. His energy shifted slightly, like his earlier stresses started to trickle back into his awareness.

"You know you don't have to do it all alone, right?" I asked. "I meant it when I said I would help."

"Ava, ya don't need to do dat. Ye've got enough going on— with your sister here, your opportunities at the atelier. I can handle what I've taken on. I always have. Ya just caught me in a moment, dat's all."

"I know you *can*," I said. "But it doesn't mean you *have to* struggle all alone. You've got people in your life who would love to help you. You just have to ask for it."

He let out a sardonic laugh, flicking his cigarette. "Mmhmm, pot meet kettle." He raised an eyebrow at me. "Tell you what—I'll ask for help the day ya do."

I stuck my tongue out at him, now almost fully dressed. "This is not about me. This is about you. But don't say I didn't offer." A few of my shirt buttons were undone, my tie dangling around my neck, but it worked. "Seriously, I am here for you, anything you need. I am happy to help. And I don't offer support to people freely . . . so consider yourself lucky."

Cillian slowly rose to his feet, still wrapped in postcoital bliss, pulling on his pants and buttoning up his shirt.

As I started organizing the papers that had fallen on the ground, he walked over and touched my shoulder. "Thank ya, love. Yer offer of support means da world to me," he said, then leaned in and pressed a soft kiss to my forehead. "If dere is anything I need yer help with, I will be sure to ask."

A knock came from the other side of the room.

"Oi?" Cillian called out, focusing on ashing his cigarette.

The doors to the room rolled open in slow motion, and my

eyes went wide in horror as I looked at Cillian. He shot me a reassuring don't-worry-about-it glance.

I smoothed my hair and checked my shirt to make sure it wasn't misbuttoned, hoping to cover up the evidence of our . . . activities.

None other than Saoirse the hostess—and did I mention yet, Cillian's daughter?—peeked her head in. "Sir," she started.

"Saoirse. Me dear," he said, waving her in as he helped me organize the papers on the table. He put his glasses back on, which suddenly made him look totally innocent. Like he hadn't just had sex in his pub.

She walked over, giving Cillian a side hug and smiling at me politely. He kissed the top of her head.

"How are ya doing, my darlin'?" he asked, giving her his full attention, hands resting on both of her shoulders as he looked at her then cupped her face gently.

"Doin' great, sir. I just stopped by to see if ye need anything from me this evenin'?" she asked sweetly, glancing at me.

"Nah, go ahead and enjoy yer time with friends. If ya can swing by the tailoring shop on yer way, only to check on how everything's lookin', that'd be great, yeah?"

That's when I realized it was Monday—he had mentioned to Lila and me that the speakeasy would be closed for the night.

She smiled at her dad before turning to me with a small wave. "Good evenin', Ms. Hawthorne. Will we still be seeing ya and yer sister at our Christmas party tomorrow, I hope?"

"Hi, Saoirse," I said, giving her an equally sweet smile. "Yes, of course. Any recommendations of what to wear?"

"Oh, Ms. Hawthorne, you of all people don't need fashion advice. Anything ya will wear will be stunnin'," she said with a smile. She was a gorgeous young woman.

"That's very sweet of you, thank you. I'll do my best," I replied.

She smiled at me before looking back to Cillian. "Love ya,

Dad," she said as she walked to the doors. It was the first time I had heard her call him Dad.

Before she rolled the doors shut, she looked back, glancing between the two of us, biting her lip.

"I didn't realize that was your daughter," I said, doing my best to play it cool. It was strange to know Saoirse's fate—she had a daughter and a grandson in Ronan. She lived to ninety-eight years old. It was creepy to know all this information. It felt wrong.

"How else do ya think those new menus I had made came to be, eh? Saoirse here wouldn't stop harassin' me at home about how the 'beautiful blonde Ms. Hawthorne' requested menus, and she was horrified she had nothin' to offer ya," he said. "Persistent that one is."

"Just like her dad, it seems," I said, looking off to where she'd stood moments ago. "She seems like a really sweet girl, especially for her age. I was a nightmare at that age."

"That's only because *you* are here. She's dyin' for me to fall in love again. She wouldn't want to do anythin' to make that more difficult. Quite a bit of sass, but a total romantic, dat one," he said, shifting his focus from the now fully reorganized papers to me.

"I like her," I said, still staring at the doorway.

"I'm very lucky. She's special," he said, holding my arms. "And so is dis one," he added, placing a soft kiss on my lips before turning me around and hugging me from behind, wrapping his arms around my waist, one hand resting on my hipbone, his face buried in my neck.

"Thank ya for helping me with me . . . paperwork," he said, squeezing my sides.

I squealed in response.

"I'll help you with your *paperwork* anytime," I said, turning back to him. "Seriously, anytime."

He pulled me close, and we danced around the tables to no

music. For the first time, I didn't want to run away. I wanted to fully live in this moment with him forever.

As we danced, I let myself melt into him, feeling his breath, the beat of his heart against my chest. A calm washed over me, my chest felt warm. I didn't feel the need to plan or control every second. There was something real here. Something that felt far beyond the anger I had been trying to hold onto.

I'd been so furious at him earlier. So ready to walk away. I'd told myself I couldn't trust him—couldn't trust anyone—but now . . . now that anger seemed so small, as if I'd been clinging to it just to avoid the deeper, scarier thing beneath—the possibility that I might actually want to let him in. That I might actually care for him.

That was ridiculous, wasn't it? He was Ronan's great-grandfather. He lived in another time. Yet he was the man I'd just slept with, only hours after finding out everything he hadn't told me.

This moment should have felt impossible. Wrong. Maybe even dangerous. Had what I'd just done affected the future somehow? Was there any way we could be together? I had so many questions. But instead of asking them all, this felt like the only real thing I'd known in a long time.

Now, with his arms around me, I wasn't afraid of the feeling. I wasn't afraid of him. And that terrified me—because I should be. I should be running from all of this. From him. From the past.

But I didn't want to.

I had no idea where this would go, what it meant, or what the consequences might be. And yet, here I was, choosing to stay. Because the only thing I knew for sure was how I felt about him.

For once, I didn't need all the answers. What I felt for Cillian was enough. I trusted that, no matter how impossible everything else seemed.

Of course, if this had any chance of becoming anything, I'd have to start figuring things out—time travel, the future, the risks—so I could be sure I'd be able to see him again. I wasn't ready to let this go.

Later. Later, I could figure everything out. I could unravel the time travel. I could get the answers I needed. I could figure out what I had to do to make sure Cillian and I could continue to see each other. To be together.

He pulled me closer, his lips brushing my cheek, and we swayed in silence, letting everything else fall away. Not forever. But for now.

19

I closed the door to our hotel room behind me, the smell of musk filling the air as much as it had the day I'd first arrived. Lila was lying in the just as musky robe on the bed, scribbling on a stack of papers, her hair wrapped in a towel.

All I could do was stare across the room, trying to process everything that had just happened.

"Ava?" Lila asked, half-concerned, half-excited.

I shook my head, tossing a bag of chips onto the bed. "I grabbed these for you from the vending machine." I figured it was the least I could do for luring her here during the holidays than ditching her every day since we'd arrived.

"Ooo, my favorite. Cheetos. Thanks, sis."

"Yeah, anytime," I said, my voice hollow as I cleared the pile of clothes from the chair in the corner and tossed them into a nearby suitcase. I needed the chair more than the clothes did.

Lila looked at me with a smile. "Sooo, are we going to talk about what happened today?"

"What do you mean by that?"

She gave me her best bored look. "Please. You're glowing . . .

slash you look terrified. Something happened at the interview?"

"Oh, the interview—I almost forgot about that."

"Tell me *everything!*" she squealed.

I continued staring in front of me. I had no idea what I was feeling. So, for now, I was sticking to shell-shock.

"Well, let's see ... To start, I accepted the job."

"Oh, congratulations, sis! That is so exciting."

"Let's just say that's the *least* interesting news I have for you," I said. Then I started down the actual list of events. I held up one finger. "So ... Saoirse, Cillian's daughter, is the hostess with the cute black bob from the speakeasy."

She gasped like the world was ending. "What? She's been there all along? And he never mentioned it? How did you figure that out?"

I held up a second finger. "Cillian's last name is Broderick."

Lila cocked her head, looking confused.

"Meaning ... Ronan Broderick's great-grandfather is—was Cillian Broderick."

Another life-ending gasp from my sister. "Oh my gosh! How is that possible?"

I held up a third finger. "Saoirse *raised* Ronan after his mother died in a tragic accident and taught him tailoring, so he could take over the atelier."

Another gasp.

I raised a fourth finger, still staring forward. "Cillian named his tailoring shop—which eventually became the bespoke tailoring house, aka the atelier—after his dead wife. Her name was none other than ... you guessed it ... *Aislinn*."

This gasp was part horror, part heartbreak. Her eyes were as wide as saucers now, hand covering her mouth.

Holding up a fifth finger, I continued, "I stormed over to the speakeasy, and I was so pissed at him because he hadn't mentioned anything about his wife or daughter that I didn't even think about the nine twenty-five p.m. thing. I got right in. No broom closet."

Her jaw dropped even wider.

"And . . ." I said, holding up a sixth finger. "I had sex with Cillian."

She threw herself back on the bed and squealed in excitement, followed by another gasp once the weight of the complexities began to settle.

I held up a seventh finger.

"Seven? What? What other news could there possibly be?" she asked, now sitting on the edge of the bed.

I finally broke my gaze from staring straight ahead and looked at her. "I think I might be falling in love with Cillian."

I stood by the hotel window, watching the snow cover the city like a blanket—thick, smothering.

Behind me, Lila had spent the last twenty minutes furiously taking notes from our earlier conversation, like she was preparing for some big court case, or maybe just trying to help me untangle whatever existential, time-traveling mess I'd landed myself in. She really was such a great little journalist. Relentless, annoyingly persistent, and alarmingly thorough.

"So, let me get this straight," she said, tapping her pen against her lips, eyes narrowed like she was about to crack the mystery of the century. Literally. "You slept with Cillian. Realized you're falling in love with him. Found out he's your new boss's great-grandfather. And now you're . . . just going to work for the family business and pretend it never happened?"

"Basically," I said, trying to mask the mix of foreign emotions I couldn't quite seem to identify.

She let out a breath. "Ava, this is serious."

I turned to face her. "What do you want me to say, Lila? That

I'll throw away everything I've worked for just because I have feelings for a man who lives in 1925? One I'm not even sure I can be with after Christmas—or tomorrow—or unless it's exactly nine twenty-five p.m. and I luckily get through that velvet curtain and it isn't a broom closet? Except for today, when it lets me in at some random time, like the rules just suddenly changed?"

"That's not what I'm saying." She paused. "I'm wondering, are we even asking the right questions? Like, have we *really* tried figuring out how this whole time-travel thing works? We only asked Christopher a few questions that he never really answered."

"Because you let him off the hook!" I said. But as soon as she said it, I realized I hadn't *really* wanted to actually know the answers. That was why I hadn't pressed. When I wanted something—anything—in life, I went out and I got it. That was who I was. If I had truly wanted to figure out the time travel rules of this magical speakeasy, I would have already found a way to get my answers.

Hearing my sister ask the question only made me realize I'd been too scared to ask myself, let alone someone else. Let alone *that* bartender. Scared that if all of this was just Christmas magic—and it would end in a few days—I might not be able to handle it. To emotionally survive it. A part of me would have rather just woken up one day and found the speakeasy closed for good, because that might hurt less than admitting how much I cared for Cillian . . . only to learn we could never be together. That wasn't the answer I wanted, so I had simply refused to ask the question.

I thought this could just be one of those "ignorance is bliss" situations, or what therapists might refer to as "complete and utter denial."

But now that I had finally let myself open up to him in this way, to feel what I was feeling now, I knew I needed answers.

Real answers. So I could figure out my future and if it involved him in any capacity.

"Okay, Mrs. Investigator, what questions should I be asking then?"

She ran the pen down her list. "Can one of you step fully into the other's world? Would you want to go back to 1925 if it meant you could be with him? Could he come here? Would he be willing to? What about Saoirse; would she come, too? 'Cause that would definitely change the past... present.

"Does the speakeasy only open during the holidays? Is it every holiday? Through the end of the year? Is this truly just a Christmas magic thing, like Chris had insinuated. If so, is this a once in a lifetime Christmas thing, or is this a yearly Christmas thing? Is it open forever and you could be in a relationship as long as you go to the speakeasy? Or"—she paused, eyes wide— "is this a *Monsters Inc.* door situation? Like, one day, it's just ... gone? Someone shreds it and then the portal shuts forever because we did something in the past that messed up the whole timeline."

Did my sister just compare my love life to *Monsters Inc.*?

"Okay, okay, I get it ... I've thought about a couple of those, you know," I admitted, folding my arms in defense. "You heard the stupid bartender. He said don't go through the other door. The risk is way too high. I am not about to disappear into the void completely, or ask Cillian to do the same. I don't even think I should tell Cillian about all of this. It might make him implode or something. I don't know." I stopped myself, laughing bitterly. "You see how insane I sound?"

"You sound like someone who's in love with their soul mate," my sister smiled. "One who is trying to find a way that she can be with him, no matter the cost."

I sat on the edge of the bed and stared at the floor. "That's the worst part. I don't even know how this happened. But I care about him. And it's definitely not just lust or fantasy—it's him.

He sees me in a way no one else ever has. And I see him. I think he might be the only man alive—or dead, or across all of time and space—that I'm remotely compatible with."

She reached over and touched my arm. "So why not fight for it, sis?"

"Fight for what?" I said, exasperated. "For one of us to abandon our entire life and hop timelines? On the off chance we don't accidentally unravel the space-time continuum and cause the world to implode? Or disappear into the void? Sure. Sounds like a foolproof plan."

"This is so tragic," Lila whispered.

"Yeah, it might actually be more tragic than the love of your life dying," I said, thinking back to that first date with Cillian when I'd genuinely thought *that* was the worst-case scenario. But this? This was worse. The love of my life was alive and breathing right in front of me—except he was technically dead most of the day, unless the broom closet randomly decided to turn into a speakeasy, maybe only during one month a year, allegedly around the holidays.

"What am I supposed to do? Spend the rest of my life sitting in front of that broom closet, opening it every five minutes to see if I can get back to The Velvet Clover? Or set up shop in the speakeasy and get trapped in a loop? Staying night after night in 1925, with a cot I sleep on in the back? Just so Cillian doesn't slip through my fingers? That isn't a life. That's a tragedy. And totally pathetic."

"What about the fact that you got into the speakeasy at a different time? Do you think there are other times we can get through?" Lila asked.

"I have no idea how to explain that one. Or any of the other questions on your list. Maybe there is some other reason that the speakeasy opens."

"Maybe we can ask Christoph—"

"I don't want to deal with that guy's little games!" I snapped.

"He isn't giving us any straight answers, and I am sick of his shit."

Lila sat next to me on the bed, rubbing my back. I wanted to shove her hand away. I was already feeling too claustrophobic. But I let her do it.

"Sis," she started, "if you really feel this strongly about Cillian, you may want to consider telling him. He may know more than he's letting on. Or he may be able to come up with a solution on what to do about all of this. Plus, if you feel this way, I'm sure he feels the same. Maybe even stronger. And he deserves to know the truth, especially if there is a ticking clock with the whole Christmas thing."

"Yeah, you're probably right," I admitted. And she was. If the roles were reversed, I would hope he would tell me. "I just don't want to tell him at the wrong time and have it ruin things. I'll consider telling him . . . when the time is right." I shook my head at the thought of having to speak those words to him.

"The most infuriating part of all of this is that I don't even know what I'm fighting against. Christmas magic? Mr. Santa Hat? Physics? A wrinkle in time? "

Silence settled between us. Lila didn't have an answer, and I didn't blame her—because there wasn't one. It felt truly impossible for Cillian and me to be together in any sort of real way, which meant my only choice was to make sure I didn't fall too hard. But that felt just as impossible as this cosmic joke I'd been picked up and dropped into.

Was it tragic? The most. Could I put on a brave front and still move forward with my career as originally planned, knowing this fun would have to end eventually? Of course. I was a professional. Would it be the hardest thing I ever did? Certainly. In fact, besides how I felt for Cillian, that was the only thing I was certain about these days.

"Either way, when it comes to my actual life—my job at the atelier—I have to be realistic," I said, shifting gears. "I have a future there. With Ronan. I made a commitment, and whatever this thing is with Cillian, I can't let it derail everything I've worked for." I was committed to my future at the atelier, confident I could take it beyond anyone's expectations. I believed in the company's vision and saw its potential—a clear focus on growth, innovation, and ushering in a new era. Plus, their PR hiring budget was surprisingly generous, which meant a nice bonus for me.

"You're my hero, Ava. I don't know if I could walk into the atelier every day knowing what you do. But if this is where you see your future, then I support you. And maybe"—Lila hesitated—"maybe there's a way through this mess neither of us can see yet. I'll keep thinking about it. Maybe even write about it; see if anything clicks."

I wanted to believe her, but deep down, I'd run through every possibility, every potential loophole, everything I knew about alternate realities and time warps, and nothing felt certain. All I could do was not fall any harder, wear a brave face, and focus on the life I could build. The one I could control.

Even if it broke my heart.

Still, a small part of me—a part that was growing louder—wasn't ready to give up. Not yet. I didn't know how or when, but I would keep looking for a way. Because if there was even the smallest chance that time could bend in our favor, that Cillian and I could be together, I had to try.

20

"I just need to stop by the atelier for a quick errand before they close," I said as Lila and I made our way through the snow-packed streets the next morning.

Since the speakeasy was closed on Monday's we'd meant to go to a fancy dinner last night, but after drowning in questions and half-baked theories, we were too fried to move. At some point, we'd just passed out.

"I don't care what we have to do as long as we have a white Christmas," Lila said dreamily, dancing behind me.

"There is no way we won't at this point. The weather app says it will be snowing pretty hard straight through until Christmas Day. So, no need to worry about that," I assured her.

"By the way," I added, glancing at her, "I booked you a flight for tomorrow morning."

She blinked. "You did?"

I nodded. "Yeah, just in case. I figured you'd want to be back in time for Christmas with the girls."

"Right . . . of course," she said. "I mean, I'm excited to see them and everything, but . . . are you sure you don't want me to stay? With all you have going on with Cillian and the speakeasy . . . Simon and the girls have said a million times that it'd be totally fine if I stayed through Christmas. Especially to support you."

"Lila, I would love it if you stayed. You don't have to for me, though. I am sure you miss them. It's got to be hard being away from your family during the holidays."

She looked down at her boots, nudging a pile of snow with her toe. "It's actually been really nice to get away. Like . . . really nice. To write. To hang out with you. Gosh, am I just the worst mother in the world for saying that out loud?"

"Of course not. Moms deserve to have a life and enjoy it outside of their children, and not feel guilty. Remember what Mom said the other day?"

"Yeah, yeah, of course. You're right. I can miss them and still enjoy my time away."

"And be a great example for them. To encourage them to live their dream life." I rubbed her back. "Well, if you decide you don't want the flight, it's totally fine. I can move it or cancel it. I just didn't want you to feel stuck here."

"Thanks, Ava. You are a great sister." She gave me a grateful smile, and we kept walking.

"So, what do you have to pick up from the atelier?" she asked as I held the door open for her. I slapped her butt and ignored her question as we escaped the falling snow.

"Oh my goodness, this place is beautiful," Lila said, her eyes wide as she took in the atelier for the first time. I had tried to describe to her how amazing it was, but seeing it in person was something else—the blend of industrial charm with dark velvet drapes—funny how I hadn't noticed they were exactly like the ones from the speakeasy until now—like all the clues had been hidden in plain sight—polished wooden furniture, and bright, airy windows that created a warm, inspiring atmosphere that made you feel like you were stepping into a dream.

"Isn't it?" I went straight for the wooden table with the ties and the gorgeous pocket watch that I had seen yesterday during my meeting.

"I can't believe you're going to work here. Can I move here with you?" Lila begged, as if she had the option. She weaved through the tables and consoles, touching the few jackets on display.

"You can visit anytime you want," I said with delight. "If your life in Colorado with Simon and the girls wasn't a thing, I would totally ask you to move in with me."

"What about this shirt for Simon?" Lila held up a clean, white button-up.

"I love it," I said, standing on my tiptoes to see it from across the room.

She checked the sleeve. "They don't have price tags on the clothes. How much do you think this is?"

I judged the shirt for a second. "Probably about a thousand bucks."

"For a friend of Ava's, it's seven hundred even," Ronan called as he came from the back. "But great eye for price, Ava," he said with a wink, kissing each of my cheeks before pulling me in for a hug.

Lila's jaw dropped, her eyes wide, as she hung the shirt back up on the stand. Shuffling over to meet Ronan, she gave me a knowing look—*he looks like Cillian, and wow, he's beautiful, too*. I raised my brows in silent agreement.

"Ronan, this is my sister, Lila. She is in town from Colorado for Christmas. Lila, this is Ronan Broderick, whom I have told you about, that I will now be having the great honor of working with."

Ronan leaned in and gave Lila a couple of cheek kisses, his European charm on full display.

"Don't worry; I am not here to harass you with PR ideas, which will be coming first thing in the new year," I said. "I'm strictly here as a customer doing extremely last-minute Christmas shopping. I need this bow tie," I said, holding up the one I'd spotted yesterday.

"Bad girl," he said playfully, checking his watch. "This is much too last minute to be shopping for loved ones. Especially a man you care about. But luckily for you, you work here now, which means you are family. So I will make an exception." He patted my shoulder.

I rolled my eyes at his assumption that I was shopping for a man, though he was right. "Thank you. You are a lifesaver. Lil!" I called to my sister, who had wandered off somewhere.

"Yes?"

"Grab that shirt for Simon," I yelled.

"No, Av, it's too much. Plus, you have gotten me way too much stuff this trip already. I'm not letting you do that," Lila shot back from the front of the store.

"It wasn't a question," I sang, rolling my eyes at Ronan. "We will take both. I owe her for missing both of her baby showers and all her kids' birthday parties for work," I whispered to Ronan.

"I'll help Sofia gift wrap these in the back," he said with a laugh, disappearing to the back room, taking both items with him.

Lila sat at the workbench across from me. "Ava, you shouldn't have done that."

"I want you to come back with something for the poor man. After all, you left him alone with the kids on Christmas," I said.

"Hey! You told me he'd be fine and it wasn't a big deal."

"I'm kidding. You know that. But is it a sin to have ulterior motives?"

Lila looked at the workbench covered in bolts of fabric, marking chalk, and pins. "What's this?" she asked, grabbing the same history of the company coffee table book that Ronan had showed me at our last meeting.

"That's the book I told you about," I said, my voice hushed. "The company history, Cillian's story, Saoirse, it's all in there."

She grabbed the book, her jaw dropped. "*This is it*?" she mouthed, checking to see if Ronan was coming back.

I nodded, encouraging her to take a peek.

She started flipping through the pages, stopping to flash me the one that had stopped me in my tracks—the image of Cillian by the fireplace in the speakeasy.

"Wow, he looks really happy in this one," she said. Pausing again, this time at the picture of Saoirse. She pointed to it. "Wow!"

I stood across from her, nodding in agreement. "Crazy, right?" I whispered.

She continued quickly flipping through the book, researching, taking in as much as she possibly could before Ronan's return.

I looked around the store more. I really did love the pocket watch Cillian carried. This one that was next to the ties was gorgeous. Why had pocket watches gone out of style? They were extremely functional, especially when you had no cell service in certain speakeasies and didn't ever have the time because you were time traveling to another decade. I was just considering purchasing it for myself when . . . .

"All right!" Ronan's voice cut through the room.

Lila slammed the book shut, her eyes widening as if she'd just been caught with weed in high school math class. "Come," he said, gesturing for both of us to join him at the other end of the workbench.

"Here is the gorgeous shirt for your gracious husband. Tell him thank you from Ronan, for letting us have you in New York for Christmas," he said to Lila, putting a box wrapped in matte white wrapping paper with a black ribbon in a matching bag and handing it to her. So chic.

I gasped. "Ronan, that is gorgeous wrapping. Very nice touch."

Lila gave a little curtsy, bowing as she took the bag from him. "Thank you, sir," she said. She was such a dork.

"And here is your hand stitched black tuxedo bow tie, for your someone special. To our new Queen of PR, Ms. Ava Hawthorne," he said, handing me a smaller bag wrapped the same way as the first.

I handed him my American Express card, but he waved it away with a dismissive gesture. "Your money is no good here, Ava. You can't convince me otherwise."

I scoffed, feigning offense. "Ronan, no, that's too much. At least let me earn it."

He smiled, shaking his head. "No need. We'll be making plenty more than that in the years to come. Now, Merry Christmas. Go celebrate with this hunky mystery man of yours."

He walked us to the door, pulling us both into hugs before we left the store, thanking him for his generosity. We waved goodbye as we made our way down the street and back to the hotel.

"That was so nice of him. I can't believe he gave all of this to us for free. Does that kind of stuff happen a lot when you are in PR?" Lila asked, mesmerized by the wrapping of her husband's gift.

"It doesn't hurt to be in control of a company's public image, that's for sure," I admitted.

"He really is a spitting image of . . ." She trailed off.

"I know. I can't believe I didn't notice it before," I said, shaking my head.

We continued walking for a block before either of us spoke again. There was something strange about the silence, though.

Lila seemed off. She felt . . . different. Like she was lost in thought, but not in the way she usually was. I brushed it off, assuming she was just processing everything she had seen in the book, like I had been after seeing it yesterday.

"I'm kind of surprised you got Cillian a gift, Ava . . . Aren't you totally against Christmas presents?" Her tone was uncharacteristically casual. "I'm pretty sure Elliot told me once you refused to buy him anything . . . ever." She let out a laugh, but it sounded hollow, forced.

"That is indeed true, yes," I said plainly, sensing the weirdness in her but choosing not to comment.

She stopped in her tracks. "Well, that must have been some good fucking sex."

My jaw dropped wide enough to catch a snowflake in it. "Did you, my holy saint sister, just say 'fucking' and 'sex' in the same sentence?" I whispered, like it was a sin to say it out loud in public. "Geez, I must be rubbing off on you."

"You just got a Christmas gift for a man from a hundred years ago who doesn't even technically exist," she said, gesturing to the bag. "How could I *not* say those two words?"

"When did you become the voice of reason when it came to all of this? Besides, how do you know it's for Cillian? It could be for anyone." I raised my nose. "Maybe I bought it for myself? Ever think of that? What's wrong with a single girl buying herself a little Christmas gift? Huh?"

Lila rolled her eyes, lacing her arm in mine as we scuttled across the packed, ice-covered streets, dodging traffic. "Well, even though it's out of character for you, he's going to love it, Ava. It's perfect for him." Her tone softened a little, almost back to normal, but I couldn't shake the odd feeling I'd noticed in her after she'd seen the company history book.

She seemed distracted, like something about the pages had left her with even more questions. But I didn't push it. I assumed it was better to let it go for now. If anything was seriously off, she would tell me. Lila was a terrible liar and had always been horrible at keeping secrets. Whatever it was, she wouldn't be able to keep it from me for long.

We walked arm in arm the rest of the way to the hotel, but the thought that the first gift I'd bought in over ten years was for a dead man messed with me more than I wanted to admit.

21

"AND . . . THAT IS PERFECT," I SAID, CURLING THE LAST PIECE OF Lila's hair before we headed downstairs that evening for The Velvet Clover Christmas party, circa 1925.

Lila turned to look at herself in the mirror, gasping at the finished product—her long blonde hair in retro finger curls, with deep red lips that went perfectly with her hair. She wore a silver silk embroidered dress with fringe at the bottom, a headband with a feather, and my fur shawl.

It hit me that this might be Lila's last night here, if she decided to fly home tomorrow morning. It made the evening feel even more precious and special.

I had one side of my hair pinned back, leaving all my curls hanging on my right with a side part, wearing a deep blue velvet, long-sleeved, floor length dress, paired with a dark smoky eye.

"Well, we definitely scream 1920's Christmas cheer," I said, squeezing her shoulders from behind as we both looked in the mirror.

I checked the time. Almost nine fifteen.

"Agreed," she said, still in awe of her reflection.

She grabbed her clutch, I grabbed Cillian's gift, and we headed downstairs to the party.

I was surprised to see there were actual people in The Fitzgerald Hotel restaurant tonight. So Chris Kringle was way too busy to entertain us with our—my—usual antics. Or any of Lila's investigative questions that she would be too shy to ask when it came down to it. That I would end up asking. That he would end up dodging completely.

At exactly nine twenty-five, he nodded us over, and we snuck behind the velvet curtain before anyone noticed we were there. It was like it had become a cute little routine we had going, just the three of us. Was Santa-Hat-Wearing Chris Kringle growing on me? No, he couldn't be. Impossible.

The speakeasy unfolded before us as it had every night prior. It was somehow even more magical than it had been all the nights before. As usual, it was packed with people—no doubt over capacity, though that hadn't been much of a concern back then. I was sure there were no fire codes in 1925, considering you could still get away with murder pretty easily. But alas, I wasn't a cop, so none of that was really my problem.

Saoirse was ready to greet us as soon as we walked in. Her smile grew even bigger when she saw us. "Ava! Lila! Welcome. I was so hoping ye'd make it this evenin'." Her usual professionalism softened a bit, and her teenage self shone through as she stepped around the hostess stand to embrace my sister and me with a warm hug.

"Lila, I was telling you earlier that Saoirse here is actually Cillian's beautiful daughter."

The comment lit Saoirse up like a Christmas tree. Like the sliver of recognition meant something to her.

"Yes, of course. You are so beautiful. And so *young* to be working every night. That is very impressive," Lila commented.

"Thank ye, ladies. I love being around da bar with such a great group of people. Plus, it keeps me close to me dad," she said with a smile, glancing at me at Cillian's mention. "It is jampacked in here tonight, but Eddie told me that Mrs. Carrington here requested we reserve you a table. Can I show ye yer way dere?"

"Oh, yes, please," Lila said, clapping her hands, bouncing on her toes.

We passed through the packed crowd; women, as usual, sitting in men's laps. People were literally stacked on top of each other. Everyone was either drinking, smoking, or dancing —or all of the above.

A live band played jazz in the corner, couples danced between the tables, and there was a swarm of men standing around the bar since the seats were all taken. The place was a total haze of smoke, musk, and whiskey. It was energizing in a strange way—magical.

"People really take the holiday seriously here, huh?" I asked.

"Ya have no idea, Ms. Hawthorne." Saoirse's eyes got big as she sat us at our table, tucked in the quietest part of the speakeasy. Thank God.

As we took our seat, I noticed it was close to the door that Kringle had told us not to go out of. Maybe we would be able to peek out of it when patrons came or went.

"Eddie'll be over soon, or of course, feel free to head up to da bar at any time to order. He's quite busy tonight. Enjoy, ladies. I am so glad ya made it this evenin'," she said, placing her hand on the table and pausing for a moment, like she was about to say something else, but she didn't before turning and heading back to her stand.

"Well, on the plus side, she clearly fancies you," Lila offered. "She'd be so stoked to have you as a stepmom."

"Not that that's a possibility, but yes," I said sarcastically. "I'm so relieved that my dead boyfriend from 1925 has a dead daughter who approves of me, so that when we have a fake relationship that doesn't exist, it will somehow matter."

"Touche," Lila said, staring at her menu.

I'd never wanted to be a mom—or a stepmom for that matter. That had always felt like the absolute last thing on my to-do list. But with Cillian . . . and Saoirse . . . it didn't feel so unbearable. In fact, the idea of the three of us sitting in a corner booth at the speakeasy, Saoirse curled up beside me, her head on my shoulder, while Cillian changed the song on the gramophone, looking over at us like we were his whole world, hit me in a place I hadn't expected. It felt warm. It felt right. Like something I hadn't realized I'd been searching for.

I shook it off. That would never happen. It couldn't. I had already accepted this when Lila and I had talked through it all. But when I was here, I couldn't help but imagine it. Couldn't help but want to find a way to make it possible. It all felt so real.

"You look pretty, sis," I said, looking at Lila, her face lit only by the candlelight on the table. "I'm so glad you came with me on this trip. I will miss you when you leave tomorrow."

There was a slight hesitation before she smiled at me. Her fingers briefly tensed around the menu. "So am I. It has been good for us. A wild turn of events . . . but I am so glad I came. Even though I miss Simon and the girls, I think it's been good for me to get some time away. I feel like I've hit the reset button. Speaking of, have you called Dad yet?"

I gave her a stupid look for asking a stupid question.

"Ladies," Eddie, with his perfect timing, and his burgundy shirt and suspenders, called to us as he found our table from across the bar. He let out a whistle and made his way over to us. "Quite da crowd, eh?"

"I'll say!" Lila shouted back to him.

"We appreciate you saving us a table, Eddie. Being in all of that"—I gestured to the rest of the craziness of the speakeasy—"would have been my worst nightmare."

"Anytin' for a woman who lights up Cillian in the way ye do, Ms. Ava," he said, placing a warm grip on my shoulder. His hands were so big, if he squeezed, he could have crushed it. "What are ye ladies goin' to go with tonight? Whiskey? My Eddie's Christmas Speci—"

"No, no," Lila jumped in right away, wagging her finger then tapping her temple. "I am pretty sure I am still drunk from those," she said, letting out a laugh. "Not that they weren't amazing," she affirmed.

"Eddie, we will get the ladies their own special bottle of champagne," a voice so distinct it could be no one else but him.

Cillian walked up behind Eddie, placing a hand on his shoulder, a lit cigarette dangling between his lips.

"Let's put it on ice for dem, Ed. Only da best for these two. Eh?"

"Yes, sir." Eddie saluted before fulfilling the captain's order without question or hesitation.

Cillian stood tall, in a tailored black tuxedo. Black studs ran down the front of his shirt. As he put his hand in his pocket, I could see his suspenders peek through. He was a spitting image of 1920's male perfection. But better. Perfection of any decade. His angular cheekbones and jaw, his piercing blue eyes, his hair neatly trimmed.

I searched his face for even the faintest trace of the stress I'd seen yesterday, but there was nothing. He seemed calm. Collected. Like the mini emotional meltdown from the day before had never happened. I chalked it up to one of three things: one, he just needed to feel like someone was in his corner and knowing I was there for him was enough; two, he was a damn good actor and didn't want to show cracks in front of his bar guests during the holidays; or three, the sex had somehow erased every ounce of tension from his life. Though unlikely, I couldn't help but hope that number three had been the solution to his problems.

"I like this white scarf you're rocking, Cill," Lila said, pointing to his chest

"Rockin'?" he asked, leaning in as if he'd misheard.

"You know, like stylish. Classy. Must be a Colorado slang thing." She laughed nervously, glancing at me. "But really, you look"—she clicked her tongue—"wow."

He gave her a small straight smile, patting her back gently in thanks. I could visibly see his resistance to receiving compliments. That was an Irish thing, as well—physically rejecting any sort of compliment. "Well, thank you, Lila. That's very kind of you. You look lovely yourself; this color suits you."

He slowly brought his attention to me, sitting with my legs crossed at the ankle, my hands resting in my lap. Everything he did, how he moved, it was like he was in slow motion. It made me want to watch. Have to watch. To look. To wait for what he would do next. He put me in a trance, captivated me so I couldn't look away. But it wasn't just his physical presence that held me—it was the way he understood me without words, like we shared a language only the two of us could speak.

It was only now that I realized that the last time I'd been with him, we'd been naked in this place, having sex. As the thought crossed my mind, it was like he was thinking the same thing, giving me a knowing look. He was in my mind. Infiltrating my every thought.

He reached out for my hand. "Ava." I expected him to kiss my hand, but he pulled me to my feet and brought me in for a passionate kiss, lacing his fingers around the back of my neck. The other, with his cigarette, wrapped tightly around my waist. The familiarity of his touch made something stir inside me, a reminder of how perfectly we fit together.

I could feel Lila's look of shock that was plastered on her face.

I pulled back, giving him a look before wrapping my arms around his neck and pulling him in for a hug. He let out an audible laugh and buried his face in my neck. It felt like I'd just seen him yesterday, and somehow, like it had been a hundred years. Like I missed him even when he was right in front of me. Like, one day, one minute without him was already one too many.

My heart ached beneath it all, at the reality of the situation. But while I was here, the rest of the world and its problems could just fall away, if only for a little while.

"I am so glad ya made it. Ya smell amazing," he said.

In response, I squeezed him tighter before releasing him and holding his face with both hands, planting one more kiss on his lips. I grabbed one of his suspenders and snapped it against his chest. He wasn't fazed. All I could see in his eyes was desire. Desire for me.

"Would you like to join us?" I offered as I sat back down in the booth.

"I will be back in, say fifteen minutes? Just need to take care of a few hooligans, shake some hands, and kiss some babies. Politics, you know. Then I am all yers, both of ya. Eh?" he said, looking at me, then Lila, then back to me.

"Yes," I said.

"Good. In case I lose you to the dance floor with Eddie tonight," he said to Lila, "I am expecting the two of you for Christmas Eve and Christmas Day."

We both smiled at him, but Lila's smile faltered. She looked away.

He disappeared into the crowd, already being stopped by half the room wanting to talk to the boss.

I looked at Lila. She looked sad.

"You can stay, sis. You really don't have to take that flight," I said.

"I know, I know. I need to decide what I am going to do. But let's not talk about that right now. Let's talk about *that*." Lila looked at me, eyes wide, gesturing toward Cillian.

I threw up my hands in disbelief at what a dream he was. "I know."

"He is literally *perfect*," she said.

"I know," I repeated.

"Have you decided if you are going to tell him tonight?" she asked. "It doesn't really seem like he wants just a fling, sis."

"I haven't decided yet. We already get such a small window of time together. I don't want to freak him out and ruin it. Maybe I could tell him if I come for Christmas."

"But if you don't, and all of this ends on or after Christmas, he'll be absolutely devastated," Lila said. "Really, you shouldn't worry about scaring him off. You could tell that man you're a unicorn, and he'd probably build you a custom stable and learn to muck your unicorn poop out himself, just to keep you around. He's so in love with you."

"He is not."

She gave me a bored look. "I think you should tell him. I would want to know," she said as Eddie came over with our bottle of champagne on a bucket of ice, as Cillian had instructed.

Lila's words lingered, and I couldn't help but wonder what it would be like to tell Cillian the truth tonight. How would I even say it? *Hey, by the way, I'm actually from one hundred years in the future. Oh, and I'm working for your great-grandson.* A chill ran down my spine at the thought.

Did he really need to know? What would the truth even give him, besides heartbreak? The same heartbreak I was experiencing. I couldn't burden him with that. But his feelings were involved. And so were mine. He looked at me like I was his present and his future. But if I told him the truth, would he feel betrayed? Would it break something between us? Everything with us had been so amazing. I would hate to destroy it with the truth.

I knew I had to tell him eventually, and I would. But I didn't know if I could muster that courage tonight. I pictured myself opening up to him, finally telling him, only for him to look at me like I was crazy. I could see it now—his disbelief, his rejection, how it would feel like I gave everything away to him, only to have him shut me out. Abandon me. To walk away and leave me. No, thank you.

I glanced behind Lila at the door. The one we only *hoped* led to 1925. A guest was just about to leave, drink in hand and a fur scarf slung over her shoulder. As she opened it, a soft gust of cold air swept in, curling around my ankles. I watched as she stepped over the threshold, and for the briefest moment, I could've sworn she didn't walk *out* so much as she dissolved into something. Not a street. Not snow. Just . . . darkness. A shifting, humming void that swallowed her whole. Then the door clicked shut again as if nothing had happened.

I blinked and shook it off, turning my focus back to Lila— and to all the other problems waiting for me beyond that mysterious door that led to who knew where.

A glass of champagne later, Lila started to mingle with other guests. Cillian joined me at our table exactly fifteen minutes after he'd said he would. He was punctual; I'd give him that much.

After what felt like an eternity of canoodling and kissing, we finally came up for air.

"So, how did Mr. President do with his political duties out there in this rough-and-tumble speakeasy?" I asked.

"Oi, it isn't easy business, but someone has to do it?" he said, kissing my nose.

I nodded. "Well, you seem like a natural."

"Nah. It's just me job," he deflected. "Ya being in public relations, ye've got to be far better at politics than some man who came out of da war."

"I'm good at it when I choose to be, but that's rare," I said, turning toward him in my seat.

He placed his hand on my cheek, rubbing his thumb gently on my skin. His touch was soft, despite the calluses on his hands. He was so gentle with me. He was also capable of killing people in a war. I wished everyone could see this side of him, this soft, sweet side of him. I felt lucky—*so lucky*—that I was the one who got to witness his true self. It made me feel special.

Should I tell him now? The thought made my heart race. What if it scared him away? What if he thought I was insane? What if it broke me? What if he broke my heart?

The words were on the tip of my tongue, but instead, I went with the safer route.

"I have something for you," I said, keeping my eyes locked on his. My palms started to sweat.

"You didn't get me a Christmas gift, Ava," he said in a tone that implied he hated receiving gifts as much as I *usually* hated giving them. But for him, I wanted to give him something that would make him smile. Something that would make him happy. Make him feel as special as he made me feel.

"You're gonna shut up and open it." I said.

He threw his hands up in surrender. "All right, go on then," he said, settling back in his chair and waving his hand as if to say, *Go ahead; give it to me.*

"Eek," I said before I realized I'd officially sounded like Lila when she got all girly and squealy.

A surprised look crossed his face, like seeing this side—a softer side of me—was a shock to him as much as it was for me.

I pulled the gift out from behind my back. His brow twitched at the box as I handed it to him.

He looked at me as he ripped off the wrapping paper gently. He opened the white box to reveal the hand-crafted bow tie. "Ava," he said, not able to take his eyes off of it. "It is . . . it's beautiful." His voice was just above a whisper before he cleared his throat. He pursed his lips before looking at me. His eyes started to swell with tears. He sniffed and pushed it down.

"Here." He handed the tie to me as he unfolded the collar of his shirt. "Will ya do me the honor of tying me bow tie for me, love?"

"Of course I will," I said, grinning from ear-to-ear. "You like it?" I asked, wrapping it around the back of his neck. Somehow, tying a man's tie was even sexier than untying it.

He stared into my eyes. "It is the most beautiful gift I 'ave ever been given. Thank you, Ava," he said, placing his hand on my knee, giving it a warm, long squeeze. "Ya know I planned on giving ya yer gift on Christmas Day. It's kind of da rule."

"That just means you haven't done your shopping yet. And since when do you follow the rules?" I asked.

"It's tradition."

"Fair . . . Well, you should feel lucky I got you anything. This was the first Christmas present I have bought in . . . Jesus, probably over a decade," I said.

He looked shocked.

"Relax. I'll tell you what, next year, I will give you your gift on Christmas Day for your *tradition*," I mocked. *Next Christmas*. I'd said it like it was no big deal, like that kind of future was even possible. But was it? I didn't *know* if I could ever come back. Coming back tomorrow was not guaranteed. Not really. Next Christmas certainly wasn't.

I shook the thought off before it could root too deeply.

"There," I said, straightening the bow I had just tied. "It's perfect."

He leaned in and kissed my cheek. "Come," he said, standing and grabbing my hand, guiding me to the separate room where we had dinner one night and sex the other. What could be next for the room that already held so many firsts for us?

He paused and looked at me before rolling the double doors open to reveal a man taking photos. The camera alone resolved any remaining glimmer of doubt that I had about this truly being 1925. It was basically a box with a mirror and a lens. A man stood under a black curtain, holding a flash box. So retro.

"I want a picture with you, and now that I have my bow tie, I feel complete," he said.

"A *picture*? Are you sure?" I asked, my voice shaky. A knot tightened in my stomach as it hit me. If I took this photograph with him, could I be messing with time? Could I actually change the future if there was physical proof I was in the past? Would this photo show up in some history book at Barnes & Noble? Or worse—the atelier's company history book? A photo was physical, tangible proof of me being here. And that made the repercussions of my actions here feel more real than before.

I couldn't shake the feeling that every small decision, every interaction, might be unraveling something bigger in the future, something I didn't understand. Until now, it had been abstract. But a photo? That was too real.

"Come on; have you ever had your picture taken? It is quite fun," he said, his fingers laced in mine.

"A few times, I guess," I lied. Only a million with my iPhone.

He took me straight to the front of the line, no one questioning the boss.

"Chester, I would like a picture with this beautiful woman," he told the photographer.

"Yes, Mr. Broderick sir, step right up," Chester said, adjusting his lens.

"Wow, this camera is so cool." I stood behind it and reached out to touch it. Cillian was already standing by the fireplace, waiting.

"Chester, could I try taking one? I've never used one of these before," I asked, half-mesmerized by its antiqueness, half-stalling. If I could drag this out just a little longer, maybe they'd forget I was supposed to be in front of the lens.

He cocked his head in confusion, but he flashed a look at

Cillian, who only nodded to him, silently communicating, *If you don't let her do it, I will fire you.*

"Of course, miss. Put yer head under this curtain here, I will hold the flash box. All you need to do is look at the screen, center Mr. Broderick in the lens, and when you are ready, press dis button here." He handed me a small, corded device with one red button that looked like if I pressed it, a bomb or some sort of explosives would go off.

"Okay, just act natural, Mr. Broderick," I said, winking before putting my head under the curtain, bent at the waist to fit beneath it. I angled him front and center as he lit a cigarette that was now dangling from his mouth. He leaned back, hands in his pockets, the fireplace behind him. "Oh, you look *so* handsome," I said, and at that moment, as I snapped the photo, a hint of a smile crossed his face.

"Perfect, miss!" the photographer said. "Yer a natural."

As I saw Cillian through the lens, I gasped. *This* was the image. The cigarette, the tuxedo and white scarf, and the damn bow tie that I had gotten him.

My breath caught. Had this photo always been in the book? Or had I just created it? Did that mean Lila and I were always meant to be here and our fate was already destined, since I had already seen it in the book?

My pulse raced as I stayed under the curtain, frozen. If Cillian and I took a photo, would it show up in Ronan's book tomorrow—more tangible proof that I was changing the future?

Compose yourself. I slowly stepped out from under the curtain, my hands shaking.

"All right then, come. Oi," Cillian said, waving me over with two fingers. "You've had your fun, darlin', now it's our turn."

"No, I really shouldn't," I said, brushing him off with a wave. "I don't think I photograph well." A total lie. I photographed like a damn super model.

Cillian tilted his head, his brow raising slightly. "I hardly believe that's possible, Ava, love. Come. Don't be scared."

"I'm not scared," I snapped, sharper than I'd meant to sound.

He was right; insecurity was off-brand for me. I couldn't have him seeing through me, to start questioning. I could always steal the picture later. Sneak into the atelier and grab the book tomorrow, destroy the photo before Ronan had a chance of seeing it. If it did, in fact, show up. I didn't really see any other way to get out of this.

Whatever. Here we go.

"Come, come, Ava." He grabbed my hand.

"Yeah. Yeah, of course," I said, as I walked over and stood by his side, giving him a look. "Are we smiling?"

He looked at me in confusion. Of course, no one smiled in pictures back then. Today. Now. *Whatever.*

"Okay, I'm ready," I said, staring blankly into the picture box. I felt Cillian's strong frame next to me as his hand settled on my waist, pulling me in close. His warmth radiated through the thick fabric between us, the energy sending a shockwave through me.

Chester took the photo. "Got it," he said. "Beautiful couple you two are."

Cillian looked at me with those eyes—those *fucking eyes* that communicated so much without a single word. My breath hitched. Then he leaned in and kissed me.

Chester's shutter clicked again—a bright flash, capturing the moment in an instant.

———

Hours blurred into a haze of drinking, laughing, and kissing. My anxiety over the picture drifted to the back of my mind. I would deal with it when I was back in 2025.

The band began to play a slow song, and Cillian stood. "Will you do me the honor of another dance, Ms. Hawthorne?"

I smiled. "I will, Mr. Broderick." I took his hand as he pulled me to my feet.

He drew me close, holding me tight to his chest. It was safe here, I reminded myself. I let myself relax, surrendering into him. I brushed my cheek against his, my lips grazing the sharp edge of his jaw.

He led our slow dance with footwork far fancier than I could follow.

"Can I tell ya something, Ava?" he asked.

"How you got so good at dancing?" I asked, glancing down at his feet, trying to keep up.

"No," he said, slowing us to a near stop. He slid his hands to either side of my hips. "Every time I've needed ya, ye've been here," he said, his voice low. "Like ya arrived out of nowhere. When I didn't even know what I needed, ya just . . . came into my life."

"What do you mean?"

"Every time ye've come to da speakeasy . . . either moments before ya arrived, or earlier in the day, I prayed to whoever runs this fuckin' world, to whoever decides our fate here on Earth, and I asked for you—someone—to come. Even before I knew ya, that first night ye came . . ." He trailed off, shaking his head like he thought I'd think he was crazy. It was cute that *he* thought *I* would think *he* was crazy, when I was actively choosing to time travel to see him each night.

I said nothing. A chill ran through me—not entirely fear, but definitely not comfort. What were the odds? What were the actual chances that someone in the 1920s had been unknowingly calling me into their life, decades before I was even born? Was it romantic? Yes. But it also made the hair on the back of my neck stand up. Like something—or someone—was orchestrating all of this. That I had absolutely no control over my actions. I wasn't sure if that thrilled me or absolutely petrified me.

Nope . . . it petrified me. Definitely petrified.

All I could manage was a small smile. I needed him to keep talking because I didn't know what to say.

He continued, "I asked for someone like ya to come into me world and shake things up. Then dere ye were, sitting at me damn communal table." He gestured toward the corner where we'd first met.

"I've been carrying so much for so long, trying to keep everythin' together, keep everyone at arm's length. I hadn't realized how much I needed someone who could see me, *really* see me—not the image I put out there, but the man beneath it all. And you . . . ye're exactly that."

"Really?"

"Yes. Yesterday, when ya showed up during the day, I didn't even realize I'd been asking for ya. But once ye were here, on some random afternoon, when we weren't even open—ya were exactly what I needed, what I had asked for just moments before. Like some answered prayer."

That word, *need*, I couldn't believe he would ever utter that word, especially when it came to a woman. When it came to me. He needed me? I didn't think he would ever need anything, from anyone, ever.

"You don't *need* anything," I said, dismissing everything he had just said to protect my heart from breaking, knowing that the truth of our future together was likely impossible.

He grabbed the sides of my face, his callused hands rough on my skin. I didn't care. It only made him that much more swoon-worthy.

"I need ya, Ava. I fucking need ya." His words were thick with desire, like I was a requirement. "I need you more than I need oxygen, water . . . food, or warmth. I have needed ya more than I 'ave ever needed anything in me life."

Somehow, I didn't find him weak when he said it. It sounded corny, but it was simultaneously the sweetest nectar I'd ever heard. If anything, it made him seem stronger than ever.

I placed my hand over his. I pulled his palm to my mouth and kissed it. This was so corny. So cringy. I used to hate people who acted like this, who said things like this. But with him? I loved it.

He'd asked for me, and I'd appeared? He had called out, and somehow, I had been brought here? Was that the only reason I'd found my way to this speakeasy? Was that why I'd made it through during the day? Because he had called into the void and asked for something? For me? And I was the answer?

All this time, I thought I was here on *my* timeline. *My* agenda. *My* free will. But what if I wasn't? What if it was him all along, asking for me? Was that why I'd felt the strange pull to the speakeasy? Even when I knew, against my better judgment, I shouldn't come back? Shouldn't get involved? But it felt like I couldn't stay away. Like there was an invisible cord tying me to this place. To him.

My heart ached with how badly I wanted to believe it—that we were connected by something bigger than logic or time. Something I couldn't understand but felt in my bones. That thought, that same hope, equally terrified me.

And underneath it all was the heaviness of what I hadn't told him. The truth.

This is it, Ava. You have to say it. It's now or never.

My pulse quickened.

It's not fair to either of you to keep it from him. He deserves to know the truth.

I took a deep breath. "Can I tell *you* something?" I asked, trying to keep my words steady.

Doubt started creeping in. *He won't believe you. He'll think you're crazy. What if it messes everything up? What if it breaks something in history you were never meant to touch? What if he leaves you?*

Concern flashed across his face as he scanned me like I was hurt. Like he wanted to protect me. Clearing his throat, he said, "Yes, of course. Are ya okay?"

I couldn't help but love that his first thought was for my safety. Men.

You can't wait any longer. I inhaled deeply, steading my nerves.

He deserves to know the truth, even if it shatters everything.

I really needed to work on my pep talks.

"Yes, of course, I'm fine," I said, my eyes drifting to the floor as I searched for the words. I was never at a loss for words. I was in public relations, goddammit. I knew how to make a bad situation sound like a positive.

But this . . . this was different. There was no way to make this situation sound positive. Not even neutral. There was no twisting this image. There was no angle. No spin. No clever way to frame this mess as anything other than what it was. A mess. A tragic mess.

"I . . . I am not from here," was the best I could manage.

"I know that. Ye're from San Francisco, yeah?" he said calmly, still scanning my face for any hint of danger.

I closed my eyes, taking another deep breath to steady myself. If I didn't tell him now, I might lose the only real connection I'd had in ages—ever—even if it was just for a week. He had been so open, so vulnerable with me. I couldn't hurt him.

"No, Cillian," I said, my voice firmer now. "I wasn't born in the 1800s or early 1900s. I was born in 1992. The year I'm from is 2025 . . ."

His expression shifted from concern to utter confusion. And rightfully fucking so.

I braced myself.

"Lila and I both. We're staying at The Fitzgerald Hotel. Some annoying, too-jolly, Santa-hat-wearing bartender snuck me into the speakeasy that first night I was here, and it wasn't until a few nights later that I knew for sure . . . that I had . . . time-traveled. I thought this was just a 1920's-themed speakeasy, where everyone does hardcore role play. Like some murder mystery party or something." I had said the words, knowing full well how crazy I sounded.

His brows knitted together, as if he was trying to track what I was saying. I guessed that finally confirmed if he knew anything about the time travel. He looked absolutely clueless.

He said nothing, so I kept talking, the words tumbling out faster than I could organize them. I should have written down some talking points.

"The Aislinn Atelier I told you about, I took the job."

His brows raised, a flicker of excitement, before the confusion deepened.

"More on that later. But when I was there, telling them I accepted the position, they showed me the company history . . . and you were in it. That's when I found out your last name, and Aislinn's name. Saoirse, and her daughter, and grandson, who runs the atelier now, in 2025. I saw it all." I paused for a second, trying to calm the fear bubbling up in my chest. "That was why I came here during the day. I was shocked I got through. The only time the speakeasy opens is at nine twenty-five each night. Or so I thought. Other than that, it's just been some broom closet in the hotel restaurant we're staying at."

I watched his eyes narrow even further.

"Okay, maybe that's too much information," I said, my voice shaking. "But I had to tell you. I couldn't keep this from you any longer, not when I have real feelings for you." I took his hand, placing it on my chest, letting him feel my heart race beneath his palm.

"I originally planned to have a fun week with you and then

head back to San Francisco—back to my real life. But after the last few days . . . spending time with you, being here at the speakeasy, getting to know you—I haven't been able to stop thinking about you. About what starting a life with you would be like.

"You've been so . . . *there* for me. And then I found myself wanting to buy you a goddamn Christmas present." I let out a breath, shaking my head. "I've been trying to figure it all out. Whether this is really 1925 . . . or if it was all just some elaborate, messed-up Christmas magic prank from that ridiculous bartender.

"I've never felt this way before, Cillian. I don't know how any of this is supposed to work or what's even possible, but I want to try. I *need* to try. I want to be with you, no matter how complicated or insane it all sounds."

The words poured out faster than I'd expected, but they felt true—the truest thing I'd said in a long time. Also the scariest. The most vulnerable, for sure. My heart was pounding, but not from fear. From *knowing*.

"I didn't realize I felt as strongly as I did until yesterday, after we . . . after everything." I looked into his eyes, grounding myself in them. "I told myself I could live with the fact that there might be no way for us to have a future together. That I could just walk away and be okay. That this was just some Christmas fling that I would leave behind. But now? Being here with you like this, I'm clear. Completely. I can't lose you. I want to find a way for us to be in each other's futures."

I wasn't just falling for him—I had already fallen. It felt like I'd stepped through that mysterious door across the bar and was in free-fall, plunging into an endless void. Into nothingness.

There was a long pause. Cillian stared at me, his eyes locked on mine. No blinking. No movement. As if we'd been suspended in time as the world continued to spin around us.

There was only silence. I could see him trying to piece everything together.

He opened his mouth, about to speak. To finally say something. But no words came. I couldn't read a single thing in his eyes. I couldn't tell if he was about to say something comforting or if he thought I was completely batshit crazy.

Did he think I was crazy? Probably. I couldn't blame him. Maybe I was.

His lips parted as he started to speak again. "Ava, I—"

But before he could say another word, a sharp bang echoed from the other side of the bar—the main entrance where guests came and went. The same door where I had watched a woman vanish into thin air.

That sound sliced through the air, pulling us abruptly from our fragile moment, reminding me once again how thin the veil between our worlds really was.

Guests started screaming, their panic rising in the air like a suffocating wave. Cillian's gaze locked onto mine, and it felt like time slowed to a crawl. Then I saw something in his eyes—a depth of recognition—that sent a chill racing down my spine. Like in that split-second, he was trying to communicate everything he was thinking without a single word. The intensity in his stare said it all: something bad was about to happen. And whatever it was, it was here.

Chaos erupted around us. The music stopped abruptly, the once lively atmosphere now replaced with frantic footsteps, the sound of broken glasses, and muffled shouts. People were scrambling to the exit, but there was no clear path to safety. The door on the far side of the bar—the main entrance—was now a blur of movement, with figures darting in and out, evaporating after crossing the threshold, trying to flee from whatever danger had entered. I could feel my pulse quicken, my chest tightening as the air grew heavier.

Cillian didn't break eye contact, but his expression had

shifted. There was a tension in his jaw, the muscles working as if he were preparing—bracing—for something. Like he was already aware of what was coming.

Guests screamed, their voices rising in panic. Cillian pulled me in, pressing his lips to mine in a desperate kiss, his hands cupping both sides of my face. Before I could process it, he pulled away. The first wave of police officers flooded into the speakeasy—five, then ten, then twenty. People screamed, dropping their drinks, while others rushed toward the exit.

I caught Lila's eyes from across the room. She was already making her way toward me, moving fast through the madness, pushing through the crowd of people. Just as I looked back for Cillian, his hand slipped out of mine. My heart stopped as I turned toward him, only to see a police officer yanking his arms behind his back, cuffs clicking around his wrists. Everything was happening in slow motion, like some cruel dream I couldn't wake up from.

"No. Cillian!" I screamed, reaching out for him. My voice was lost in the pandemonium as cops and terrified patrons wedged themselves between us. I fought through the crowd, my hands outstretched, desperate to reach him. I had to follow him.

Cillian's eyes remained steady on me. Unshaken. Calm.

"Stay calm, Ava," he yelled, his voice clear and commanding above the chaos. "I will find ya. I will be back, all right?" His eyes locked onto mine, wide and intense.

I nodded, but my whole world was crumbling.

I stopped fighting, my body going still. "Okay," I whispered to myself, covering my mouth with my hand to hold back the scream threatening to spill out.

Lila finally reached me, her eyes wide with panic.

"Come on, Ava! We have to get out of here. If we get arrested in 1925, we have no idea what they'll do to us. They might drag us through that door, and we might never be able to come back!" Lila's voice was sharp as she grabbed my arm and pulled me toward the back exit.

My eyes stayed fixed on Cillian, a sinking feeling in my chest telling me this might be the last time I'd ever see him.

The cops hauled him out, but in that moment, he turned toward me—blood trickling down his face, his eyes still locked on mine. Then he was swallowed by the crowd as the cops dragged him toward the exit across the bar, disappearing into thin air like everyone else from 1925. Vanishing completely.

The velvet curtains closed around me, and the world went dark. Everything went numb. I couldn't feel anything except Lila's hand gripping mine, yanking me through the door, pulling me back to 2025, before I had time to process what I was leaving behind.

22

I woke up next to Lila. She was already staring at me, her brows pulled together in the way they do when she's trying not to panic. Her face scrunched, like she'd been rehearsing what to say the moment I opened my eyes.

I blinked against the light, hoping—stupidly—that maybe it had all been some long fever dream. That I'd finally woken up and things would be fine again. But the look in her eyes told me everything I needed to know.

It had been real. All of it. And I was still here.

"Are you okay?" she asked.

I stared at the sliver of light trying to force its way through the curtains. The world outside felt distant.

"He'll be fine," I snapped, though I wasn't sure I believed it. Maybe if I said it enough, it would start to feel true. "He saw this coming. He has a plan. He has to." I felt numb. My denial sounded pathetic, even to me.

Inside, my heart was in a free fall, but I couldn't show it. Not now. Not when everything was so uncertain. My mind was racing, thoughts scattered, but I clamped down on them. I had to be tough. I had to shut it down.

This was why I didn't let myself get real feelings for someone. Because when you cared, everything became fragile. Delicate. Everything could fall apart when you least expected it. The second you let your guard down, you became breakable. I couldn't afford to be broken right now.

Flipping on my PR crisis mode persona, I shoved every emotionally fragile ounce I had left deep inside. I couldn't show fear. Not in front of her. Not in front of anyone.

"What time do you have to leave for the airport?" I asked, grasping something—*anything*—to distract myself from the heartbreak that felt like an open wound.

Lila hesitated, reaching for her phone. "Well . . . that's the other thing." She turned the screen toward me. A red alert banner flashed across the top.

WINTER WEATHER WARNING: ALL FLIGHTS TO AND FROM NYC CANCELLED DUE TO SEVERE WEATHER CONDITIONS.

I blinked. "Wait, seriously?" I got up, rushed over to the window, and peeked out at the narrow gap between the buildings. Snow was already piled high on the street, and it kept falling.

She nodded. "I've already checked five different airlines and all three airports out of New York. Everything's grounded through at least tonight. Most likely tomorrow. I can't get home. I just texted Simon and the girls to let them know. They are fine, just wanting to make sure I am safe. I'll call them later."

A bitter laugh escaped me. "Perfect. We're snowed in. On

Christmas." At least now I wouldn't be alone. That was something. And maybe Lila would finally stop wavering and feeling guilty about whether she should go home or not. Now, she could just be present and really be here.

Lila shrugged. "Guess New York decided I'm staying whether I like it or not."

I glanced at her. She seemed almost excited to stay.

"I'm selfishly glad you're stuck here. I'm really grateful you'll be with me through this shit show, Lil. But I'm sorry you'll miss Christmas with your family."

"It's all good. Mom sharing what she did gave me some peace of mind. Her comment about having my own life, and that being inspiring to the girls, really helped. I'm excited to stay, knowing I did everything I could to get home. I guess it's a sign from the universe. It's meant to be that I'm here with you. Speaking of, do you think we should still go tonight? Cillian said we should join them for Christmas. Or do you think the speakeasy will be shut down? It might be dangerous to go back."

"Of course we'll go. Why wouldn't we?" I snapped, trying to sound normal, even as everything inside me cracked. Sometimes, complete denial really was the only PR strategy. It made everyone around you question their own instincts. Wonder if they were crazy, even when you were the crazy one. Which, if I'm not mistaken is what most therapists would call gaslighting.

Lila sat in silence.

I paced back to the window, staring at the mostly closed curtains like I was staring at a skyline that wasn't visible. Damn this viewless room.

My mind flashed to the speakeasy. I'd gotten in once when it wasn't nine twenty-five p.m. Maybe the clock wasn't the only way in.

Cillian had said that when he'd needed me, I'd come. Which was odd. What if I could get in again? What if I figured out what was happening before tonight? I wasn't ready to admit how badly I wanted answers. Or how much I had to see him, to make sure he was okay.

"Ava, did something happen before the cops came?" Lila asked.

I stopped pacing. It killed me to have to tell her—to embarrass myself like this—but she'd been around for all of this mess so far. Plus, she had kids. That had to raise your tolerance for embarrassing moments, right? Might as well let her see it through.

"I finally told him. Everything. About the time travel. What year you and I are from. The atelier. Ronan. All of it."

I cringed just thinking about it. My chest burned at the memory. It was the first time I'd let myself be that open, and it felt like I'd swallowed glass. Sharp, lodged in my throat and between my ribs.

She gasped, "You did? Oh, Ava, I am so proud of you. What did he say?"

"He didn't have time to say anything. I talked too fucking much, and right as he was about to say something, shit hit the fan and the cops showed up."

Her hand shot to her mouth. "Oh! I am so sorry, Ava."

I had given him my heart, my truth, laid it all out there. And now, it was falling apart. What if I had pushed him away with the truth?

My mind was spinning with worst-case scenarios, imagining him rejecting me or pulling away.

But then the cruelest thought hit me—none of it even mattered. He was from a hundred years in the *past*. This whole thing—my feelings for him, everything—was pointless. None of it was *really* real. He didn't belong here. I certainly didn't belong there. And I was never supposed to. How could I have been so stupid to think I could have a future, even a week of a future, with someone who would never truly be able to be *here* with me?

Suddenly, everything felt pathetic. There was no "us." There was never going to be an "us."

I looked away from the sliver of light in the window to my sister, my face expressionless. "He told me he needed me."

Lila's eyes widened.

"I told him I wanted to make it work. To be with him. To find a way."

"Av, that is *huge!* Major progress in the vulnerability department," Lila said. "That sounds like the closest thing you have had to a real relationship in a long time."

"Well, look where that got me," I said. "Oh, I forgot to mention, I somehow got roped into taking a picture with him. I tried to stall by taking one of just him, only to realize it was the photo from the company history book at the atelier. Then we had one taken of the two of us together, since I had no way to get out of it. I'm almost positive it might end up in that book at the atelier. Which means, for one, what we do in the past definitely affects the future—and maybe even the other way around. It also means either Ronan sees it and has a full-blown psychotic break, or I break into the atelier and destroy the thing."

She winced. "Okay, yeah . . . this is not ideal. But we'll have to deal with it later. It's Christmas Eve—Ronan probably won't even be at the atelier for the next few days, anyway."

She reached out, grabbing for my hand. "Ava, listen to me. It's okay to feel this way. You're not weak for caring, for opening up to someone. You're human. Yes, it might hurt like hell right now, might be terrifying, because you don't know if Cillian is all right, but that doesn't mean it was a mistake. You didn't do anything wrong by letting him in."

I swallowed hard, trying to convince myself to believe her, though every part of me felt like my whole life was unraveling.

"I told him everything, Lila! That means I actually care about him. Like I imagined some sort of delusional future together and admitted that to him. But none of it matters. None of it is even possible. I just can't believe I got so pulled into all of this. It's so embarrassing."

"Don't let this break you, Ava. You are strong. You have a future—with or without him. And who knows? There might still be a way. Nothing's certain yet."

I caught a hint of uncertainty in her eyes, the same hesitation she'd had since yesterday at the atelier. Something felt off, but I couldn't put my finger on it. Her brows furrowed like she wanted to say something but couldn't. She started to pick at her nails. "Well, let's at least go back tonight. We've gotten in every night at nine twenty-five, no problem. Who knows? Maybe he was able to pull some strings or pay the cops off. It's worth a shot."

I didn't answer right away. I flopped back down on the bed next to her, sighing. "Yeah. Fine. Let's do it. We'll try. But if it's not open tonight, I won't go back again. I can't." I couldn't.

"Should we try going earlier today? Just in case it's open and we could get through and check on Cillian sooner?"

"No. I don't think I could handle staring at that broom closet again. I'd rather wait until we know we can get in for sure." I might have an actual breakdown in that closet if I tried to get in and couldn't.

The only thing worse than showing up and him not being there, or it being nothing but a broom closet, was showing up and having him think I was insane. The idea of facing him—of him knowing how badly I'd believed in some ridiculous, impossible future—was too much. He knew the truth. And I wasn't sure I wanted to know what he thought about it.

Who knew if he'd even let me back into his bar after my unhinged confession? I was already humiliated by how exposed I'd made myself. I wasn't about to risk adding public shame on top of it—in front of a room full of dead people, no less.

Both of us sat there in silence, until she finally said, "So . . . what should we do today, then?"

"Anything." Anything to distract myself from this Christmas "magic" nightmare bullshit.

I couldn't believe this was happening on Christmas, of all days? It felt cruel, like the universe had a twisted sense of humor I didn't understand. I always did have the worst luck with Christmas. Once your father has left you on Christmas, it's like you become a crap magnet for every kind of holiday disaster after that.

———

Lila had been writing all day, tucked into the corner of a coffee shop, lost in her own world. I, on the other hand, couldn't focus to save my life. But I wasn't going to sit there and spiral, so I forced myself to open my laptop and get caught up on work. It wasn't that I felt productive, or even remotely capable of being productive, but the noise of the café and the distraction of busy work helped. A little.

I did my best to wrap up my projects at Atlas & Grey, mostly going through the motions. I jotted down notes for campaign ideas to support them in Q1 of the new year, once I officially stepped away. But it all felt like a blur. Every email, every task, passed through me like fog, like I was watching myself from the outside, detached and numb. But it was easier to distract myself with work than to face the feeling of the gaping hole in my chest, the uncertainty. I wasn't sure how much longer I could keep pretending everything was fine.

I thought a million times about trying to get in earlier but couldn't bring myself to do it. I didn't want to stand outside that curtain looking pathetic, staring at an empty broom closet until the speakeasy opened.

Nine twenty-five p.m. was our best chance of getting in. It hadn't let us down yet. So I would wait. And wait. And fucking wait. Count down the minutes and wait until I could see if he was alive. Count down the seconds until I could see if Cillian was all right. If *we* would be all right.

God, I was becoming a *we* girl. Just like my sister. We this. We that. I was an *I* girl, dammit. Not a *we* with some dead guy.

Once Lila and I hit our limit on how much work we could realistically do on a Christmas Eve, I took her to West Village to walk around. We ended up stopping at one of my favorite spots, Dante, for an old fashioned. I was trying to pass the time and distract myself until nine twenty-five, when we could go back to the speakeasy and see if Cillian was all right. It felt like the longest damned day of my life. I tried to act like I was having fun. I tried to enjoy the city. Lila, of course, saw right through me. She knew better than anyone when I was faking it.

Flowers, green art deco walls, and antique lighting filled the restaurant. I scanned the bar and caught snippets of conversations—a couple laughing too loud by the corner table, a bartender polishing glasses, a group of suited men leaning in close over their drinks.

Lila was trying to squeeze past a tight corner table when she accidentally bumped into someone.

"Oh, I am so sorry," Lila said, stepping back.

"Lila! What did we talk about with the *I'm sorry*?" I snapped. I turned my attention to the woman she'd bumped into. "My sister has a little substance abuse problem with that word that we are trying to detox her from."

The woman smiled, pulling her attention away from what looked like a manuscript spread before her. "It's okay. I totally get it," she said before focusing back in front of her. Blonde hair, sharp eyes, and a suit jacket that made her look like she owned the place—or at least this corner of it.

I nodded toward the pages, elbowing Lila. "Writing a book?" I asked her.

She looked up again, pen still in hand. "Trying."

Lila and I exchanged glances.

"So is my sister," I said, nudging her. "She just started writing a rom-com during our trip here to New York. Used to be a journalist before the kid tornado hit."

Lila blushed tomato-red. "Ava . . ."

"What? Someone's gotta brag about you." I smiled.

"No way," the woman said warmly. "I actually used to be a Senior Editor at Regent House Publishing. If you ever want support with your manuscript, I'd be happy to take a look—or make connections where I can."

"Wait. Really?" Lila blinked, stunned. "Ava, did you hear that?"

I nodded.

The woman tucked a strand of hair behind her ear. "It's no trouble. I've helped a lot of first-time authors get their foot in the door."

"Wait—did you say Regent House Publishing?" I asked.

"Yes, I was there for years before stepping away to write full time. You know it?"

I turned to my sister. "Lil, I'm pretty sure that's where Mom publishes her books."

"Oh my gosh, you're so right."

The woman's brow lifted. "Who's your mother?"

"Clara Hawthorne," Lila said. "Have you heard of her?"

She laughed. "Heard of her? I edited *A Choice of a Lifetime.* I'm Sarah Jones," she said, reaching out to shake our hands.

Lila's jaw dropped. "You're *the* Sarah Jones? The way our mom talked about you, I assumed you were in your forties. No offense."

268 | ARIA DEVI

"Not quite. And none taken." Sarah grinned. "What a small world. Well, if your manuscript's even a fraction as strong as hers, I think you'll be just fine. Your mother is an amazing writer. She's had a very large impact on my journey. She had a quote. What was it? 'The choice of a lifetime is about choosing yourself. Even if it feels impossible.' That line literally changed my life."

She glanced between us. "And you are?"

"Ava Hawthorne," I said. "This is Lila Carrington. We are sisters and Clara's daughters."

For a moment, none of us said anything—just letting the weird coincidence hang between us. Only in New York. Only on this day. Only in this damn restaurant.

My gaze drifted back to Sarah's jacket. It was fabulous, without trying too hard. "By the way," I said, nodding toward it, "I need to know who made that. It's incredible."

She looked down at herself. "Oh, thank you. My friend Emma made it. She's one of the only female bespoke tailors in the city. She's done a lot to modernize the industry; keeps the craftsmanship but updates the cut, the feel, the whole attitude. Her stuff is very refined without being dated, you know?"

I perked up. "What a small world. I'm about to take a job with an atelier. It's over a hundred years old, and they're finally ready to modernize and bring a PR team in house. I've been working on bridging that same gap: keep the soul but bring it into the now." I decided to leave out the part about the charming, dead, hundred-year-old boyfriend whose great-grandson currently ran it.

"Then you really need to meet Emma. She's made that her whole mission—honor the past, but don't stop innovating. You'd be surprised what people are willing to wear and what they are willing to pay when it actually fits the modern world they live in now."

I nodded. Not just for the tailor recommendation, but for

the reminder. *Honor the past, but don't stop innovating.* It was a great marketing angle.

Lila tapped my arm, unable to contain her excitement. I could already tell she'd be texting Mom the second we walked away.

Sarah scribbled something on the back of a receipt and handed it to me. "Lila, this is my number. Reach out anytime about the manuscript. I'm happy to help. And Ava, that's Emma's info. Just tell her I sent you—I'm confident she would love to meet you and collaborate."

I slipped it into my coat pocket and smiled as a thank you.

"Thank you, thank you, thank you!" Lila said.

"Have a wonderful Christmas, ladies. Good luck with the atelier. And the manuscript," Sarah said, waving, before returning to her project.

"Thanks, Sarah. It was great to meet you," I said casually.

As we walked away, Lila whispered, "Okay, that was fate. I am texting Mom about this right now. She will flip!"

And maybe it was.

Or maybe it was just New York, where magical speakeasies, hundred-year-old ghosts, and freaky coincidences with familiar publishers all live on one little island like its normal.

"Can you believe that was mom's editor?" Lila asked.

"It's incredible. What a score for your book," I said, doing my best to sound excited. And I was. But my sadness kept hold of me, my mind drifting back to Cillian. During our conversation, it had almost escaped me. But the second we sat down at the bar, reality—or delusion—rushed back in.

I ordered two old fashions.

"Can I do anything?" she asked, knowing she'd have time to be excited about her new connection later.

"No," I said way too harshly, running my finger over the edge of my coaster.

"Okay . . . but are you sure that *you* are okay?" she asked, picking at her fingernail again.

"I'm fine. But why are *you* acting weird? You have been since the other day at the atelier." I said with an edge.

"What? No, I haven't. I am just worried for you. I can see you really like Cillian. I just don't want you to get hurt by all of this," she said, looking down.

"I won't give him the power to hurt me," I barked. The second the words left my lips, I knew it was a lie. "I don't give that power away to anyone, especially a man. *Especially* one from 1925."

"Oh, okay." She cowered a bit. "Just know that I love you. And I'm here for you . . ." She paused like she was calculating whether her next words would get her throat metaphorically ripped out. Fair. "But sometimes it's okay to open yourself up to love. There's a difference between giving your power away and sharing your strength with someone. I think there's real power in being seen—really seen—by someone who loves you. I think there is beauty in actually needing someone."

"I never said I needed him. I am not going to fall apart for him. I'm not some weak, desperate girl, Lila. I'm not pathetic."

She placed her hand over mine. "You aren't fooling anyone, Ava. And that doesn't make you weak. It definitely doesn't make you pathetic. It's beautiful to watch. I've never seen you as magnetic as you are when you are with Cillian. When you are soft, kind, and sweet. It's magnificent to watch."

That couldn't possibly be true. I had worked my whole life to be the opposite. To protect and shell and mask. To become hard. Untouchable. Mysterious. That was what had made me successful.

I checked my watch. Eight fifty. *Finally.*

I downed my drink, slammed it on the table—just like Cillian would have—and threw cash down on the bar. That cash could have bought us a car back in 1925.

He is fine. He is fine. He is fine. I know it.

"Come on, then," I said, grabbing Lila by the arm as we turned to leave.

As we stepped toward the door, I glanced back over my shoulder. "Thanks again, Sarah. Seriously."

She gave us a small wave from her table. "Good luck, both of you. And tell your mother I say hello. Actually, tell her I say thank you."

Lila beamed and waved back. "We will!"

Then we slipped out into the Christmas Eve cold, and I hailed a cab to take us back to The Fitzgerald Hotel.

23

IN THE CAB RIDE OVER, ALL I COULD THINK ABOUT WAS CILLIAN—his presence, his absence. The ride felt four hundred times longer than it actually was, every passing second stretching into a small eternity. My heart raced at whether or not Cillian would be on the other side of the door when we entered the speakeasy.

After sitting in a shocking amount of traffic for Christmas Eve, we arrived back at the hotel, heading straight for The Velvet Clover. But there was no Chris Kringle in sight tonight. I would have bet actual money he'd be here—let's be honest, the guy didn't exactly scream *family man*, and Christmas Eve probably ranked as his personal Super Bowl. This should have been his one shining moment of the year. What a missed opportunity for him.

As I pulled back the velvet curtain and reached for the door handle, I paused for a moment, letting out a slow breath.

Was Cillian okay? Was he in jail? He had to be okay. Was he even thinking about what I had told him? Did he have a plan to put me in an insane asylum the second I came through the door of the speakeasy?

Should I expect a deserted wasteland? An illegally run speakeasy that had been looted and vandalized by the cops and locals? Or would it be Christmas Eve at The Velvet Clover as if nothing had happened?

I had no idea what I was walking into, but I knew one thing for sure—I wasn't ready for whatever it might be.

I glanced over at Lila. She caught my eye, her brow furrowing, but she stayed quiet. We counted to three, a silent agreement, before pushing the door open.

Alas, as we walked in, it was as if Christmas had swept in and erased everything. As thought last night had never happened. The Velvet Clover was pristine, its usual charm untouched by the chaos of last night.

The one and only thing out of place was Saoirse not waiting at the hostess stand to greet us. No Eddie behind the bar. The gramophone was stationed where the band usually played. "White Christmas" was playing.

Lila and I looked at each other, then to the left and right. We walked past the hostess stand and into the greater bar area.

Lila grabbed my arm. "Sis, look! There they are, by the tree." She pointed to the Christmas tree in the corner, piled high with even more gifts than before.

I quickly sent up a silent plea—*Please, let Cillian be here. Let him be fine.* I wouldn't believe anything until I saw Cillian's beautiful blue eyes.

As I circled around the tree, the back of Saoirse's head came into view, her bob looking as sleek as ever, a gift propped on her hip. She stood next to Eddie, hand placed on his shoulder. Eddie was sitting on a wooden bar stool, smoking and drinking. What looked like two or three other patrons stood with them. No Cillian in sight.

My heart raced. Panic.

As we walked over to them, Lila grabbed my hand, holding it tight, non-verbally reminding me to breathe. It was like her mom instincts had kicked in—she knew I couldn't speak. I could feel her silent message, letting me know she's got this. All I felt was fear—fear for Cillian. Whether he was all right, and if he was, whether he would want anything to do with me.

"Hey, everyone," Lila called out, her voice bright so we didn't surprise them. You never knew who might be armed and trigger-happy in 1925, I suppose.

They all turned at the sound of Lila's voice, their faces lighting up with pure joy as they recognized us.

"Lila! Ava!" Saoirse squealed, setting the gift she was holding on the floor before rushing over to greet us with hugs. Then, as if she could see the worry in my eyes, she turned back and called, "Dad, look who's here! I told you she would come. I told you they'd be here."

And there, stepping out from behind the tree, holding three gifts, was Mr. Cillian Broderick. The man I had feared might be gone forever. The man I was falling in love with.

It took everything in me not to break down and collapse on the floor in relief. I hadn't expected that level of emotion, but seeing him alive, seeing him okay, so real and present, hit me harder than I could have ever imagined.

He stood there, his eyes locked on mine, and within seconds, he was standing before me like he had teleported, unable to get to me fast enough. When he hugged me, the world around us melted away. The warmth of him filled the hole in my heart. His scent alone made me believe that all was right in the world, that we would be alright.

I kept my composure as best as I could, pretending everything was fine, until the buzz of conversation returned. Lila slipped away to join Eddie, Saoirse, and the others, leaving us alone.

"You are okay?" I asked, touching his face to make sure that it was real. To make sure that he was real. I looked for some sort of injury, anything that might have happened to him. "What the hell happened last night?"

"I'm okay. I'm okay," he said, pulling me into him again, his hand bracing the back of mine, holding me close. His voice was low and steady, reassuring me. "I was able to pay da coppers off. I've got a solid relationship with the chief, so they won't be botherin' us here anymore. It was just a big misunderstandin', really. Some rookies on the force were lookin' for a reason to throw their weight around. They didn't know what they were doin'. 'Cause it was a holiday, they had nothin' better to do."

"Jesus, I was so worried about you," I said, covering my mouth with my hand to hold back tears.

"Eh, eh, eh," he said softly, grabbing my face in his palms. "We're okay. I'm okay, Ava."

My gaze shifted from the floor to him, my heart still racing, but this time for a different reason.

"What about . . . everything I told you last night? Have you had time to think about it?" I held my breath, waiting for his response.

"Well," he said, pulling away to light a cigarette, offering me one before he lit his. I shook my head. Smoking would just make me even more anxious. Out of control was not a good look on me.

"Lucky for us," he said, taking an inhale then blowing out smoke, "I had a lot of time in a jail cell last night to think about it."

"And?"

"And . . . I am findin' a workin' solution."

"What does that mean?" I pressed. "You don't think I'm clinically insane?"

"Well, my darlin', ye *are* insane," he said, taking another drag, a playful smile tugging at his lips. "But the thing is . . . so am I, love," he added, the smile fading, his voice turning serious. "That's why we work. And why we'll *continue* workin'."

He wasn't running. I hadn't scared him off with the truth.

Almost as quickly as the relief hit me, the questions started flooding in. What was the solution? What did he know? What were we going to do? What could he possibly do about time travel—about *any* of this?

We were running out of time—literally—if this, in fact, was a freaky Christmas magic thing. The clock was ticking.

"Well, I'm glad you think we'll work," I said, pulling back just enough to look him in the eye. "But I can't sit around hoping you'll be able to solve this with your limited 1925 resources and internet access. I need answers."

He opened his mouth to speak, but I cut him off. "When I go back, I'm going to find Chris Kringle and figure this out," I said. "He showed me this place. He has to be the one with the answers."

He grabbed my shoulders, and pulled me in to kiss me. If we weren't in a public place, a moan would have escaped me. Lucky for him, I had self-control. Though I was pretty sure that was exactly what he was aiming for—distracting me from the problem, or trying to calm me down.

"Love," he said, "I know we need to figure this out. And we *will*. But I need you to be patient and to trust me." He pulled back slightly, his expression shifting. "More on that tomorrow," he added with a crooked smile, cupping my face with his free hand.

Why was he not more worried? More urgent to figure this out?

"It's Christmas Eve," he continued. "And around here, we open all of our gifts tonight. As you can see," he said, turning me toward the tree, his hand on the small of my back, "there are many gifts to open."

I tried to focus, my head spinning. He was fine. *Cillian was fine.* Maybe that was enough for tonight.

"Fine," I said. "But tomorrow, we need to figure all of this out. I'll be expecting a little more urgency from you."

Once again, Christmas was ruining everything. An inconvenience stealing what little time we might have left—and for what? So we could all open presents no one needed, most of which would end up in a landfill by next year?

I couldn't believe how laissez-faire he was being. Or maybe he was just calmer under pressure than I was. Chris Kringle had been nowhere in sight at the restaurant. And it wasn't like I could storm off into the snow and demand answers from the universe. So I figured my time was best spent here, with Cillian, for tonight. Who knew, maybe I'd think of something while I was here— some way to fix this, to stop the clock from running out? But, if not, at least I'd have tonight. At least I'd have *him* for one more night, if after Christmas, this all disappeared. But it wouldn't. It couldn't. Maybe he did have answers. He didn't seem scared or nervous. Maybe I could trust that he really would figure it out.

"Yes, we will, me love," he said, kissing my cheek, interlacing his fingers in mine, and walking me to the small group of people.

Eddie greeted me, grabbing me a seat next to Saoirse and Lila, while Cillian poured me a glass of whiskey.

Saoirse introduced me to the other patrons, three oddball regulars of the speakeasy: one man, Callan, in his fifties who lost his wife last year; Declan, a young kid, mid-twenties, who didn't have a family around after the war; and Kiera, one of Saoirse's friends.

I greeted them all with smiles and handshakes. Cillian returned to passing out gifts. He had bought gifts for all these lonelies? And not just gifts, but incredibly personalized and custom gifts.

For Callan, an engraved flask. For Declan, a custom cigarette case. For Kiera, a gorgeous silk scarf. For Eddie, a gramophone record player. For Saoirse, a camera—apparently she loved taking photos.

That last one made my stomach twist. Photos.

The photo of me and Cillian flashed in my mind once again. If that picture ended up somewhere it shouldn't—like Ronan's coffee table book—how the hell was I supposed to explain that? Me, standing beside his great-grandfather in some vintage photograph taken decades before I was born? Lil and I may have to pull an *Ocean's Eleven*-style heist—sneak into the atelier, steal it, and burn it.

I forced a deep breath. I couldn't afford to spiral right now. One problem at a time. I could cross that bridge when I got to it.

In no way had I expected Cillian to get gifts for Lila or myself. For God's sake, we'd known each other for all of a week.

"For lovely Lila," he said, handing her a box wrapped in gold paper with a red bow. His sleeves were rolled up, once again showing his perfect forearms, a cigarette bouncing between his lips.

"You got *me* something?" Lila asked in disbelief, as she ripped open her gift, revealing a box, which held a leather bound journal with a fountain pen. Her jaw dropped as she looked at him.

"For all yer writin'," he said with a grin.

"Cillian, this is the sweetest gift. I cannot wait to use it. Thank you so much." Tears welled in her eyes.

He pulled her up and into a hug, patting her back. I couldn't help but smile at the sight. It was beautiful. They had their own little dynamic. It was special. It made me happy to see two people I cared for so much get along.

"Now. Let's raise a glass and toast," Cillian said. "First of all, everyone in this room is family. I wouldn't want to spend Christmas with anyone but all ya sound, good people. To the moments that make time stand still, to the laughter that fills the night, and to the people who make the journey worth every joyful and challenging step. May we always find each other in the most unexpected of places, and may the spirit of tonight carry us through the year ahead. Here's to love, to life, and to the joy of being together . . . and escaping the coppers so we could all be here in this lovely speakeasy on Christmas Eve together. Cheers."

We all clinked glasses, and cheered, and clapped, and drank.

"Everyone, I want Ava to open her gift without all of ya present, so exchange gifts amongst yerselves and have a good time."

They all booed, Eddie whistled, but nonetheless, they started to mingle as Cillian came up to me. He pulled me to stand, and guided me across the room to the communal table. That damn communal table.

"Drinks are free, of course. Ya can serve yerselves. Eddie is off tonight," he called behind him.

They all cheered.

Eddie yelled, "Yeah, no askin' me for nothin' tonight. I'm leavin' to spend time with me family, so don't even try!"

I glanced at Lila at the mention of family, but she seemed fine. Like she had come to terms with being away from the girls and Simon. I hoped being here with everyone made it a little easier on her.

Cillian stood over me as I sat in the communal booth where we'd first met. "Ya didn't think I was goin' to forget yer gift, did ya?" He squatted down in front of me. The tie I'd gotten him hung untied around his neck.

I grabbed it and pulled him in for a kiss. "I don't need a gift. I don't believe in gifts. This was a special case," I said, rubbing my fingers over his tie.

"Too bad, because I got ya somethin'." He pulled out a gift that was hidden behind his back. The wrapping paper was almost identical to how his tie had been wrapped—matte white with a shiny black bow.

I frowned, tilting my head.

"I guess the shops wrappin' style hasn't changed much over the last hundred years. I suppose that means I have pretty good taste for being *old-school*," he said with a wink.

"Like they say, if it ain't broke, don't fix it." I laughed.

I untied the ribbon and unwrapped the box, revealing a pocket watch with an ornate "A" engraved on the cover. Shocked, I looked up at Cillian.

"Now, I had this hand crafted specially for you. Obviously, I had to put a rush on it." He winked. "But me watchmaker owed me a favor. I wanted ya to have somethin' meaningful that you could wear with all of yer suits. And so ya could keep proper time when ya are here."

"I-I . . ." I stammered. A PR professional at a loss for words. The irony.

I paused and stared at it. A tear streamed down my cheek before I looked back at Cillian, still crouched down in front of me, his hands on my legs.

"This is the most beautiful and meaningful gift I have ever received. Thank you, Cillian."

"May I?" he asked, grabbing the box from me before taking it out and hooking the silver chain through the button hole on my vest. Like it was a necklace that he was wrapping around my neck, Ava Hawthorne edition. "You hook it like dis," he said, showing me. His eyes darkened, a look that made me think he was thinking less about buttoning my vest and more about unbuttoning it.

Then he popped the watch open. The face was gorgeous and intricately detailed.

I gasped, "It's so beautiful." I ran my finger over it as it lay in his hand.

"Just like you, Ava Hawthorne," he said with all the certainty in the world. "My love."

He dropped the watch into the pocket of my jacket, patting it gently. "Now, no matter where either of us are, ye'll have a reminder that time doesn't change love; it only deepens it. That not everythin' in life is meant to be figured out with the mind. Some things are meant to be felt, to be lived, and to remain a little mysterious. Sometimes the beauty lies in the not knowin'." He paused, his gaze locking with mine. "We'll talk tomorrow. We'll figure everything out. I promise. Eh?"

I wanted to say that I didn't accept that love could survive on mystery alone. That he was corny for saying it. That not knowing our future freaked me out. That there was no way we could ever work out. That nothing could ever come of this.

"At least tell me what you're working on," I said. "As far as a solution."

"Ava, I need ya to trust me."

I wanted to fight him. To force him to tell me. But I knew it wouldn't do much good. I had to try to trust him. I had to. And, in the meantime, I would do what I could to figure it out on my end of the portal.

I pulled him in and kissed him—a long, slow, sweet kiss— as he kneeled before me. He wrapped his arms around my waist and melted into me. I wanted him to take me right there in the booth. But I was pretty sure sex in public was frowned upon on Christmas Eve with people around, no matter what decade you were in.

I buried my face in his neck, breathing him in. I'd let him hold me for now. Let his promise that, tomorrow, we would figure it out together, get me through the night. Tomorrow, I'd deal with the questions, the unknowns. Tonight, I'd bury all of it.

For tonight. I chose to trust him.

24

"GOODNIGHT, EVERYONE! WE WILL SEE YOU ALL TOMORROW FOR Christmas Day breakfast!" Lila called behind us as we left for the evening, heading back to the future.

Each time I left 1925 to go back to 2025, I couldn't help but feel like I was leaving my real future behind. Like my future was in the past and the present seemed like nothing more than a distant memory. One I was becoming more and more indifferent to return to.

I glanced at her. "You think we actually can? Get in during the morning?"

"We said we would. I am banking on either Chris Kringle being there to help us get through or some sort of Christmas miracle."

"We shouldn't promise we'll be there if we aren't sure about it," I said.

She smiled. "Sis, since when have we ever been sure about any of this?"

"That's fair," I said.

"See you tomorrow!" Eddie and Saoirse called to us. Cillian waved, standing in a way that made my heart race double time.

We got back to the hotel room, where we both collapsed on the bed; Lila from a fun time and myself from swooning over Cillian all night. Tomorrow, he and I would talk about our future, if we even had one. While this thing between us didn't make sense on paper, in theory, or in time, he said he had a plan. At least an idea. Which was more than I had—until now.

But I wasn't going to sit around hoping the universe—or Cillian—would hand me answers. I needed to start digging. Maybe poke around the speakeasy again. Try to get in first thing tomorrow morning. Maybe track down Christopher—shit, I didn't get his actual name. Well, how many Christophers could there really be in a New York City phone book? I could spend tonight googling stuff about time travel until I ended up on some conspiracy forum that actually helped me make sense of all this.

On the plus side, Cillian wasn't scared off by the complications. And let's be real, this was borderline science fiction. That made it easier to breathe. Easier to believe that, if there was a chance we might figure this out, that we could. Together.

Cillian was different. Not just from other men, but from anyone I'd ever known. He saw cracks in the rules and walked through them like they didn't matter. He made impossible things seem like they might not be so impossible after all. He was different. We were the same kind of different.

"How are you feeling?" Lila asked, in a way that sounded like she was waiting for the other shoe to drop. She'd been acting off—on edge—like she knew something but wasn't telling me. I had just chalked it up to her missing Christmas with the girls.

"I'm terrible," I admitted. "The man I love—I mean, the man I'm falling for—I don't know what the hell our future will look like. If it'll look like anything at all."

She sat up, propped on her elbow and gasped. "Ava Rose Hawthorne, are you officially in *love*?"

I slapped her arm before burying my face in the pillows. "I'm not!" I screamed.

"You are. You are past the falling. You are in it!" she said, shaking my body. "You *love* Cillian."

I held the pillow over my face, covering my smile, only allowing her to see my eyes, shaking my head.

"You are! I can see it in your eyes. Did you tell him?"

"No. Because I don't . . . I can't say it yet—not until I know what's going to happen. Not until I know what we're going to do. I'm not going to expose myself like that. Besides, tonight wasn't the right time to say it.

"Anyway, we have to talk about everything tomorrow, first. He said he had some ideas. So, depending on how that goes, I'll tell him."

"Tomorrow?" she asked, cringing. "How can you even hold that in? The first time I knew I loved Simon, I blurted it out like an idiot. I couldn't even contain myself."

"Well, that is the difference between you and me." I winked.

"Totally . . ." She looked up to the ceiling, and then my words clicked. "Hey!" She laughed.

"Kidding, sis," I said, grabbing her face to kiss her forehead. "I wanted to say it, but it isn't that simple. We are navigating a one-hundred-year time difference here. Honestly, it is more complex than any PR nightmare I've had to deal with."

"Ava, this isn't a business thing. This is a heart thing. You won't be able to fight it if he is for you. Which he clearly is."

"I just don't know what kind of solution he's going to bring to the table," I said. "I'm not about to drop the L-word unless I know for sure he feels it, too, and we can actually be together in some real way."

Lila rolled her eyes. "Oh, come on. Did you see him tonight? Over there, giving you this?" She tugged on the chain of my pocket watch hanging from my suit. "The man was practically bowing at your feet. He definitely L-words you."

"Fine, maybe he likes—"

"Loves," she corrected. "He totally loves you."

"Whatever. Either way, we'll figure it out tomorrow. But I'm not just going to sit around waiting. I'm going to start digging—Google, old archives, whatever I can find. If Chris Kringle shows up again, I'll press him for answers. Then I'll sort through it all with Cillian. Maybe then I'll say it."

Lila said nothing. She started picking at her nails again.

"What? Why have you been so up and down?"

"What do you mean?" she asked defensively. She could never tell even a half-decent lie. Every time she picked her nails, she was lying. As if she was physically rejecting it.

"Every time he gets brought up, you get weird," I said sharply.

"I do not!"

"You do know I can tell when you're lying, right?" I snapped. "You started getting weird after the atelier . . ." I stepped closer. "Lila, what did you see? What happened?"

I was practically a professional in my own right at interrogation. Lila didn't stand a chance.

I watched her eyes dart toward the floor, her lips parting like she was about to say something, but nothing came.

"Lila." My tone sharpened. "Tell me."

"I . . . uh . . ." Her face flushed. She took a shaky breath. She was hiding something.

I leaned closer, lowering my voice. "Lila, don't make me ask again. I don't have time for you to hide information about this. We are already on a time crunch here, if Santa Hat wasn't bullshitting us with the Christmas magic comment."

Her eyes widened. She opened her mouth, but still— nothing.

"Lila. Now."

"I . . ." Another shaky breath. "Okay, fine, I'll tell you."

Her voice was so small it made my stomach twist. Whatever it was sounded bad.

"Lila!"

The words erupted out of her like a volcano. "Fine! When we were at the atelier the other day and, you know, I was looking through that book. The one on the workbench at the atelier —"

"Yeah, coffee table book. History of the company. I remember," I cut her off, trying to get the point out of her.

"Well, I was skimming through it, and I stopped on that page with Cillian."

"Well, duh, I could have guessed that. What did you see?"

"I . . ." More damned stuttering.

"Lila, get on with it," I pressed.

"Okay, so I was looking, and the book, and the page with Cill—"

"Fucking tell me—now!" I snapped.

"I saw his obituary, and it said Cillian died on December twenty-fifth . . ."

"So?"

"It said he died on December twenty-fifth . . . 1925. Which is this year . . . for him." She didn't even look me in the eye as she said it.

"No. *No.* There is no way," I said, rolling my eyes. "I never saw that when Ronan showed me the book. That wasn't there. I know it wasn't. I would have noticed it. Seen it myself." I shook my head in disbelief.

Had I missed something? Could I have overlooked it? Maybe I had been too focused on the other parts of the book. No. She must have misread it.

"I'm just telling you what I saw. After he got arrested last night, it made me worry that something might actually happen to him. But after seeing him today, he was fine, so I didn't even mention it. I thought maybe . . . maybe it wouldn't happen like that. I thought maybe you changed things, that it wouldn't play out that way. Because of you. Because of us being there. Like maybe we changed the future by being there. That's why I didn't say anything. I'm sorry, Ava."

"Stop saying you're sorry!" I snapped, then took a breath. "Well, clearly, he is fine—you just saw him. I am sure last night changed things. I bet if we checked the book now, his obituary may not even be there."

"Yeah. Maybe. Totally. Of course," she said with her head down, picking at her stupid nail.

"There's no way that's possible. There is just no way that is true."

"Ava . . . I know what I saw," she said sheepishly.

"There is no way I wouldn't have noticed that in the book."

A pause.

"Maybe you are right. Maybe after yesterday, it changed things. But if not . . . you don't think that maybe your conversations with him . . . or us being there . . . changed something in the past, do you?"

"Oh, so now you are saying *I* am the cause of Cillian's death that you are claiming is tomorrow? Is that it?" I yelled.

"No, I didn't mean it like that." She cowered, like she had when we were little and I would scream at her. I winced at the memory that I didn't even know was stored in my subconscious. "I didn't mean it like you were the cause. I was just wondering if maybe it wasn't there until you told him everything about us, that we are from the future. It's a stupid thought. I shouldn't have said anything."

"Yeah, Lila, it *is* stupid. I know what I saw, and his obituary was *not* in that book. I also know that I am *not* the reason for his death. He is not dead. There's no possible way that's true. Who dies on Christmas when they are in their thirties? You saw him, he was completely fine tonight. Totally healthy. Totally alive.

What you saw is not real. If anything, us being there made it so he *didn't* die."

A look of hurt crossed her face, like a wounded animal. An innocent animal who couldn't defend themselves against a voracious predator. Aka me.

"Yeah, you are probably right—"

"I'm definitely right," I corrected.

"Right," she said. "Maybe I got the date wrong. I was in a rush, and Ronan came out right then. I must've misread it." She tried to mask her sadness, but her big doe eyes gave her away.

"It's all going to be fine. Let's just go to bed. Cillian is not going anywhere. He will be just fine. If there was any risk to him, it would have been last night when the cops came to arrest him. He and I can talk through everything tomorrow, get it all straightened out before Christmas ends, and it will all be fine," I said with a confidence that I wholeheartedly believed. I *had* to believe it.

"You're right, Ava. I am so sorry for even bringing it up."

"Lila, stop fucking apologizing!" I snapped then took a deep breath to steady myself. "It's fine. I forced it out of you. Thanks for telling me. Let's just . . . go to sleep."

Within minutes, Lila fell asleep in her clothes, her hair and makeup still done.

She slept, and slept, and slept.

And me?

I didn't sleep a fucking goddamn wink.

25

DECEMBER 25 — CHRISTMAS DAY

After not sleeping all night, I gave up around four a.m. and got out of bed. I needed to move. To do something. Anything to quiet the noise in my head and the ache in my chest. At some point during the night, I thought it would be a good idea to try to sneak into the speakeasy. See if I could figure out how it worked. To find some clues. Or a solution—any solution—for how Cillian and I might have a future together. Depending on how that went, if I was met with another dead end, I could at least go on a run or find some gym to work off all this anxiety.

I crept through the quiet hotel lobby and the empty restaurant. It was a lot creepier here without anyone around. I went straight for the curtain. I tried not to think about whether I would get in or not. The less I thought about it, the less disappointed I'd be if it turned out to be the broom closet.

I pulled back the heavy black velvet curtain, my hand hovering over the handle. *Here goes nothing.*

I stepped through the door and, to my pleasant surprise—

and quite honestly, shock—I felt that all too familiar wave of cold air enveloping me, the same one that simultaneously felt so welcoming. And I knew I was back. Somehow, I had made it back to The Velvet Clover of 1925. I considered it a Christmas miracle.

Naturally, with it being barely four thirty on Christmas morning, there wasn't a soul in sight. The chairs were flipped upside down, resting on the tabletops. The bar was spotless, free of whiskey spills and beer stains. It was like a snapshot frozen in time. No sign of Eddie, or Saoirse, or Cillian. It was so quiet, so still, you could have heard a pin drop.

"Hello? Is anyone here?" I called, my voice echoing through the space.

Silence was the only response. Okay. Time to start sleuthing. Clues. Answers. Anything.

I searched the drawers of Saoirse's hostess stand, finding some of those leather menus, a few coins, a headband, some pearls, and what looked like an old movie ticket to *The Phantom of The Opera*. Nothing else.

I walked through the bar, scanning every surface for a note, a letter, a newspaper—anything that might indicate what the hell was going on in this time-traveling speakeasy. The bar itself was spotless. Not a glass out of place. No receipts in the register.

I ducked behind it, rummaging in the drawers and shelves. A few empty bottles. An old matchbook with *"The Velvet Clover"* embossed in gold lettering. Cute. I threw it in my pocket. No dates. No names. No help.

"Jesus, did Cillian train his cleanup crew at the CIA?" I whispered. This man left no paper trail.

In my scouring of the place, I stumbled upon a small back office, one I hadn't noticed before. The door was cracked open. I stepped inside. It was unmistakably Cillian's office. *Jackpot.*

Maybe I could find a clue as to what his brilliant solution was to all of this.

A single wooden desk sat against the wall, a dusty filing cabinet, and a coat rack with nothing hanging from it. A bookshelf lined one wall, with old ledgers, and one framed photo of . . .

Holy fuck. There it was. It was me. And him.

The photo of us at the Christmas party the other night. We were kissing. He looked happy. And me? I looked hopelessly, pathetically, disgustingly, delusionally . . . in love. I grabbed the picture and held it close to my face in disbelief. He'd framed it —our photo, right there in his office.

Then, out of nowhere, a sharp, stabbing pain hit me in the chest, like someone had driven a knife right into it.

"Ahh!" The sound ripped out of me as I doubled over, dropping the photo on the desk, clutching my chest with one hand, stomach with the other. "What the hell was that?" I breathed. It felt like I'd been stabbed, punched, and had the wind knocked out of me all at once.

I checked my pocket watch. Four forty-five a.m. I needed to get out of here. I couldn't be caught in here. And I had a feeling Cillian would be an early riser, especially with Christmas Day breakfast just around the corner.

I found a dusty ledger sitting on the desk, the pages were old and yellowed. I flipped through it, scanning each entry. Most were mundane: food deliveries, performance schedules, inventory checks. I opened the desk drawer. Inside was a journal—leather-bound, and tied shut with a piece of twine.

I hesitated then undid the knot. *Fuck it.* I didn't have time to honor his privacy right now. It wasn't that I didn't trust him. But I'd rather ask for forgiveness than permission in this scenario.

The entries were sporadic and fragmented: *Eddie—check car engine. Saoirse—new gloves.* Just a bunch of half-thoughts, scattered Christmas gift ideas, lists, random phrases. No dates. Nothing helpful.

"Dammit," I muttered. Did he even have any idea what we were going to do or had he just been yanking my chain?

I noticed, near the back of the book, was an envelope, slightly worn and thin at the edges. I turned to it carefully.

It was a letter.

Saoirse. Open Christmas Day.

Cillian's handwriting. No mistaking it after seeing his handwriting everywhere in the office. I stared at it, heart pounding in my chest. It was sealed. With a thick, old-fashioned, red wax seal, stamped with what looked like a clover.

"Shit."

I ran my finger along the edge of the flap. I *could* open it. It would have answers. I knew it would. Probably all of them. They would never know who opened it. There weren't security cameras back then—now.

I seriously considered it then realized I had to do it. I had to open it. To get the answers I needed. The answers *we* needed.

Just as I went to rip it open, my hand froze.

I couldn't.

It wasn't mine. Whatever it said, it wasn't meant for me. But just the fact that it existed meant something, right?

I slid the letter carefully back into the journal and closed it. Retied the twine like I'd never touched it. My chest ached, like I was so close to an answer that was morally inaccessible.

I stood there for another moment, staring at the desk before leaving. At the photo of us.

He was my future. He had to be my future. I wouldn't feel like this if he weren't.

Then I turned and walked out.

I couldn't open that letter. And that killed me. God, I

wanted to open it. But I couldn't break trust between Cillian and his daughter. When had *I* become so morally sound?

There was only one place left to check.

I made my way to the communal table, to the side of the bar Chris Kringle had told me not to mess with. To *that* door.

I paused. His warning rang in my ears: *Don't go out the other door.*

I had no idea where this door led. Maybe to the streets of 1925. Maybe straight into Cillian's arms. Maybe into a black hole. All I knew for sure was what I'd seen. People didn't leave through this door. They vanished. Like vapor. Gone. Into the void.

I stepped closer. What if that was the point? What if that door wasn't an ending but a beginning? What if, on the other side, there was an answer? A way forward? A way to him? To us being together?

My hand shook, hovering just over the handle. *If there's even the slightest chance . . . If this could somehow lead to an answer. To a life with Cillian.* I didn't care if it was foolish. I didn't care if I disappeared. Because what was the point of any of it—of existing at all—if it meant I couldn't be with Cillian.

The metal was ice-cold as I wrapped my fingers around it. I took a big breath in.

I turned the knob.

Then . . . nothing.

I pulled. It didn't budge.

I twisted harder. I yanked it. It felt more than locked. It was sealed. It felt sealed by—God, I officially was starting to sound like Lila—Christmas fucking magic. It was as if an invisible force held it shut, an undeniable magic keeping me trapped inside this little pocket of time.

"Are you kidding me?" I yelled, slamming my hand on the door before I tried my last resort—kicking it down. I kicked and kicked. Nothing. The door may as well have been made of steel.

Of course! Of course, this wasn't some neat little story with all the answers waiting behind my magical Christmas speakeasy door. That would have been way too fucking easy.

I stood there for a moment, taking my hand off the knob. Maybe I could will the damn thing open with my mind.

I stared at the door. "Open," I demanded.

It did nothing. "Please?" I asked the door. Nothing.

Well, it was worth a shot.

I guessed stepping through that door wasn't meant for me. Whether it was some kind of magic holding me back or just a really stubborn deadbolt, I had no choice but to let it go and trust that I wasn't supposed to go through it.

———

I stepped back through the door to 2025 with nothing. Nada. Zip. Zero. Zilch. No progress when it came to finding a way for Cillian and I to be together. Just the usual dizziness that came from moving through one hundred years in a matter of seconds.

Now I was in more need of a workout than ever.

Since I still had hours until Christmas breakfast, or when Chris Kringle might arrive at the hotel for his shift, I figured I had a little time to burn before I could continue my sleuthing. A workout usually helped in moments like this. Not that I found myself in moments like this often.

Unfortunately, this stupid hotel didn't have a gym, and most Equinox's were closed today. Wasn't there any company that didn't buy into this whole closed for Christmas bullshit? Employees just loved a reason to get a paid day off.

It was this day. This stupid holiday.

Funny to think that a week ago, my biggest problem was Elliot—not wanting to be alone for Christmas so I wouldn't have to face my mother's endless questions. Now look at me.

Hopelessly in love with a man from one hundred years ago, with no way to be with him.

How did that saying go? *If we all threw our problems in a pile and saw everyone else's, we'd grab ours right back.* Yeah, well, today, I'd happily trade mine for the past version of my problems. She had no idea how good she had it a week ago.

Maybe I was simply eternally cursed when it came to men at Christmas. Jeff had started it all that day he'd left. Honestly, that guy deserved an award, the "Which Father Can Fuck Up Their Family's Life the Most" award. He would take the gold. Every year. Forever.

But I digress.

For now, my only option was a run—a run on the snowy, icy streets, but a run, nonetheless.

I wondered if Lila was still out cold. I had hurried to bundle up and slip out of the room this morning like a church mouse, not wanting to wake her. Just because I couldn't sleep didn't mean she should suffer. Even after she'd said that crazy shit last night about Cillian. I wondered if I had dreamed it all, but then I remembered . . . I didn't sleep, so that was impossible.

I shouldn't have yelled at her last night; she was only trying to help. I couldn't help it. I was terrified—scared of what she'd seen. Scared it was true. Scared of what I didn't understand. Scared I had messed with time, and the past. I was scared that all of this—whatever this was—was all my fault.

That was the weird thing about sleep, about dreaming, about time traveling—after a while, you forget what's real and what's just a fantasy.

I couldn't believe what Lila had thought she saw. There was just no way anything had happened to him. I had seen him with my own two eyes last night. Cillian was fine. Nothing had felt off this morning in the speakeasy. I felt confident that us being there had changed the future. And I was sure—positive, really—that if I went to the atelier right now, his obituary would be nowhere to be found.

The air was frigid. But I needed movement more than I needed warmth. The snow crunched beneath my tennis shoes with each stride I took. No one was out. The streets were empty. It was eerie. This city, that was always so full of life, felt completely vacant on Christmas morning. Like a ghost town.

One block.

Five blocks.

Twenty blocks. I ran and ran until I was numb. Faster, faster, faster. Frozen.

I stopped at Gramercy Park, debating whether I should turn around and run back. As I slowed to walk around the gated space, that familiar pang returned—that same stabbing pressure I'd felt in my chest back at the speakeasy, once again doubling me over.

"Ow!" I screamed.

What the hell was this pain? Fear? Concern? Or was it my denial finally starting to crack?

What if Lila was right?

What if Cillian really was gone? Dead? Gone for good? What if last night had been the last time I'd ever see him again? What if I really *had* messed with something in the past, and now it was changing the future? No. No. If anything, I saved him from doing something risky.

Then the fear was washed away by a wave of anger. How could Lila say what she'd said? Like I had something to do with that obituary magically appearing? She was my sister; how could she say *I* was the cause of his death?

I shook my head and started running again, doing my best to outrun the cocktail of fear and anger gnawing at me. I couldn't afford to let doubt win. Not now.

Maybe this was the Universe. God. The stars and the moon. The founder of the simulation we lived in. The man (or woman) with the video game remote control up there in the sky —whoever it was—having my back. Removing the problem for me before I moved to the city and had to deal with ending it myself. Maybe this was just its way of helping me avoid another relationship catastrophe.

Maybe whoever it was, whatever it was, the greater forces that be *was* throwing me a damn bone for all my hard work. I could move to a new city. Focus on my career. Focus on me. Not Elliot. Not Cillian from 1925. Not some man I'd inevitably siphon off some of my power to, just by simply coexisting with. This way, I could focus on *me*. Me, myself, and I. I could double down at the atelier for the next ten years and establish myself in a way that I'd been striving to my entire career. Maybe I could make this atelier truly legendary.

Who knew? Maybe Cillian would turn out to be just one big distraction—a pain in my side, pulling me away from my goals. I could never guarantee anything would work out between us, anyway. He could lose interest at any time. He could cheat on me. He could leave me just like Jeff had left my mom. There were no guarantees when it came to men.

Plus, who knew if, after today, the portal would close forever? What kind of relationship could that even be? One that only existed in the cracks of time, when fate decided to let me steal a moment with my beloved through some random door I stumbled upon? Or only during Christmas? Fuck that. The fact that I was having this conversation with myself was *insane*, for more reasons than one. I should check myself into the nearest loony bin.

Fuck men. Fuck Elliot for breaking up with me, despite me staying in that relationship out of pity at the end, for what? To save him the embarrassment of breaking up with him before the holidays. Fuck Cillian for being from one hundred years ago. Granted, that wasn't totally his fault, but still, fuck him. Fuck Jeff for being a deadbeat my whole life and treating my mom like shit. Leaving us all for a shiny new family. Fuck all men.

Why had I been so eager to throw away any freedom and semblance of power I'd reclaimed after my last relationship, only to jump right back into bed . . . or another century, with another man? Giving away even more power than I started with? No. Not me. Not the Ava Hawthorne I worked far too hard to create, just to blow it all on something so unrealistic. So unreliable. On something that didn't even exist.

But those feelings—the confusion, the fear, the anger, the pull—they coursed through my body, sparking something inside me I couldn't ignore. An invisible cord seemed to tug at me, pulling me forward. I had absolutely no idea why, but I needed to get to the atelier. *Now.*

So I ran. I ran, and ran, and ran.

Suddenly, something felt off. Like maybe time had shifted while I'd been traveling through it. Like everything I thought I knew was wrong. The atelier was the one place I might get answers, or at least some clues. At the least, it was the one place I could trust to be there no matter what time of day it was.

My chest burned from smoking too many cigarettes all week, mixed with the cold air, but I didn't care. I couldn't stop, not now. Then, like my legs had a mind of their own, they stopped and, suddenly, I was standing outside the atelier, heart hammering, wondering if I was about to find relief or just more questions.

There I was. Staring at my reflection in the window of The Aislinn Atelier. But the face staring back wasn't mine. For a split-second, I could have sworn it was Cillian's beautiful face looking right at me.

"What the . . . ?" I muttered, rubbing the partially steamed and snow-covered window with my gloved hand. As I did, I saw only a crystal-clear view of myself in the reflection.

Shivers ran down my spine. I couldn't shake the feeling that I wasn't alone.

I cupped my hand to the window, looking at my future. Right there. This was it. And for so many reasons, I couldn't wait. I couldn't wait to help Ronan and Sofia. To get in the trenches with them. Making this company something epic that would be remembered forever. At least I had this opportunity going for me.

But beneath it all was the ache of knowing I'd be reminded of Cillian every single day. No matter what our future held, I would be constantly surrounded by his spirit that was weaved and stitched into this place. No matter what happened between us, there would always be that quiet, persistent twinge of pain. I just hoped the atelier would be worth that pain.

Past my own reflection, the store was empty. No Ronan. No Sofia. I could see the table nearest the door, the one where I'd found Cillian's tie. But next to it, where the watch stand had held that beautiful pocket watch yesterday, it was now empty. Gone.

Wait.

The pocket watch was gone?

I stepped closer to the glass, heart pounding. It couldn't be. Could the watch I saw just yesterday on that same table—the same one with the engraving—be the exact pocket watch Cillian had given me last night, a hundred years in the past? Had it been the same one? I hadn't even realized the engraving was identical. I'd assumed the "A" stood for Aislinn or maybe atelier when I had seen it on the stand. But now . . . now it was gone.

And I had it.

"A" for Ava.

It was the same watch. The exact one. Which meant what Cillian had given me in 1925 was the one that *used* to be here, in this time. Now that it was in my possession, it no longer existed on that table in this version of reality. It had vanished. And now it belonged to me.

My heart plummeted past my stomach and, God, it felt like it fell straight out of my ass.

Which meant . . . what we did at the speakeasy wasn't just a fun fantasy. It wasn't a dream or a time-locked memory looping each night. It was real. Real enough to rewrite what was here. Today. Real enough to reach forward, into this world, and erase something that had once existed.

If a watch could vanish—or appear—what else could? Worse—what else already had? Maybe like the obituary Lila had sworn she'd seen—the one I refused to believe—did exist. Because it hadn't been there when I'd looked at the book. Maybe it had appeared for her because something *had* changed.

And if the watch no longer existed here, in this time, then that confirmed our suspicion: what we did together in the speakeasy—our choices, our actions—they didn't just stay trapped in some pocket of the past. They changed things. They changed *this*. They changed the future. This version of the present. *This* reality.

I rubbed the corners of my mouth, trying to stop my thoughts from spiraling. My mind raced through everything I'd done at The Velvet Clover, tracing each thread that might be tugging at the fabric of this timeline.

Had me leaving Eddie a fifty-dollar bill that first night caused some sort of weird ripple? Maybe he'd bought something he never would have—something that, even in the smallest way, shifted the economy. Had sleeping with Cillian set off a wave of events that would change his entire future? Had I influenced Cillian to change the bar's menu, and that affected . . . what? The supply chain? Did the meal he and I had, change the chef's entire career somehow? Some domino I couldn't even see but had still managed to knock over. What if

I'd said something I wasn't supposed to? Or touched something never meant to be moved?

And the worst part—I'd dragged Lila into it, too. What if just by being there, she'd shifted something? Said one too many "I'm sorrys" to the wrong person.

It felt like I'd ripped the Sharpie out of the universe's hand and started scribbling all over a page of history in permanent marker. And *if* the past could affect the future we live in now, did that mean Lila was right? That before me, Cillian hadn't died until later—years or decades later, even. But *because* of me . . . he was set to die today?

Did *I* cause Cillian's death?

If I went back into the speakeasy today with my sister, was I going to have to watch the absolute love of my life die right in front of me? Or worse . . . was he already dead?

No. It isn't possible. I know it isn't. Not possible. Not possible. Not possible. Cillian is fine. He is alive. He is alive. He. Is. Alive.

He has to be.

I repeated it over and over and over with each step as I sprinted as fast as I possibly could back to The Fitzgerald Hotel. Back to The Velvet Clover.

26

I BURST THROUGH THE DOOR OF OUR HOTEL ROOM. "LILA, WE need to go check the speakeasy right now—"

I stopped in the doorway. She stood there with her luggage packed, putting on her coat.

"Where the hell are you going?" I asked.

"Av, I just got a call from Simon," she said, her eyes red. It looked like she had been crying. "Violet got really sick last night. She has a fever and has been throwing up for hours. He had to take her to the hospital this morning."

"Oh my God. Is she okay?" I asked, still frozen in the doorframe.

"I don't know," Lila said, shaking, searching the room for something, rubbing her temple with her palm. "I checked, and there were some flights back up. I was able to book the last seat on the next flight out of JFK. But I—I have to go right now."

"Do you want me to come with you?" I hated to admit that my first thought was that maybe I could just run from all of this. Just disappear—ghost Ronan and the atelier, never go back to the speakeasy again. Pretend none of it ever happened. Pretend Cillian never existed.

I knew running wouldn't fix anything, no matter how tempting it was. I wasn't about to become Jeff—running away from responsibilities and the choices I'd made. Even if a small part of me wanted to. This time, not becoming him was motivation enough to stay.

"It was the last seat on the flight, Ava. And you couldn't do anything about it even if you did come," she snapped.

"Well, neither can you, Lil," I snapped back, anger rising at how she didn't want me to escape this mess with her. I was a little jealous—jealous that she had a reason to leave, to run away, while I'd be stuck here, alone on Christmas Day, despite all my best efforts not to be. Forced to face this shitshow by myself.

"I'm her mom, Ava! I can't just keep playing here in New York with you if something is seriously wrong with my child. I know you couldn't understand, since you have no responsibilities outside of yourself."

"Lila," I said. A threat. I could feel my jaw clenching, the heat rising behind my ears. No way was I going to let her talk down to me like that. She would be smart not to say anything to push me over the edge right now.

"What? It's true. All you do is work and now, apparently, date men who don't even exist in 2025."

I scoffed, "*Excuse* me, you were the proponent of *all* of this. 'See you tomorrow at Christmas Day breakfast,'" I mimicked her from the night before. "That was *you*, not me. You have been the one pushing me to pursue things with Cillian."

She said nothing, which pissed me off even more.

"At least fight back if you are going to throw shots, Lila," I said, hoping that would get her to stand up for herself.

But now she looked even more defeated.

I had won the battle. But just for good measure, I let out another string of words.

"Lila, it's not my fault that you chose to get married, have kids, and become a housewife with no real dreams or vision for your future. You don't need to be bitter because I am living the life you wish you had!" My tone alone could have shattered glass.

She froze, her eyes went wide. Horror. Her throat bobbed. She looked at me like I was a monster in a movie. A cruel, evil woman who said cruel, evil things. Oh my God. I was Miranda Priestley in *The Devil Wears Prada*. A cunty ice queen bitch. And on Christmas, no less.

For the first time in my whole entire life, I regretted what I had just said. There was just silence between us. Then more silence.

What felt like an eternity later of staring into each other's eyes, not knowing what to say, she stifled the shock and rolled her eyes as she wrapped her scarf around her neck. I could see that my words were beyond repair. It felt like what I assumed it was like for Brad Pitt to tell Jennifer he was leaving her for Angelina—fucking excruciating and awkward as hell. And kind of terrifying.

"Ava, my Uber's here. I have to go," she said, storming toward the door, slamming it behind her not even a second later.

I paused before opening the door. "Lila, wait!" I shouted after her.

But she was gone.

"Fuck!" I screamed, resting my head on the same door she had just walked out of, and rightfully so. I slapped it with my palm so hard that everyone on my floor could hear. Good morning and merry fucking Christmas, Floor 4.

I slowly turned back to the room, the empty room. Like whatever was left in there was a scary sight I was going to have to face eventually. And it sure was. There wasn't a trace of her. It was like my sister had been nothing more than a ghost. Like she had never been there at all.

I had to reset for way too many reasons. But mostly, to look halfway decent before launching myself into a wild goose chase to figure out what the hell was going on with Cillian.

I tore off my clothes and jumped into the shower, the hour I'd spent in that frigid New York air suddenly catching up to me, settling deep into my bones. My fingers burning as the water blasted down on me, scalding hot, like molten rocks slamming into my frozen skin. I didn't care. Part of me wanted it to hurt. Wanted it to melt me down like candle wax, to burn off everything I'd become and send it swirling down the drain. Let the sewer rats have me. I probably belonged down there with them, anyway.

I just destroyed my sister verbally. Absolutely annihilated her, like I would have done with one of the guys I worked with. The difference was, they could take it. They were used to my outbursts. They expected it. My sister, clearly, did not. And we had made it through the whole trip doing so well.

Why did I always have to push things over the edge? I couldn't help myself. I always had to have the last word. But whatever. She was family—eventually, she'd have to forgive me. We'd had worse fights—I thought. And we'd always found our way back. My sister was related by blood; she was required to forgive me. Wasn't she?

I hoped.

And yes, this felt different. But I could fix it later. I would have to. After I dealt with whatever state Cillian was in. After I figured out this whole watch disappearing in one realm and reappearing in another thing. After I tried to undo the damage I might or might not have created in the past—present.

I rushed, throwing on a gray, wool suit, stuffing my new pocket watch in my pocket, smearing on some makeup, and running a brush through my hair. While hurrying to get ready, I considered if I just pretended I didn't know what version of reality might be waiting on the other side of that velvet curtain, then maybe everything would just be okay. If I could will it into being fine. Into Cillian being fine. Or maybe the whole thing would just vanish. Like if I ignored it hard enough, all my problems would disappear.

———

The lobby of the hotel was still quiet. So was the hotel bar. The only soul in sight in either place was Jeremy. Goddamned Jeremy. The non-helpful bellhop, concierge, doorman, valet kid. He was sitting behind his concierge desk, scrolling on his phone.

I walked through the lobby and straight back to the bar. I stepped over the velvet rope blocking the restaurant's entrance. I was really finding a rhythm of sneaking into this speakeasy. They really needed better security in this hotel. Maybe they should promote Jeremy to lead bouncer.

As I approached, a heaviness settled in my chest. It was all I could feel—fear of what I might find, fear of what might have already happened.

Cillian was the only person I wanted to see. But what if the past had already been altered too much? What if this was my last chance to see him at all? What if I was too late? Every step felt heavier than the last, and I knew the consequences—whatever they might be—were waiting on the other side of the velvet curtain.

I rubbed my pocket watch as I moved toward the curtain, hoping, praying everything was still okay. Either my gut instinct was right, and something had happened to Cillian, or I would be right on time for having Christmas Day brunch as planned, and we would figure all this out together.

I pulled back the velvet curtain, taking a deep breath. I wished Lila was here with me. Everything felt off without her—too quiet, too hollow. Too sad.

Pushing the thought aside, I stepped through the curtain and opened the door to the speakeasy. There it was—The Velvet Clover. The rush of air. But this time, the usual hum of music was gone, and the silence hit me like a wave. I checked my watch. I was right on "time" for Christmas brunch. But the room was quiet, like it had been earlier this morning when I'd snuck in, only now the lights were on. The Christmas tree was lit in the corner, but the space lacked its usual energy—it was still.

Saoirse wasn't there to greet me, though I hadn't been expecting her to on Christmas Day. I took a few steps in, scanning the room, and there they were. Eddie and Saoirse, standing side by side, facing the Christmas tree, just like the evening before.

"Hey, you two," I said, doing my best to bring the same level of Christmas cheer Lila would have so naturally brought with her, and failing miserably.

They both turned to look at me. Their faces didn't hold any Christmas cheer.

Eddie waved me over. Saoirse seemed like she was trying to smile but couldn't quite get there.

I walked over to them, my heels clicking in the silent space with each step. "What's up? What's going on?" I asked calmly. "Merry Christmas."

Saoirse managed a polite smile and nodded. "You, as well, Ava. Is Lila with you today?" Of course she would ask about her right off the goddamn bat.

"She had to head home. Family emergency," I said, sighing. "She sends her best to you both and thanks you for everything. She will be back," I said, crossing my fingers behind my back.

My mind flickered to the irony. In PR, I had become a master of crafting perfect narratives, even if they were only half-truths. Those half-truths, they had allowed me to live with myself.

But this? I wasn't sure if I was saving face for my sister or just protecting myself somehow.

Eddie and Saoirse both looked down at their glasses of whiskey. Whiskey this early? They looked . . . disappointed. Then, I couldn't help but wonder if maybe they never really liked me. Maybe they only tolerated me when Lila was around.

"Ava," Saoirse said, "please, sit."

"I'm fine. What's going on?" I asked.

Eddie rubbed his eyes, and then the back of his head.

Saoirse pursed her lips. "Something terrible has happened."

No. No. No.

I braced for the worst possible outcome, like I always did when a crisis hit at work. It usually ended up being less severe than I'd imagined, and I'd end up relieved. But that never stopped the anxiety from creeping in.

"What? Did the cops shut down the speakeasy again? Something with the tailoring shop?" I was grasping at straws—any explanation that wasn't my worst nightmare. Anything but what my gut was already screaming at me.

She looked at her shoes. Her little black Mary Janes. They couldn't be more than a size five. She was such a petite little thing.

"It's . . . my dad—" she said, her voice catching.

Fuck.

It was still weird to hear her refer to him as Dad. She almost always referred to him as Cillian or sir.

Eddie walked toward her, as if that would support her getting the words out.

My heart started to race.

"Is he . . . okay?"

"Ms. Hawthorne, there has been a terrible accident regarding Mr. Broderi—" Eddie choked up.

"We weren't able to ring you—none of us had your telephone exchange," Saoirse said.

I shook my head, touching her arm. "It's fine. What happened?" I asked, remaining as calm as possible. This was my specialty—crisis management. I had been training for this moment my whole life. Or so I told myself—probably a little too overconfidently.

Eddie left for a moment then came back with a whiskey in a crystal glass to match theirs.

Saoirse wiped a tear from her cheek. "He was driving . . . early this morning, to the speakeasy."

"The coppers said they thought it was around four or five in the mornin'," Eddie added.

What felt like a rock dropped into the pit of my stomach. *Shit.* I could tell by their tone that this was not fucking good. Then it hit me—the stabbing pain in my chest earlier, that sharp pang when I'd been here this morning—it happened right around that same time.

"What happened?" I asked, my tone sharper.

"He went home right after you and Mrs. Carrington left last night. He never sleeps much. So it made sense that he was awake. I figured he was on his way to prepare for breakfast," Saoirse said.

"Eddie, Saoirse . . . what happened to Cillian?" I asked point blank. "I can't do anything with all of this beating around the bush."

A look of pain filled both their eyes as I looked between them.

I dropped my head, already knowing what was coming. Lila had been *right*.

I pulled Saoirse into a hug, and as soon as she hit my chest, the sobs started pouring out of her. I let her go, giving her space to catch her breath.

"They found . . . his car . . . this morning on 5th Avenu—"

Saoirse's voice cracked. She paused, her breath shaky as each sob caught in her throat. She grabbed the edge of the table nearest her, her fingers trembling, trying to steady herself, but her body shook with each gasp. "I . . . it . . . it caught on f-fire," she managed to say, her words stuttering and breaking apart. Tears streamed down her face.

"Po-policemen were slow to arrive with da holiday," she continued, her hands shaking. "Someone phoned it in. One of the police officers who knew me father was able to identify da vehicle." Her voice was barely above a whisper. "Everything inside of it bur-burned to ash . . ."

My hand flew to my mouth as I struggled to catch up with what she'd said. My hands trembled, the impact leaving me breathless, unable to speak. The speakeasy turning, spinning around me. *No.*

Despite Lila warning me, telling me . . . I didn't believe it. I didn't believe her. But she had been right all along. I was . . . *wrong.*

Saoirse reached into her coat pocket and held her hand out, her fingers curled tightly around it. "This was found near the crash," she said. "It . . . it was the only thing that survived the fire. We thought you should have it."

She opened her hand. It was the pocket watch. *Cillian's* pocket watch, scorched and blackened at the edges.

"Ms. Hawthorne, I am so sorry to tell you dis, but . . . Cillian is . . . he's dead, ma'am," Eddie said as if it was the only way I would fully believe it.

The glass of whiskey slid through my fingers, falling to the ground, shattering into a thousand pieces of crystal, whiskey flying across all of our shoes.

Not possible. Not possible. Not possible. The words from my run reverberated in my head.

"No, he can't be," I whispered.

"I'm so sorry, Ms. Ava," Saoirse said. "Cillian, me father, he was so different with you. You two had somethin' . . . somethin' so rare. It's hard to explain, but ye . . . you were his world, Ava. I could see it—" Her voice cracked again.

I nodded slowly, staring at the floor. "Don't. I'm fine. It's fine." I panned my eyes to her. But it wasn't fine. I wasn't fine. This wasn't fine. I was *anything* but fucking fine.

Tears welled up in her eyes again.

Before they could well up from deep in the reservoirs of my own suppressed, locked-away feelings, I managed to say, "I . . . I have to go. I'm so sorry—" Then I turned and ran out of the speakeasy as fast as I had come in.

"Ava, wait!" they called after me, but I couldn't. I couldn't stay with them. I needed to leave. Now.

What had I been thinking? Allowing myself to fall for Cillian. To fall for a dead man. Now, in more ways than one. It'd been reckless, naïve, and plain stupid. I had convinced myself that what we had was real, but it wasn't. I couldn't even comprehend what was happening.

He left me. He wasn't alive. He never had been in the first place. I knew he had already been dead . . . technically, in 2025.

And yet, the pain of his death now being real, today, in this moment . . . it completely shattered me. It was a deep, crushing weight that suffocated everything inside of me. Like being gutted, like a deer left wide open in the snow—still warm but completely emptied. It wasn't just grief; it was the kind of pain that bent my soul. Twisted it and smashed it into a million pieces. A pain that made my chest collapse, leaving me breathless, unable to move. Unable to think. How could I feel this way for someone who had never really been alive to begin with?

How could I have been so stupid? How could I have let myself believe in something so fragile? Reality crashed into me, and I couldn't breathe through it.

27

I SLAMMED MY HAND ON THE CONCIERGE DESK. "WHERE THE FUCK is that bartender?" I demanded, fury coursing through my veins.

I was pissed. Pissed at Chris Kringle for dodging every question I'd asked about that damned speakeasy. For vanishing the last few days—during Christmas, no less. But more than that, I was pissed at him for ever suggesting I go in that stupid place to begin with.

More than all of *that*, I was pissed at myself. Pissed I hadn't press harder. That I hadn't gone looking for answers sooner. That I'd trusted Cillian would find a way for us to be together in time. I was pissed that I'd kept going back, night after night, like some starry-eyed idiot chasing some Christmas magic without ever demanding the truth.

I had to find Chris Kringle. I needed real answers. If anyone knew anything about the speakeasy, about Cillian, about why the hell all of this was happening, it was him. He had to be involved. He *had* to be. Maybe . . . maybe there was more to the story. Something bigger. Something that could explain the unexplainable.

I suddenly had the feeling that everything I needed to know was locked behind that bar, behind that maddening, jolly man. And I wasn't leaving without the truth. Even though now, now it was too late.

Jeremy, jack of all trades, master of none, jumped out of his skin, most likely deep in some useless online game or scrolling through social media, being a little internet creep.

"Shit, miss, ya scared me," he said, standing quickly, the phone flying out of his hand and on to the counter in front of him. "Sorry, which bartender are ya inquiring about, Ms. Hawthorne?"

"The fucki—" I exhaled a breath. "The bartender. The one who looks like a jolly do-good man at the holidays. He has a belly, wears suspenders. He's had a Santa hat on every night this week," I said, gesturing to my head.

A look of confusion was his only response.

Useless. This boy was useless.

I leaned on the desk, closing my eyes. "He told me his name was Christopher." Which had to have been some stupid alias for the holidays to mess with me.

His blank look was even more evidence of his utter stupidity and incompetence.

"Ms. Hawthorne, I have worked 'ere nearly every day this year. Heck, I 'ave worked here for the last five years. I know all the bartenders—all the employees, for that matter. I am confident none of them are named Christopher or match dat description ya are sharing with me," he said with a dumb look on his face.

I dropped my head back, scanning the ceiling as if the answers to my problems were somehow written up there. Nope. Just a wood-carved, Irish ceiling staring back at me, indifferent to the chaos unfolding in my life.

"I really am sorry I can't be of more help, miss. Maybe I can offer you a free drink in the bar for Christmas? I can make it m'self, as I am the only one on shift today."

I cut him my best eye daggers, about to say something probably a little too harsh, when my phone started to ring. I grabbed it from my pocket.

"You have to be kidding me," I muttered.

"Jeff (Deadbeat) Hawthorne" was displayed on my phone.

"Ma'am?" Jeremy asked hesitantly.

"I'm fine"—my preferred half-truth of the day—"I'll figure it out later," I told him, turning before I rolled my eyes at the general incompetence of every employee in this place.

My phone felt like a lead weight as my "father's" name lit up the screen.

I stared at it, wishing I had a penny to toss. Heads, I'd answer. Tails, I'd block him forever. A festive little game of Christmas Roulette.

Lila's voice echoed in my head: *Maybe he's changed.* But I didn't care if Jeff had changed. I didn't care if he never did. But maybe if I answered, Lila would forgive me one day for being a complete psycho. And maybe—I hated admitting it—I wanted someone to take all this out on. And who better than the man who had started it all?

Here goes nothing. I picked up.

"Yeah?" was all I said, pulling the phone to my ear.

"Ava?" Jeff's voice was near breathless, in shock that I'd answered, I assumed.

"This is she," I said, acting like I had no idea who was on the other line.

"Hey." He sighed. "Ava, it's your dad. Jeez, it's so great to hear from you."

"Well, actually, you called me," I said dryly.

As he launched into whatever pre-rehearsed speech he had prepared, I threw him on speaker and pulled the phone away from my ear to open my messages. I didn't have all day to make moves to figure out what the hell had happened to Cillian. The love of my life who had just died—well, one hundred years ago today. I was such an idiot for not figuring this out earlier.

"Of course," Jeff said, doing his best to recover. "I just meant it's nice to hear your voice." He followed it up with a nervous laugh.

My fingers hovered over Ronan's contact card in my phone. I typed:

> When did your great-grandfather, Cillian Broderick, die?

Why was I asking? Maybe I was clinging to the impossible, hoping this was all some mistake. That maybe I could do something in the present to change the past—just like I had before, with the watch. Or maybe I just didn't want to believe the truth.

Was it wildly inappropriate to text my new boss a personal question on Christmas Day? Absolutely. Did I care? Not at all.

"Yeah, what's up? I am kind of busy. Now is not really a good time," I said to Jeff, unearthing all the angst I had as a teenage girl. He literally could have called me any of the other eight thousand seven hundred fifty-nine hours in a year, and he chose this one. The one when I'd found out my boyfriend had just died. I kept my eyes on my screen, waiting for an answer from Ronan.

"Well, it's Christmas Day. I just wanted to call you and see how you're doing." His voice sounded hopeful. Slightly pathetic.

"Yeah, of course, how could I forget the annual call I get from my unfaithful, unloving, un-devoted *father*?" I said, leaving seconds of silence on the other end of the line. Sometimes, I pictured me at his funeral years from now, with that etched on his tombstone. "*Here lies Jeff (Deadbeat) Hawthorne. Unfaithful, unloving, un-devoted father.*"

"Ava, you have every right to be as upset with me as you

are," he said, his voice cracking. "And I know we haven't talked, so you wouldn't know . . . but over the last few years, I have done a lot of therapy. Working on myself personally."

"Yeah, I know what therapy is. Patty's suggestion, I assume?" I interjected. The woman he'd left my mom for and the wife he'd built a fun new life with, decades ago.

He cleared his throat. "Actually, it was my idea. I wanted to heal the things within me that led me to do what I did during the earlier seasons of my life. To you girls. To your mother."

"And your way of doing that is calling Lila one time a year," I said. Not a question.

"I needed to resolve everything within myself before I could try to be a part of either of your lives again in any real way—"

"And if we don't want you to be a part of our lives? If you missed your chance?" I asked.

"Then, of course, that is fully your choice. But the least I can do is apologize and own up to everything I have done that has caused you pain in your life."

I stayed silent. I had to admit he did sound . . . different. There was a softness to his voice that hadn't been there before. Maybe he was getting older, realizing what actually mattered in life. Realizing how much of an asshole he had been. Regretting leaving his wife and kids for the next newest, younger woman, who was now, too, getting old and wrinkly.

"I am sorry, Ava. I would love to say that I did the best I could. But I didn't. I was scared. We had this perfect life, your mom and I, and you girls. I never grew up with a healthy example of love when I was a child. I self-sabotaged, thinking the other grass was greener. I couldn't admit it to myself for a long time—until recently—but I messed up. I would take it all back if it meant I could have a relationship with you and your sister." His voice cracked again.

"And again, your way of doing that is by calling us one time a year?" I asked. Part of me wanted to believe him—wanted to hope that he might be different. But the louder part of me was screaming that this was the same old story: words without action.

I pictured Lila, always hopeful, ready to forgive, only to be disappointed time and again—missing lunches he'd said he'd make, waiting for phone calls that never came. I wouldn't let myself become vulnerable to his little games.

I checked my phone again for a text from Ronan. Still nothing.

"I didn't want to assume you would just let me back in. I wanted to clear the air with each of you before trying to mend our relationship. I didn't want to start calling you every month or every week if it wasn't what you wanted—"

I couldn't take this bullshit anymore. He had no idea what it had been like for us. To constantly be let down. To constantly be told one thing and shown another—a promise made, then a promise broken, again and again.

"You ruined men for me!" I shouted, this time, my voice cracking.

The silence that followed was louder than anything.

It was true, wasn't it? He was the reason I hated men. The anger, the abandonment, it all started with him. It all came rushing back like a tidal wave, drowning any rational thought I had left. Nothing he said could take back the years of hurt he had caused, nothing could undo the damage he had done to me. To Lila. To my mother.

An image of Cillian flashed in my mind. The part of me that had opened up to him, to someone who felt like a spark of hope, felt like a chance at something real. Someone who wouldn't leave me. Wouldn't abandon me, like Jeff. Or Elliot. Someone who would be a constant in my life. Someone who was safe. But now? Now that was gone, too. Cillian was now just another man who had slipped through my fingers. And at Christmas, no less? Just like Jeff had. The irony.

My mother or sister couldn't have written it into their next book better if they had tried.

Another piece of me lost to a version of a man I could never fully trust. Couldn't rely on to show up and be there for me when I needed him most.

At least, with Jeff, I expected his shittiness. But Cillian? Cillian had been something I had dared to hope for. Ironically, something that had never even really existed. Yet, I had still put my hope in him, my trust in him that he would find a way for us to be together. And now that hope was just another thing that had been ripped away from me. Another man whom I had loved—gone.

I swallowed hard, the lump in my throat feeling like it might choke me. What was the point of engaging with men at all? Every time I let myself trust even a fraction, let myself believe I could rely on them for a moment, I was always left disappointed, shattered, and more alone than before. That had been proven time and time again.

"Honey—"

"*Don't* call me that," I barked.

"Ava! Wait," he said.

I stopped right as I was about to hang up the phone. Something kept me from clicking that red button. That same sliver of hope I had held onto as a little girl, that he would become the dad I always wanted and hoped for. And needed . . . *Needed*. I had needed him.

"I know I can never begin to understand the pain I've caused you. But my wish is that you don't close yourself off to the love of a good man. All men, for that matter, because of a deadbeat dad who didn't yet have the emotional awareness and tools to see the truth of his actions. You deserve love, and to be loved by a man far better than me."

I stood by the hotel lobby window, staring out at the New York City street filled with Christmas lights and piles of snow.

The irony of him calling to resolve all this—on Christmas, no less—wasn't lost on me. A full-circle moment, giving me one more reason to become that much more bitter during the holidays.

A stinging sensation rose from my stomach up through my throat, then to my nose and eyes. At least he was owning his shit—that was a first. My eyes stung as I blinked, and one single tear streamed down my left cheek.

"Honey—"

"*Don't* honey me, *Dad*." I hadn't called him dad since I was five years old. It felt weird to even say the word. "Don't use some twelve steps of forgiveness program bullshit on me. It's way too late for that."

Maybe he *had* changed. Maybe Lila was right. I had to give it to her; she had been right about Cillian all along. Maybe she was right about him.

"Honey." This time I let him say it. "I am deeply sorry. I hope that if you can never find it in your heart to forgive me, you can at least find it in your heart to open up to other men who are better than I have been to you. There are some really great ones out there. They would be so lucky to be with you."

I sniffed back a tear, forcing the burning and stinging in my eyes and nose back down into that lockbox deep in my chest.

"And what if I don't need men? I've managed just fine without them . . . well, for pretty much my entire life." I wasn't really looking for an answer; I meant it more as a backhanded jab.

"Well, of course you may not *need* one to survive, Ava. Clearly, you are fine without. You are a self-sustaining woman. But when it is the right one, you will *want* him. When you find the one your heart longs for, wanting and needing won't feel like a weakness. It will feel like an honor. A strength. You won't believe you ever lived life without them." He choked on his own words. When did Jeff get so soft?

"Ava, you are a strong, successful woman. I see all the stuff online about you. But that strength will ten-fold when you have an amazing man backing you. Don't let your stupid old dad be the reason you block your potential to really love a man."

As he spoke, something inside me shifted. A tiny crack in my armor. I hated that a part of me—a microscopic sliver— wanted to believe him. I wanted to believe that kind of love existed, something that wasn't a constant disappointment or a letdown. Something that wasn't a man leaving at Christmas. His words made me feel . . . something that, after today, after Cillian, I didn't know if I would feel again.

Hope.

I allowed myself to picture it—being supported, cared for, loved the way he was describing. A small echo of it resurfaced —when I'd been with Cillian. I'd felt this when I'd been with Cillian.

But I shoved it back down. *No. Don't let him in. Don't. He hasn't changed. How could he?*

As the silence stretched on, a part of me wavered, wondering if maybe he was right.

No. I couldn't let my guard down. Not after everything— after all the disappointments, the years of lies, the heartbreak. For *decades*. A man who had abandoned me for selfish reasons, who'd only now come back when it was convenient for him? I couldn't let myself believe in any of it. In any of him.

I sniffed, choking my emotion back, shifting into autopilot —*Ava Hawthorne, the PR professional*. No emotion. Just business. Just for ten more seconds. I could do this.

I cleared my throat. "Jeff, I appreciate you calling. Thank you for your kind words. I accept your apology. I hope you have a nice Christmas. Wish Patty a Merry Christmas, as well." I pulled the phone away from my ear to end the call.

"Ava, one second. Please," he said, his voice muffled as I pulled the phone away from my ear.

I paused. Hang up and don't hear from him for another year? Or hear him out?

Lila's words echoed in my mind. *What do you have to lose by just hearing him out?* Damn Lila, haunting me at the worst times.

"Yes?" I said in my best public relations voice. Seemingly calm. Seemingly unaffected.

"Would you mind if I called next month . . . just to check in? See how things are going? To chat? Would that be okay with you?" He sounded like, if he had a tail, it would have been between his legs. But it was an effort. More of an effort than he had made in thirty years. And that . . . that was progress.

"Sure . . . Dad. That would be fine." The corners of my mouth turned up ever so slightly.

At the end of the day, results spoke louder than words. He meant to call, but only time would show if his actions matched his words. In both life and business, I was the kind of person willing to give others the chance to prove themselves, through action.

"Oh! That is great. Just wonderful, sweetheart. Thank you. I love you, Ava. Merry Christmas, honey."

I hung up before saying anything else.

I bit my lip. I wanted to stay angry at him, but my small grin turned into a smile that turned into another tear rolling down my cheek. Effort. He had made an effort. That was all I had ever wanted from him. All I'd ever needed from him—was effort.

I checked my phone again. Still no text from Ronan.

I needed to get out of this lobby, away from Jeremy.

"Ms. Hawthorne, are ye all right?" Jeremy called from his post.

"Fine," I barked, walking past his stand toward the restaurant. I held my head high but covered my face with my hand, pretending like I was scratching my temple to hide the tears running down my cheeks.

"If I can do anything for ya, please do let me know . . ." His voice trailed off as I tried to escape.

I replayed Jeff's words over and over again in my mind. I couldn't believe it—the hope his words had sparked in me. The promise of effort. For the first time since I was a little girl, I wanted to believe it. I wasn't sure if I was ready to let him in fully. Even if I was just being as pathetically delusional, as Lila had been in the past with my dad's empty promises, I didn't want to shut myself off completely. I didn't want to live like that —hardened and alone. Not anymore.

I had to go back. I had to help Saoirse and Eddie. I couldn't just leave them. I couldn't just walk out on them when they needed me the most.

As I walked back through the bar and toward the velvet curtain, I pulled it back, grabbing the door handle, longing to see the familiar sconces and candles lighting the bar and the Christmas tree. I turned the handle of the door and stepped into the speakeasy.

But, this time, instead of the warmth and life of the space I had visited already twice today, there was only silence. No Saoirse or Eddie. No Christmas tree. No speakeasy. Just the cold, dark storage closet. Buckets and brooms. Rolls of silverware. Mops and rags. The world I had left behind was gone. Saoirse, Eddie, and the speakeasy were gone. Cillian was gone.

I stepped inside, and the door clicked shut behind me.

And I lost it.

No. No. No.

It hit me all at once, like getting slammed in the chest. I couldn't breathe. I couldn't think. I was pissed. Panicked. Terrified. And underneath all of that, absolutely fucking heartbroken. The kind of heavy, gut-punch ache that made it impossible to stand. Impossible to breathe. Impossible to live.

Everything in me was unraveling, and I couldn't stop it. The air felt too thick. The room too small.

I had to get back to the speakeasy. I had to.

Cillian was gone. Dead. Dead in 2025 and 1925. And I was alone.

My phone dinged. Then dinged again. Ronan. And?

I hesitated, the heaviness in my chest making it feel impossible to lift my arm. But I had to look. Maybe there would be some answer about Cillian—the truth of what had happened, or a sign that I wasn't completely alone in this mess.

My hand shook as I unlocked the screen, the bright light stinging my eyes. Two messages.

One from Mom. And one from Ronan.

Mom:

> Merry Christmas, baby. I wish you were here. I hope u & Lila are having a fun time in the Big Apple. I saved your spot on the couch. Call me when you can. Love you always. - Mom

She was sweet. Being home with her and her pie—even with all the annoying questions about my love life—sounded pretty good right about now. But I couldn't answer. Not yet. Not until I saw what Ronan had said. I clicked on his name.

Ronan:

> Such a wild coincidence. I just looked at his obituary last night. He passed away on Christmas Day. 100 Christmases ago today.

Fuck. No. No. No.

I collapsed to the ground, my back hitting the shelves. One tear after another slid down my cheeks until they flowed in a steady stream, wetting the lapels of my suit.

The thought—that maybe he was still alive, that somehow this could all be reversed—had been eradicated with Ronan's confirmation. I had killed Cillian. I had changed the future by being in the past. And now, he was dead. He had an obituary in the present. Now. Just like Lila had seen in the book.

Cillian was dead. Gone. Just like that. I would never see him again. And the speakeasy was now a broom closet. It was Christmas. If all of this was just some kind of Christmas magic like Chris Kringle had said, that had to mean I would never be able to access the speakeasy again. The portal might be closed forever.

It hit me like a freight train. I had spent so much time in denial—of the signs, the ticking clock, the truth Lila had tried to tell me. And for what? To protect myself from fully opening up to Cillian? So I could be some strong independent woman who didn't need a man?

My heart shattered into a million jagged pieces, just like the whiskey glass I'd dropped at the bar an hour ago. Broken.

It wasn't fair. Life was better with him in it, so much better.

I tried to push the thoughts away, but the memories kept flooding my mind like some stupid 1920's silent film. His smile. That damned smile he only showed to a select few. Dancing with him. The way he held me, the way we fit together, like it was meant to be. His hands, rough from years of work and war, holding my face gently, like I was something precious. Something fragile. The way he kissed me, looked at me, like he could lose himself in my eyes. Every second we had spent together was seared into my brain like a film I couldn't turn off, playing over, and over, and over again. And now, it was all gone. Just like him.

Jeff's words rang in my mind. *When it is the right one, you will want him. When you find the one your heart longs for, wanting or needing won't feel like a weakness. It will feel like an honor. A strength.*

My chest heaved in and out. Hyperventilating. I imagined my life. The rest of *our* life together. The memories *we* could have had. The good times. The fights. The businesses we could have built. The Christmases we would have shared. Growing old together. Dying together in our old age, in a bed together, like *The Notebook*. Like Ally and Noah. Being taken away together through love. A vortex of a lifetime flashed in a split-second. *Us*. The life we could have had together. I didn't care if it was in 2025, or 1925, or some other dimension altogether . . . I would settle for fucking 900 B.C. I would live in any time period on any planet if it meant I got to be with Cillian.

I punched the wall beside me, and a roll of silverware fell and hit my shoulder, bringing me back to the moment. This shitty, unbearable version of reality. Without him. How every moment would be from now on—just me, all alone, knowing he was gone. Knowing I had lost him forever. Because I hadn't done what I could have to figure all of this out.

I had tried to protect myself from this. From the moment I'd met him, I knew there was no real way for us to be together. Or, at least, that's what I'd told myself. But now that the chance was actually gone, now that he was *dead* . . . it hurt even worse. It had all become real. And I realized just how much hope I'd secretly let myself feel, hold onto. That somehow, some way, we might have found a way to be together after all.

You won't believe you ever lived life without them.

I couldn't live without him. I mean, I could. But I didn't want to. The idea of living this life alone now sounded awful. I thought of tomorrow, next week, next month, moving to New York, my career, my future. Without him. The idea of not having Cillian as a part of each future memory I would make nearly killed me right here on the floor of this stupid broom closet.

Pain radiated through my chest. Was I having a heart attack? I tried taking a few deep breaths, trying to slow my heart rate, calm myself. To control my out of control mind. Where were these emotions coming from? There was a raw power within me I hadn't even known existed. A power in these emotions. Jesus Christ, it scared me.

Breathe in. Breathe out. Breathe in. Breathe out, I repeated to myself for who knew how long, until I was able to.

"This has got to be a joke," I said out loud. I'd finally fallen in love, actual true love with someone. I opened my heart to him. Bought him a fucking Christmas present. Then he *died*. My worst fear in life was realized.

"Thanks for the bone you gave me . . . a real winner," I said up to the sky, to whoever was up there, controlling all of this unfair bullshit.

The broom sat in the corner. "What are you looking at?" I said as though it were a person mocking me.

I needed to talk to someone. But everyone who liked me— even a little—was either mad at me, trapped in 1925, or dead. So, I figured this broom was my only real confidant.

I took a few more deep breaths. "You know . . . love is a bitch. Love doesn't care. Love doesn't care about responsibility. It doesn't care what is good or bad. It doesn't care if you have a one hundred year age difference. Love. It just is. It consumes you. With love, we have no fucking chance," I said, looking to Mr. Broom, waiting for his response.

"I know, I know. It's fucked up . . ." I responded as my new friend, Mr. Broom, over there in the corner.

It was then that I realized I was sitting on the floor of a disgusting, greasy broom closet in a nine thousand dollar suit, with mascara covering my cheeks, crying about a man who was from 1925, who had been dead long before I was even alive. And in that pathetic sadness, I scraped my lifeless carcass off of the floor, used one of the napkin wrapped silverware sets to wipe off my mascara, and walked my ass out of this godforsaken hotel.

28

I WALKED THROUGH THE SNOW UNTIL I FOUND THE FIRST BAR that was open on Christmas Day. It was a small hole in the wall sports bar, with a few old, single, men drinking alone, and that was about it. *Perfect.* I would fit right in.

"Oof, hon, you look like you need a strong drink," the bartender said as I took a seat at the bar. She had to be in her mid-fifties. Short brown hair. I guessed a spunky empty-nester divorcée.

I glared at her, but I couldn't blame her. She was spot on. I had done my best with the dried mascara streaked down my cheeks with that sad excuse for a cloth napkin. I had never real-ized that once mascara was mixed with salty tears, it became a permanent marker on skin.

I had always prided myself on never letting myself cry with makeup on. It was too expensive, too time-consuming to ruin over a man. Yet here I was, becoming the pathetic woman I had pitied just a mere week ago.

"What can I get you, darling?" Her tone was warm. Like somehow she knew what I was going through. But she didn't. No one would ever know. Because I could *guarantee* no one in this bar had ever fallen in love with someone who'd died a century ago—and also today.

I stared at the wall of liquor. "Whiskey . . . Irish." The least I could do was honor Cillian with that.

She smiled, reaching up to pull a bottle from the top shelf. She poured a generous amount in a glass and set it in front of me. "It's on the house, sweetheart," she said.

I raised a brow, biting my cheek to hold back what came next. I'd learned recently that once a single tear slipped, the rest followed, pouring endlessly. Like once the emotional floodgates opened, I couldn't shut them off.

I raised my glass to her and, like Cillian would, I drank the entire thing in one go. My throat and eyes burned.

She didn't blink as she refilled my glass. I let it sit this time, running my finger along the top ring of the glass, like Cillian used to do.

"You talk to a lot of people every day. Bartenders probably know people better than psychologists," I said assumptively.

She blinked once, waiting for my question. She had one of those paradoxical vibes. Like she might cut you, but she would hug you afterwards.

"What are your thoughts on women 'needing' a man these days?" I air-quoted.

She shrugged, grabbed a rag, and started cleaning the bar around me. "Is this question for you or a hypothetical, darling?"

I shrugged. "Strictly hypothetical . . . but probably both."

She smiled. "Over the years, I've seen all types of people sit at this bar. Many of them come in here all proud and independent. Seemingly tough. But I *see* underneath all that hard exterior. That stone wall they have built up. Behind everyone's hard, crab-like shell they have built to protect themself, who they want the world to see them as, behind *all* of that is a gentle, very sensitive little child who would love nothing more than to share their life, their memories, their good and bad times, their heart, with another person." She poured herself a glass of whiskey to match mine. "It's what we all desire deep down. Love. True love. And that—love—is nothing to be ashamed of."

I stared at my glass.

She continued, "We women have been convinced by society that we don't need men to be happy, to make money, which is true. That bullshit messaging started back in the 'We Can Do It' days, when the men were off at war and we had no choice but to step up. And we did. But, somewhere along the way, we started to believe we had to do it all alone, forever. But we all need people. We are social creatures. We may not *need* men to survive these days, but there is no gift richer than a man loving a woman who loves herself."

She held out her glass. I wasn't sure what we were cheering to, but I clinked mine against hers, anyway, and we both took a drink.

"Letting that type of love into one's life isn't about losing yourself or giving your power away . . . or whatever bullshit they've programmed you to believe. It's about finding someone who makes you feel like you can be more than you are, a greater version of yourself than you are, alone. And that, my friend, is not a weakness. That's strength in knowing what matters. *That* is real love."

I gave her a toothless smile and nodded, still staring down at my glass, doing everything I could not to break out into tears at the recognition of Cillian being exactly *that* in my life.

"Success will not be your greatest challenge in life, my dear," she said, scanning me. "Finding someone to share it with, darling, is the biggest challenge for most I meet. You have to wonder: what is all this success you kids chase these days, if you are all alone at the end of it? If you have no one to share it with?"

"I found it . . . you know?" I said. "The one to share it with. I never fully let myself need him or try to find a way to be with him, because I was terrified of losing him. Terrified of what that would mean about me. I was afraid of looking weak. I was afraid of rejection, afraid of getting hurt, afraid of him leaving me—whatever you want to call it. Then he died." I looked at her, searching for some reaction, but she remained still. "So, I guess it's a good thing I didn't let myself need him too much, right? I mean, what's the point of becoming that susceptible to potential pain and loss when you will eventually lose them one way or another?"

Her eyes softened. "To need is not weakness; it is the recognition of what makes us whole."

What was it with all these bartenders talking in riddles in this city?

"Yeah, I guess," I muttered.

"Don't they say it's better to have loved and lost than to never have loved at all?" she added.

I rolled my eyes. "Oh my God, can you get anymore Hallmark?"

She raised her thin brows. "Sweetie, men *know* they need women. Shit, they wouldn't be able to forward their genes without us, let alone upkeep a nice house and pick their shit up off the floor. They would go off the rails not being able to get blowjobs alone." She laughed. "In what world did we, as women, start to believe the falsity that *we* could, or would, want to live without *them*. At the very least, for the benefit of how they make our lives easier or better, like fixing the leaky faucet or carrying the heavy stuff we don't feel like lifting. Driving us places or patiently listening to us when we need an ear. Who else is going to help us keep the balance? Make us laugh at the end of a long day, rub our feet, or remind us to take care of ourselves?" She shook her head. "We've been sold the idea that we can do it all alone. But, baby, we don't have to."

"You would make a killing as a therapist. You should really reconsider your profession," I told her.

"Nah, I have found I can do much better work at this bar here, where all the *real* troubles surface." She winked.

I stood and took out my credit card to pay for my drink, not totally sure where I was heading next.

"Your money is no good here." She smirked. "You can't convince me otherwise."

Her words stopped me cold. They were the exact ones Ronan had said when I'd tried to pay for Cillian's tie. *Cillian.* Cillian was gone. Ronan wasn't. I realized there would be a thousand little moments like this—things Ronan or a random bartender would say or do that would remind me of him. Of Cillian. I felt the loss all over again.

It hurt—God, it hurt—but beneath the sting was the faintest flicker of comfort. Like maybe Cillian was still here in some way. Still watching. Still with me. From heaven, or limbo, or hell—I didn't know. I wasn't sure I wanted to.

"Thank you . . ."

"Pam."

"Thank you, Pam. For the drink and the advice," I said as I pushed the door open and entered the cold once again. All I could think, as the wind hit my face, was how much I hoped that when Cillian had died, he'd gone out with a cigarette and a joke. Maybe even remembering that story he'd told me on our first date about the Native American man who'd said, "Today is a great day to die. And therefore, I shall live."

I had to remember that he wasn't afraid. Not of dying. Not of loving. Not of needing.

But I was. Maybe I still am.

29

I woke up in my hotel room completely disoriented. The last thing I remembered was Pam and the bar. I hadn't been drunk, but everything after that was a blur. I was still in my suit from the day before, and my head ached. Where the hell was my phone?

I searched my bed before remembering . . .

Remembering the one thing I'd hoped to forget. Hoped to wipe from my memory.

Cillian. He was . . . *gone*. Dead. Forever.

It shattered my heart all over again.

I wondered how much it would cost me to get a lobotomy.

I lay in bed, staring at the ceiling. It felt like there was no point. No point to any of it. There was no speakeasy to visit him at. I hadn't realized until now just how much joy there'd been in that place. In him. The joy he had brought to me and my life. The excitement it had created in my day. The spark it—he— had lit up in me.

The mere idea of living a day without him was soul crushing. Like the zest of a new job, a new city, a future—all of it—was tasteless, joyless. There was no point if I didn't have him to tell about it. Like that brilliant bartender had said, *What was the point of any of it if I didn't have anyone to share it with?* God, I should have been going to her for advice all week rather than dealing with Chris Kringle. At least she gave me something to work with. Some wisdom to make all of this a little more bearable.

I rolled over onto my side into the fetal position, throwing a pillow between my thighs. There, next to me, was a pile of paper. Handwriting filled the pages.

I propped myself on my elbow to get a better look. I recognized the perfect loopy penmanship.

Lila.

There were enough pages to be a near-finished book—at the least, a solid screenplay. How had I missed this on my bed after she'd left yesterday? It was like the pages had magically appeared this morning. This had to have been what she'd been writing this whole time. Jesus, she had written a ton.

I collected the papers, organizing them as I sat up in bed, leaning against the headboard behind me.

A bright pink sticky note was stuck on the first page:

It's not complete yet, but I wanted you to read what I've come up with so far. Thank you for being my lifelong muse, sis.
—Love, Lila

P.S. I'll take your names out of it if it ever becomes a major motion picture (I know you like your privacy).

The top margin on the first page read, "*The Velvet Clover – A Christmas Romance.*" Was this about . . . me?

I started to read:

What else would an uptight PR executive from San Francisco do but visit New York at Christmastime with her sister? She was too buttoned-up for her own good, too proud to admit she was lost in her own life. But something about the city—maybe it was the snow, maybe it was the Christmas spirit—started to soften her edges.

I rolled my eyes and laughed. "Seriously, Lila?" I muttered. This was about me. Unless she knew another "uptight PR executive from San Francisco visiting New York with her sister at Christmastime." I had literally told her *not* to write about me. But, of course, I read on. How could I not?

I read through the pages and the mention of the jolly bartender, the hidden door, the speakeasy, then a familiar name caught my eye—Cillian. My heart skipped and broke at the same time. This wasn't just my story. This was *our* story.

. . . it was the place where everything began, where two unlikely souls found each other against all odds.

He noticed her before she noticed him. Of course he did. How could he not? She walked into the room like a mistake waiting to happen. But the kind he wanted to make twice. The kind he'd make a million times over, or chase through time itself, if it meant getting even one more second with her.

I kept reading.

. . .

. . . she was scared, of course. Not of him. Of herself. Of what she might find if she let someone truly see her. Truly accept her. Truly love her.

My tears blurred the words. Somehow, Lila had communicated moments that mirrored emotions I hadn't even admitted to myself.

They didn't fall in love loudly. There were no grand declarations, no sweeping gestures. Their love unfolded in the quiet—between glances that lingered a little too long, in silences that said more than words ever could.

He didn't ask her to let him in. He just waited. Waited while she built walls so high even she couldn't see over them. But still, he showed up. Not with promises or perfect lines, but with presence. Steady. Constant. He saw her for who she truly was and still accepted her, despite it. Because of it. And she hated it. Hated that someone had seen her—truly seen her—and hadn't run. Wouldn't run.

They fought it, both of them. In their own way. Sarcasm was her armor. Wit was his. And yet, beneath it all, there was a gravity between them. A deep unexplainable connection. An unspoken pull that neither of them understood but both felt. Every moment they shared felt like it could collapse time itself—like the past and future didn't matter when they were in the same room. Like nothing else mattered. Time stopped when they were together.

She would never admit how afraid she was. Afraid of needing someone. Of wanting something real. If he noticed, he never called her out. Never made her wrong. Never rushed her. He just looked at her like she was worth the wait. No matter how long it took.

And he was the only one who ever made her believe that maybe, just maybe, she was.

. . .

Tears ran down my cheeks, soaking the pages. I kept reading, unable to stop. It was the most beautiful love story—mine and Cillian's—written exactly as it happened, but with a tenderness that could break anyone's heart. Even mine.

Somehow, Lila had seen us more clearly than I ever could.

He looked at her like she was the only thing that mattered in the universe, with a depth so intense that it left anyone in their wake with weak knees. As if his gaze alone could pull her into his world and keep her there forever.

From the moment their eyes met, it had been clear—they didn't need words, didn't need time, yet in those moments together, it felt as if all the years and decades they hadn't spent together had already been lived. Their souls recognized each other as if they'd loved across lifetimes. Across timelines. As if they had already lived a million lives, in a million forms, side by side. Time blurred, and they both knew, without a doubt, that their connection had existed long before their separate worlds had ever brought them together.

My heart pounded, reading as fast as I could, waiting—desperately waiting—to see how it would end. Hoping, praying, that maybe Lila had written our ending. The ending where we would find a way. Our happily ever after.

Tomorrow, they would find it. A way. Across timelines, across boundaries. To meet in the middle of impossibility and carve out a life that belonged only to them. They would rewrite the rules, bend time itself, and choose love over logic. Because love like theirs wasn't meant to fade into the past. It was meant to defy everything.

. . .

I turned to the last and final page.

There, Ava stood at the door behind the velvet curtain—the door that had brought her back time and time again to The Velvet Clover. She was ready to step into 1925—to meet Cillian, to find a way for them to be together, to finally open her heart and share how she truly felt. She lingered at the threshold, hand trembling just above the doorknob. She took a deep breath, turned it, and—

The words stopped there. The story ended mid-sentence, cut off. No resolution. No ending.

I grabbed the stack of pages, flipping through them again, hoping to find another one, a missing page—anything that would tell me what happened next. But there was nothing. Just blank paper. No answers. No closure. The story ended at the moment it was supposed to begin, before we could ever let ourselves fully give in to the love that had always been right there, waiting for us to claim it.

I stared at the last sentence.

Cillian was gone. Really gone. And this, this story—our story—was all I had left. A beautiful but cruel reminder of what I'd had and lost. The love I never fully let myself feel, because I was scared.

I pressed the pages to my chest. My sister. She had written this for me. For us.

After everything I'd done—the yelling, the harsh words—she had still left this for me to find. I could hardly believe she had taken the time to write this. I'd been so selfish, pulling her away from her family during the holidays, only to push her away when she needed me the most. And yet, here she was, giving me something real, something she had poured hours of love into . . . something I didn't deserve. It wasn't just a gift. It was her way of telling me she still saw the good in me, even when I couldn't see it in myself. That thought almost broke me.

I laid the papers down on the bed, my heart breaking harder than I thought possible. He was gone. The story was unfinished. And so was everything between us.

I finally found my phone and snapped a picture of the pages, sending it to her, my tear stains visible on the page.

> I'm such a bitch. I'm so sorry for yelling at you. I was emotional. This is the best gift I have ever been given. Please forgive me.

She responded right away.

> You are a bitch. But I love u anyway. It's your Christmas gift. I wanted u to be able to read about the beautiful love u have with Cillian from my point of view.

> To see how special and rare it really is, to truly let love into ur life.

> Anyway, I forgave u as soon as I left.

> You know I can't hold a grudge for long. Or at all

> Also, stop saying "I'm sorry" . . . it kind of makes u sound pathetic ;)

I smiled and typed:

> How is Violet?

Better now, thanks for asking.

> Thank god.

I love you, Lil. Let me know when you can come visit me in New York. You, Simon, and the girls are welcome anytime.

I love you, sis. Thanks for being my muse.

> Even tho I told you not to write about me ;)

> This would make a great movie tho.

I still need the ending. xx

I stared at her message. This *was* the ending. Cillian was gone. There wouldn't be some sweeping final chapter, tied up with music, and snow, and a kiss under twinkling lights and a mistletoe. No reunion. No redemption arc. No happily ever after. Just me, alone on Christmas, in New York City. The exact thing I had been trying to avoid from the beginning.

I swallowed hard, phone in my hand. I wanted to respond with something light. Something sisterly. She had enough going on with Violet and reuniting with her family on Christmas. Plus, what could I say when the story was over, and now the author would have to make something up that was far less tragic than reality, just so that she could sell the movie rights one day?

I would tell her everything later. I would fill her in on my great tragedy. For now, I'd keep it light.

I am on it.

I lied. Or half-truthed. No, actually, that was a full lie. I wasn't on it. There was nothing to be on. Cillian was dead.

By the way, what happened after I left? Is Cillian . . . I mean . . . is he ok? Did u get back in and figure it out?

I stared at the message, my fingers frozen over the screen, but I couldn't bring myself to respond. I couldn't bring myself to tell her that he was dead.

Instead, I threw my phone across the bed and grabbed the stack of papers and flipped through them until I found one of the pages that was stuck in my mind.

There was something rare about their love. The kind of rare that doesn't shout but changes you quietly and completely.

It wasn't built on need, not at first. They were whole before they'd found each other. Independent. Fierce. Strong. Maybe a little too strong. But when two whole people fall in love, something unexpected happens: the love doesn't fill a hole—it creates one.

Not because they were broken. But because the soul, once it's touched by something that real, that divine, begins to need it. Not in a desperate way. Not in a way that diminishes who you are. But in the way your lungs need oxygen. In the way your heart needs a beat. A new requirement needs to survive.

Needing someone like that doesn't make you weak—it means you've known a love deep enough to reach the soul.

It's not codependency. It's soul-dependency.

And when that kind of love is gone, it doesn't just hurt—it changes the shape of your existence. The crack—that hole—it creates never truly goes away. Never truly heals. Because it wasn't just something they wanted. It had become part of how they breathed. How they existed. It was what they needed.

That was Ava and Cillian.

The kind of love you don't get over.

The kind you don't want to.

The kind you can't forget, no matter how hard you try.

The kind you never really let go of. Not all the way.

It was the kind of love you need.

Another tear streamed down my cheek. I ran my fingers over the page, hoping I could summon him like a genie in a bottle, simply from touching the words.

I did. I needed him. I needed Cillian. Like air. Like water, oxygen, or warmth. Every part of my being felt lost without him.

But somehow, reading Lila's words—*soul-dependency. The kind of love you never really let go of. Not all the way*—something clicked. Like some invisible cord tugged at me. On my soul. A deep knowing let in the possibility . . .

That maybe it wasn't over.

That maybe needing him wasn't the end—it was the beginning. A signal. A thread I hadn't allowed myself to tug, to use to get to him.

I scrambled for my phone to check the time. I couldn't find it anywhere in the bed. I remembered I had the pocket watch. Really handy, this thing. Even in 2025.

I clicked the button on the top of the engraved case cover to check the time.

Nine twenty-five a.m.

Before I shut it, I noticed the inside cover. There, engraved on the back, was a message I hadn't noticed when Cillian had gifted it to me.

> *When I needed you, you were there.*
> *When you need me, I will find you.*

Holy shit.

Cillian had said that every time he needed me, I had shown up at the speakeasy.

I closed the case slowly, the weight of those words holding me, grounding me. Then I realized, *I need him. I need Cillian.*

Could it be possible?

Before I could let myself think, before my logical mind could stop me, I jumped out of bed, throwing my pocket watch back in my jacket pocket.

I sprinted down the hall, skipped the elevator that was so old it took an eternity to go only four floors, and went straight for the stairs.

I need him.

I need him.

I need him.

I need Cillian.

I ran down the stairs. I ran across the lobby to the restaurant. A few patrons were seated, having coffee. The bar was dark, closed for the morning.

I slowed down so as not to draw attention from Jeremy. I didn't need him thinking I was crazy—well, crazier than he already thought I was—running for the broom closet, looking like a raccoon in yesterday's clothes, dried mascara, my hair a mess.

I stepped up to the velvet curtain and took a deep breath. *Cillian, I need you. I need you. I need you.* His engraving said when I needed him, he would find me. Just like when he needed me, I was always there.

Cillian, just like all those times you needed me and I was there for you. Now, I need you. Please, I need you here with me.

Despite everything—the logic of death, the finality of it, the permanence of it—something about this moment felt like a defying reason, just like the speakeasy had made no sense to the mind. How Lila had told me time and time again that I would never be able to make sense of any of it with my mind. Maybe, just maybe, Cillian could defy that same logic and find his way to me. Despite the circumstances. Despite logic.

I hoped. I even prayed. And in one moment of faith . . .

I slowly pulled back the velvet curtain and pushed open the door to 1925.

30

I HELD MY BREATH AS I TURNED THE HANDLE, CLOSING MY EYES AS I opened the door to the speakeasy. My heart hammered in anticipation of what I would see, who I would see. What would be on the other side of the door. Maybe I really would be able to change the past from the future, just like I had the other way around, with the photo and the pocket watch.

I slowly opened my eyes, and my heart sank, dropping past my stomach, into my feet and, this time, into where I assumed hell resided. Where I might actually rather be than here right now. At least, in hell, Cillian and I could be there together. Like we had planned.

Before me was the same dirty broom closet that I had sobbed in the day before.

All of the hope that had filled my body only moments ago evaporated and left me empty. Emptier than before.

He *lied*. Cillian had *lied* to me.

I *needed* him.

And he wasn't here.

My mouth hung open, hand still resting on the handle. My other arm dangled limply by my side. I was an idiot. He'd left me. He'd left me here alone. He had died. Cillian was dead in 2025 and 1925 and all the years in-between. And me needing him wouldn't change a thing. I was too late. I had waited too long to see it. To admit it.

Maybe that was the one thing time travel, non-linear timelines, and alternate realities couldn't defy or change: death. It was the only guarantee. The only constant. The only permanence.

I blinked, shaking my head in disbelief, looking at the broom closet in front of me. I couldn't believe it.

I needed him.

I *needed* him.

And he wasn't here.

He was gone.

He was dead.

It was like I had to keep telling myself to believe it.

A dark, angry laugh escaped me. Then I slammed the door with all my might. Patrons peeked their heads out from their booths at the ruckus. I didn't care.

As I came back from behind the curtain, standing at the bar was none other than Christopher. The incredibly unhelpful and unreliable Mr. Santa-Hat-Wearing, Rule-Enforcement Bartender, Chris fucking Kringle. And yes, he was still wearing the Santa hat, even though it was the day after Christmas. For Christ's sake.

He stood there with his usual dumb smile.

"*You!*" I sneered at him, stalking over to the bar. "Where the hell have you been? What kind of sick joke have you been playing? What the hell is all of this? Some kind of disgusting prank?"

"Oh! Why, 'ello, Ms. Hawthorne. Did ya have a lovely Christmas?" he asked without faltering for even a millisecond in my blaze of fury. How could he be so fucking jolly?

"No! I am terrible. You sent me on a wild goose chase all

week, trying to figure out what the hell was happening back there." I pointed toward the velvet curtain. To the pathetic broom closet. "Then gave me no answers! And yesterday, I asked Mr. Does-Every-Job-Here Jeremy about you, and he said he didn't know a Christopher, that *no one* by that name has worked here since he started *five years ago*," I said, my brows raised high. I slammed my palm on his bar. "Explain yourself!"

He just stood there, that stupid grin still plastered on his face.

My breath came in heavy pants. It felt like fire was blazing out of my nostrils, like I was some sort of dragon. My heart was pounding as the anger, confusion, and heartbreak swirled inside me.

"Because of you, I fell for someone who doesn't even exist! A man who is dead! He . . . *he* . . . was everything. All because of that stupid magical Christmas speakeasy you sent me to. And now I don't know what the hell is real anymore and what isn't!" I slammed my palm against the bar again. It was either that or this man was getting slapped, and little lady Lila was not here this time to protect him from a proper, and much deserved, ass-whooping.

I could feel tears prickling at the edges of my eyes, but I refused to let them fall. Not yet. I clenched my jaw hard, trying to dam the tears from spilling out.

"I see ye're upset, Ms. Hawthorne," he said with his stupid smile still plastered on his face. "Ms. Ava, do ya remember what I said to ya that first night we met?"

I gave him a bored look. "I don't remember. And I don't care. For all I know, you drugged me that night, and I am still on the same crazy trip, sitting in that broom closet, tweaking out. For all I know, this has all been a terrible nightmare. A hallucination. And honestly, I hope it is. I hope I wake up tomorrow and come down from whatever drugs I am on and it was all a dream."

He ignored me, pausing to pour a glass of whiskey—Irish. The same kind that Cillian drank. Had drunk. How could he possibly pour that and drink it in front of me? This man had to be some sort of sick sociopath.

"That night, I said to ya . . . dat people tend to fight the hardest against the thing they need the most."

I glared at him, shaking my head in disbelief. "I've had enough with this city's riddle-speaking bartenders and time-traveling disappearing acts, old man. What on earth are you saying? I didn't need or deserve what I just got. Can't you give me *one* real answer?"

He chuckled almost as if he were enjoying a private joke that no one else was getting the punchline of. "I think, my dear Ava, ye've spent so long runnin' from what ya need, ye didn't realize it was exactly what ye've wanted all along."

"What the hell does that mean?"

"But alas . . . I believe ye've finally figured it out," he said, handing me the glass of whiskey and nodding toward something behind me.

I grabbed the glass. "What are you trying to say?" I asked, turning to follow his gaze.

And standing there, time folded in on itself, the world narrowing to just the space between us. It was as if he'd stepped right out of one of my memories and into my current reality.

There, in front of me . . . was Cillian.

31

His piercing blue eyes were locked on mine, sending a jolt through me, as the entire room—the entire world—outside the two of us vanished. It was just us, suspended in that moment.

My heart skipped so many times I swore that it had stopped beating altogether. I wasn't sure if I was dreaming, or awake, or had just teleported to 1925 without knowing it.

But there he was. Cillian, all of him. Here. Standing in front of me. In the year 2025. In the future. My *present*.

His normally stoic face softened, the corners of his mouth lifting into the faintest smile. He arched a brow. Then he reached into his coat pocket to pull out a cigarette and lit it before finally saying, "Ava, me love, there is no need to get upset with Sir Christopher here. He has been the one helpin' me out. If anything, ya should probably be thankin' the man."

At the sound of his deep voice—the voice I thought I would never hear again—it took everything in me not to run straight into his arms . . . or collapse on the floor.

Instead, I looked back at Kringle, who was already retreating toward the kitchen, giving us space.

I called after him, "Hey, you. I'm not done with you! Is your name even Christopher? Who are you?"

He paused in the doorway, a mischievous glint in his eye. "Let's just say, Ms. Hawthorne, dat I was a Christmas miracle." He winked.

"Unbelievable," I said, rolling my eyes, though the faintest hint of gratitude slipped through.

"Ye're welcome, Ms. Ava." He pressed his hand to his chest, right over his heart. Then, just like through the "other door" of the speakeasy, the one he'd warned me never to go through, the door where I'd watched 1925's patrons disappear night after night—he slipped behind the restaurant kitchen door as if it were a gateway to somewhere else entirely, evaporating into nothingness. Vanishing into the void.

I stood frozen, staring after him. It really was Christmas magic. It had to be.

Then, slowly, I turned and began walking across the restaurant toward Cillian, who was now smoking inside. I figured I could tell him later that it was no longer legal. I couldn't take a cigarette out of a man's mouth after he'd just found himself one hundred years in the future. He probably needed it, just to keep his sanity.

It felt like I was stalking prey, like if I moved too quickly or touched him, he might run away, turn to dust, or vanish. At this point, anything was possible.

He held my stare, unwavering, as I closed the distance between us, now just a few feet away. I handed him the glass of whiskey I assumed Chris Kringle had poured for him. He took it, drank it, then set it down on the table beside him.

"Explain," I said.

He shook his head, taking another slow inhale. "There really isn't a need to explain." He paused, exhaling painfully slowly before locking eyes with me. "But I will."

I took a deep breath in and held it.

"The car crash—I faked it. Covered it in petrol and lit the whole thing on fire so there'd be no trace of me. No remains. Nothin' anyone could question. I needed the world to believe I was gone. Except for the pocket watch. I left dat so there would be no question that it was me in that burning car."

I flinched at the thought of him burning to death in a car.

"It wasn't until ya told me about da door—the portal, the time travel—that I understood what it actually was. That it could be more than just a doorway back to yer current reality. That it could become a passage *through*, not just *to*," he said. "Before that, that door only led me back to 1925. But once I *knew* —once I understood, once I believed—*dat* awareness changed everything. From what I figure: that's the rule of it. The light of awareness is what makes time travel possible. What makes multiple dimensions and alternate realities possible. The *awareness* of da portal—the awareness of da time travel— allows it to be so."

"I can't believe you figured all of this out in just a few days." Lila and I hadn't even made that much progress in a week.

"Well den, I guess ya should have told me sooner, me love." He winked.

I narrowed my eyes on him. "That doesn't explain how I got through the first night. Before I knew about it. Or believed it."

"My best guess is that Chris Kringle was yer guide—yer initiation of sorts. Until ya experienced it for yerself, until ya truly believed it was possible, through yer own direct experience, until ya saw enough proof that yer mind couldn't deny it. Once that door had been opened—not just the physical door, but the door of yer mind—ye could come and go without him."

"But *you* didn't see any proof, so how did you get through without me?"

"Because I fully believed ya, without a shadow of a doubt. Ya simply tellin' me was enough. You became the key that unlocked it in me mind. The moment ya spoke the words, it opened that door in me mind, and I believed it, then I felt it, too. I knew it to be true. Then I could come and go without ya. That's how I found my way here to you."

"Well then, how come I could get in sometimes and not others?"

"That, me darlin', was our love—our deep connection. Our soul's bond. Like I said before, whenever I needed ya, called for ya, asked for help, or invited you in, ye came. You were there."

"So, when the portal wouldn't open, that meant you didn't need me?"

"No. It just meant I wasn't actively askin' for ya—for help. Invitin' you in. The portal beyond nine twenty-five, whether a.m. or p.m., only opens when one of us invites the other through, whether our consciousness is aware of it or not."

"So, I wasn't coming and going on my own free will? It was because you invited me in, and I just convinced myself that it was my idea?"

"Of course you have free will. But yer soul wanted to answer the call. It's like the mind's way of protectin' itself, makin' sense of things it can't fully grasp. When I invited ya through, yer subconscious took over and made it feel like yer own decision, yer own choice. Yer own life circumstances leadin' ya there. That way, the experience felt natural to ya, not forced. I guess even the boss in the sky knows Ava Hawthorne won't do anythin' she is forced to do. Unless it is her idea."

"So, you are saying all I had to do was ask for you, and you would come?" Meaning, he had finally been able to come to me . . . because I had finally admitted I needed him, because I invited him through by simply asking for him.

He let out a deep laugh. "I guess ya could say dere's great power in the invitation, my dear Ava."

"How the hell did you figure all of this out?" I asked.

"Our new friend, Christopher, was a big help."

I frowned. "Why couldn't he have just told me all of this? It would have saved me a lot of damn time. How did you get answers out of him? I tried multiple times, and either he wasn't here or he just gave me the runaround."

He smiled. "Now, gettin' answers out of *dat* man, me dear, dat was the real Christmas miracle."

I rolled my eyes. "Okay, so you didn't actually die in 1925? You just disappeared from there? Are you staying? Can you stay? Can you get back?"

He stepped closer, grabbing my shoulders. "No, I didn't die. I *chose* this. I chose *you*. All you, Ava Hawthorne, need to know now is that I'm here. And I'm here to stay. With you."

I swallowed, then whispered. "But how could you leave it all behind? Your life. Your time. Saoirse. Your businesses. Everything you have ever known."

"I didn't leave anythin' behind. Not really. Saoirse knew my plan all along. Her reaction—that I'm sure you saw—was real, as she was terribly sad for me to leave. But she knew that if it meant I could be with the woman I loved . . ." He paused, waiting for my reaction.

I didn't give him one, even though my heart started pounding so hard I could have sworn he would be able to see it beating double-time in my chest.

He continued, "I knew it would be worth it for us. She is ready to run the atelier, and Eddie will help her with the bar. She was all set to publish da obituary once I was gone. I had it pre-written and included it for her with a letter to be opened on Christmas Day with all da instructions."

The letter from his desk . . . had been his obituary? The obituary he had written for himself? Maybe that was when it had appeared in the book—when Lila had seen it—because he had written it back then, that's how it had shown up in the present.

"Ava, I didn't really leave anythin' behind, because we don't ever *really* leave anythin' behind. Not truly. Time isn't as linear as we think. Clearly." He grinned. "It folds, it breathes, it loops back on itself. And the soul . . ." He touched his chest with one hand, then placed the other hand on mine. The warmth from his touch felt like the jolt of a defibrillator bringing my still and broken heart back to life. "The soul doesn't belong to any one place or era."

I blinked back tears. "You're way too progressive to be from 1925," I said, trying to humor my way past the vulnerability I didn't want him to see. "But doesn't it hurt? Letting go of your life like that? Leaving it all behind?"

"Is it much different from what ye're doing? Leavin' your life in San Francisco behind?"

Fair point.

"Of course, it's challengin' in some ways. And will be. But pain or fear of the unknown—of the future—isn't always a sign to hold on tighter. Sometimes, it's the invitation to loosen the grip. To surrender. Attachment to what we think *is* makes us believe we lose things. But what's real can never be lost. And me love for ya is not only real, but it's something worth fightin' for. Travelin' to the future for."

I stood there, stunned by the simplicity of it. The beauty in it.

"I didn't abandon anythin'," he said. "I am just followin' where love has called me next. And because of the love that I had lost in Aislinn and Eoin, I knew I wasn't willin' to lose this love. It's rare. So rare. I was just willin' to do whatever I had to do to keep it." He reached for my hand, his fingers brushing mine before he took my hand in his, his grip firm and reassuring, as if there was no question he was staying.

Part of me still fought it—the fear of uncertainty burning a hole in my heart. I had to try, just a little, to talk him out of it. To test whether he truly wanted to stay. To make sure he wasn't making a mistake he'd regret later—only to leave me all alone, abandoning me once I was in too deep. I refused to end up like my mother after Jeff had left, with two children and no career.

"Aren't you the least bit nervous of culture shock?" I asked. "Do you have any idea what 2025 is like? iPhones, and social media, and greasy fast food, and don't even get me started on what COVID-19 was like."

"Me love, I fought in a war . . . *that* is culture shock. I can handle 2025. Just like ya handled 1925." He grinned.

"But you don't even know how to operate a smart phone. You've probably never flown on a plane. You've never had to deal with TSA. Oh, and you aren't allowed to just shoot people on the street now, you know? They can track your DNA through your fingerprints," I said, making sure he was aware of *that* crucial factoid as soon as possible. "You will also need an updated wardrobe." I was actually the perfect person to help him with that last one.

He let out a laugh. "I am very well aware of da incompetencies I will need to catch up on, but I have time. And I have you. That is all that really matters to me."

"You also know you can't smoke that inside nowadays?" I pointed to his hand then crossed my arms. "It's illegal."

He glanced at his lit cigarette. "Well then, maybe this decade isn't for me, after all." With a mock dramatic sigh, he took a step toward the speakeasy door as if he were about to walk through it then paused and shot me a mischievous wink. Instead of leaving, he walked over to a nearby table and stubbed out the cigarette in a glass, as if he owned the place. He was just as confident in 2025 as ever.

He cleared his throat, now stalking toward me. "Okay, have we handled all yer objections as to why I wouldn't be able to survive in 2025 with ya?"

"What about the atelier? I'll be working there, and Ronan is bound to recognize you."

Got him.

"Sorry, love. Who's Ronan?" he asked.

"Right." I shook my head, realizing I had a lot to bring him up to speed on. One hundred years, to be precise. "Your great-grandson, Ronan. He runs your atelier now."

He cleared his throat. "So, we will tell him. The truth. Just like I did with Saoirse, eh?" he said, getting closer and closer. I could now smell his musk and tobacco. And *him*. My heart melted at his smell.

"He's going to think we're both insane. If he sees you here—alive—it won't make sense to him. Hell, it barely makes sense to me." I paused, biting the inside of my cheek. "I thought it was weird seeing you outside of the loser table. But this? Seeing you in 2025? It's freaky. Like watching some kind of alien that just landed on Earth."

"Communal table," he corrected. "If we can accept all of dis and get past it, so can Ronan," he said, remaining annoyingly casual, even at a time like this.

"Stuff is a lot more expensive now . . . inflation has been a real bitch in the last one hundred years." I was grasping for anything I could to make sure he really wanted to stay here. "Drinks and apartments are like . . . really expensive."

"Well, it's a good t'ing I have plenty of money," he said, now so close that my face was in his hands.

"Ava."

I looked to the left, avoiding his eyes, staring out the window, trying not to let the tears come at the sound of my name on his lips. The voice I never thought I would hear again. I failed. A tear rolled down my cheek. *Fuck.*

"I love you," he said, squeezing my face so hard that I probably looked like a chipmunk. I tried to pull away, but he didn't let me move an inch. "Eh, eh. Don't pull away. Look at me. I love ya."

The tears streamed down my cheeks.

"From the moment ya walked into my damn pub and sat at

me communal table, I haven't gone a second without thinking about ya, or how I could find some way to be with ya," he said. "Saoirse tells me ya say we needed menus, I got dem bound in leather by the next night, for God's sake. I shut down the whole damn pub for a night just to have a date with ya. I hired a band for ya. Ye gave me inspiration to change the atelier to honor my late wife. The moment I met ya, I knew I would find a way to be with ya. No matter the cost. I may not have consciously known you were from the future, but I knew you weren't from my time. Hell, look at ya. The way ye walk, dress, talk, it was all different. Foreign. Like seein' a teacher on a date or an alien who just discovered Earth." He winked.

Okay, those were some *great* call backs, I had to give him that.

"But, I knew there would be some sort of cost to being with ya. I knew I wanted to pay it, however big the fine." He continued to hold my face tightly in his hands.

I clenched my jaw to stop the crying, to stop the new kind of crack that was splitting my heart in two. Hearing him confess that he had known, on some level, all along, that he had somehow understood the depth of what we were, even before it fully made sense to him, was overwhelming. It was everything I didn't know I needed to hear. I wanted to crumble in his arms, let the tears fall, but I inhaled, determined to hold it together.

"And every time, Ava . . . every fucking time I needed ya, without even knowing it was ya that I needed, ya showed up. Ye were there for me," he said, lacing his fingers in my hair, pulling the back of my head closer still, leaning his forehead against mine.

I closed my eyes to blink out the tears that had flooded them.

"I know ya don't need anyone, and that is fine. But I need ya, Ava. I know that. God, even if a part of ya *wants* me, even a little, just give me a chance to be with ya, to give ya everythin' ya didn't know ye wanted or needed. I want to give ya the whole world. Just like ya have for me."

My heart cracked, and cracked, and cracked with every word he spoke. But *this* crack didn't feel like breaking. It was my heart breaking open. Open to his love. The rawness, the vulnerability of his words, the love, it started seeping into the crack and filled it until it overflowed.

"Oi. Me love. The love you and I have is eternal. We have trust. We have transparency, and truth." His eyes wide, his words were now rushed, like we were on borrowed time. "What we have is true love. It is rare. So fucking rare that we had to travel one hundred years to find it. This type of love supersedes time, and space, and all limiting constructs. And now that I have found it, I am not going to let it go. I refuse to let ya go."

And just like the first time we danced together, something about his hardness—his strength—softened me. I tilted my head then nodded the little I could in his hands. I mentally reached for something sassy, cunning, sardonic, rude, clever. *Something. Anything.* But nothing came. All of it had melted away under his loving look.

His eyes held a truth so pure, so absolute, that it stripped me completely bare. All I could see in his eyes was the truth. The truth of his words. The truth of his love.

Then all the layers—the walls I'd carefully built, the sharp edges, the hardened shell I'd spent years constructing—shattered in an instant.

I was left stripped. Vulnerable. Naked. Yet, somehow, I didn't feel afraid.

Finally, I let out in a whisper. "I love you, too, Cilia—"

Before I could finish saying his name, he pulled me in for a passionate, primal kiss. Like it was our first, and last, and every one in-between. The lips of the man that I thought I had lost forever, I got to experience once again.

I let go and let myself feel it all. Peace. Calm. Safety. And most importantly, love.

I pulled away. "Cillian, I . . . I need you," I admitted, letting the tears stream down my cheeks. Somehow, those three words felt harder to say than *I love you*. "I didn't want to admit it, but once you were gone—today, when I came down to look for you —I finally realized I *need* you. And not that I can't survive without you, but I would rather have you in my life. When you were gone, my life felt empty, purposeless. Life is better with you. You give my life meaning." I let out, "I need you, Cillian." My voice broke as I finally said the truth I had buried for so long. "I need you. Not because I'm weak. But because I'm strong enough to know that I don't want to face this life without you. I love you."

"And I need *you*, Ava Hawthorne." He nodded in understanding, pulling me into his chest as I buried my head in his neck, wrapping my arms around him, never wanting to let go.

We stood, hugging each other, holding each other in a warm, loving embrace for what could have been another hundred years, and it still wouldn't have been enough time together.

Home. I was finally home.

EPILOGUE

"Ava! Ya ready, love?" Cillian called to me from the living room.

"Yes, just touching up my lipstick, then I'll be out. Can you put on Niall's coat for me?

"Yes, ma'am, I sure can," he said, grabbing Niall from the floor, already in his tiny baby suit with a cute tie.

Our home felt like a dream. Perched high above the chaos of the city with floor-to-ceiling windows that let the skyline pour in like a painting, every inch reflected a piece of us. I had insisted on making it feel like The Velvet Clover, to bring a piece of Cillian's life with him to the future. Our new present.

While Niall's little playpen added some much-needed youth to the place, a well-worn copy of the red book with the wolf and the arrow through its chest from Barnes & Noble that Lila couldn't shut up about rested on the coffee table, the cover bent from being read and reread. Yes, I had officially joined the ranks of converted romantasy readers. Don't knock it till you try it—it's actually pretty good stuff.

"Can ya believe it has been two years since ya started at the atelier?" Cillian asked as he strapped Niall into his mini wool jacket I'd set out earlier.

"No. Can you believe it's been two years since you left 1925?" I asked, tapping the liner into my lips with my finger, walking over to my two favorite men in the world. I laughed then paused. "Do you ever miss it?"

"Nah. Time's just geography. Ye're me home." He held Niall on his hip, and turned to look out the window. "Eh, sometimes I miss pieces of it," he said. "The quiet. The pace. Saoirse. But I know she's happy knowin' I found and chose love again. That I found a way forward."

I slipped my hand into his. "You did more than move forward, Cillian. You've built a whole new life."

He kissed my temple. "Because of ya. And you," he added, nodding to our son, who was now babbling something about a squirrel.

I didn't think I'd ever want to be a mom. Turned out, I didn't actually hate kids—I just didn't like any of them that weren't mine. Niall was so cool. Half-me, half-Cillian. How could I not be completely obsessed?

Of course, Saoirse. She was the exception. I would have loved to be her mom. I thought of her often. Wondering where she was now, what chapter of her story she was in. I wished she were with us. That she could see the life Cillian and I had built. That she could be a part of it. That she could meet Niall. Sometimes, I felt her here, with us, in spirit.

"Well, at least now I know how to operate a MacBook Pro," Cillian said, sounding like someone's grandpa, even though he hadn't aged a damn day since arriving here—besides a few gray hairs, which I was pretty confident were because of me.

"You're so old." I laughed and tickled Niall's belly. Our little guy squealed and kicked as I squeezed his chubby baby leg.

Any mother's kryptonite. "I love you both so much. The two most handsome gentlemen in the world."

I glanced behind them. On the fireplace mantle sat *the* photo—our photo from the speakeasy. Proof that it had all happened. That I hadn't dreamed it. That love, miracles, and maybe even Christmas magic were real.

I smiled, touching the chain hidden beneath my jacket. The pocket watch Cillian had given me that I wore every day. It hadn't ticked since the day he'd arrived in 2025. It had just . . . stopped. Like time had been holding its breath, counting itself down until we found each other. And then, when we had, it had exhaled. Like its job was done. Like we were finally where we were meant to be. Where time no longer mattered, because we were together.

The love of my life stood there, wearing the bow tie I had given him two Christmases ago—and technically, one hundred years ago—eyes soft on me. I was grateful. Beyond grateful.

Interestingly enough, I'd discovered I didn't totally hate Christmas after all. In fact, I actually enjoyed it—the music, the decorations, the time spent with loved ones. Sure, I still saw it as a boost for Q4 sales, but beyond the corporate hustle, there was a magic to the season that was undeniable. And, nowadays, there were few things I loved more than spending Christmas by a tree with my family.

What? People change.

"You're an amazing mum and wife, me love," he said, his voice deep.

"And you," I said, kissing his cheek, "are the most wonderful father and husband."

———

We arrived at The Aislinn Atelier just after eight. The place was filled for the Christmas party. A-listers, our best clients, and some close family and friends.

Ronan welcomed us as we came in. "Ava, you look stunning, as always," he said, kissing both of my cheeks.

"Cousin." Cillian winked at Ronan, shaking hands and pulling each other in for an embrace.

Ronan had taken the news surprisingly well when we'd told him. Actually, it had been his idea to tell people he and Cillian were cousins. He had even insisted on Cillian being involved in the expansion of the atelier, something that turned out to be one of the best moves the company had ever made. We just had to tweak the company's origin story a bit—shift a few dates, adjust a couple details. Nothing too crazy. As we moved forward, we had adopted Sarah Jones's tagline, "Honor the past, but never stop innovating," as our guiding light. That mindset proved to be incredibly impactful . . . and lucrative. Since then, sales, bookings, and press coverage had all exploded.

We never did get back into The Velvet Clover. We would visit The Fitzgerald Hotel once in a while for old time's sake, but the speakeasy door never opened again. I checked once—okay, maybe twice . . . fine, five times—but it was never more than the broom closet. Whatever magic had existed there was gone, or maybe it was simply no longer meant for us. I always did take a minute to say hi to Mr. Broom while I was there. He's doing well. So is Jeremy.

I'd come to accept that the doorway to another time didn't open just because we *wanted* it to—it opened because we were *ready*. Because we *needed* it, for a season, to find each other. And now that chapter of our lives had closed. Its purpose was fulfilled, beautifully and completely—for Cillian and me to find each other. Or find our way *back* to each other.

Mr. Christopher Kringle never appeared after that day, either. Believe me; I looked. I even tracked down the hotel owner online once to ask for him. No record. No trace. Just like that, he was gone. Maybe he really *had* been a Christmas miracle. One of Santa's little elf spies. Or maybe he was something else entirely. But I liked to think he'd come into my life just long enough to annoy me for a bit, and change it forever. And then he had left the way all magic does—quietly and without asking for anything in return. Somehow, I was okay with that. Because what we found—the rare, impossible gift of true love in each other—was more than enough.

"Great turnout, yeah?" I asked.

"Magnificent turnout!" Sofia popped up out of nowhere—per usual—never more than a few steps behind Ronan. "Happy two-year anniversary." She grinned, pulling out a cupcake from seemingly thin air, complete with a lit candle.

"To you, Ava, for your *work-iversary*. And to both of you," she added, glancing between me and Cillian, pulling a second cupcake out from behind her back. "For your *love-iversary*."

Cillian laughed and clapped his hands together.

I rolled my eyes, blowing the candles out with Niall. "Thank you, guys, but not necessary."

"Very necessary," Ronan insisted. "You were the catalyst for the growth we have had over the last few years. We couldn't have done any of it without you, Ava. The entire team and I are so grateful for you."

Cillian placed a loving hand on my lower back, as Sofia and Ronan drifted to mingle with other guests. Even through layers of fabric, his hand warmed me just like it had the first time he'd touched me all those years ago in the speakeasy—like fire on my skin.

"Eh, me love," Cillian said gently. "Look."

And then I saw them.

My parents, both of them, were standing just off to the side of the champagne bar, across the room. Jeff held a glass of sparkling water like it was his comfort blanket, while my mom was deep in conversation with one of the design interns, animated and glowing, as usual, in the emerald atelier gown I'd gifted her last Christmas. We'd expanded into women's fashion, and she was by far my best advertisement.

"Oh, Niall, look—Grandma and Grandpa made it," I said. He waved and babbled excitedly at the sight of his Nana and Papa.

"Come on," Cillian said, taking my hand. "Let's go say hello."

Since Niall had been born, they'd agreed to get along. And, surprisingly, it had worked out really well. They stood close enough to seem like they hadn't spent the past three decades divorced. And tonight, they seemed like they were on their best behavior—for me, for Niall.

The three of us walked over together.

My dad, in his usual sport coat and loafers, pulled me into a tight hug. "Honey, this place is amazing. I'm so impressed," he said, smiling.

"Thanks for coming, Dad."

Cillian stepped forward. "Jeff, it's great to see ya," he said, offering his hand.

But my dad ignored it and pulled him into a hug, too. "You," he said, clapping Cillian on the back, "are one hell of a man. It is so wonderful to see you again."

Cillian let out a laugh, "Thank ya, Jeff. Ye, too."

"My big man, Niall!" my dad said, turning to him with a big grin as he held up his hand for a high-five.

Niall swung his little baby arm in the air but completely missed. We all laughed.

I looked at my dad—really looked at him. Our relationship had changed so much. He was actually showing up now. Calling every week. Committing to plans and following through. And I had forgiven him. Fully.

I felt the weight of years lift. My dad was here, on Christmas, for the first time since he'd left all those years ago. It was such a beautiful full circle moment. His effort, no matter how small, was enough for me. I was so grateful he was making equally as much effort to be part of Niall's life.

"Hi, sweetheart," my mom said, stepping away from her other conversation—ever the social butterfly—and leaning in to kiss me on the cheek. "You look amazing, sweetheart. This place is just wonderful."

"Thanks, Mom. You look great in this dress. Fits you perfectly," I said, smiling, scanning her.

"Oh, this old thing," she said, spinning around like she wasn't in her mid-sixties. Then she turned to Cillian, her face softening.

"You," she said, placing a hand gently on his shoulder. "I can't tell you how grateful I am for you. You've brought so much peace into my little girl's life. Into all of our lives."

Cillian forced a smile, his Irish discomfort with receiving compliments never fully going away. You could take the boy out of the Irish speakeasy, but you couldn't take the Irish speakeasy out of the boy. "Oh, well, thank ya, Clara. I do me best. But truth be told, she's that and so much more to me."

She leaned in and gave him a kiss on the cheek. "We are so happy to have you as a part of this family."

Jeff and Mom exchanged a quick glance and a polite smile. So grown-up. So mature. Some award-winning divorced grandparent energy.

"Oh! And how could I forget my favorite person," my mom said, reaching out to take Niall from me. "The whole reason we're really all here . . . Of course, for you, too, honey," she added, looking at me.

I smirked. "Please. You wouldn't have even RSVP'd if Niall wasn't on the invite . . ." I paused. "And honestly, neither would I." I laughed.

"Oh, you!" Mom said, waving me off.

Jeff chuckled.

I felt a lump form in my throat. A good one. A ball of emotion. Of happiness. Somehow, this—my parents standing here, civil and smiling—was its own little kind of Christmas miracle.

Before I could fully process the moment, a familiar squeal rang out from behind me.

"Surprise!"

I turned, only to see Lila and Simon walking toward us.

"Oh my God, how did you get here? When . . . ?" I asked, rushing toward them.

"Cillian flew us out." Lila grinned. "He insisted we surprise you and said that we could stay for the week. Hope that's okay? It's New York—we couldn't say no," she added with a laugh.

"Of course. You're always welcome!" I said, pulling her into a hug.

I turned to Simon, who gave me a warm smile and raised his glass. "And you, too, of course. It's so good to see you both."

"Wouldn't miss it for the world," Simon said. "Lila's been buzzing about this trip for weeks. And so have the girls," he said, nodding toward them. They were already floating around at the dessert bar.

"Ava. Cillian. I have good—well, *great*—news that I had to tell you both in person," Lila said, bouncing her usual Lila bounce.

"Well, go on," Cillian said with that stupidly charming grin of his.

"I was talking with my literary agent last week, the one who helped me get *The Velvet Clover* published through Penguin Random House." She shot me a knowing look.

The same story she had gifted me the day I'd thought Cillian was gone. The one that meant the world to me. She had gone on to finish it with our true happy ending. Then, with our permission, Lila had published the book but tweaked it to keep our story private and anonymous, preserving the heart of our love without revealing everything. The backbone of our story was there, but the rest remained just between us. It had become an instant bestseller.

"Yes? And . . .?" I coaxed.

"Well, the screenplay I adapted from the book just officially got picked up by Netflix. They're making your story into a movie!" she squealed.

It had been so surreal to have our love story out in the world, touching people without revealing who it was really about.

I smiled, biting my lip as I glanced at Cillian.

His jaw dropped. "My goodness. Lila . . . that's incredible. We're so happy for ya," he said, pulling her into a hug.

It was official. Cillian and I were *"we"* people. Singular pronouns had almost completely disappeared from our vocabulary, just like I'd always hated about Lila and Simon.

"Did you hear that, Niall? Your mom and dad are gonna have a movie made about them!" I said as he sat on my mom's hip. Both of my parents laughed, probably assuming Lila had dreamed the whole thing up and loosely based the characters on us. They had no idea how close to home it really was—and I wasn't about to freak them out by mentioning the time-traveling speakeasy.

Niall clapped his hands in delight, squealing something unintelligible that we decided definitely meant: *Hollywood, here we come!*

"We 'ave to celebrate." Cillian waved over a server, who brought us six glasses of Irish whiskey. We all held our glasses up, letting the Irish toastmaster have his shining moment.

In his deep, sexy, beautiful Irish-accent, he began, "To Lila —for documentin' and so beautifully capturin' a journey of a lifetime, and for makin' us look much sexier than we are in real life. Thank ya for dat," he said with a wink. "And to love— defyin' all odds, time and time again."

I smiled, marveling at how far we'd come. Here we were, my entire family together on Christmas. Cillian and I—together, whole, building a business, building a life, and raising this little person that was half of me and half the man I loved. I had found the man who brought out my best. The man I chose. The man I *needed*. My anchor. My home.

Even now, after everything, I couldn't imagine standing on my own without him. And I wouldn't want to. Together, we stood, brought together across time by Christmas magic and true love.

The End.

ACKNOWLEDGMENTS

I took a trip to New York City during the holiday season while editing my first book, *The Other Woman*. I stayed in a little Irish place called the Fitzpatrick Hotel. Sitting in the restaurant, I thought, *How cool would it be if this place had a hidden speakeasy?* That thought—paired with my search for a Christmas book I'd actually enjoy reading—sparked the idea for *The Velvet Clover*. Thank you, Fitzpatrick Hotel, for the inspiration.

Alexander, I never thought I'd finish one book, let alone publish three in a single year. None of this would have been possible without your endless support and love. You cheer on my big dreams and (somehow) push me to dream even bigger. I spent years searching for a man who made me feel so safe in our love that I could finally write a book boyfriend similar to the love I get to experience every day with you. You were my inspiration for Cillian, and I stole too many lines from you to count. If this book had a bibliography, you'd be officially cited.

I'm honored to thank Allison Lutz, my editor, for spotting my blind spots and encouraging me to write better. These books would be nothing without your watchful eye. Kristin Campbell, you joined me on this project to round it out and make it shine. I could truly feel your heart in every grammatical tweak and plot hole flag. Without you two in my corner, I don't think I'd sell even one copy (well, maybe I would, but no one would read past page one). It takes a village.

Mitch Rosacker: you helped me take this book from the depth of a kiddie pool to that of an ocean—expanding its reach and mystique. You helped me transform "Christmas magic" into a cosmic portal of interdimensionality: a quantum love experiment stretched across multiverses and infinite potential realities. In the end, all we know for sure is . . . love wins.

To Chelsea Lauren and Chelsea Fiegel: thank you for reading this book before anyone else. Your time and willingness to be early readers means so much. Sharing work before it's "ready" can feel scary, and the two of you made it easy to hand it over and say, "Critique me!"

To my family and friends: you are always the first to support me. You buy my books—some of you bought more copies than you'd ever need—and many of you even read them, which shocked me. Some of you, I'd have preferred you didn't. But that just shows how much you love me, and maybe one day I'll stop cringing when I think about it. You know this, but I'll say it again: your love and support mean the world to me.

To all of you who have read my books: it's difficult to put into words (even for a writer) how much your support means. Without you, I'd be speaking to the void. Sometimes I wonder if I still am. But knowing that my words land on even one pair of eyes (yours—right now, in this moment) is enough to keep me going, to keep me writing. Each day I sit at my wooden desk to face a blank page, I think of you.

For you, I will always keep writing.

ABOUT THE AUTHOR

Aria Devi is the bestselling author of *The Other Woman* and *Wanter Dynamics & The Love We Are*. *The Velvet Clover* is her third novel. She lives and writes in Austin, Texas.

You can follow her on TikTok, Instagram, and Substack at **@ariadevibooks**.

instagram.com/ariadevibooks
tiktok.com/@ariadevibooks

THANK YOU FOR READING

If you enjoyed this book, please consider leaving a review on Amazon—your words help other readers discover the story.

YOUR NEXT READ BY ARIA DEVI

If you loved The Velvet Clover, don't miss The Other Woman—
a gripping novel about love, betrayal, and the choices we make
that change everything. Get it on Amazon.

www.ingramcontent.com/pod-product-compliance
Lightning Source LLC
Chambersburg PA
CBHW021954130726
47903CB00014B/1353